HEART
PAYMENTS

Also by Gerald Jay Goldberg

THE NATIONAL STANDARD

THE LYNCHING OF ORIN NEWFIELD

126 DAYS OF CONTINUOUS SUNSHINE

GERALD JAY GOLDBERG

HEART PAYMENTS

THE VIKING PRESS   NEW YORK

For Nancy

Library of Congress Catalog Number: 81–65285
ISBN: 0–670–36466–5

PART I

OAKLAND, 1976

35. BOY ON VENICE BLVD.

Los Angeles, 1959
Paper, twigs, string, gold stars on cardboard
Size: 9 x 12 inches
Coll. Mrs. M. Dorfman, New York

Venice is burning. The force of the explosion crumples Thrifty's metal awning like a napkin. In the middle of the hose-drenched street, a car with rear tires blown off squats on its rims. The traffic lights don't work. Sticks of flame cover the background, fringe the roof of the Bank of America, loft gold stars into the smoke-black sky. Crisscrossing the boulevard are long strings of hose. The firemen hold their lines in silence. At a bus stop on the picture plane, a young boy in breeches and coat of forest green velvet sits cranking his melodeon. He wears lace ruffles at wrist and collar, silver buckles on his shoes. He smiles and, smiling, seems altogether as gay as a seaside, as brilliant as cut glass. Two sweet white birds have appeared out of nowhere and hang in the charred air above his ringlets.

WEST HOLLYWOOD, JUNE 11, 1976

Henry Tattersall finally showed up looking small, trim, red as a scar, and admitting to squinty eyes and straight black machine-tooled gangster hair. Except for the sunburn, all the rest was an old story. His wife was relieved. Although Henry had taken the day off to go to the beach at Santa Monica, he couldn't swim. For someone who couldn't even float, the beach was no place to be on a blistering June day—the first molten sparks of what proved to be a heat wave and unusual in the city for that time of year.

Dorothy Tattersall knew her place and stayed home in West Hollywood, curled in the sea-blue shadows of their lanai, sucking a peach pit, Woodward and Bernstein on her lap. In the Lincoln Sitting Room, Nixon was down on his knees. Good God, the President of the United States weeping, sobbing, out of his mind! And there beside him kneeing the carpet was that terrible man. Whenever she thought of him, he was always Kissinger, never Henry Kissinger. His villainous Blue Danube accent seemed to mock the only war she ever really cared about. They were shoehorned together into the smallest room in the White House—Nixon and Kissinger haunch to haunch—and still those two brilliant young reporters had been able to find out what was going on in there. Like her Henry, no doubt they too had their sources.

I suppose Harris was after money, he called to her from the kitchen. Tattersall's voice was unmistakably resigned to life's crap. She could never understand how her husband knew about Harris and such things. Removing the peach pit from her mouth, she smiled, remembering that she had put the letter down on the dining room table. She got up, smartened the back of her bleached summer cut where it had flattened against the green chaise. In the kitchen, she watched him unpack. You'd better put something on that burn, darling.

Henry had asked for two bags at the store, one inside the other, providing double strength. He didn't want to risk any

4

accidents on the bus coming home. Unpacking, he showed his wife Old English bread crumbs, Mazola oil, three lemons, two ears of corn, two cans of Coors, scallions, a bottle of Canada Dry club soda, a ripe cantaloupe, and three quarters of a pound of freshly fileted petrale sole. Though bone white, the fish nevertheless revealed subterranean subtleties of pink and gray gratifying even to a nonswimmer. Henry's fingers skillfully peeled back the corn's husk, exposing golden kernels sitting in neat rows. Lovely, said Dorothy. He stripped the second and uncovered a cob full of tank traps and potholes.

Henry sucked his teeth philosophically. Somehow things didn't always work out for him. He was not a practicing Christian but, theologically speaking, he would probably have been most at home in the eighteenth century, when evil was not denied but kept in perspective. His unspoken dream was that, once revealed to Tattersall, the big picture would show a basically benevolent setup. Life, however, had steeled him to the fact that it might not.

Dorothy Tattersall said that she didn't want corn anyway and quickly declared her diet, her dental apertures. She loved her husband. He looked so wistful, she could have kissed him. Maybe the skin won't peel, she soothed, trying to cheer him up. Henry recalled one summer when he was a kid that overnight he had turned mahogany. Pointing to an area on his badly burned chest just above his left nipple, he mentioned the word tan. We'll use vinegar, darling, said Dorothy. I'm sure you'll be able to get some sleep.

Henry shrugged. He found himself admiring his wife's tits and thinking that he liked it better when they whispered suck rather than comfort or wisdom. A great tan wasn't all you got at the beach. Tattersall, you horny bastard, he lightly chided himself as he walked his erection out the kitchen door, why not try a little vinegar on *that*?

The printed return address on the envelope said HARRIS PRODUCTIONS. There was no stamp, no address, no postmark, only *Tattersall* in flaming ballpoint. He supposed that Harris Productions, not finding him at home, had produced the contents. He tore open the envelope. *Hey, Henry,* said Harris, *I got an idea who ripped off your rastler. I'm out of town for the weekend but tell you all about it on Monday.* Gott im Himmel, *it's honeymoon time again! Laba-laba-ooooo. Later.*

The coincidence impressed Henry. Earlier that afternoon, while dipping his toes into the Pacific to cool off, he had idly, almost without thinking, splashed his way down the beach to Venice and Market Street. It was as if he had been drawn back by some bottled message rolled up out of the sea, as if he thought that after all this time the Rembrandt might still be found in Asher's old house. But not even the house was there any longer.

The new Café des Artistes on the oceanfront should have prepared him for the rest. Pausing at its side entrance, his bare toes cooling in the shade of its pretty green candy-striped awning, Henry was amazed at the changes. Now there were expensive art galleries on the block, a boutique called HERS. Across the street, where the shabby Edgewater Hotel had stood, were luxury apartments with ocean views. Asher's house had been demolished and was now a fenced-off vacant lot. A posted sign promised The Catch, specializing in the fruit of the sea. There were no more winos carpeting the sidewalk. No more boarded-up windows and broken glass. The old people he had enjoyed listening to during those weeks when he had had the house under surveillance had been blown off their benches by death and real estate developers. Henry generally approved of things being cleaned up, straightened out, but this Market Street made him feel as depressed as wet socks.

He glanced over the letter again. Tattersall rated Harris basically reliable, but after eight, nine years of disappointments he was not about to sour his stomach with hope, excitement, rich expectations. There was just a chance they were shacked up at his place. He found Harris in the book and dialed. So good of you to call Harris Productions, said Claude Rains. It was Harris on the answering device. Terribly sorry darlings but Mr. Harris is away this weekend on location. Do leave your name and number at the sound of the tone, and he'll be back to you as soon as he possibly can. Now there's a dear.

6

Lifting the receiver from his ear, Henry put it down gently in its cradle. The Tattersall style, grace under pressure. It would be Monday, then. All these years he had waited for news, waited so nonchalantly that it must have seemed at times as if he had forgotten, or didn't care anymore, or had fallen asleep. His patience was legendary in the insurance business. All the top L.A. companies that specialized in covering artworks knew that he never gave up the big ones, even years after they had dropped him from a case. Taking the long view, Henry had managed to convince himself that his failures were only postponed successes. And indeed sometimes they were. It had taken him three years to track down Terborch's *Lady in the Window*, five to wrap up the strange disappearance of the dragon netsuke in jade.

Ever the professional investigator, Henry mulled over Harris's message with typical Tattersall sang-froid. He had always known that recovering the missing Rembrandt was just a matter of time.

SANTA MONICA, JANUARY 4, 1966

WELCOME TO SANTA MONICA, said the beat-up sign hanging on the telephone pole. Fantastic, said Dan Asher and turned up the music on the car radio. Amidst the rock and roll, someone had slipped in "Love for Sale." It was like coming upon a forgotten photograph in the family album. Erroll Garner at the piano making time dance to a human tune. Dan Asher hammered out the rhythm on his steering wheel as he drove up Ocean Avenue.

It was a great morning. The sun twinkling on the Pacific as if it were a tray of rings. The park along the top of the palisades bursting with people. Bums, jugglers, elderly types in straw hats, bare-chested joggers in flimsy shorts, mothers with tots. As Dan Asher waited for the light on Colorado to turn green, a tall, heavyset woman in dark glasses crossed to the park in front of his MG. He smiled. He liked the stiff, no-nonsense way she moved her arms. He admired her blouse. That's a super blue, he called. She glanced at the long-haired creep in the convertible heap with the disgusting bumper stickers. Drop dead, she advised. Although the light had changed and the cars behind him had already begun to blow their horns, Dan Asher couldn't stop laughing. He was laughing so engagingly that she had to smile in spite of herself.

At the corner of Santa Monica Boulevard, he hung a right and cruised slowly past the meters looking for the right one. All he could see was a bunch of red tongues. The parking space he wanted was about to be occupied by a fourteen-foot adventure in moving. Not on your life! He gave the driver of the U-Haul an ultimatum. The MG's horn sounded a bit thin, unconvincing, embarrassingly like a whine. Say, shouted Dan Asher, could you move up a little? There's plenty of room. The truck obligingly pulled up and he swung in behind it, inheriting twenty-five minutes on the meter. More than enough time for what he had to do.

The five-and-dime store around the corner on Second Street was a favorite of his. Even when he didn't know exactly what he wanted, he could usually find it there. As soon as he opened the door, the two young salesgirls up front looked at one another as if the king of the shoplifters had just walked in. Dan Asher tried an ingenuous wink. He was, after all, a regular.

Although he had no time to chat and went right to work, he could hear their tittering behind his back. Who knows, he wondered, what it is that excites the teenage dears? Marissa doted on his blue eyes, his ponytail. Her schoolgirl pals thought he sounded like John Lennon on the phone. It was probably good for them to have someone over thirty they could trust. Dan Asher was fifty and still credible. Puberty's darling.

He went shuffling in sandals past the long five-and-dime counters, hunting for something as if he knew it was there. He saw what he wanted beside the can openers. From amidst the kitchen decals of field and stream, he impulsively plucked a Giant White. Of course its feathery antennae were an anatomical lie, but it was one that appealed to Dan Asher. There was always room in his work for centaurs, for minotaurs, for a butterfly Moby Dick.

On the King's way out, Little Miss Acne leaned her titlets caressingly over the cash register to see what he had. Dan Asher showed her the earthy gap between his two front teeth and a mass of wrinkles and stains. That's a nice butterfly, she said. He nodded, dipped into his pocket, and paid up.

Wait a sec! She held out her hand. Don't you want your change? Scooping it up, he gave her palm an avuncular stroke and, charmed by her giggle, promised to call again.

Women, he thought fondly as he closed the door behind him. How invigorating.

LOS ANGELES, JUNE 23, 1967

Good evening. This is the eight o'clock news. A gleaming Air Force One touched down at Los Angeles International Airport at 7:40 this evening. The President, looking wonderfully fit in black tie and dinner jacket, was accompanied by a large number of Secret Service men. He immediately boarded a military helicopter for the short trip to the Century Plaza. The parking lot at the rear of the hotel had been cleared for the occasion and served as a landing field. There was a Democratic welcoming committee on hand to escort the President through the back door. Apparently neither he nor daughter Lynda Bird was aware of the ten thousand chanting demonstrators massed in front of the hotel's main entrance.

California National Committeeman Eugene Wyman said, "I feel that although people have the right to demonstrate, it should be done with dignity. And nothing should ever be done to embarrass the high office of the presidency."

NEW YORK, 1951

Dr. and Mrs. Milton R. Shaw
announce the marriage of their daughter
Gretchen
to
Daniel Asher
on Saturday, January twenty-seventh
Nineteen hundred and fifty-one
New York City

SANTA MONICA, JANUARY 4, 1966

Parked up the block on Santa Monica Boulevard, his red '59 MG pleaded guilty to seven years of graceless aging, a dented red fender, a woolen gas cap. The cap had once been fifty percent of a flamboyant comedy team of brown, yellow, and peach argyles created by his second wife, the late lady Madeleine. The cornball sign on the MG's bumper said DIRTY OLD MEN NEED LOVE TOO.

Who else but Mona would have come up with such heart-breaking news? And his daughter, Marissa, clapping her hands, had cried Neat! He hated to hurt their feelings. Mona was great for causes. She was Peace and Freedom. She wanted all L.A. to know where they stood on Vietnam and Mayor Sam, the draft and Proposition A. Dan Asher saw himself as more of a private person. Secretly, he would have preferred deadpan bumpers sworn to *omertà*. Perhaps sensing his weakness, she turned him into Another Mother for Peace. Although he loved Mona, he couldn't deny that she often broke out in unappetizing plans that involved others.

Stopping, Dan Asher peered into Baumgarden's Stamps and Coins, surveying a window full of dust-covered glassine envelopes containing, for instance, eighteenth-century Spain's José Delgado in rose, carmine, amber, and grass. No doubt better known to most as the celebrated Pepe Illo who regularly fought death at five in the afternoon. Brains, balls, grace, wit, taste —he had it all—and still he was ripped open like third-class mail. Adiós, Pepe.

He saw nothing he wanted behind the glass. Not this time, Baumgarden, rectangles are a dime a dozen. He was currently in the market for septagons, octagons, something like that. He saw what he had in mind on top of the Crocker Bank building, and his butterfly took off. He watched it hover in the sky-blue center of Crocker's hexagon like Castagno's white-winged holy ghost etched against the heavens. Not bad if you happened to live in Florence in the quattrocento, but not much for Los Angeles in 1966. Still and all, he was getting close.

Dan glimpsed his mustache mirrored in the store window, the shimmering of silver-flecked highlights, his bushy-brown horse-shoe damp in the noonday sun. It was going to be another hot January day. Even his faded ice-blue workshirt began to heat up, stick to his skin, weigh him down. Dreaming a benzene ring, he allowed his butterfly to crack the nucleus and perch asymmetrically, unstably, on one of its six carbons.

Son of a bitch, it worked! He felt like leaping up and dancing, singing, weeping for joy. He felt a sudden urgency to get back right away to the studio with his butterfly. He felt he had better move his ass lickety-split. He felt his whole body break out in a cold sweat. All at once, he felt terrible.

When it came, the stone fist slammed directly into his heart, into his left shoulder, and shock waves roared down to his elbow, pounding out heat, then numbness, then pain. His eyes squeezed shut, his face twisted against the crushing pain. Although halfway to the car, he realized that he was not going to be able to make it. . . .

Dan Asher found himself sprawled out on the Second Street pavement wearing only one sandal and trying to catch his breath. His tongue stuck in his throat like a plug. Then he was breathing again, sucking up thin pale scraps of air. He wondered how long he had been lying there. He wondered if it was five o'clock. The tower of the Crocker Bank building loomed above him, showing a huge clock face and no hands. He felt sorry for Harold Lloyd. Nothing to hang on but the Crocker emblem. Tears filled his eyes. The pain was strangling him.

Someone in white shoes was shouting in his ear, but he couldn't make out a word. He wanted to go home. He wanted to go to a hospital. He searched desperately for his car and saw it at the end of the block, radiant in the sun. It was as though an old and dear friend had suddenly turned up looking as wonderful as remembered. He tried to move toward the car and knew even before he tried that it was impossible. The pain crushed him to the pavement as flat as a manhole cover. He had no strength. He lay there motionless—a hostage bound and gagged and sentenced to death—while the hot Santa Ana wind played with his hair.

OAKLAND, 1976

DANIEL ASHER: Collages 1943–1967.
The Oakland Museum, 1976.
Introduction by Mordecai Bell.

It is time now, almost a decade after his death, to reassess the achievement of Daniel Asher and his place in the history of modern art. His work, unknown by many today, was first exhibited to acclaim in 1943 at Peggy Guggenheim's Art of This Century Gallery in New York. It was Duchamp then who praised these early collages as "courageous." That word, I believe, epitomizes the artist's entire career.

In an age bereft of traditional sources of value, Daniel Asher placed his faith in the act of creation. At a time in art history when greatness and largeness were not infrequently confused, he chose to find whips in crickets' bones and chariots in nuts. It has been said that "Matisse was in the line of heroes who strike up a tune in the face of death." The brilliance of Daniel Asher's last work—its sudden burst of joyous color—must surely place him in such a line.

Everyone knows how the reputation of Paul Klee has suffered over the years from the "small work, small worth" syndrome. It is hard for some people to believe that major art can come pint-size. It is harder still for some to accept that a major artist can devote himself exclusively to collage and a life of pasting, sticking, fragments, and debris. And yet Asher did just that.

Selecting scraps of the real world, he arranged them so cannily that they not only exist as themselves but fuse paradoxically into that other reality, the imaginary world of art. The hallmarks of his work are order, economy, and resonance. The genius of Asher was his ability to take a single quarter note and make it ring like grand opera, to take a star and produce a universe.

SANTA MONICA, JANUARY 4, 1966

Stumbling out of the bar's blackness, he was earnestly trying to explain. He wove back and forth on the sidewalk, blinking in the sunlight. He was tall, thin, black, and he wore his lightweight cream-colored shirt out of his pants à la Sukarno and the Indonesian gentry.

Without warning, he raised his voice angrily. I am talking to you, sir, pay attention. Except for slurring the last word, he might have been a TV anchor man. I have been all over, he said, and everywhere I have been I have run into this same stupid kind of behavior. It seems as though when you are black they assume you cannot think. That's all right, that's all right, indeed keep them closed, for under the cloak of blackness I talk to your unconscious mind and speak pain and souls and things you cannot see with your natural eyes. I am talking about the rich man who I can tell you is so high up with his fine women and push-button phones that he has even forgotten that he has forgotten the poor faceless poor man way down here below.

The poor man is zero in America. Seven days a week he scuffles for his tiny piece of the pie and one morning he gets up and his eyes are open. It doan mean shit, he tells himself. He tells himself, You bust yoa ass and break yoa heart for what?

The one so high and the one so low, but both just flesh and blood. The theme is universal, I know.

Throwing his head back, he looked wildly about and began to shout. I, too, am human, sir! His voice welled with tears. I demand respect. Is it too much to wish to preserve your natural shining dignity? Is that too much to ask? Goddamn you, have you heard one single word I've said? He tripped over the large figure sprawled on the pavement, caught his balance, turned back, and, bending, sniffed.

Pheweeee! The sharp riveting smell of rubber cement. I warn you, sir, take care. Remember Watts! The fire next time, you poor dead honky. You, sir. I am talking to *you*. Pay attention.

LOS ANGELES, JUNE 23, 1967

The June 23rd issue of the *Los Angeles Free Press* (vol. 4, no. 25, copyright 1967, $5.00 per year) promised a monster rally, a celebration.

Fifty thousand demonstrators to begin gathering at noon in nearby Cheviot Hills Park. Look for picnicking, rock groups, the fine vibes of Phil Ochs, John Carpenter, and the Mucho Guerrillas doing their theatrical thing. At 6 p.m., the nation's best-loved pediatrician, Dr. Benjamin Spock, keynotes the event. At 6:15, Mr. H. Rap Brown, the new director of SNCC, will tell it like it is. Then more speeches until 7, at which time an army of 50,000 peace-loving hippies, straights, heads, squares, kids, pets, and baby carriages will move out along Motor Avenue to Pico Boulevard and then, marching hand in hand and kneecap to hubcap, parade smartly up the Avenue of the Stars to the Century Plaza, arriving just in time for the President's gala $500-a-plate dinner. And won't he be surprised!

SANTA MONICA, JANUARY 4, 1966

White shoes trudged Broadway with the heavy tread of the uncoordinated. Not only his shoes were white but the socks, the pants, the shirt, the peaked cap—a walking blizzard. Isidore Siegel from Venice, rounding the corner of Second Street on schedule. Whatever else Tuesday might bring to Southern California in that turbulent first decade of his retirement, it was sure to carry Siegel to the Bay City Rollers. The black bowling balls flowing across the green knife-smooth lawn spoke to him of civilization, class. Robinson's shoe department it wasn't, but then what was? His mind danced nimbly over history, sidestepping the store's few unpleasant cracks and cranks. Siegel's palmy days had been lived among Robinson's elegant customers, thick carpets, foreign tongues, sateen-covered chairs, the crystal chandeliers from *Gone With the Wind*. That was the sort of perfumed world he had left behind for a lousy two-bit pension and Medicare.

Dressed like a nurse, Siegel looked like the patient. He was frail and pale, had a red network of spidery threads in his cheeks; a wicked twitch shook his eye. But his younger brother, Mo, was actually the patient. One morning Mo got up with multiple sclerosis, and he had been dying ever since. Mo spent a large part of each day trying not to fall out of his chair. His brother watched him every minute like a security guard, even read him detective stories, and on Tuesdays when Mo's ex-wife came to visit her ex-husband, Siegel in white trudged off to join the Bay City Rollers and make something of what was left of his life.

That Tuesday there was a body blocking his happiness. Some big kid decked out in Salvation Army remnants lay stretched across his path. Siegel did not deny their right to dissent, but he had little use for these beltless flower people.

It was the winter of '66. It was the winter in which our newspapers discovered that the youth of America had grown stiff, rebellious, eager to offend. Teenagers were burning flags, burning draft cards, and seemed to hate the very law itself and everything that said military-industrial complex. It was the winter after Watts and before Century Plaza. *Time* had just saluted General Westmoreland as their Man of the Year, and Siegel had saluted *Time*. The kid on the sidewalk was saluting nobody because he was flat on his ass, stone still.

Close up, Siegel could see that he had misjudged the fellow. This was no kid but a middle-aged bum reeking of shit. Siegel knew well how violent death had a way of routinely opening sphincters in the rat holes of Limehouse, in the parlor cars aboard the boat train to Calais. Mo's brother was no stranger to murder, having encountered it previously on the moors, the links, and the vicarage rug. He observed no bloodstains. He was experienced enough not to touch the body, the telltale small paper bag, the loose thong sandal that had fallen into the gutter, anything. The victim's face was an unpleasant gray. Slowly, the murdered man's eyes opened—startlingly blue—and spittle bubbled on his lips like peroxide on an open wound.

Out into the street rushed Siegel, his white cap flying, his white peak pointing the way, his thin arms windmilling the air as he hailed car after passing car sealed against the heat.

Stop! Wait! Please!

PART II

OAKLAND, 1976

51. BENEATH THE PIER
(The Museum of Crime)

Los Angeles, 1961
Paper, cigar bands, metal washer, postage
stamp on cardboard
Size: 9 x 7¼ inches
Coll. Mrs. M. Dorfman, New York

The air is dank beneath the pier, the ocean choppy. Tied to one of the thick slime-streaked wooden supporting posts is a young woman. She could be Mexican, South American perhaps. She is gagged, her chemise torn, her raven curls disheveled. The flood tide has already brought the water to her waist. She struggles to free herself, the veins in her neck bulging, her eyes white with terror.

Nearby, two men sit stiffly in a rowboat. They have black beards and are dressed in cutaway coats so perfectly tailored that it is evident they have not been rented for the occasion. Their top hats gleam like polished marble. Their leonine faces are somber, befitting an official event. Across their chests they carry ceremonial bands that suggest they may be representing some foreign government. One of them wears a single silver earring. Their arms are folded resolutely, their minds made up.

Above them, the pier is completely deserted. A long black limousine waits in the moonlight, its windshield by now misted over. There seems to be someone sitting in the back. Stamped on the rear door a small triangular device bears the image of a griffin argent.

LOS ANGELES, MAY 7, 1967

LOSS PUT AT $2.5 MILLION

Rembrandt Stolen from County Museum of Art

A Rembrandt masterpiece purchased last year for an estimated $2.5 million by industrialist Newton Ward was stolen from the Los Angeles County Museum of Art late Friday afternoon.

The painting, "Jacob Wrestling ‚with the Angel," had been on loan to the museum and was until recently on display there. It was about to be sent to the Chicago Art Institute, site of a major Rembrandt exhibition opening later this month. The theft occurred while the painting was being prepared for shipment.

"Our storage facilities are as secure as any in the world," said J. Martin Donleavy, director of the newly built museum. "When we opened in March of '65, every precaution was taken to protect our treasures. We have the latest safeguards, the most sophisticated devices. Frankly, I just can't understand how such a thing could have happened." Donleavy termed the loss a "disaster."

According to police estimates, the painting disappeared Friday from the downstairs shipping room sometime between 4:30 and 5:00 p.m. When an immediate search conducted by the museum staff yielded no results, outside authorities were called in. Thus far no ransom attempt has been made.

The oil painting, 90 × 50 centimeters, has been called by experts one of Rembrandt's finest treatments of a biblical theme. It was painted in 1647 and depicts a young Jacob draped in an animal skin wrestling with a blond curly-headed angel who holds his leg.

The canvas, viewed by thousands here since last November, had been jimmied from its frame, which was found badly scratched on the floor of the shipping room. No one has official access to this area but employees. Museum officials declined to specify the number of guards on downstairs duty at the time of the painting's disappearance.

Newton Ward expressed hope that the work would soon be returned undamaged. "I am sure that Martin Donleavy and the police are doing everything in their power to recover my painting. Needless to say, I am upset."

The police indicate that they have few leads in the case, and as of now no suspects have been named.

—*Los Angeles Times*

WEST LOS ANGELES, SEPTEMBER 18, 1964

They met for the first time at the Mark di Suvero opening at the Dawn Gallery in Westwood. Miles Dorfman, a curator at the Los Angeles County Museum of Art, was fascinated by the rough monster poles within the sleek, narrow space, amazed at the combination of delicacy and strength that the sculptor managed to achieve with his massive beams poised giddily in air.

Yeah, nice, said Hawk, and then went on to discuss more important matters. He explained that the two most crucial influences on his own work at the moment were Duchamp and Wong.

It was Wong who created the instruction painting:

A. Steal Rembrandt's *The Polish Rider* from the Frick Collection.

B. Hang it up in the Hunting Department at Abercrombie and Fitch.

C. Ask the salesman if he has a matching quiver and arrows in stock.

It was Hawk who conceived of the instruction painting:

A. Steal Wong's stolen Rembrandt.

The good-natured Miles laughed in spite of himself and, seeing the artist's outstretched hand, forked over a buck for expenses.

SANTA MONICA, JANUARY 12, 1966

You haven't met my cousin Charley yet, Mr. Asher, but he looks a lot like Douglas, my oldest, who was here yesterday. Charley's a good boy. An engineer. He's coming today with his wife, Sue Ellen. Drove all the way from Hobart, Indiana, just for my birthday. How about that! We Thomases are what you call a close family. Thank God that don't mean I have to live in Indiana. Small towns are not exactly my idea of heaven. Five minutes in any one of them and I'd be ready to climb the walls.

Now Charley, on the other hand, says there's always something doing in Hobart. You take 1944, for example. Charley says in 1944 a pretty young bank clerk for the Hobart Savings and Loan told police that a man wearing a Halloween mask crept into her bedroom. Had this little can in his hand and sprayed some wonderfully sweet-smelling fragrance into the air that paralyzed her legs. Once the story got out, fourteen other ladies in town came down with the paralysis. All of them claimed it was the most beautiful smell, the strangest experience they could ever imagine.

You see what I mean about small towns, Mr. Asher? Come to

think of it, I guess Hobart is lucky that guy wasn't spraying something terrible like the diarrhea.

Elbert Thomas grinned and made shrill little wheezing sounds that resembled metal hangers scraping on a metal rack. That was Elbert laughing, having the time of his life. Elbert choking was a mouth like a fish. He clutched the top of a nearby chair. Suddenly the color of his face matched the whiteness of the walls. Gasping air, he managed to suck the pink back into his cheeks.

All right. Okay. Just fine, Mr. Asher. No cause for alarm. He straightened up, wiped the tears from his eyes with his pajama sleeve. Nothing like a good laugh to lighten the load. Now don't you feel better?

Propped up on two pillows, Dan Asher glanced at him for a second. Then he turned back to the sheet-shrouded mound at the other end of the bed where his feet were buried.

Atta boy, said Elbert. Sure you do. He was full of encouragement. He himself had lived through four heart attacks, and here he was in retirement still going strong. Taking each day as it came. By now Elbert had come to believe in himself as a survivor, but he remembered how the first couple of attacks had nearly knocked the wind out of his kazoo. Small wonder Mr. Asher was in the dumps with his first. He felt sorry for the man, took pity on the long face, the sad eyebrows, the bad teeth, the droopy Mexican mustache, the cautious way he moved his body as if it were booby trapped and might explode at any minute. He tried to cheer him up with riddles.

How about this one? Tell me what you call a young woman who rings your bell in the middle of the night wearing nothing but a pair of peppermint-striped panties and high-heeled shoes? Staring out the window, Dan Asher asked him what time it was. It was eleven fifteen. Visiting hours, he said, did not begin until noon. There was still plenty of time. Elbert repeated the riddle and, unable to hold back any longer, said Welcome. Get it, Mr. Asher? She's called welcome. Once again Elbert wheezed, choked, and laughed himself white. He dearly loved a good riddle.

Dan Asher thought, The Mouth says plenty of time but he's

dying. Poor old bastard. The best jazz says gonna live forever, don't believe in death. But in this place everything tells me believe: the gauges, the stainless steel trays, the green oxygen tank in the corner, the intravenous tube in my arm, Felstein's bedside manner full of bullshit optimism, this stiff thing with the ties in the back that they hung on me like a white shroud. Oh, Christ! Where's my pants? My butterfly? I've got to get the hell out of here before they kill me.

At twelve sharp in walked the Thomas family, eleven strong including the Indiana branch. They filled the room with their noise, their presents, their wall-to-wall smiles, their many happy returns of the day. 'Lo, said Elbert weakly. He had washed his face, buttoned up his pajamas. He sat on the edge of his bed drooping forward like an invalid. Although the doctor had told him he could go home tomorrow or Friday, he wondered if it might not be best to wait until the weekend. Walking still pooped him out. Mrs. Thomas, a squat woman with a bulldog chin, thought it over for her husband and said Sunday. Elbert stood up, hugged Mrs. Thomas, kissed Sue Ellen, shook hands with Charley.

The Thomases held their birthday party in the lounge at the end of the hall in order to give Mr. Asher some peace and quiet. It was Elbert's idea. You sure could use a little of his hair, cracked Charley on their way out. Douglas had flashbulbs and took pictures of everyone, arranging them into groups of threes and fours like furniture. It was a good party. Returning to his room with a small piece of the birthday cake wrapped in a napkin for Mr. Asher, Elbert was pleased to see that there were two visitors with him.

One girl looked about sixteen and scrawny. She had the long legs of a high-jumper, and her short skirt only made them seem longer. She said hi. I'm his daughter, Marissa. The other daughter was older. She had curly brown hair that hadn't been combed in days, a pockmarked face, and no lipstick. Her heavy brocade gown came to the floor, but nothing could hide the fact that she

24

had a body that might move men to tears, to distraction, to the barricades like La Pasionaria's voice. No, no, said Marissa, giggling pleasantly. She's not my sister. That's Dan's friend Mona.

Elbert was pleased to meet them both, but he had to admit that he had a little problem. If A says to B, Give me one of your pencils and I'll have twice as many as you have, and B says to A, Nope, you give me one of yours and we'll both have the same, then how many pencils does A have and how many B? Marissa said, Wait a minute, hold on, do that again. Dan Asher said, Don't encourage him. Mona went over to the old man and whispered something in his ear. Elbert's face said nothing. Then turning to his roommate, he said, She's smarter than you are.

Mr. Asher's two visitors stayed on with him for a while, chatting, and Elbert wandered off to the other side of the room and tried not to listen. He heard Mr. Asher asking about Marlene Dietrich. The young girlfriend said that she was downstairs waiting in the car. I've got to go, she said, and kissed him goodbye. Looking up, she caught Elbert staring at her and walked straight up to him. Don't be jealous. You, too, she said, kissing him on the cheek. She left instructions with him to take good care of her friend. Marissa said, Thanks for the cake. On the way out, Mona confided, I like your puzzles. Elbert's face had the pink glow of a plastic sponge. Come again tomorrow, he called, and I'll have a new one for you. It was a promise.

SANTA MONICA, JANUARY 5, 1966

OAKLAND, 1976

DANIEL ASHER: Collages 1943–1967.
The Oakland Museum, 1976.
Introduction by Mordecai Bell.

The artist's parents came from Russia. His father, Julius, owned a small clothing store in the Bronx known locally for its selection of smart fedoras and sporty caps. It was Mr. Asher's fondest dream that his only son might one day enter the business. Poetically speaking, I believe he eventually did. Hats —especially bowlers—were to become an integral part of his haunting artistic vision. It was once suggested (v. "The Small Miracles of Daniel Asher," *Art News*, Feb. 1953), that these hats probably owe a debt to Max Ernst's 1920 work, *The Hat Makes the Man.* Knowing what we do about Asher's background, such a claim seems largely dispensable.

As a child, Asher delighted in drawing not only all the usual subjects so dear to the young such as baseball players and airplanes but also, according to his mother, who is now eighty-six and confined to a nursing home in the Bronx, such uncommon images as wheelchairs, can openers, and hats. Skill in naturalistic detail came easily to him without formal training of any kind. If family legend is to be believed, there was one exquisite depiction of a Tyrolean feather so lifelike that it led to his father striking the lad when he claimed it as his own. Unfortunately, none of these youthful Düreresque drawings could be included in this retrospective. Most have been either lost or destroyed.

WEST HOLLYWOOD, JUNE 14, 1976

On Monday the store opened at ten. It was then a little past eight. After a slow, shuffling Sunday, Mrs. Devonshire was

26

making an early start. Not that she actually intended to buy anything at the Broadway, but she could always kill a couple of hours there. No, really, she said. It's not so bad. I'm glad I've got a place to go.

Tattersall raised his head. Aside from her, he was the only one on the bench. It wasn't the worst that Henry had ever heard at that particular location, but it was probably not the last from her either. This was a frail woman in a large straw hat, a flimsy print dress, the hair gray, the face gray, and the bare arms as thin as glass tubing. Clutched in her lap a torn pocketbook and a plaid knitting bag that bulged with something heavier than wool. Tattersall guessed food stamps, a worn cardigan sweater should the temperature at the beach dip below 75 degrees, a navel orange for lunch.

Glancing eastward beyond Barney's Beanery, beyond Bekins into the sun, he could find no bus. The wind blew soft and desert dry. Henry had known it to make some people as jittery as a long drumroll. He resumed his newspaper.

BEVERLY HILLS, SEPTEMBER 5, 1959

Marissa was seven in 1959. She had just lost another mother and didn't yet have a place to live. Temporarily they were staying with Max Roth in Beverly Hills. Max came as a surprise to her. He had a sweet smell, a funny way of talking, a swimming pool all to himself. He seemed to her as remarkable as the palm trees, handsome enough to be an actor.

Genug, he told Dan. I agree one thousand percent. There is only one Kunsthistorisches, one Charlot, one Gustave Mahler, one Brown Bomber. I agree! I agree! Agreed *The New York Times* is *The New York Times* and in a class alone. But please, dear friend, you should have seen what this was like before. A rag! A scumbag! There was a time when I myself would not have read *The Los Angeles Times* without a gift subscription. Today we see noble principles on every page and the largest circulation west of the Rockies. The gallery coverage you will find to be sincere.

WEST HOLLYWOOD, JUNE 14, 1976

Ecosystem. Once Los Angeles had only youthful strata from the Quaternary and the Tertiary periods and, following the full moon, grunion. The air was as silver as snail tracks. Since then orange groves have come and gone, leaving signs everywhere. Stern orders in the sky.

Hold up two fingers. Save someone's life. Meet Spyder. Come to the Valley of the Sun. To Marlboro Country. To Caesar's Palace. Flip open a box. Don't ask me why I smoke. Promise her anything. Discover the magazine for today's California. Ask your dealer. Do it pronto. Get yours. Signs on the walls blazoned Picfair Bowling, a New American Hamburger, Bekins. The typography clashed like opposing teams.

At the corner of La Cienega and Santa Monica, a billboard flaunted a woman wearing a two-piece bathing suit. She squatted in a giant frying pan, her back a flag of raw and brilliant red. The color matched Tattersall's sunburned face at the bus stop below. Close your eyes. Tighter. Henry closed his eyes as if shutting the door on a room where a shrill, stubborn argument had been going on for a long time.

Getting off at Doheny. Crossing to Melrose. He strolled slowly. The Theatre Vanguard, a few small boutiques filled with clothes that were so old they had become fashionable again, a quaint clock shop with a bronze sundial in the window, a plant store called The Bad Seed. On its cinderblock side, a modest blue arrow with the message Blue Dart Messenger Service and below that, without capitals, *harris productions*.

Tattersall followed the arrow down the narrow alley to the

rear. Both names appeared on the door of the boxlike one-story structure and in the curtained window a sign. OPEN it said —four bugle blasts in Day-Glo orange on black. The door was locked. He brushed off the stoop and sat down between two large wooden jardinières that were being held together by rusty metal bands. Leaning back against the door, he spread his newspaper across his lap.

So much was still unresolved. Rumors of steroid traces in the urine of East German women swimmers. The density of the shadows in the Hays-Ray affair. A first-ballot nomination for Jimmy Carter. Death, of course, nicely tied things up, but the paper did not regularly carry obituaries. You had to be either a well-known national figure or a hanging. Phil Ochs was a hanging.

> Folksinger and popular composer of 60s protest music such as "I Ain't Marching Any More," Ochs was called by many "the next Dylan"—a prediction, unhappily, never realized. Dead at 35 in his sister's closet.

The chill of the stoop in the gloom-shrouded courtyard. Through thin seersucker trousers, Tattersall felt it and rose. Troubled by Ochs's haste. In connection with his work, the private investigator had come to know many artists over the years and found them generally to be too hasty, too sensitive for their own good.

OAKLAND, 1976

DANIEL ASHER: Collages 1943–1967.
The Oakland Museum, 1976.
Introduction by Mordecai Bell.

An outstanding student, Asher received a scholarship to attend Princeton University, where he was a member of the Class of '38. Presumably as some sort of compromise with his father, he followed a pre-law program. His former roommates and the few teachers at Princeton who still remember him speak of a shy, quiet, intense young man.

When finally it came time for Asher to apply to law schools, he told his father that he would wait a bit before beginning graduate work. He did not tell him that two years earlier at the Museum of Modern Art he had seen the famous show entitled "Fantastic Art, Dada, Surrealism," and that he had made up his mind to become an artist.

WEST HOLLYWOOD, JUNE 14, 1976

The two dwarf lemon trees in the jardinières were in all stages of the growth cycle simultaneously, a time-lapse montage of each tree's history. The bud, the blossom, the deep green bulb, the yellow fruit, the brown-stained rotter side by side, clinging to the tough, twiggy branches. Uncared for, never sunned, irrepressible trees, bemused into fruit by mild temperatures, their lemons glowing dimly beneath the soot. Here it should be noted that agriculture is one of California's largest industries, worth over three billion dollars to the state in 1975.

Tattersall cleaned out the cigarette butts and gum wrappers from the jardinières. Without knowing why, he was reminded of something the woman at the bus stop had said about outliving her children.

Looky looky looky! So excited he just couldn't sleep. Up and out at the crack of dawn. It was Harris, snapping his pudgy fingers and dancing down the alley with a shuffle step. See you got my message, Henry. Press the flesh.

Henry's alleged excitability was a misunderstanding so profound that he felt physically drained. Harris, on the other hand, appeared radiant. His face was tanned, his eyebrows thick, and his teeth were white and strong. He had the smile of a lecher, the freckled and balding scalp of a scoutmaster. The yellow floral-print shirt he wore was opened to the breastbone. The delicate gold chain around his neck was new. Something was always new with Harris. Lose sight of him for a second and there he was back with a new friend, a mind-boggling deal, the latest dance craze, or tinted glasses. He had an aging effect on Tattersall. The question was what else he had.

Preamo, reported the informer as he opened the Blue Dart door and suggested that they conduct their business within. Grade A preamo. Tattersall wearily brought up the rear. Only yesterday the word had been "dynamite."

The Blue Dart Messenger Service was a desk, a telephone, an answering device, a half-empty jar of macadamia nuts, one beat-up file cabinet, and, in the corner, a large dieffenbachia —each dark green leaf as broad as a book. It was nothing more than a front for Harris's dreams. They hung on the walls, the framed covers of five paperback thrillers on which he had acquired movie options for little more than breathtaking promises. While waiting to make just the right deals for his properties, Harris made pocket money by delivering messages. He had one for his friend Henry: the Marquis Gallery on Camden Drive in Beverly Hills.

Last Friday, he had delivered a package there. No one was in the office to sign for it, so he looked into the storage room in the back. Against the wall was a three-tiered wooden rack. And what do you suppose he saw there while casually checking the inventory? What do you suppose, Henry?

All right, snapped Tattersall, cut the crap.

Up on top and shrouded in the corner was grappling Jacob shooting for a takedown on some out-of-towner with wings.

The investigator looked at him and frowned. How, he asked, how could he be sure that it was Jacob? From the top drawer of his desk, Harris produced a creased postcard reproduction of the Rembrandt painting. He knew one hundred percent, he said. It was Jacob, all right.

Tattersall appeared just a little disappointed. If *Jacob Wres-*

tling with the Angel turned up in any gallery in Los Angeles, he had had a hunch that it would be Roth's. This new development, however, did not at all rule out Asher. Slipping his informant a twenty, Tattersall confided that he was not optimistic.

Harris looked at the bill as if it were a subpoena. You've got to be kidding, he said. Rembrandt is money in the bank. Right now that hot painting is waiting for you on Camden Drive, and it's worth millions. Come on, Henry, is this the best you can do for preamo? Henry nodded reassuringly and made a promise to him on the way out. We'll see what happens, he said. And now tell me about married life.

Oh, said Harris, it would never have worked out. Cynthia is a lovely and talented girl, but definitely not right for the part. The search goes on.

Henry stared in silence at the gold chain around the informer's neck. What the hell, he thought, no one's perfect. In his back pocket, he himself carried a small black comb.

LAPD—File 21350 x (Century Plaza Riot)
Typescript of Press Conference held by Inspector Thomas Cassell (PRD)
Parker Center
22 June 1967
Q: Could you tell us, Inspector, why Chief
   Reddin was against the Police Commission
   granting a permit to the Peace Action
   Council for tomorrow's march?
A: We have information that led us to believe
   that a potentially dangerous situation may
   exist here.
Q: What sort of information?
A: Our special agents—these are specially
   trained undercover operatives working in
   the field—our agents have learned that extremist groups intend to use the occasion
   of the President's visit for acts of civil
   disobedience.
Q: Do you have any reason to believe that the
   President's life is in danger?
A: We intend to do all in our power to see
   that it isn't.

Q: Does that mean that you think it may be? Have the police uncovered a plot against the President, Inspector?
A: I can't comment on that.
Q: What sort of security precautions are you taking?
A: It's probably one of the largest—I guess it's the biggest security operation in the Department's history. We'll be working closely with the Secret Service, the FBI, the hotel security guards, and city park rangers. All time off has been canceled, and there will be in excess of 1,000 officers available for duty in and around the Century Plaza area tomorrow when the President arrives. I might point out that two years ago even at the height of the riots in southcentral Los Angeles, no more than 496 policemen were on duty at any one time.
Q: What is the President's schedule?
A: We understand that he'll be flying here directly from Washington and arrive in Los Angeles on Friday at 7:30 P.M. How he'll travel from the airport to the Century Plaza is not known at this time.
Q: A spokesman for the march has said that the demonstrators have no intention of massing in front of the hotel or disrupting anything but the killing in Vietnam. Does that reassure you?
A: The only quasi—comfort we can take is from the Weather Bureau's prediction of a remote chance of drizzle.

THE BRONX, JULY 23, 1952

Dan Asher hated hospitals. His sister died in one. Marion's obituary seemed to be hanging on every wall, neatly framed and matted. He would gladly have settled for an old copy of *Screen*

Gems. He glanced around the waiting room for something else to read. The elderly couple in the corner making less noise than ferns, the woman dozing, the hollow-eyed man leaning forward on his umbrella handle. Dan Asher wiggled his toes, slid a finger into each shoe. His socks were still damp from the puddle that he had stepped into when they had gotten out of the taxi.

From his rolled-up raincoat on the chair beside him, he drew a crumpled pack of Camels. It was empty. The idea of a cup of coffee appealed to him, but the idea of sacrifice appealed to him more. Goddammit, he was not going to be left completely out of this thing! Upstairs poor Gretchen laboring, bearing down, wailing her sweet heart out, her golden hair pasted crazily to her forehead with sweat, her legs bound in stirrups, her dimpled thighs being ripped apart; downstairs her Dan doing his small bit of suffering for the cause. Asher felt embarrassed by his own nonsense. This sort of flutter was not like him at all. He went to find out if there was a place in the hospital to get some coffee at that hour of the morning.

There was nobody at the front desk but Freddy Martin playing "The Lamplighter's Serenade."

A moment after dark, around the park . . .

The sax section was definitely nasty, oozing around the park like Uriah Heep. It was Music till Dawn, tuned to a whisper but not low enough for Dan Asher. He reached over to the small portable and turned it off.

On the desk beside the radio lay a folded copy of the *Compass* that he picked up. Stevenson was saying he'd run. Dan Asher was glad to hear it, preferring Princeton in the White House to West Point, but he had no illusions about where the rest of America would be standing in November. He hated the mindless mass hysteria of politics. On the other hand, he adored Jane Arden on page 12. She was bathed in moonlight, drenched in candlelight, dining alfresco in black strapless chic, a single strand of pearls around her neck, an orchid on her gown. She looked great! As trim as a propeller. But all the time she was really thinking inside her balloon, WHY DIDN'T THE PARKS COMMISSIONER WANT ME TO SEE

HIS PAYROLL RECORDS? Dan Asher had to have her.

The big woman who suddenly appeared behind the desk wore her hair braided over her ears like two Wagnerian pretzels. There had been a changing of the guard since he and Gretchen had arrived. This one demanded to know what he was doing. Dan Asher was very carefully tearing out the comic strip and putting Jane Arden into his pocket. For your information, she said, that's my newspaper. Given her position regarding private property, he was frankly surprised that she read anything as liberal as the *Compass*. He had taken her for a storm trooper.

He folded the paper, handed it over, and indicated that he was about to become a father. It worked like a charm. The tight military line of her lips dissolved into a lullaby. She wanted to know everything: the name of the obstetrician, the patient, the crib, the carriage, the pediatrician, the diaper service. Was he excited? He certainly was. He decided he had done her an injustice. He could have listened to a fine voice like hers for hours, and she had something to say about coffee too. The White Tower around the corner was open all night. Dan Asher hesitated. Go ahead, she urged, go ahead. These things take time. It's not going to happen any quicker if you're sitting in there. She was right, of course.

He stood at the front door gazing out and saw that the heavy rain had dwindled to a fine mist. A wind had blown up. The street looked deserted now, a death ship with only running lights, going nowhere in the dark. Turning, he flickered a faint smile deskward, but his new friend was busy on the telephone. He slipped quietly back into the waiting room and sat down again. His chair was still warm. He might have allowed his sister to die in one of these places, but he'd be damned if he was going to budge from his wife. He was far enough away from her as it was down here.

Opening a copy of *The Christian Science Journal* and, sure enough, the first article he came to was entitled "Beyond Death." For God's sake, don't worry, Gretchen! You can do it. Chin up. I'm with you, cutey. Nothing to worry about. Remember, if it's a boy, Michael, a girl, Marissa. Push, honey, push!

35

CERTIFICATE OF DEATH

No. 66-781-0025

Type or Print in Permanent Ink

Deceased—Name First Middle Last		Sex	Date of Death Month Day Year	
1. Madeleine Benedict Asher		2. F	3. 6 / 30 / 59	

	Race	Age Last Birthday	Date of Birth	County of Death
DECEASED	4. White	5. 40	6. 5 / 9 / 19	7a. Manhattan

City, Town, or Location of Death	Inside City Limits	Hospital or Other Institution (If not either, give street and number)
7b. New York	7c. Yes	7d. 432 Sixth Avenue

State of Birth (If not in USA, name country)	Citizen of What Country	Married, Never Married, Widowed, Divorced
8. Minnesota	9. U.S.A.	10. Married

Surviving Spouse (If wife, give maiden name)	Social Security No.	Usual Occupation
11. Daniel Asher	12. 059–12–2326	13. Dancer

Residence— State	County	City, Town, or Location	Street and Number
14a. New York	14b. Manhattan	14c. New York	14d. 432 Sixth Ave.

Father—Name First Middle Last	Mother—Maiden Name First Middle Last
15. Joseph Alfred Benedict	16. Margaret Tate

	Informant—Name	Mailing Address
PARENTS	17a. Daniel Asher	17b. 432 Sixth Avenue

Part I. Death was caused by: (Enter only one cause per line for (a), (b), (c).)

	Immediate Cause	Approximate Interval between Onset and Death
CAUSE	18. (a) Drug Overdose (Phenobarbital)	
	(b) Due to, or as a consequence of:	
	(c) Due to, or as a consequence of:	

Part II. Other significant conditions (Conditions contributing to death but not related to cause given in Pt. I(a).)

	Autopsy	If Yes, were findings considered in determining cause of death
19a.	19b. Yes	19c. Yes

Accident, Suicide, Homicide, or Undetermined (Specify)	Date of Injury
20a. Suicide	20b.

Certification—Medical Examiner or Coroner—
On the Basis of the Body and/or the Investigation, in my
Opinion Death Occurred on the Date and Due to the
Cause(s) Stated.

Death Occurred Hour	The Decedent was Pronounced Dead				Date Signed
	Month	Day	Year	Hour	
21a. 5 P.M.	21b. 6 /	30 /	59	11:30 P.M.	21c.7 / 2 / 59

Certifier—Name (type or print)	Signature	Degree or Title
22a. W.W. Thomson	22b. *W. W. Thomson*	Coroner

Burial, Cremation, Removal (Specify)	Date—Month Day Year
23a. Cremation	23b. 7 / 2 / 59

Funeral Home	Address
24a. Frank E. Campbell, Inc.	24b. 1076 Madison Avenue, New York

Funeral Director (Signature)	Registrar (Signature)
25. *Joe Smith*	26. *Thomas B. Stern*

CERTIFIER

BURIAL

SANTA MONICA, JANUARY 13, 1966

Mona hated hospitals. According to Dan Asher they depressed her. I wish she wouldn't come today, he told his friend Leland. He had spoken to her that morning, but he didn't think it had made any difference. Perhaps if Leland would call and tell her that he was right there in the room and everything was fine, she might take the day off. Leland called, but there was no answer.

Seated, the painter Leland Sonderman was as tall as some men standing, and his beard swagged down like Spanish moss. Dan Asher respected him as an artist. He admired his courage in choosing to be an oil painter in an acrylic world. He envied the children and couples that were his subjects—always at home in their airy rooms and easy landscapes. He did not, however, care for his work. Dan Asher would absolutely never have told him that, and Leland, of course, did not mention that he knew. Friendship may thrive even in such dark, fastidious soil.

It was Leland who had gotten Dan Asher the job at UCLA the previous year when he needed the money. Leland taught studio courses there. Dan Asher had never before taught anywhere and was surprised at how much he liked it. He celebrated the end of his first quarter of teaching by having a party for his class in the university's sculpture garden at the foot of Lipchitz's *Song of the Vowels*.

Following the party, the chairman of the Art Department had a visit from a student who did not smoke pot and did not drink Almadén California Mountain White Chablis. The chairman, an amiable man of the world, took the news of the party in his stride. If charges were being made against Mr. Asher, he insisted that he have something in writing. The chairman hoped that the letter would never arrive, but it did.

Leland was furious. He demanded that his friend's side of the story be heard before any final action was taken. Summoned to the chairman's office, Dan Asher frankly acknowledged that it had been a good party. Leland's position in the department was awkward for a time after that. Prepared as he was to make allowances for genius, he said nothing to his friend.

In the hospital room, Leland told of plans for an artists' antiwar tower on Sunset. Dan Asher was not surprised to learn that Mona was a member of the organizing committee, but he had heard nothing about it. The subject was dropped. Leland reported that he had run into Max Roth, who sent his regards, promised to visit. Dan Asher did not think he would. We have a very special relationship, he explained. Let's just say Max feels that I've done him an injustice, and I'm the one who's been robbed. It had been five years since Asher's last exhibition at the Roth Gallery.

What's past is past, said Max, when he arrived with his wonderful smile and marvelous voice. He was looking more prosperous than ever. His dungarees were custom-tailored perfection and his black boots as sleek as seals. He was glad to see that someone had already brought the patient the new book by Ed Ruscha. Who else but Edward would ever have thought of doing such a thing? said Max in admiration. What a mensch! Every building on the Strip recorded once and for all in *unbarmherzig* black and white. I call that a beautiful thing. Outstanding! The copy of *The Sunset Strip* in his hand was apparently not for Dan Asher after all. For Dan Asher he managed to find something else. In his suede pocket a 3 × 5 photograph of the Lissitzky 1920 book jacket for *Dialogue de Deux Mondes*.

Max's polish was a gaudy juggling act that Dan Asher noted without applause. He recalled a long-ago dinner at the dealer's house when the doorbell rang and in came two well-known collectors. Max checked his watch, announced that the Abelsons were late and, laughing, asked what they wanted to drink. It was by chance that Dan Asher afterward learned that they were actually one week early. The mystery of how two extra veal chops were obtained at that late hour had only briefly captured his imagination.

How unnaturally clean he looks, how pale. Max was sorry he had come. Abrupt changes in other people's lives unsettled his own and sometimes even made it seem less interesting. I myself, he asserted, am not a perfectionist. Only last year such high-mindedness killed Albert Schweitzer, plugged Ambassador Stevenson in the heart. Live and let be, my friend. You cannot solve all the world's problems overnight. As for Dan Asher's own financial problems—what with hospital expenses and school supplies (how is the little star-struck darling?)—Max hinted that he might be of some help. *Salud y pesetas*, he said on the way out. Call me at home as soon as you are once again tip-top. The private line.

They sat talking softly through the waning afternoon. Once a nurse passing by in the hall looked in. How you doom, Mr. Asher? She was big and black and ugly, and her heavy lips barely moved when she spoke, as if her teeth were incriminating evidence. Here now, lemme straighten this out for you. Dan Asher decided that he would live. Loving her kindness and the unexpected delicacy of her thick fingers as they caressed his sheet, stroked his pillowcase smooth. He could always find something in a woman that he adored.

As soon as she left, he got out of bed to join Leland at the window. It's all right, Dan reassured him. Relax. Exercise is wonderful for the heart, they say. A bit wobbly, he held tight to the sill and leaned his forehead against the cool glass. There they were below making their music. Eight of them dancing together with tambourines and finger cymbals and seeming as out of place on the Santa Monica pavement as camels or yaks. Dan Asher relished the contrast. What he didn't care for was the crushing repetition. Infinite human beings turned into the same shaved head, the same saffron robe, the same gaunt fanatical look, and chanting the same Hare Krishna 1,728 times a day. Not an artist in the bunch.

One of them had a framed portrait that he held high above his head in the direction of the hospital windows. Dan couldn't make out the face, but he knew very well who it had to be. Elbert Thomas, his mouth gagged and his eyes blanked out as if Greek marble. After that the rest was easy for him. The octagon stop sign on the corner he painted solid gray. An elderly woman rode toward it on a bicycle. He clamped a set of earphones on her head, trailed a conveyor belt behind her loaded with scented soaps and shampoos and oils and incense sticks, the products labeled Celestial Glow. The horses appeared out of nowhere. Eight black-plumed stallions before a black-wreathed coach standing motionless in the middle of the street. Having forgotten about them, Dan was astounded. He had not expected to come upon the same eight animals that had carried off Pepe Illo waiting patiently for him.

Alone. When he awoke, Dan Asher was alone. Leland had gone home, and now he lay with his sick heart in the darkening room. The linoleum floor smelled of pine needles and formaldehyde. Dan Asher felt himself shrinking, shriveling up like the afternoon light. Cut off from the things of this world that he loved with their shifty colors. Mona's rose flesh that he had kissed and stroked a thousand times and watched come alive hot pink under his palms. Her low voice with its throaty jackpot promises. Her dear ways that he loved. Invisible in the late afternoon gloom, the tears unfocused his eyes. He reached for a tissue. Blew his nose.

At least he knew that he could count on her. If the worst came to the worst, Mona would take care of the kid. Gretchen had turned out to have less mothering in her than a hot-water bag. But he was not going to say anything harsh about a living mother at a time like this. The selfish bitch! She could keep her blood money for all he cared. There was probably a local group that would handle his cremation cheap. Spread him out like a benediction over sea, desert, or high above the timberline. A nice variety of choices.

In New York there had been the Chapel Society. Madeleine was a dancer, so he had given her a bouquet of a dozen long-stem beauties and the sea to dance upon. Madeleine's mother hadn't much cared for having a cremated daughter. She was Catholic. But she hated to fly, and by the time she arrived from Minneapolis it was too late. He had done the best he knew how with the body, the dead wood of that sweet face. Done the best he knew how for the mother, telling her that death was by natural causes. Standing in Grand Central Station on that gloomy platform and trying to calm the distraught woman, reason with her that if in the beginning it was dust that we came from then surely we could be shaped up out of dust at the final bell. Body and soul.

And if it were not so, would I not tell you?

Mrs. Benedict stared at him. You kike bastard! she screamed, pushing him back and tearing at his upturned collar with her black woolen hands. Never before or since had he seen so much loathing in a human face.

Dan Asher wondered if he would ever work again. Bedridden and old, Matisse with a pair of scissors had cut out bathers, pomegranates, monkeys and acrobats, kings and dancers and Chinese fish. Why not Dan Asher? He was only half a hundred and still pumping. Fleetingly, hope chucked him under the chin.

Then it was Mona that he began to worry about. He wondered if something had happened to her. Not an accident. She was a skillful driver, so not an accident but a busted clutch, a dry radiator, an empty gas tank because she used machines without mercy, without having the least feeling for them. He had not wanted her to come today, but he was troubled that she hadn't, surprised that there had been no call, no message.

And then there she was standing in the doorway, looking outrageously young without lipstick, and breathless and desirable, and she had come just for him. Dan saw her hesitate for a split second as if she had entered the wrong room, didn't recognize the old man lying in the shadows. Staring at the made-up bed next to his own, she asked, Where's Elbert? Did he go home?

Dan told her, Dead.

PART III

OAKLAND, 1976

31. HOTEL CALIFORNIA

New York, 1958
Paper, mirror fragments, 5-centime coins,
sheet music, coffee bean on cardboard
Size: 8½ x 11 inches
Coll. M. Roth, Los Angeles

*Outside the window, the low balustrade is ornamented with
bronze-colored circular shields bearing the inscription* RÉPUB-
LIQUE FRANÇAISE. *Above the window, the sign of the coffee
bean. The window itself is long and vertical. The drapes, covered
by a pattern of stars and planets, are tied back and reveal an
adolescent girl completely naked staring out through the blue-tinted
glass.*

*It is always raining outside the Hotel California, always sad;
always there is a slight chill in the air. Deep within the blueness of
the room, a man whose face is hidden beneath the brim of his
Borsalino sits cross-legged on the edge of the unmade bed, a*

cigarette holder between his lips. The mirror behind him is cracked. Pasted to its frame are the words "O Manon, ma jolie, mon coeur te dit bonjour" from the old love song.

SANTA MONICA, FEBRUARY 7, 1966

Sounds transformed into visual images. Fascinated, Dan Asher watched the two silent C.C.U. television screens. The patients' names were taped to the frame. Goldman fluctuated wildly, his peaks and valleys a farce. Costomski appeared to be dwindling off into the straight line of eternity. Bates, Lopez, and the rest signaled okay.

Standing with his back to the screens and the nurses' desk, Dr. Felstein said, The worst is over. Now, with a new diet, a new exercise program, new habits, there's no reason to think that Dan in time will not be able to do all the things he has always done. How soon can we fuck? asked Mona.

The resumption of normal sexual relations. Yes, said Dr. Felstein sternly. He was almost the same age as she was.

BEVERLY HILLS, JUNE 15, 1976

Street-corner peddling is forbidden in Beverly Hills. Bernie the Flower Man was the exception. There was probably nobody from one end of Camden Drive to the other who knew that his real name was Wachs. Bernie the Flower Man was an institution, a celebrity. Cops cruising Camden and Brighton Way let their eyes police 270 degrees. Bernie sat on the northeast 90 degrees as if established by a plebiscite.

His white cart with its sky-blue awning had already made the local television news twice, once when they were doing a feature

46

on aging and once when a smogless day appeared on the weather. On aging, bald Bernie chewed on his cigar stub and said, I like what I'm doing here, and I've got no place else to go. So I guess I stay here with my flowers until it's time to go. Then, he said, I'll go. On the weather, he showed pink roses, red and white camellias, yellow daffodils, and bronze mums if you had color. Tattersall idly checked the merchandise. Very colorful, but he didn't care for the smell. Indiscriminate floral sweetness made him as restless as the beach did.

Bernie glanced across the street and replied, Sure. Sure I've been in there. You like flowers, you like art. But they show people with three eyes and heads like buttons. Who cares about such losers? I'm for the old stuff. Van Gogh, ships, flowers. You know what I mean.

Tattersall knew. Not everyone likes modern art, he agreed. He wondered how they managed to pay the rent over there. Bernie couldn't say, but he did know that they had people going in and out all day long. Don't ask me why, but that's a fact. Tattersall shrugged and suggested that maybe Mr. Marquis knew better than either of them what the public wanted.

There ain't no Mr. Marquis. There's a Mr. Mark Hofstedler, Bernie pointed out. But he's dead. Then there's Mr. Mark number 2 who runs the show, and believe me he's a wonderful young man.

Bernie noted Tattersall's white shirt, the tie, the narrow seersucker lapels. The clean-shaven cheeks belonged on a witness stand. A *wonderful* young man, he added. What about some carnations?

Bernie watched him go. Crossing the street and ambling up to the gallery window and looking in. The Flower Man muttering. The Flower Man peering after him and muttering, Get yourself a fink somewhere else, you FBI son of a bitch!

OAKLAND, 1976

DANIEL ASHER: Collages 1943–1967.
The Oakland Museum, 1976.
Introduction by Mordecai Bell.

It was sometime toward the end of 1939 that Asher rented a cheap one-room apartment in Greenwich Village. He lived on Jane Street near the river and was fascinated by the life of the piers—the longshoremen, the people arriving from all over the world, the giant ships. "I'm thinking of stowing away on one of them," he wrote to a former Princeton classmate. "I have such a desire to see Europe! By the time I can afford to go, there probably won't be anything left of it."

Although he never did get to Europe, Asher was able, ironically, to meet a number of the most important European avant-garde artists in New York. They had come to America to escape the war. He haunted the galleries where their work was shown and met the celebrated Mondrian at the Dudensing Gallery, Kurt Seligmann at the Julien Levy Gallery. Seligmann liked the intense young man and in turn introduced him to Duchamp, Tanguy, Masson, and Max Ernst. For an aspiring young artist, it was exactly the right historical moment to be in the city.

The collage show organized by Peggy Guggenheim in 1943 included, in addition to well-known European artists, the work of the young Americans: Pollock, Motherwell, Baziotes, and Asher. Of this group, it was Asher's collage entitled "Sadness in the Ring" (whereabouts currently unknown) that was especially well received.

Asher's first one-man show was held in 1946 at the Külicke-Reid Gallery in New York. The collages exhibited were small and dark. Their images were as crowded together as the shiploads of refugees that he had seen arriving. No single common theme linked all the works (as would be the case in later exhibitions), but the vision was consistent and singular.

In an idyllic setting, whether party or picnic, something inexplicable, discordant, has occurred off to one side and nobody seems to notice. In the collage *Strings* (cat. no. 3), for example, children fly kites or play games with gyroscopes, yo-yos, chestnuts on shoelaces. One is reminded of Breughel, of course, except that in Asher's world the tree in the corner dangles a small white bird with a rope around its neck.

The critics, intrigued by this new talent, were uniformly enthusiastic. Daniel Asher had just turned thirty and, with his first show a success, would no longer have to support himself by taking odd jobs. "A *frühe Geglückte*," his dealer, Hans Külicke, called him. "That's what Asher was," he recently told me, "a wonderful young success."

The Hotel Victoria
Kingston, Jamaica
April 14, 1964

Dearest Dan,

I was in the Museum of Modern Art last week, and, not seeing your *Don Juan* anywhere, I got worried and asked at the desk downstairs. The cute-looking fairy there said no, it wasn't on exhibition just now but yes, they still had it. Well, that was a relief! Anyway, since I happened to be by myself with some free time on my hands—which is a real rarity these days—and being in the neighborhood I thought why not, you know, for auld lang syne, and walked over to East 57th Street and the Külicke-Reid.

They still have the same silly zebra-striped awning out front that we used to howl at. The one you said was just right for a whorehouse. (You see, of course I haven't forgotten.) For a minute there on the sidewalk it might have been 1953 again with nothing changed, but once inside I felt like John Glenn out in space.

It's a different gallery now. They're showing bronze beer cans and pictures of creamsicles and Dick Tracy. I mean really cartoons, and when I spoke to Hans he said they were specializing in pop art these days. He said they were no longer handling your work and hadn't been for more than three years. I looked at him, and he said that's right, three years, and he didn't think anybody was just now. I couldn't believe it. After all the exhibitions and the articles and the Venice Biennale. You're in the Museum of Modern Art, for crying out loud!

I could have sat right down on the floor and wept, I felt so bad. It hurt me terribly. You remember how easily I used to be hurt. Still the same old softy, I guess. Then I remembered that letter I got back last year with *Not At This Address* scrawled on the envelope, and there was the *s* you've always been in too much of a hurry to close and your uncrossed *t*. I never thought I'd forgive you for that, but you can see what sort of marshmallow I am. Look, I know damn well you're still at the old address in Venice, so no more bull. Just take this money and use it for whatever you need, and don't think twice about it because there's plenty more where that came from.

You can't imagine how things have changed for us since Richard did the Charles Jourdan ad. Everybody wants him now—Klopman, McGregor, everybody—and when he tries to cut down on the workload by upping his prices, they only want him more. He's here in Jamaica doing a new campaign for Schenley. As for me, I've been busy taking pictures of my own, and I'd be doing that right now if I wasn't sitting on this balcony in the sun writing this letter.

Does my photography come as a surprise to you? I thought so. You'd be amazed at how serious I am about it too, but not the commercial stuff like Richard's. You know how I've always been more interested in people than things. That's why I've been shooting my subjects mostly in kitchens recently. Somehow to me people in kitchens seem much more real than out in the streets. And the sunlight through kitchen windows can be beautiful. Did you know that Walker Evans could spend a whole day waiting for the exact nuance of sunlight? It reminds me of you. I remember how absorbed you used to get when working and how excited when things fell into place. Would you believe that I'm a little like that myself now? Really, there are times when I feel as if I'm right on the edge. I'm so tired and frightened I want to stop, but that's usually just when things begin to get good. I wish you could see what I've been doing and tell me what you think. I know you'd be straight with me. You always were.

You *will* take the money, won't you? Please, as a favor to me. Use it to buy something pretty for Marissa and give her a sweet kiss for me. She must be a big girl by now. Let me know if she needs braces on her teeth or anything.

Affectionately,
Gretchen

P.S. The other night we were at a Chinese restaurant and when I broke open my fortune cookie it predicted an older man of great wealth and charm who is sincere. I'd already met one middle-aged charmer so I said no, thank you, one per lifetime is just right. Don't think I'm not grateful for the experience, darling, but I was only a baby at the time and bound to make all sorts of crazy mistakes. Fortunately I was lucky and Richard turned up. You aren't still angry with me after all these years, are you? You know it wasn't my fault. I couldn't help myself and I simply couldn't stay, but I *was* terribly fond of you, Daniel.

Dear Gretchen. How he had worshiped her. The thin delicious squiggle of a pale blue vein near the corner of her right eye. Dan Asher had to shout to be heard above the music. Marissa, he called. Hey, Marissa! Turn down the damn phonograph and come in here a second.

Marissa appeared with her nose in a copy of a book bound in the gloomy red livery of the Venice public library. Come on, honey, move your ass. Look here. This came for you. He showed her the check. Trying to whistle, Marissa made a wuthering sound and said, Five hundred dollars. Wow!

From your mother, explained Dan Asher. Do you want to keep it or send it back? Marissa looked down at her book. Helpless Philip was once again compulsively dragging his club-foot after the disgusting Mildred. Whatever you say, Dan. I don't care. Okay, he said, folding the letter and the envelope and tearing them up. We keep it.

BEVERLY HILLS, JUNE 15, 1976

Some doors are glass or propped open and cry out for you to come in. Some are as forbidding as bank vaults. Framed between Rájan's elegant shoes for ladies and Clareboudt's handsome accessories, the door of the Marquis Gallery was weeper's black, heavy, and exclusive. Tattersall pushed his way inside.

The gallery was practically empty, except for the middle of the glistening parquet where a padded bench held a portly, distinguished-looking man in his sixties and an agreeable young fellow who behaved so attentively that he might have been a nephew fearful of being disinherited. The corpulent older man had manicured nails, gray sideburns, a neatly trimmed salt-and-pepper beard. His suit was pin-striped, acres of blue pin-striped cloth. The cane between his legs was black. He leaned forward on it to examine more closely one of the works hanging opposite. When he opened his mouth, out came Orson Welles.

The voice took Tattersall by surprise. It was as if the dapper young Welles of the Mercury Theatre had been murdered and replaced by this gross parody who anyone could see was a fraud. He was studying a 1954 pen-and-ink drawing of an old, rather silly-looking, nearsighted painter in a beret and the naked model—a young woman easeful and indifferent—who sat voluptuously before him. He was saying, Yes, I understand that sense of disgust, the self-loathing that he must have felt at being old and cheated, and not simply of the sex, though of the sex too, but of the dreams, those perfect and unuttered possibilities that each man thinks are to be his at some time in his life and never now will be. The young man sitting beside him said, That's it, Orson. Good Lord, you've said it well. Did you know that when he drew that he was seventy-three?

A boyishly endearing smile softened Orson's face. Wise old bastard, he said. He knew. He knew that when you're seventy-three they come as nurses, models, not lovers.

52

Henry looked again. Impossible. So what if his name was Orson? It could only be a coincidence. The private investigator went around the walls from sketch to painting to print, making his way casually toward the storeroom in the rear. It was a first-class show. Under the circumstances, he didn't mind dawdling en route. The exhibition covered Picasso's career from early to late, an impressive collection for a museum, let alone a private gallery. One or two of the works he thought he recognized from the lecture series he and Dorothy had attended at the County Museum. The blue and rose periods were Tattersall's favorites. There were only a few sketches from these early years and, not surprisingly, none of the priceless paintings.

There was, however, a remarkable pastel done in 1900 that he couldn't take his eyes off. The scene was a bedroom with a couple entwined, the man groping between the woman's legs while she laughingly held him off. If Henry were a rich man, he would have had that at home and hanging in the place of honor over their twin beds.

The flapping of rubber and the jingling of clamps. Someone passed behind his back on the way to the rear of the gallery. Tattersall was puzzled. No one ever wore galoshes in Beverly Hills. A blond woman in leather slacks sat down at the desk in the far corner before the entrance to the storeroom. Her wrists and arms were heavy with bracelets. Obviously, she worked in the place. Walking over, Henry asked for the price list. She was glad to oblige, handing him a plastic-covered pamphlet. She suggested that he might also like to help himself to one of the catalogues from the pile on her desk.

The catalogue was a handsome book-length volume with color reproductions—an expensive promotion that was as ambitious for a private gallery as the show itself. It presented seventy-five Picassos from 1900 to 1973, consisting of oils, gouaches, prints, drawings, and sculpture. If none of the works was on loan, the gallery's financial investment must have been in the millions.

Is everything here for sale? he asked innocently. Everything, she said, including the catalogue. That will be three dollars. Paying up, Tattersall expressed an interest in seeing the gallery director. Mr. Hofstedler was occupied at the moment, but perhaps she could help. Was it one of the Picassos? Or perhaps he was interested in the School of Paris? We specialize in the School of Paris, you know. Modigliani, Utrillo. . . . Her *r* rolled like a paradiddle. The School of Paris, admitted Tattersall, and was invited to follow her into the storeroom.

It was just as Harris had said. A three-tiered wooden storage rack against the wall and in the corner on top a canvas draped in a white sheet. Look at this, she said, calling his attention to a small Soutine, a portrait of a young man with a bony face and sad blue eyes. She sighed and said, I don't know what it is about those eyes . . . From the middle of the rack, she pulled out a Modigliani nude for his inspection. The looping curves and warm colors of an oriental bazaar. She said, Isn't it lovely? Despite her getup, her complications of heavy eye makeup, jangling bracelets, and hair lacquer, she seemed to be genuinely moved—an excellent saleswoman. Is that a Chagall up there? Tattersall wanted to know. He didn't bother to wait for her answer. Standing on tiptoe, he reached up into the corner and took hold of the sheet.

The ringless fingers that clamped his wrist were stubby and hot. Tattersall noted that the watch had a blank burgundy face with 14K hands. The cuff links looked solid gold. I'm afraid not, said the young man he had seen talking outside in the gallery.

He was tall, surprisingly tall, and had no difficulty sliding out the painting next to the covered one Henry had been aiming at. It was a picture of five sullen Indians with war paint, amber beads and earrings, noses like Roman generals. As you can see—he smiled pleasantly—the top shelf is where we keep our Indians and cowboys. My father loved the West. Are you looking for a Chagall?

Henry said he might be if the price were right. Unfortunately Mark Hofstedler had no Chagalls on hand at the moment, not even a print. Mark—everyone called him Mark—was such an affable, open-faced, sweet-smelling, paunchy young man that it was hard not to like him. He looked like someone who, despite all his efforts, would have difficulty keeping the armpits of his

54

fine shirts free of stains. Mark couldn't say for certain, but his hunch was that a Chagall might be found. You just never know. Something is always turning up on the art market. That's what makes it so damn exciting. He took Tattersall's number and promised that he would be in touch if anything developed.

As they returned to the gallery and walked toward the front door, Mark wanted to know what he thought of the show. Very nice, said Tattersall, and, pointing to the Picasso pastel he had so admired, he wondered aloud where it had come from. *The Lovers?* asked the gallery owner. He seemed surprised at first, then embarrassed.

I'd like to, he explained, but look at my position. It really can't be done. Let's just say that it came from a private source who prefers to remain anonymous. People like that with important work for sale don't care to tell the world their business. They expect the same sort of complete privacy that you yourself would in a similar situation. You understand, don't you? Henry said that he did.

But if, for example, you had asked me about that still life over there, Mark continued, I wouldn't mind in the least telling you that it was originally part of the Gertrude Stein collection because it now happens to be the exclusive property of the Marquis Gallery, which is true of most of the work on exhibit here.

That would explain it, thought the investigator, glancing across at the still life. He's a middleman. Are those brown bananas? asked Tattersall. Croissants, replied Mark.

Stenciled on the rear of the building that housed the Marquis Gallery *Unauthorized Cars Will Be Towed Away.* The Mercedes convertible parked in the alley was the perfect blue of Persian miniatures. The license plate was ART 2. For the same twenty-five dollars it could have had two more letters. Tattersall, who had problems identifying the make of an automobile, rarely forgot a personalized plate. He filed away ART 2 along with NBC 4, ICM 5, CHESS, DELI, TACO, LA RAZA, EL CID, SMOOTH, DOLL,

YENTA, NOSH, NEUTRA, ME 4 YOU, I BITE, HUMBUG, BABS, BETH, BARBY, TOD, HUN, CHAYIM, MATH, METRO, BOOZE, BONES, BRUINS, BONSAI.

A fancy small sports car once led him to a piece of pre-Columbian sculpture that had been ripped off from a gallery at one of the Claremont colleges. A graduate student who had gambling debts at the wheel and RUNT on his plate in the rear. Someone using tar had changed the letter R to C. It was a childishly clumsy job that Tattersall had preferred not to look at. He was reminded of a tasteless joke he had once heard about Van Gogh's ear.

LOS ANGELES, DECEMBER 19, 1976

SECLUDED PARADISE

The importance of elegance in a Bel Air setting and rustic privacy on a tree-lined estate only minutes from Westwood Village is yours with this luxurious Mediterranean home featuring four bedrooms, four baths, plus two maids' rooms with baths, baronial living room boasting oak beams and hardwood floor, tranquil den, plus basement recreation rooms with fireplaces for all your creative or entertainment needs. Paneling and parquet abound. The custom-designed pool has its own wet bar, and the gardens with their aviary must be seen to be believed. The metal fountain in the delightful brick courtyard is by Claire Falkenstein and as the French say *formidable!* Three-car garage. Security system throughout. Closed-circuit TV.

Reduced for immediate sale. Call: (213) 494-5437.

—West Views

VENICE, OCTOBER 24, 1964

Market Street under shackling iron clouds. The Asher place turned out to be a deconsecrated Baptist church, a run-down, weatherbeaten, gray-clapboard building surrounded by a few small factories and stucco shacks. Despite the recent rain, the lawn out front resembled shredded manila envelopes. The gray peeling signboard that had once announced the title of the weekly sermon no longer held news of the Sabbath. Its glass frame had disappeared.

Climbing the high wooden staircase to the front door, the powerful German shepherd nosed each step suspiciously. Mona, tender of small animals and children, tightened her hold on the dog's clothesline leash and knocked. It was only after she had knocked a second time that the door was opened by a thin kid with purple shadows under her eyes who might have been pushing the outer limits of twelve. Her tee shirt said LOVE ME OR LEAVE ME.

Hello, dog. The kid welcomed the animal with a gingerly pat on the head. You're a big one, aren't you? She glanced up, gave the owner of the wary animal a cool, appraising look, and said, Hi. Mona concluded that here was a precocious, poised, fearless little thing who had probably already begun years of guilt-free masturbation. I'm looking for Daniel Asher, she explained, and was invited in.

The walls of his studio were painted white and covered with pictures of birds and shells, tarot cards, letters, photographs, and old posters announcing shows by Asher in New York, Frankfort, Stockholm, Paris, Chicago, and Los Angeles. There were brown water marks on the ceiling where the roof leaked. The windows were narrow secular rectangles, but superimposed amateurishly on top were amusing Gothic wooden arches. Two beat-up leather couches and some nondescript wicker and black-canvas chairs were huddled together in the middle of the studio. Mona walked over, stepping around the clutter of loosely piled books and stacks of *Scientific American, Artworld,* and *Art International.* With the ocean only half a block away, the air in the house smelled unmistakably of seaweed and damp. It was just the sort of queer place that she might have expected him to live in.

Behind a wooden railing where the altar had once been, she noted that he had set up his worktable, using a couple of sawhorses and an unpainted door. There was a draftsman's lamp clamped to its side, and the working surface was as immaculate as an operating table. Perfect, thought Mona. She guessed that the two of them lived in the rear, the old sacristy probably the kid's bedroom. She wondered if there was anyone else on the premises. The girl's mother, according to Mona's boss, Miles Dorfman, had been a dancer with Martha Graham before committing suicide.

When the kid returned, she reported that Dan said he'd be there in a minute. She stroked the dog's ears and asked what his name was. Marlene, replied Mona, and explained, He's a she. Oh! Hands on hips, the kid scanned the animal's expressive face for a clue and then turning to Mona gave her what looked like a slow, sly smile of sexual complicity.

Do you like the Beatles? she asked. They were singing "Do You Want to Know a Secret?" All right, said Mona without enthusiasm. But I prefer Bob Dylan. The kid nodded and said, Dan doesn't much care for them either because he's into jazz, but I'm teaching him.

Teaching me what? Asher wanted to know. As he came over, he wiped his hand on his pants and extended it to his visitor. Hello, I'm Dan Asher.

The nicotine stains on his teeth were the least of it. Mona had never seen anyone quite so smirched before. His white corduroy pants and blue workshirt were spotted with coffee, streaked with grease, stippled with paint. White bits of plaster clung to his face, to his blue knit cap. The man's ability to attract stains seemed to her extraordinary, but his indifference to them bordered on genius. He was staring down at her, his eyes spotless blue and disturbingly insistent.

I'm Mona, she introduced herself, Mona Block from the County Museum, and she was glad to meet him at last. She was surprised that they hadn't run across one another before this at the museum or on La Cienega. *Putting his arm around her, Miles whispered, See that guy with the ponytail across the street in the black sweatshirt and boots?* Or at somebody's opening. I don't get to many openings, he admitted matter-of-factly. Don't have the time.

I've got to go, announced the kid, feeling that the two of them had already forgotten about her. Her father said, Take care. Always, said the kid. She and her friends were taking part in a Bikeathon. It's for cerebral palsy, she told Mona, and added coolly, Twenty miles. You want to pledge something?

Mona thought that ten cents a mile sounded about right. The kid wrote down *Mona Block* on her list of sponsors and then realized that she had no idea how she was going to get paid. Dan offered the possibility that Mona might still be there when she got back. The sound of her name on his lips appealed to Mona. If not, she said, I'll leave the money with your father. Mona also told her that it looked like it might rain.

You'd better take your sweatshirt, Marissa, said her father. Oh, Dan! The kid tossed her long blond hair like a whip. Take it, he growled, or I'll kick your ass in. Stomping off, she returned almost immediately with a sweatshirt tied around her waist. She gave Dan a peck on the cheek. All right, tough guy, she said. But don't think I'm going to wear it. The kid had his number and knew it, and her father, to judge by the bemused expression on his face, knew it too.

Galloping away thunderously on her heels, she raced out the door. Mona could find no dancer in those legs. Sometimes, she knew, these genetic things skip a generation. Her own case was a perfect example. The closest her mother had ever been to an art museum was a visit with her father to Canton, Ohio, to see the Football Hall of Fame.

Does she want to be a dancer like her mother? asked Mona, and felt terribly young and stupid when Dan Asher revealed that the child's mother had never been a dancer. She should have known better than to trust Miles. It wasn't the first time her boss had been weak on details. He was a sweet guy who owed his curatorial success more to charm and persuasiveness than to scholarship. Mona decided to stick to first-hand information —that she had been a schoolgirl when she first saw some of his work at the San Francisco Museum, that years later in 1960 she had been quite impressed by his Los Angeles debut at Max Roth's gallery, and that she hadn't seen anything new of his in a long time.

As I said on the phone, she explained, that's why I'm here. To see what you've been up to. I don't think I've seen a show of yours since '61. Dan Asher admitted that he hadn't had one. Is Roth still your dealer? The artist thought the question over and replied, He says he is. . . . For the first time he seemed unsure of himself, and she liked him better for it. I don't know . . . He owes me some money. Dan Asher rubbed his hands on his shirtfront as if he were cleaning them of Roth. Come on. He took her around by the shoulders. I'll show you what I've been doing.

He flipped a switch, and from above a bank of baby spots flooded his worktable with light. There were two large brown cabinets nearby that had open shelves filled with a jumble of trays, jars, paint cans, small boxes, clipping files, and portfolios. Given his work, Mona had anticipated the tidiness of a Kandinsky rather than this disorganized flea market.

On the shelves were all sorts of feathers, bones, buttons, marbles, tickets, foreign coins, pipes, steel engravings, picture postcards, playing cards, tarot cards, baseball cards, business cards, flowers, sequins, and glass. An intriguing assortment of colors, textures, and shapes. Mona had never before seen a round seven of spades. Please don't, cautioned Asher irritably. I know exactly where everything is here. Sorry, she said, and quickly returned the card to the shelf.

On the table he placed before her works from a new series that he thought he might call "Pompes Funèbres." Did she like the title? Mona couldn't care less. She was interested in his art, not his literature. Dan Asher did not want to alienate her by arguing the point. An L.A. County Museum show now might do wonders for his maimed prospects, his dwindling bank account.

Look at this, he said. Tugging excitedly on the sleeve of her blue denim jacket, he said, Look at this. The collage on the table was relatively small, as was usual for him, about the size of a piece of ordinary typing paper. A man in a black trilby and heavy overcoat stood with his back to the viewer. On the ground beside him was a coffin. The blanket covering it was decorated with the Greek letter Ω in gold. It had been cut from a watch clasp. A swatch of wallpaper with a pattern of small white plus signs filled the rest of the surface. In the context, the rows of identical white crosses took on the grim redundancy of a veterans' cemetery. And this, said Dan Asher, hastily placing another work beside it. Look at this.

Mona nodded and made tactfully appreciative sounds but said nothing. There was no doubt about the high level of his craftsmanship, but finally she found these new pieces a bit too gloomy, too stark, too static for her taste. If perhaps the mystery at the heart of his work had deepened, the conception seemed to her more abstract, less compelling. She pointed to the one remaining work in the portfolio. Is that from your Museum of Crime? The wooden pile that the woman was tied to was streaked with emerald green and her swirling hair was drenched with sea spray. Oh, yeah, he replied. Old hat. Then, noting the top hats of the two bearded men in the rowboat, he shrugged his shoulders apologetically and laughed.

Mona was familiar with the Museum of Crime series from his last exhibition at Roth's, but she had never seen this particular collage. She was taken with its drama, its energy, the visual excitement. Dan Asher gazed fixedly at the collage for a time and appeared to have forgotten all about her. Under the bright lights, the flecks of plaster that spotted his cheeks and stippled his handsome Zapata mustache looked like pancake batter. Mona felt no inclination to laugh, which surprised her. Still and all, said Dan Asher as he turned and looked into her eyes, it's got something, you know. Care for some coffee?

The kitchen at the rear of the house was a makeshift affair. Instead of closed cabinets, a freestanding network of open shelves held pots, pans, dishes, silver, and groceries. It divided the space into kitchen and dining room. On the windowsill, in the thin gray afternoon light, two half-gallon jugs of California Chablis and Mountain Red Burgundy took on a rich jewel-like glow. The humming sound was coming from the back yard where an oil company had one of its pumps working, the crossbeam dipping its neck stiffly like a wooden horse. Speckling the kitchen floor were drops of plaster that led to the sink. Mona observed that beneath it the wall was freshly plastered.

When the coffee was ready, they sat at the dining-room table and Dan Asher poured. We had a flood, he explained. The hot-water pipe rotted away. I had to put in a new one. He seemed rather proud of the fact that he took care of the plumbing and plastering and carpentry and electrical problems himself. Mona found his touch of vanity endearing, given the sloppiness of the plastering job. As long as he didn't regard doing household repairs as an act of social egalitarianism or a test of manhood, she didn't mind at all.

Who does the cooking? she asked. The answer was they both took turns. Marissa enjoyed making spaghetti with clam sauce and stuffed meat loaf, and he had a few specialties of his own. Mona said she hoped that coffee wasn't one of them. You're not much good at it, you know. The matter-of-factness of her voice annoyed Dan Asher. Ordinarily even the very young ones loved to mother him.

Next time, he promised, you can handle the coffee. Mona smiled and admitted that it wasn't one of her specialties either. I do herbal tea, she informed him. I do a blend with clove and marshmallow root that's called Crescent Moon. You might like it. Dan Asher didn't say so, but he was sure that he would.

There was a great deal about her that he adored already. Her wonderfully low, breathy voice. Her hair cascading to her shoulders in an artless rush of small brown curls. Pale green eyes that glistened with emotion. The way she held her coffee mug in two hands and rested it lip to luscious lip while listening to him tell about the old Edgewater Hotel down the block where once years ago a number of distinguished suicides had occurred. And those jeans she wore that clung to her like a suntan, with not a line—not even the faintest, made by panties spun out of angel's breath—to hint at anything underneath but Mona, bare and beautiful.

Dan Asher abruptly got up. Oh, no, he told himself, he was not about to ruin his chances at the museum by frightening her away. No, he had no intention of getting involved in something like this again. Absolutely not, not another irresistible child half his age.

Dan Asher didn't suppose she wanted a second cup of his lousy coffee, but he asked anyway. She didn't. Anything else? he offered. Cheese? A glass of wine? I think there may be a few pickled artichoke hearts left in the refrigerator. Mona smiled no. Walking behind her, he placed his fingers lightly, ever so lightly on her shoulders and, bending over, said in a voice as tender as a caress, I have a few things in the next room you might be interested in. Mona turned and looked him squarely in the eye. I've got all afternoon, she said agreeably.

LOS ANGELES, JUNE 25, 1967

"Lord knows," said Police Chief Tom Reddin, "they were told enough times to leave before we went into action. But the group had no intention to conform to the conditions of the city permit that allowed the march.

"Their permit allowed them to march past the hotel to make their point and then to march back to where they started. The trouble began when they stopped in front of the hotel and some of them staged a sit-in.

"But even at the start of the march they were passing out literature advising people how to violate the dictates of the permit and recommending violations of the law, pure and simple violations.

"We had to do what we did. Our concern was the protection of the President, and we didn't want anything to happen that would endanger or discredit him."
—Los Angeles Times

VENICE, OCTOBER 24, 1964

His bedroom resembled a battlefield, the bed and bureau two scarred old campaigners down on their luck. She marveled at his indifference to the clothes on the floor, the shoes, the magazines, the unmade bed, the battered cartons piled in the corner. The smell of stale cigarette smoke hung in the air. On top of the dusty bureau—amidst the dirty socks, a white clamshell filled with cigarette butts, his dingy yellow comb clotted with long brown hair—was a clutter of mostly oversized picture books, some of them exquisitely bound. Trained in art history, Mona should have known more French than she actually did, but she knew enough to gather that the largest of them contained a selection of the gems from the Bibliothèque Nationale's collection of illuminated manuscripts. She noted a book of Old Testament miniatures, a photographic essay on Sainte-Chapelle.

In the mirror above the bureau, Dan Asher caught sight of the plaster spotting his face. He picked up a sock and dabbed at his nose, his cheeks. Those boxes over there in the corner, he began. See them? She said she had. Not too long ago, he explained, his father, who was retired, died. The old house in the Bronx where he had grown up had recently been sold. His mother was moving into an apartment and didn't have room for any of this stuff. I still haven't been through all of it, but look here . . .

Tossing the sock on the bureau, he went over and began rummaging in the carton on top. It was full of books, papers, photographs, grade-school report cards. Two shoe boxes contained old picture postcards. There was a baseball glove bearing the name Mel Ott. What's the *Nassau Herald*? asked Mona. Oh, yeah, he said, seeing what she had been looking at. My graduation yearbook.

Reaching over his shoulder, she lifted it out. Class of 1938. It amused Mona to think that in 1938 she hadn't even been born. She found it hard to believe that he had gone to Princeton. Her Princeton was largely derived from F. Scott Fitzgerald, her image of Princeton men an oleaginous blend of the social graces, the big money, patrician good looks, and booze. Their style was as smooth as Formica, whereas his was as wrinkled as a raisin. She located his picture in the yearbook and was amazed at how young he looked then, how good-looking, how much his daughter Marissa resembled him. He had ridiculously short hair and a supercilious expression that mirrored the look of his classmates. She liked him much better now. Mona felt genuinely sorry for Hebrew Asher in 1938 among the Princeton Wasps.

Ah, he said, straightening up, here we are. He handed her two white pieces of cardboard that age had yellowed around the edges. I was eight and in bed with the measles when that was done. The first one she looked at was a drawing in profile of a cowboy on horseback, a rifle hooked to his saddle and a scarf about his neck. The other was full face, a Robin Hood type with a bow and a pointed cap from which rose a very long, twisting feather. Both figures were stiff, disproportionate, and, with one or two minor exceptions, just what Mona would have expected from a child that age. Glancing up, she caught him looking at her. It was a curious, puzzling look, and she wasn't sure what to make of it. She congratulated him on the horse's raised front hoof, the shading of Robin's feather to suggest thickness.

Dan Asher was spellbound. Her seriousness, that sultry voice, the light dancing voluptuously on her gold hoop earrings. His familiar room took on a special look, a precious aura that he would never forget. Afterward, it was impossible for him to recall exactly how it had come about. It wasn't that Dan felt she wouldn't mind if he kissed her, but rather that she seemed to expect it of him.

They came together as easily as clasped hands, and their lips touched with such exquisite delicacy that they might have been sipping a piping hot brew or one so rich that they hoped it would last forever. Mona made no movement to draw away. She seemed so relaxed, so sure of herself. Dan Asher was just a little dazed to find this bold young charmer in his arms, ecstatic at the way their bodies fit together. Wait, he cried excitedly, letting her go, don't move.

He returned from inside with two napkins and a handful of blue feathers. His long, sure fingers moving with incredible swiftness, he spun an exotic blue-petaled flower and placed it above her left ear. It was an act of magic that delighted Mona. There, he said, turning her toward the mirror. He stepped to the side to admire her and was struck by the resemblance. Manet's Olympia. She could pass for Manet's Olympia, and he told her so.

It's true, he insisted. With that fantastic expression. And the flower in your hair . . . Not quite, said Mona. She continued to gaze imperturbably at herself in the glass as she removed her jacket, unbuttoned her white cotton blouse.

Dan couldn't believe his eyes. She dropped her blouse to the floor, unpeeled her pants. As if to atone for the few pockmarks on her face, the rest of her skin was perfection itself, an unblemished garden of delights. Oh, God! She is absolutely . . . Dan felt his heart going everywhere at once. He could barely breathe. Not even with Gretchen that day-warmed summer night on the beach at East Hampton, or frisking under the water with Bernadette in her shower on East 10th Street, or the very first time he had . . . no, never . . .

Mona was searching for a ribbon in her pocketbook but couldn't find any. She hopped on the bed. The sheets felt cold and damp. Come here, baby, said Mona, and the big German shepherd jumped up and curled at her feet. Marlene is no cat, she said, but if Titian could use a dog, so can I. Mona fluffed up the pillow and leaned back. Now all I need is a velvet bow around my neck and somebody with an armload of flowers in the background. But what the hell. You get the idea.

She looked at him, a steady, sullen gaze, completely unself-conscious. The rich blue from Mona's flower was palely reflected in the windowpane behind her head, as if Manet had been reluctant to waste the little that remained on his palette of such a magical color. Captivated, Dan Asher even adored her pock-marks, paid silent homage to her two or three other trifling imperfections. The tangled web of cocoa-colored hair under each arm that she had not bothered to remove. Her breasts that were too large for her body. And then as he came and stood over her there was a cloyingly sweet smell that to him resembled nothing so much as pink cotton candy. Asher's shirt flew from his back and, dropping down beside his own glorious Olympia, he bent his lips to hers. The dog growled restlessly.

Hold on, said Mona. Before you get too excited I want to warn you that unless you've got a condom handy you can forget it. I'm not wearing a diaphragm, she told him, and I don't take the pill. She had no desire to provide her female self free of charge as a guinea pig for some capitalist pharmaceutical company hungry to make a buck. So either it's a condom or nothing.

Dan Asher knew there was no point in scouring his bureau drawers, his medicine chest, the closet shelves in an effort to satisfy her. He was no more likely to find a rubber in the house than a crystal punch bowl or drapes. Thrifty Drug was on Venice Boulevard, but that was out of the question. He placed a kiss on the plum-colored aureole surrounding her left nipple. I'm not fooling, snapped Mona.

Dan explained the situation to her. Okay, she said, and kicked the German shepherd off the end of the bed, as long as we understand one another. Dan's tongue flicked playfully across her navel. He buried his nose in the small copse of hair below that was the dark, rich color of whole wheat. It smelled like a rose garden. Oh, rapture!

Mona caressed his hair, the back of his neck. She began to bounce lightly on the bed. She licked her lips and made soft interesting sounds. She was as active as her dog's tail. All at once her body quivered, quaked, exploded in convulsive movements, and came down in laughter like a shower of confetti. Her laughter was so unexpected that at first Dan thought something was wrong. Come here, she said, smiling and holding out her arms.

After a while, he got up and said, I'll be right back. Mona pulled up the khaki woolen blanket at the foot of the bed and covered herself. Although the one window in the room was closed, drafts of cool damp air spilled through the warped casement. The woolen blanket felt like barbed wire against her bare skin. She folded her arms protectively across her breasts. Above her head on the wall was a small photograph. She considered the intense teenage Dan Asher, his arms around a smiling young woman dressed in a glen plaid jacket with padded shoulders from the 1930s and an off-the-face hat. Coquettishly she leaned her head toward him. The family resemblance was unmistakable.

There was also an old-fashioned poster that said COME TO THE VENICE OF AMERICA. Only 14 miles from Los Angeles. Founded by the late Abbot Kinney, after touring the world over many times to find "the ideal spot." Venice is a wonderland of amusements—beach, surf and piers, mountains and sea—and a paradise for children. Venice loves her children and vies with nature in making them healthy and happy.

At the bottom of the poster, Dan Asher had pasted a passport-size photo of his daughter at six or seven, her eyes wide open with excitement and her laughing mouth oblivious of its missing incisors. Mona was charmed by the secret, tender side of Dan Asher's relationship with the child. Had he taken care of her by himself all these years?

Turning over on her stomach, Mona reached out to the window and tried to press it down to block the draft but couldn't. In the process, she very nearly knocked over the can on the sill. The unusual gold label made her think at first it was some unfamiliar imported beer. She twisted the can around. It said Gold Water. Throwing the blanket aside, Mona jumped out of bed and got dressed. She seized her leather shoulder bag from the bureau and was pulling the strap over her arm when Dan Asher came back.

This'll warm you up, he said. He was balancing two glasses of red wine and a plate of cheese and crackers. Then he saw she was dressed. What's the matter? he wanted to know. Where are you going? He seemed genuinely hurt that she was about to leave.

Here. She handed him two one-dollar bills. Dan didn't understand. The money might have been a sexual payoff. They exchanged glances, and all at once her gesture struck them both as laughable. That's for Marissa, she explained.

Dan Asher asked her please not to go quite yet. He wanted to talk to her, to find out more about her. She pointed to the Gold Water can. Don't you realize, she said firmly, that the money you paid for that is going to be used to help elect an extremist maniac who wants to drop atom bombs on Hanoi, Peking, Moscow, and turn live human beings into lampshades and fertilizer? Don't you realize that? Dan Asher said that it was a joke, that he bought the can as a joke.

Okay, said Mona. She was still not altogether satisfied, but she relented. Okay, she said. You're *not* going to vote for Goldwater then. That's definite. Dan Asher said it was. He wasn't going to vote for anybody. He hadn't voted for anybody in years. That's something, she informed him, that we're going to have to change. She picked up the dog's leash and tugged at it. Come on, Marlene.

Dan stopped her at the front door. He held her by the shoulders and gave her a long tender glance. I want you, he said. I know, replied Mona.

She walked quickly down the stairs and hurried off, his exotic blue flower fluttering away in the gray afternoon light.

LOS ANGELES, MAY 18, 1967

The ailing Matisse coughed and put down his scissors. He leaned back on his pillows. The shape he had just cut out resembled a giant coffee bean.

"Ever since the earliest times," he explained softly to his guest, "it has been represented in more or less the same fashion: a coffee bean. Do you know the red-light district of Toulon? You will find this symbol everywhere on the walls there. And each of the bordellos carries this coffee bean as its emblem. Sometimes it's painted on the wall, sometimes cut into it, sometimes . . ."

PART IV

OAKLAND, 1976

89. IN THE HEINZ PAVILION
(New York, 1939)

Los Angeles, 1967
Paper, ribbon, beads, cellophane, plastic,
National Geographic photographs, metal coil
on cardboard
Size: 12 x 15½ inches
Coll. Miss Marissa Asher

*The very air inside is golden. It is as if all the windows, the doors,
the plastic dome, the entire building has been wrapped in yellow
cellophane. The warm light kindles warm thoughts, slapstick
smiles, expectations. Except for the nagging of the machinery and
an occasional clink of glass, the hall reeks of reverence.*

*The sign that hangs symbolically over the exhibit is a Heinz
pickle. It bears the number 57. Rolling down from deep space in a
series of dramatic switchbacks, the conveyor belt carries the empty
ketchup bottles toward the picture plane. A single bottle has passed
beneath the loading coil. It is filled and labeled* Salsa de Tomate.
*Bathed in lemon and orange shafts of light, the ruby bottle flames
beneath its beaded aureole.*

Of course it belongs to the black African girl. She is bare to the waist and as innocent as a periwinkle. She claps her excited hands, her eyes closed, her shaved head thrown back in ecstasy. There is a vertical zip of light on the hoops she wears about her neck, a point of light on the bottom of the large ring in her ear.

The three men closest to her in the smiling crowd lean forward intently. One is a fur-hatted moujik, one a grim Javanese warrior in ceremonial skirt, one a Madagascan piper. On the floor before them, they have placed a ribboned box, a star-studded bottle, a jar covered with pictures of veiled women. These are souvenirs from other exhibitions at the fair. Having freed their hands, the foreigners wait to collect one more memento.

WEST HOLLYWOOD, JUNE 16, 1976

Miguel Oviedo drove his battered Dodge pickup truck down the street and pulled up in front of the white stucco house with the red tile roof. The Tattersalls lived in a Spanish dog, one of those one-story Los Angeles buildings impossible for real estate people to peddle in the 1930s when they were first built, and now everybody wanted them. Miguel let down the tailgate, shoved the bag of manure aside, and unloaded his power trimmer, electric mower, and hand mower, trying not to make too much noise. He was old but strong despite his sickness. The diabetes slowed him up only a step or two, that was all.

It was a little after seven. He liked to get an early start on a day when there was a Santa Ana blowing and the temperature could jump to 90 by noon. Pulling his hand mower into the back yard, Miguel began to work around the flagstones. He knew he should be getting more than fifteen dollars a month for a pain-in-the-ass lawn like this. If he didn't have to compete with the Japs for the work, he might be making more money from all his customers. Miguel went behind the barbecue pit that hid him from the house and unbuttoned his fly. It was his sickness. The diabetes made him pee more times a day than the church bells rang in Hermosillo, where he had grown up. Hearing the front door open, Miguel buttoned his pants quickly.

When Henry Tattersall walked into the back yard, the gardener was trimming the border near Dorothy's birds of paradise. Tattersall approached him, carefully eyeing the grass to avoid the snails. He hated the crunch of their squashed shells under foot. *Buenos días*, said Henry pleasantly. Years ago he had realized a dream when his small restaurant specializing in continental cuisine opened on Westwood Boulevard. The restaurant had failed, but he could still feel himself smile inside when out of his mouth came hot tidbits of Spanish, sweet morsels of French. Miguel looked at him and nodded. All at once his dark, wrinkled, ominous face became sunny with teeth. He said, Good morning, mister, and began to cough so hard that finally he spit up phlegm. Shit, he said, and wiped his mouth.

That's quite a cough you've got, said Henry. You should give up smoking. Miguel shook his head. At my age you don't give up more than you have to. Henry admired the idiot's doggedness, took pity on his black, cancerous lungs. Are you taking anything for it? he asked. Miguel dismissed the cough as nothing. It goes and comes. I live with it.

People could learn to live with anything, thought Henry: smog, heat, quakes, mud slides, maddening boils, loneliness. When he first became a private investigator, he never believed that he would be able to cope with the lack of finality in unsolved crimes, but he had learned to live with even that over the years. Now Henry found it ironic that he had a better reputation for patience than solutions.

My wife, he told the gardener, asked me to remind you about the snails. I have not forgotten, said Miguel. The poison is in the truck. From his pocket, he drew a folded pink paper and, opening it carefully, presented the receipt to Henry. He pointed to the number written at the bottom of the page.

Yes, of course. Henry told him to add the amount to his bill at the end of the month. It wasn't the money that was troubling him. What sort of poison is this? he wanted to know. It's not going to hurt kids or dogs, is it? There is no danger, Miguel reassured him. Only the snails. Because we've got a lot of little kids on this block, and they're all over the goddamn place. ¿Comprende? Miguel sighed heavily and said, This is not the first time, mister.

Henry wished that there was some way other than poison to get rid of the slimy things. If it had been his garden and not Dorothy's, he might well have learned to live with them. Henry hated to kill anything. True, he kept a gun in his office, but it was difficult for him to imagine under what circumstances he would ever actually use it. The .22 target automatic with pearl handle in the trim cordovan holster attached to his belt was more for public relations than protection. It was something that some clients seemed to expect of him, like a diploma on the wall in a doctor's office. More than one prospective customer had been sold by Henry's unbuttoning his jacket and casually reaching into his back pocket for a hanky.

Although anxious to get to his office early, Henry had something else to say before leaving. He walked over behind the red-brick barbecue pit and pointed to where the dichondra had been burned away by urine. There's a law against it, he told the gardener, but they let their dogs run wild. So just in case, he cautioned, I don't think you should put your poison down here.

¡Claro! snapped Miguel, and the roar of the power mower as he started it up ended their conversation.

OAKLAND, 1976

DANIEL ASHER: Collages 1943–1967.
The Oakland Museum, 1976.
Introduction by Mordecai Bell.

Although Asher was to acknowledge an early interest in the Surrealists, this period of interest, in my estimation, was as brief as a summer's shower. For his studies and temperament were to lead him in quite another direction. If he found an appealing aura of mystery in the Surrealists' work, he disdained their metaphysics, sensationalism, and dream imagery. What Asher discovered early in his career, I believe, was that solidity of shape was more important to his art than vague, unfamiliar forms, and that the logic of association was more valuable than a dreamy irrationality.

WEST LOS ANGELES, JUNE 16, 1976

The bus stop he got off at was on the corner of Santa Monica Boulevard and Beverly Glen, in front of the large Arco station. Henry stood there and waited for the light. The station attendants—young, clean-cut, unusually polite kids eager for permission to clean a windshield or peek under a hood—did nothing to whet his appetite for driving. Dorothy was the driver in their family, which was fine with him.

Henry didn't really trust himself behind the wheel of a car. What if, God forbid, he should become distracted and hurt someone by accident? It was simply that he knew he had too much on his mind to drive safely anywhere. In Los Angeles, where there were more registered vehicles on the road than in any other city in California, he wouldn't last two minutes. Henry was in no hurry. He waited, watching the kid fill out the charge form for the black Lincoln maybe '72 or '73 with California license 417 NAW. When the WALK sign finally went on, he crossed.

It felt cool, pleasant in the shade of the trestle as he passed under the Southern Pacific spur line. Between the noise of passing cars, Henry caught the liquid note of pigeons nesting above him in the metal girders. He came out into the heat on the other side and turned up Little Santa Monica, walking west along the single pair of tracks that for a few miles divides Santa

Monica Boulevard into big and little. Henry's office was only a few blocks away on the corner of Glenwood. It wasn't yet nine, and he guessed that already the temperature must be near 80 degrees. Henry didn't mind. The desert wind didn't depress him as it did others he knew. If anything, it made him feel wide awake, a little edgy maybe, as if something were about to happen.

Henry hoped so. He had only had minor success the day before in checking out Harris's story. There was a painting wrapped in a sheet in the Marquis Gallery storeroom, but whether it was the stolen Rembrandt was still up for grabs. He had tried to find out. He had asked Harris to help him, and yesterday afternoon they had gone back to Beverly Hills, but things hadn't worked out.

Henry's plan called for Harris to park his car right in front of the gallery where the car's horn would suddenly begin to blare uncontrollably. When Hofstedler and his assistant came out to see what was wrong, Henry would slip in to see what was under the sheet. Everything worked fine at first: the parking spot directly in front of the gallery; the horn going off like a disaster, rattling windows, turning heads; the people running out in droves to have a look. But despite the commotion, the heavy closed door of the Marquis Gallery never budged. Tattersall, who had no intention of breaking the law, agreed to pay the summons that Harris received for disturbing the peace. It's *there*, Henry, insisted the informer. Believe me, it's *there*! After sleeping on the problem, Henry decided that he would have to do things another way.

Tattersall's office was in a two-story wooden building with a white stucco front that faced the tracks. There were two shops at street level. The one on the right was the Apple Lighting Fixture Company. A few ugly chandeliers hung in its window like fourteen-year-old orphans who had long ago given up any hope of ever being adopted. Stenciled on the window at the left was the name Western Medical Supplies. Western Medical catered mostly to small hospitals and stocked everything from braces to bed pans to orthopedic belts to nonallergic pillows, and in quantity. Who would believe that there were so many maimed and ailing human beings in the sunshine of Los Angeles? The store had enough crutches on its walls to qualify as a religious shrine.

Henry entered the narrow glass door between the two stores. It was numbered 766½ and opened directly onto a staircase leading upstairs that was a tight squeeze for two-way traffic. The small downstairs directory in the hallway listed:

> Suite 1. Yoga Life
> (Kim Enterprises)
> Suite 2. William W. Gregg, C.P.A.
> Suite 3. Henry Tattersall

Picking up his mail from the hallway box, Henry lumped it together with the Marquis Gallery catalogue he had brought from home and climbed to the second floor. A former client—a wealthy Palos Verdes woman who collected antiques—had once complained breathlessly to him that these stairs were steep enough for a house in Amsterdam. Henry couldn't say yes or no, never having been east of Las Vegas, but he didn't really think the stairs hurt his business. Most of his customers came over the phone or through the mail rather than in the door. And the rent at 766½ Little Santa Monica was low enough for him to survive while waiting for his next case. The discreet sign outside Suite 3 said The Tattersall Service, and written below the single word "Inquiries." Shifting the mail to his left hand, Henry slipped out his keys.

His office was a single large L-shaped room that took up the front corner of the building. It already felt hot inside. The low ceiling made it seem even hotter. Henry, who usually left the windows closed to keep out the dust from across the street, dropped the mail on his desk, walked to the window behind it, and turned on the air conditioner. It leaped to life like a sprinter out of the blocks.

Not only was Henry's office neat, it was also one of those remarkably well-regulated places where everything worked. His desk digital clock-calendar never dropped a day or mislaid a minute. His delicately balanced postage scale was accurate to the sixteenth of an ounce. Beaming down on all this order was a woman holding a white parasol, Monet's tranquil *Lady in a Garden*. The County Museum of Art poster announced a 1973 exhibition of Impressionist and Post-Impressionist paintings from the U.S.S.R.

Henry, seated at his desk, ran through his Rolodex file and got the number he wanted. He called, but Ben Whitelaw hadn't come in yet. He left a message with his secretary. Whitelaw was to call as soon as he came in. Tell him Henry Tattersall. Tell him, said Henry, it's important. Then he dialed his answering service and the operator gave him his calls. That it? he asked, jotting down the last one. The operator said, You got it, Henry. Glancing over the list of callers, he decided there was nothing that couldn't wait.

He spread his mail accordion-fashion across the desk top and, leaning forward, sifted through the letters. The familiar Dutton return address immediately caught his eye. Tearing open the envelope, the investigator found a small check inside for services rendered. Less than two weeks ago he had done a routine job for them, a confidential rundown on a new major-policy applicant.

The Dutton people were always quick to square their bills, which was fine with Henry. In the matter of the Rembrandt back in 1967, however, he thought they had been just a little too hasty. At the time, they had seemed more eager to pay Ward his two-million-plus insurance than to continue paying Henry his modest per diem and expenses. But then Newton Ward owned one of the largest private art collections in the world and was probably Dutton's most important client.

For Henry, the stolen Rembrandt held such meaning, such promise, that he had never considered giving up the chase. It was the sort of challenge that made his life as an investigator seem worthwhile. Lose art, he had once read, and you lose history. Although he had no children of his own, Henry was genuinely moved at the thought of untold future generations of kids being shortchanged on their history. There was also, of course, the money. The recovery now of the Rembrandt meant that he would receive a percentage of the difference between what Dutton paid Ward nine years ago and what the painting would bring at auction in the current market—more money than Henry had ever dreamed of. The financial reward in no way compromised Henry's sincerity. He had long ago accepted the fact that reality humanized idealism rather than mocked it.

Among the bills in front of him on the desk was his blue bimonthly from the Department of Water and Power. The amount never varied more than a few cents, summer or winter. Every year around Christmas Henry would take a week off, and Dorothy would drive them up to San Francisco for the holidays to visit her family. Henry might just as well have been working night and day in the office for all the difference his absence made to the utility company. He had called them, explained that his was a one-man operation that consumed barely any local energy when he was out of town, but it was hopeless. Henry remembered the gay, nasal voice of the young woman at the other end of the phone telling him that he hadn't a thing to worry about, reassuring him tenderly as if he had a terminal illness. He ripped open the envelope. He was glaring at the bill when a velvet knock on the office door was followed by Sanford Kim.

Kim, a Korean with a crewcut, was on the short, trim side like Henry. His office was just down the hall. Yoga Life, a mail-order business, specialized in exercise books and records. Stay young with Yoga, promised Kim. Most recently he had developed a line of health foods under the trade name "Sunblest." Henry guessed that his neighbor must be doing fairly well, to judge by the variety of sport jackets he wore and his new diamond pinky ring. Having once told Kim that he had been in the restaurant business, Tattersall had lived to regret it. The Korean was now always dropping by to ask for an opinion on some experimental medley of figs and pineapples or flaked coconut and dried dates, and Henry, regardless of how busy he might be, didn't want to be rude.

Kim again, said the smiling Korean, his voice as soft as a snowflake. You forgive me, Mr. Tattersall? Henry indicated that he did. Kim complimented him on his sunburned cheeks and, tearing open a small plastic bag, handed it over. The private investigator dropped his gum into the wastebasket and squinted at the mixture. He took a mouthful and swallowed. Raisins, of course, he reported. Yes, hissed a pleased Kim, folding his arms, the natural raisin! He nodded his head encouragingly. And? Unbleached, unsalted, dry-roasted butternuts. Yes, and . . . ? Diced filberts. And? Watched closely by Sanford Kim, Henry ran his tongue over his teeth, searching for a taste that eluded him. Dried papaya? he ventured. Once again, exulted Kim, a home run. And the bottom line?

Tattersall considered his reply. Undistracted by the ringing telephone, he mulled over the latest bland, uninteresting mixture from Sunblest. He longed to tell Kim the truth, to free himself of his duties as unpaid consultant. Only some fancied notion of oriental delicacy obliged Henry to tell his visitor that the mixture was okay. Ah, Mr. Tattersall! Mr. Tattersall! said a beaming Sanford Kim. No, keep the rest. Enjoy. He retreated, backing away gracefully toward the door. Your phone. A thousand thank-yous.

Ben Whitelaw had gotten Henry's message from his secretary. She said it sounded important, Henry. How can I help you? Whitelaw, who worked for a large credit reporting agency on Wilshire, was always willing to pick up an extra $25 by passing along confidential information. Henry explained that this time he was interested in a Mark Hofstedler and spelled the last name for him. Do you have his home address? asked Whitelaw. Henry told him to hold on and he would check the phone book, but Whitelaw said never mind. I'll be back to you in a few minutes, he promised, and hung up.

In a low case against the wall were two rows of telephone books alphabetically arranged from *Airport* to *Western*, their listings covering the sprawl of the city. Tattersall, figuring Hofstedler for Beverly Hills or Bel Air or the Palisades, flipped through *Western* but without success. Maybe the family is old money and Hancock Park, he speculated, pulling out the central

Los Angeles book, but again no luck. Henry traveled as far south as *Huntington Beach–Orange County*, lightly dusting the volume as he replaced it, before satisfying himself that the art dealer was an unlisted number.

BEVERLY HILLS, FEBRUARY 12, 1976

THE WELLINGTON GUN SHOP

In Beverly Hills Since 1937

Sold to	Mr. Mark Hofstedler			
Address	32 St. Pierre Road			
	L.A. 90024 (Bel Air)			

2	S&W 38 Spls	@ 199.95	399.90
1 box cart. (50)			8.95
			408.85
		Tax	24.53
		Total	433.38

WEST LOS ANGELES, JUNE 16, 1976

As he was going through his file cabinet, Henry found among his papers under the letter "P" a clipping about a recent theft of a Picasso. The 1905 painting of a boy's head had been stolen from the Gobelins Gallery in Paris. Picasso's rose period spoke to Henry of a brave innocence that was much better than anything he could remember from his own childhood in Hollywood.

Unfortunately, there was no painting of a boy's head in the Marquis Gallery exhibition.

The clipping that he was looking for was a dimly remembered piece about a stolen Picasso and Gertrude Stein, and he had just pulled it from the file when the telephone began ringing. He glanced hurriedly over the article. He was wrong. It was a Picasso drawing once owned by Stein that had disappeared and not a painting. The article, however, gave him another idea. It was primarily about Stein and Toklas and a man by the name of Paul Lippencut who a year ago had donated a large private collection of books, holograph letters, documents, and memorabilia concerning the two of them to the UCLA library. Hofstedler himself had assured Henry that the work in the Picasso catalogue titled *Still Life with Croissants* had belonged to Gertrude Stein. Wondering if Stein knew anything about it, Henry put down the article and picked up the phone.

Listen to this, Henry. Whitelaw had come up with not one but two Mark Hofstedlers and seemed rather pleased with himself. Tattersall explained that the father was dead. Actually, said Whitelaw, it really doesn't make any difference because credit-wise they both have A-1 ratings. Then he gave the silently disappointed Henry a rundown on Junior.

Young Mark was thirty-one, married, wife's name Evelyn, operates the Marquis Gallery (which Whitelaw pronounced mar-kiss) on Camden Drive, banks at the Beverly Hills branch of the Bank of America, and owns his own house in Bel Air on St. Pierre Road. Henry jotted down the address. The department stores where Hofstedler had charge accounts were predictably the fashionable, expensive ones in Beverly Hills. Whitelaw also mentioned Mel Scott's. It was an overcarpeted, overpriced men's store that seemed just right for Hofstedler with its jodhpurs and yachting caps and well-tailored suits in blues and grays. The smell of dark wood and leather in the place was suffocating. Henry, who had been there once on business, recalled admiring the nicely matted prints of English hunting scenes and meadow pipits on the walls. I'll send you a check, he told Whitelaw. Thanks for the help.

Apparently there hadn't been even one small overdue payment at Magnin's or Saks to blemish the young man's record. Doubts settled on Tattersall like dead leaves as he leaned back in his chair. Maybe Harris was only dreaming his Rembrandt. Maybe under that sheet in the gallery's storeroom there was nothing more than another gang of Indians. Maybe Hofstedler was really a reputable dealer whose business was booming since his old man's death. But if it turned out that Gertrude Stein never owned the *Croissants*, then there was a good chance that the still life hanging in the Marquis Gallery was either stolen or forged. And if young Hofstedler was showing questionable Picassos up front, he just might be fencing hot Rembrandts in the back. But why, Henry wondered, would someone who owned an established, legitimate art gallery that seemed to be thriving want to risk everything by handling pinched goods?

Twirling his wheel of fortune, Tattersall came up with Infofact on the Rolodex and dialed the number. A woman answered, and he gave her the art dealer's name, address, and age. She seemed sure she'd have some news for Henry in a few days. Infofact was a computerized information retrieval system that allowed lawyers and insurance companies to find out any time a person's name appeared on an official record. For a small fee it was possible to learn such things as the ownership of property, outstanding bank loans, automobile accidents, arrests.

This is a rush job, Henry explained. Do you think you could have something for me by tomorrow? I believe so, she said sweetly. It will, however, cost a few dollars more. Henry left his number.

Located in Westwood, UCLA wasn't far from the office. Henry could be there in a few minutes if he didn't have to wait a half hour for the bus. The moment he switched off the air conditioner there was the sound of rushing wings. Sure enough, the clock on the desk showed 10:14. The old man was as punctual as swallows at Capistrano or elderly salmon heading upstream. Through the window, Tattersall watched him carefully cross the street to the railroad tracks, his brown paper bag filled with pieces of corn, bread, sunflower seeds, rice, clutched in his stringy hand. Henry liked this old guy who had taken it upon himself rain or shine to look out for the neighborhood pigeons and had nicknamed him Crumbs.

The doctors took out half my stomach, Crumbs had told Henry one day. But even though I was away a long time, somehow my birds made it through without me. They were so happy to see me back. I don't know what I'd do without them. It's awfully lonely when you get old in L.A. I have a daughter, but she didn't even know I was in the hospital. Maybe she knew and didn't believe it was true. It's hard to believe in anything nowadays.

Look, he had said, pointing across the tracks to the distant figure on top of the Mormon temple. The angels don't even have wings anymore. How are you supposed to know? That one could just as well be some pimply punk with a trumpet from a high school band. You know, he had added, hoping to keep Henry there a few minutes longer. You know, wings are lovely. I love to see them. Pigeons . . . planes . . . all the wonderful things that can take you away from this hole.

Henry stared down at Crumbs's birds, perhaps as many as a hundred of them with wings flickering in the sunlight as they hovered about him. He saw the claws near Crumbs's head and feared for his eyes. He did not see the fluttering beat of the birds churn the air into brilliance, a twinkling light show that surrounded the old man as he sat in his boat gliding away across a pool of diamonds.

LOS ANGELES, JUNE 23, 1967

THE GOOD SPORT
by
Dean McConnell

Oh yes, friends and fans, before the big trouble broke out Muhammad Ali was most definitely there. In a blue suit and a striped tie and a flower hanging from his lapel and signing autographs and the sun beaming down on small and large alike. Simply a gorgeous day in Rancho Park, and if you didn't know and paid no attention to the signs, you just might think that everyone there had nothing better to do than honor speed and power and grace and beauty and happy days were here again.

Not so. One glance at the hundreds of placards around the park, and that, as they say, would be that. The signs saying END THE WAR IN VIETNAM NOW, and LOVE BUILDS WAR DESTROYS, and VIETNAM FUERA, and I'D RATHER SAVE MY ASS THAN LYNDON'S FACE, and one glance would be enough to bring you down to this black earth where no one wants to play games anymore and every carefree jock is under suspicion and just may turn out to be a closet bloody Green Beret or fruit.

So you took in the signs and the marchers and the no-nonsense looks on the faces of the helmeted cops who were there to preserve law and order, and sooner or later you knew somebody was going to get killed.

But Ali was there, and Ali looked as if he would live forever. You probably couldn't get close to him because of the crowd and would have no idea how tremendous he really is, but yours truly, who is no peanut himself, as you well know, pushed his way through and barely came up to the big fellow's muscular Adam's apple. But did that stop the Sport?

I hear you're a draft dodger, champ, a dark-brown yellow chicken. What do you say to that? The pen he was holding crumbled in his hand—a puff of smoke—and as he peered down to see who it was, his face clouded over, and the mob around us that had been chanting Al-eee! Al-eee! Al-eee! suddenly became as still and gray as smog.

This here, he lashed out, is serious business. More serious than anything I ever done before. Before when I fight I used to make my body like a whup. I was always taking that pumpkin seed, taking that wheat germ, taking that four complex special stuff you grind up and mix with honey and orange juice. Running till tears come to my eyes.

Now I'm in the fight for peace and it's my mind I'm working on. I'm making my mind like a steel trap, making it like a bulldozer, like a laser beam. I'm reading. Reading everything I can get my hands on. Thinking deep. Praying hard. Looking for answers and staying up till the wee hours of the morning to find them.

Yes, you are, shouted someone in the crowd. You are the greatest! And the rest of them chanting Al-eee! Al-eee! Al-eee! And me so moved that there were real tears in my eyes as if I had been running right along with him stride for stride, and I asked him, Champ, I said, champ, will you ever fight again?

His big brown eyes narrowed and he might have been looking me through and through to see if I could understand, and as long as I live I'll never forget what he said next. Right now, he told your Sport, this is the biggest fight of my life. And the only one.

One day when all of this is over and Vietnam nothing more than a fifty-point Scrabble blitz, they'll set up a ring out there in the middle of the Memorial Coliseum, and there'll be one hundred thousand delirious fans in the stands hallooing to the heavens as the champ climbs through the ropes back into the limelight. And it will be as if he and all of us had been awakened from some ugly nightmare and returned to a better world where people once again play by the rules of the game, and no one has to be ashamed of being simply a good sport.

—*Los Angeles Today*

OAKLAND, 1976

DANIEL ASHER: Collages 1943–1967.
The Oakland Museum, 1976.
Introduction by Mordecai Bell.

The death from pneumonia of his sister Marion profoundly shocked the artist. That such a traumatic event would inevitably be reflected in his work was to be expected (v. *Homage to Marion*, cat. no. 12). His marriage to nineteen-year-old Gretchen Shaw took place in 1951. The Shaw family had been Bronx neighbors, and he had known her since she was a child. A daughter, Marissa, was born to the couple in 1952.

My first meeting with the artist occurred one year later when I had the good fortune to organize an exhibit of his work for the Walker Art Center in Minneapolis. This show subsequently traveled to museums in Chicago and San Francisco and did much, I am pleased to say, to enhance his modest but growing reputation. The innovational nature of the collages that were included now seems apparent. For example, long before the development of Pop Art—a movement that only amused him— Asher was already, on occasion, using cartoons in his work (v. *Dinner with Jane Arden*, cat. no. 15). His unique ability, however, was that he could make these small insignificant figures truly move us. European recognition for Asher began when he was selected to participate in the Venice Biennale of 1954.

Professionally, the artist seemed to be going from success to success. But his happy home life all at once disintegrated. After three years of marriage, his young wife suddenly deserted him. Asher took full custody of their daughter, and the couple was legally separated in 1954.

LOS ANGELES, OCTOBER 17, 1966

Mona's twenty-fifth birthday was celebrated at the Moujik. Dan Asher's idea. He considered the old Russian-Armenian restaurant high above Sunset a perfect choice for the occasion and made all the arrangements. For him, the run-down place contained full archives of romance, pathos, intrigue, a subtle eroticism. He delighted in its uneven floor, the mysteries shrouded beneath its lumpy and faded red carpets. He wanted to surprise his love with the spectacular view of the nighttime city, to share with her the Moujik's rosy candlelit enchantment. He wanted, in a way, to thank her for saving his life.

Immediately following his release from the hospital, he had become terribly depressed. Slumped on the couch in his damp studio, he would listen angrily to his heart and wonder how he had allowed the perfect instrument handed out to him to become so untuned and defective. What's the matter with you? Mona had wanted to know. Why so glum? He informed her that he had just gotten some bad news. I'm going to die. Pulling him to his feet, Mona said, Not this minute.

They had gone hiking in the winter desert, kite flying on the Venice beach. Dan Asher was amazed to discover that after two days of this madness he was still alive. After two weeks, he was flourishing. Their lovemaking was better now than ever before. His work seemed so too. And the lightning right jab he planted on Roth's mug was one more death-defying act.

When not too long ago a volcano erupted on Guadeloupe, the chief of police of that French island ordered the people there to "Learn to live with your volcano." Dan Asher had learned to live. For his girlfriend, the volcano was Dan Asher, and she had not found it quite so easy. But it *was* her birthday, and he obviously wanted so much to make her happy that she was determined to have a good time and overlook the seediness of the dump.

Mona glanced up at the slim blond waitress who appeared at

her elbow and smiled. She was a shy, dreamy sort. Look a customer straight in the eye and she either fainted or went blind. I could bring it now, she offered him tentatively, or later if you like. Dan Asher said that he'd let her know when.

Quida. Mona read aloud the single word printed on the waitress's pin. I like that. It's an unusual name. Ouida, corrected Dan Asher. He explained that the company that produced the pin had made a mistake. She was named after the English novelist. Ouida's face broke out in a strawberry rash of embarrassment. My mother loved her books, she revealed softly. Her heroes were all so beautiful. Not like everyday people.

She put down the two menus and identified the Monday night special as blinchiki with cheese and sour cream. Dan Asher began to tear up his menu. On the cover, the small drawing of a Russian peasant in boots, a shirt down to his knees, a wide black belt, and a bushy fur hat worn low on the forehead appealed to him. He pocketed it. The paper remnants strewn about the table resembled a torn bird. The waitress turned away and looked sick. Nothing to worry about, he reassured her, and announced that they would begin their celebration with vodka.

What was that all about? What is it she couldn't bring now? Mona wanted to know, but he waved the question aside. Later, he promised, and directed her attention out the window at the illuminated city which lay shimmering at her feet. Mona loved Los Angeles at night from above Sunset or Mulholland, the flat sweep of twinkling colored chains stretching away forever. They watched as a finger of light from a used-car lot or a movie premiere searched the sky for customers.

The lights inside the restaurant were kept romantically low, which made it easier for diners to appreciate the view and the management to reduce overhead. The Moujik also cut costs with paper napkins, no tablecloths. The red candlelit globes on the tables floated in the darkness like water lilies. Dan Asher pointed to the man with the stubby mustache smoking a cigarette behind the bar, his face a Lautrec mask footlighted from below. There was about him something of the sadness of Adolf Hitler in his Berlin bunker presiding over the last days of an empire. The

Moujik, a family operation, had been barely scraping by for years. That's the father, he said. Ouida, their waitress, was somebody's aunt. The son was the kid with no hips who had filled their water glasses.

That night, as usual, the restaurant was no more than half full. The Moujik survived only because of the faithfulness of its regulars, who night after night, week after week, returned to the same tables. They were so dependable, he told her, that if one of them died while eating it might be months before anyone realized what had happened. Mona liked that and laughed, and for a minute Dan Asher thought maybe he hadn't made a mistake in bringing her here.

When the vodka arrived, he toasted every beautiful part of her, and each time she tried to ask her serious questions he'd cover her mouth with kisses. Mona quickly tired of the game. They were simple questions, and oddly enough she hadn't asked them until now: why his first wife left him, how his second had died. He had been hoping to avoid them, and reluctant, especially tonight on her birthday, to tamper with old scars. Still and all, she deserved an answer.

Gretchen was the easier one to talk about, so he began there. She was five years younger than you are now, he said, and already a mother. It was simply too much for her. Eaten up by youth and the rage for lost possibilities. You'll note I use the plural, because the fact is she didn't know what the fuck she wanted to do but leave. And out the door she went, leaving behind the two of us—one mewling ten-month-old infant who had just learned to wave bye-bye and one corpse. Three months later when my father had his first heart attack, my mother said *that* woman did us all a great wrong. If he had been hit by a truck, she would have said the same thing. I realized then how easily I might become the ghost of her going. We survived, Marissa and I, because when dear unhappy Gretchen closed the door behind her, I was able somehow to keep it shut.

Were you, asked Mona, were you in any way responsible for her leaving? The red globe between them cracked into two and flamed in his eyes. What the hell is that supposed to mean?

Mona felt that he had made it sound as if what Gretchen did had nothing to do with him.

It didn't! His palm came down on the tabletop emphatically, knocking his vodka glass into his lap. The few drops left in it that spilled out onto his pants he ignored. He licked the colorless liquor from his thumb. Maybe . . . maybe I could have done more. I've thought about it, he said honestly. But just imagine being judged for all the human failures that touch your life. That's *some* load! It would make even Atlas's ass sag.

Mona answered his grin with a blank wall. Pulling the hair away from her eyes, the brown curls tinged with a halo of red light, she lowered her voice and asked, What about Madeleine? It was suicide, wasn't it? Why did she do it?

What could he possibly tell her about that when he couldn't even explain it to himself? The beautiful and talented Madeleine with a husband who loved her and, after years of struggle, at the very top of her dancing career. Dan Asher's hand automatically went to the pocket where he used to keep his cigarettes. Nothing. He took a deep breath.

Leukemia, he said. It was leukemia, and a shocked Mona made the round lips of *oh*. It was easiest that way. Even he might have understood what happened if it had been that. Look, he whispered. A spotlight had gone on in the center of the room, and into that warm pool of light ambled the three musicians.

They were individually even more dissimilar than Picasso's three music makers, but as a group they had for Dan Asher the same sinister gaiety. The heavy female singer wore green shoes and a green satin gown with gold frogs down the front that fastened her garment from ankles to Adam's apple. She resembled a Baroque green sofa. Behind her, the interesting-looking fellow at the electric organ had a fine nose and chin, the almond eye of the Mongol. He wore a black vest but no jacket, an opened white shirt that bared a chest of black curls tight as buds. His manner was remote, smug, ironic, sure. He might have been listening to an attempt at seduction being bungled in the next room. The third member of the group was the tall, blond, scholarly looking accordionist. He had a forehead that rose to spiritual heights, round gold spectacles, a gold tooth. The small scar at the corner of his mouth appeared pink under the spotlight. The three of them looked as if they ordinarily played and sang with different orchestras and had come together tonight by mistake.

The singer suddenly tossed her head back, a frozen smile on her face, and announced Cossack songs! Songs of passion and violence and despair. She attacked the music with Slavic intensity, each note a slashing thrust or parry. Her sound was clean, strong, true. She had a good voice. The next one I do in English, she cried, and sang of horses, men, and drinking under the cold stars. The red light of the amplifier in the background glowed like a campfire.

From behind the bar, the owner began to clap his hands in time to the music, and Ouida and the kid joined in. Here and there in the darkness a few fitful claps could be heard. Holding her arms out stiffly before her as if galloping across the Moldavian plains, the singer began to shimmy wildly. Her eyes flashed with pleasure as a guttural, animal cry of urgency leapt from the owner's throat. Mona, unaware that the Moujik advertised itself as spontaneous, looked on in absolute disbelief. Dan Asher became apprehensive, fearing that she saw the place only as rather old and silly—and perhaps him too. The minute Ouida spotted his signal, she stopped applauding and ran off.

Having finished her number, the singer removed a green lace handkerchief from her sleeve. She dabbed at the corners of her mouth, crushed the handkerchief into a ball, and lifting her heavy chin to the light cried, Zo! She swept directly to the edge of the spotlight closest to their table and leered at Mona. Perspiration could be seen blistering her forehead, black rings of makeup theatrically mocked her eyes. She took a step closer. Dan Asher considered shoving her back.

She sang a cappella, first speaking the words and then, as the intensity of her involvement grew, shifting from inner conviction to full-throated vocal power. *Hoppy brrrday do you, hoppy brrrday do you.* . . . Nothing she had done up to now had prepared Mona for this. The woman's hint of vibrato could tear your heart out; her perfect control made you glad to see it go. She sang the song as if she really cared. She might have been Mona's mother.

The manager himself seemed to be caught up in her spell, and it was several seconds before he started the applause. When Mona tried to thank her, the singer was gone. Approaching the table, Ouida carried a long rectangular box in her arms. If there was a birthday cake inside, it was no higher than a pizza pie. Mona glanced questioningly at her boyfriend, and Dan Asher beamed.

Open it, he said. It's for you. Inside the box was the artist's birthday present to his love, an intricately woven Mexican shawl that glowed in emerald, amber, and orange. She held it up to catch the little light in the room and then wrapped it around her shoulders. Oh, Dan! she said, in a voice as soft as a breath, and hugged herself with pleasure. He had thought that she'd like the shawl, hoped she would, but when the salesgirl on Alvarado Street packed it for him he could hardly have guessed that the box contained such joy. He reveled in her youthful delight, his darling's gift to him.

The evening had, after all, turned out to be a success. Mona showered him with kisses. Thrilled with her shawl, she refused to take it off despite the risks of cherries jubilee and the closeness of the room. As for the future, the subject came up only because he thought it might amuse her.

Dan Asher said, Ouida, you know, reads fortunes. Tea leaves, tarot cards, you name it. She's really very good. The waitress lowered her eyes, her fine blond hair dropping over her face like a wispy curtain. He touched Ouida's arm by way of encouragement and said, Aren't you? She appeared to wince. Mona expected her to go bald with embarrassment and wished Dan would leave her alone.

But oddly enough, Ouida was not in the least embarrassed. Yes, she was conversant with the future and perfectly at home in its mysteries. I have the second sight, she admitted. Apparently regarding herself as nothing more than the instrument of her genius, she could talk of it unashamedly. Greatness had been thrust upon her through no merit of her own. A golden visitation, an unexpected announcement, and from then on she had been blessed with prophecy.

Try her, he suggested to Mona. You'll be amazed. No thanks, she said. Mona didn't care for the idea of having her fortune told. Is it, he wondered, that she's afraid of tempting fate, of angering the gods? Is that it? Go ahead, don't be afraid, he gently teased her. Nothing bad can happen to you tonight. Not on your birthday. I wouldn't allow it.

Mona tried not to get angry. It's nonsense, she said, bogus infantile irrational nonsense. If *you* need to have someone make a fuss over your big-deal dream future, go ahead. I prefer reality.

Dan Asher was unprepared for how angry she had become. And over nothing.

19 ⟨NASSAU HERALD⟩ 38

DANIEL ASHER

"Dan"

Asher was born December 29, 1916, in New York City.

He is the son of Julius Asher and Ruth Israel. His father is a businessman, president of Asher's Clothing Co. He has one sister.

He prepared at DeWitt Clinton High School, where he was a member of the French Club, the Jazz Club, Arista, and winner of the Kerwin Fingerhut Award for Creative Writing.

Major: French; Scholarship Holder (4); Departmental Honors (3); Assistant Photographic Editor of 1938 *Bric-a-Brac*; associate member of the Gateway Club.

Asher will probably engage in the legal profession.

He is a Hebrew and an Independent Liberal.

WESTWOOD, JUNE 16, 1976

The trees wore name tags. Henry had once worn a name tag at a peace officers' convention downtown at the Biltmore. The trees were at UCLA, and their tags said heavyweight things in Latin like *Liriodendron tulipifera* and *Nyssa sylvatica*. Just walking across the campus you could get an education, but name tags on trees didn't look right to Henry. It felt as queer to him as Disney's dancing mushrooms or ducks in sailor suits.

The students tossed Frisbees in the sun, sprawled over the well-tended lawns, crowded the walks on their way to classes or to lunch. The way they were dressed they could have been going to the beach. The girls hardly had any clothes on at all. Henry, with an eye for a pretty face, asked a smiling, barefoot, blond young coed wearing a red halter where the library was. She passed him by as if he weren't there. The private investigator might have been an empty Baggie. Invisibility was good for the job but hard on his ego. It didn't hurt Henry as much here while working as it had on the beach.

Although he had never gone to college, Henry had taken an occasional extension course at Santa Monica City College. He and Dorothy, who had majored in sociology at Stanford, enjoyed such subjects as collecting rare porcelains and Turkish village rugs. Comparing the campus at Santa Monica with this one was like comparing a window box to Versailles. It took Henry a quarter of an hour and directions from two students plus a young woman selling something she called health sandwiches on black bread with alfalfa sprouts to get him to the canopied main entrance of the research library.

Inside it was cool and crowded. Examination time, said the elderly woman at the information desk. She pointed to the staircase. The Lippencut donation was in Special Collections, and that was downstairs. One flight down, behind the double doors that opened noiselessly, was a large beige-carpeted reception room with hardly anybody there.

Henry approached the librarian at the desk, identified himself as a California taxpayer with scholarly interests, and explained what he wanted. The long-haired young woman looked up from her book. She was wearing eye shadow. Henry squinted at her turquoise tank top and noted the brazen thrust of her naked nipples beneath. He assumed it was a political act. Nowadays even librarians no longer wore brassieres. It was a refreshing sign of the times that made him feel perhaps he had been born too soon.

The librarian asked him to fill out a pink information card. Then she handed him a mimeographed sheet of instructions for the use of Special Collections material and told him to wait inside, pressing a buzzer that unlocked the door to the reading room. Just a minute, she called, coming out from behind her desk. Henry marveled at how completely unself-conscious she was, how indifferent to the bounce and jiggle of her liberated breasts. He was comfortable with modesty but willing to consider the possibility that here was something new and better. You can't bring that in there, she said, taking the Picasso catalogue from him. She promised to return it when he left. Henry was not so captivated that he failed to ask for a claim check, but she said it wasn't necessary.

Two people sat at round tables at opposite ends of the long and otherwise empty reading room. One could have been a graduate student and the other had a professorial beard. Each of them was surrounded by piles of papers and brown folders. Neither looked up as Henry came in. He selected a table at some distance from both of them and sat down quietly in a seat that resembled an upturned plastic helmet. Fifteen minutes passed and Henry was beginning to worry that he had been forgotten when an overloaded cart—the Lippencut collection—was rolled slowly in and delivered to him.

It was hard to know where to start. There were books and boxes and looseleaf folders without titles numbered from 1 to 5 that intrigued him but turned out to contain only newspaper clippings from 1934 about Stein and Toklas visiting the United States. Henry thumbed through memoirs with such titles as

What Is Remembered and *Portraits and Souvenirs* and *Paris Was Our Mistress* and *The Autobiography of Alice B. Toklas*. Apparently the B was for Babette. In the boxes were unpublished letters. Toklas wrote in a small, cramped hand while Gertrude sprawled all over the page.

Tattersall found a photograph of the two of them labeled *Paris, 1922*, that matched their penmanship. They sat by a fireplace, bony Alice on one side packed neatly into a small needlepoint seat that had frail legs and Gertrude in sandals on the other side, her bulk swelling an overstuffed chintz-covered easy chair. Small bouquets of flowers placed strategically about the room complemented the floral prints the two women wore as they stared stiffly at the camera. It was a frozen moment of botanical harmony that appealed to the detective. The wall behind them, however, was what really interested him, for in addition to paintings by Cézanne there were four Picassos, and not one of them was a still life.

A book by Gertrude's brother, Leo, contained a tantalizing reference to an argument between the brother and sister and the division of their joint art collection in 1913. Leo got the Renoirs and Matisses, Gertrude the Picassos, and the Cézannes were split fifty-fifty. There was no hint of how many Picassos were involved or their titles. It wasn't until a couple of hours had gone by, and he was almost hungry enough to eat a sandwich with alfalfa sprouts, that Henry opened a thin folder of documents and came up with the answer.

He found it in a copy of an eight-page inventory of Gertrude's estate filed in Baltimore in 1948 and officially stamped J. Martin House, Register of Wills for Baltimore City. In addition to works by Juan Gris and Matisse, there were twenty-nine Picassos in the Stein collection at the time of her death. Henry counted nine still lifes listed among them. There was a still life with glasses, one with lemons, another with pears, but not one of the nine titles mentioned croissants.

An ecstatic Tattersall reached into his pocket for a piece of scratch paper and discovered the folded sheet on which he had written Mark Hofstedler's Bel Air address. Turning it over, he quickly copied down the titles of the paintings. He had just gotten to number five with pears when someone behind him bent over and whispered, Don't you believe in warnings?

Henry knew better than to make any sudden movements. His hands might have been screwed to the tabletop. Without turning his head, he glanced down at the floor, expecting deadly black leather, and spotted the toe of a harmless white buck. There was nothing to worry about. He turned and looked up into a pair of angry green eyes. The thin white-haired man they belonged to had his shirt sleeves rolled evenly to the elbows and obviously meant business. He reached across to the mimeographed sheet of instructions in front of Henry and, pointing to the bottom, tapped staccato where it said ANYONE FAILING TO ADHERE TO THE ABOVE WILL NOT BE PERMITTED THE USE OF THESE ARCHIVES. Colorless polish, thought Henry, noting the nails, but otherwise he was confused. No pens in Special Collections! whispered the angry man, whose manner suggested that he was in charge down here. Take this, he said, placing a needle-sharp pencil on the table, and Tattersall nodded his appreciation.

As soon as White Bucks had left the reading room, Henry got up and, taking the page he wanted from the Stein inventory, went outside to the librarian's desk. A different young woman was now seated there. She wore eyeglasses with thick rosy plastic frames. As he feared, she knew nothing about his Picasso catalogue, but she wanted to be helpful.

Not here, she kept saying, shaking her head melodramatically as she peered into drawers and cabinets and finally, all smiles, located the catalogue at the bottom of a small closet behind the desk. Henry had felt sure that he would never see it again. He smoothed out the corner of the cover that she had accidentally torn. Is there a Xerox machine here? he asked. There was, and for ten cents he made a copy of the inventory page, slipped it into the catalogue, and decided that the time had come to get help from an expert.

LOS ANGELES, JUNE 16, 1976

Gilbert Wright had been a curator at the County Museum of Art about as long as the Rembrandt painting had been missing. Miles Dorfman, his predecessor, had been careless, but hardly anyone actually believed that he was involved in the theft. Tattersall's guess was that the trustees hoped by letting him go they would appease the wrath of Newton Ward at the loss of his painting. Within a few months, however, Ward made clear that he was not appeased. Calling a press conference, he announced that the County Museum could go to hell. Rather than donating his priceless art collection to the city, he intended to build a museum of his own. In the end, the trustees lost a fortune in art and gained a curator. Doubtless, they would have preferred it vice versa. Tattersall, who liked Wright, suspected that his ingratiating manner was merely the way he coped with nine years of symbolizing a defeat.

Mr. Wright out to lunch. The black museum guard spoke in a bored, remote voice as if the uniform he wore were no more than an accident, some awful momentary trick of fate. He be back at three. So will I, said Henry, and went to get something to eat.

The cafeteria in the museum was bustling, noisy, full of light. A faint ripple of sour milk floating on the air reminded him of an apple-cheeked pal from elementary school known as "Slops." Although it was a weekday afternoon, there wasn't an empty table in the place. Everybody was interested in art these days. He and Dorothy had had to wait more than an hour to see Impressionist and Post-Impressionist paintings from the U.S.S.R., more than three to push their way past golden trinkets from the lands of the Scythians. Henry got at the end of the cafeteria line and waited his turn, eyeing the steaming chili lurking behind the counter and trying to decide whether to turn it loose on his sheltered taste buds. Had the kidney beans been soaked at least twenty-four hours? He was willing to pay the inflated price listed on the wall menu if the beans were tender, the paprika no more than a sprinkle. The counterman's movements were methodical rather than quick as he went from one customer to the next. A round-faced Mexican-looking fellow, he showed a pumpkin paunch covered by a tight white jacket that gaped where a button was missing. The counterman placed a wrinkled stuffed pepper on a plate and shoved it out. Wiping his hands on a rag, he looked resentfully across at Henry. You? he challenged. Henry asked himself, How far wrong can you go with plain turkey and a dash of mayonnaise? He paid for his sandwich and, forsaking the air conditioning inside, took it out on the molten plaza to eat in peace.

Built adjacent to the La Brea Tar Pits where once-glorious mastodons had been reduced (tusks and all) to a sullen bubble or two that rose darkly out of the past and disappeared, the County Museum of Art fronted Wilshire Boulevard. It consisted of three white rectangular buildings propped on slender concrete columns that resembled the spindly legs of seabirds. A year ago the legs scurried ashore when the museum's reflecting pool was drained and replaced by a sculpture garden. The raised central plaza connected the three buildings and was dotted with benches, trees, and a few large pieces of sculpture. Seated in the shadow of Rodin's *Thinker,* Tattersall munched on his dry sandwich.

Hi! The greeting was bright as a bullet. Hot enough for you today? It was a concave, one of those gaunt religious fanatics with a shaved head and a thin pigtail whom Henry had seen dancing around the city. This one wore coral beads. His peach robe billowing in the Santa Ana gusts reminded the detective of a windblown Botticelli. Henry munched his turkey and nodded.

Super hot, agreed the picturesque young man, but I see you're keeping your cool. He flashed a terrific smile. Hey, good for you. Krishna loves that. He handed Tattersall a paperbound copy of the *Bhagavad Gita* and said, I want you to have this. Henry handed it back. Hey, no! Please. I *really* do. Henry wiped his mouth with a napkin, wadded it up, and, not seeing a litter basket nearby, stuffed it in his pocket and got up. He didn't want the book, and it was too hot to argue about it.

Suddenly grabbing Henry's arm, the Krishna follower asked,

How about a donation anyhow? Sorry, said the investigator, removing the hand from his arm. He was more annoyed than angry. As he walked off toward the entrance to the Hammer Wing of the museum, where the administrative and curatorial offices were located downstairs, he could hear a faint, familiar voice in the background saying, Hi there. Hot enough for . . . ?

Gilbert Wright had returned from lunch and would see him. Henry took the elevator down to the first level, and the guard on duty in the hallway, who had been notified, passed him through. Although the curator's door was wide open when he got there, Tattersall paused on the threshold and knocked.

Mr. Tattersall! Wright called from his desk and hurried over to take the investigator by the shoulder, shake his hand. Come in, come in. It's been ages. You're looking great. Been to Palm Springs? Please, sit down. No, he said, pushing forward a low-slung, padded leather chair in a color that Henry's wife called palomino and fashionable and looked to him mottled tan. Here, take this one. It's more comfortable.

Tall, affable, with a ready smile, Gilbert Wright was in his mid-thirties, but his hairline was already receding. The hair that remained he allowed to grow long, and it sprung out of the back of his head like wires. He wore an open collar, a blue blazer, white ducks. The first thing he wanted to know from the investigator was if there was anything new on the stolen Rembrandt.

Henry said no and inquired about Miles Dorfman. Did Wright ever hear from him anymore? Now and again. He's directing a small gallery at a little college on Long Island, but as far as I can tell he seems to be happy. Folding his hands on the desk in a helpless gesture and lowering his voice as if fearing to be overheard in the hallway, he added, It's too bad. He deserved better. He put together some really first-rate exhibitions while he was here. Still at Hofstra, thought Henry. It's his wife, said Wright, who's got the good job. She's now a senior curator at the Brooklyn Museum.

Wright's windowless air-conditioned office was wonderfully cool, and the chair Henry sat in turned out to be as advertised. Leaning back, he began to relax for the first time that day. This was the same office that Miles Dorfman had once occupied. Nine years ago it was from this very spot that *Jacob Wrestling with the Angel* had disappeared, the two struggling gladiators whisked out the door, never to be seen again. Tattersall automatically glanced about the familiar room, still searching by force of habit for the one clue that might have been overlooked, even though he had a pretty good idea of the Rembrandt's present whereabouts. Swiveling around in his seat, he turned to the curator and, placing the Picasso catalogue before him, asked if he had seen the show at the Marquis Gallery.

Wright hadn't. He was so busy organizing a European Moderns exhibition that he didn't have a minute for pleasure. People like Miró, Bacon, Dubuffet, Kitaj. The first major American museum show of contemporary European painting in almost two decades, but you can see what it's doing to my hairline. Busy, busy, busy. He leafed through the catalogue and gave an *ah*! and then a surprised *huh*! and then *mmmmm*. Lovely, he concluded. As they say, the man's a genius. Noting the show's closing date on his desk calendar, he returned Henry's catalogue. Thanks for the tip. If I can, I will.

Then Tattersall told him why he had come. Opening the catalogue to the reproduction of *Still Life with Croissants*, he explained that the gallery owner said it was from the Gertrude Stein collection, but he didn't think so. He showed Wright the copy he had made of the inventory of her estate. The curator found it most interesting. Perhaps, he suggested, Ms. Stein sold the painting before her death. It was a possibility that for some reason hadn't occurred to Henry, a base not touched, a visit to the witness stand with his fly open.

From a bookcase built into the wall, Wright removed a wine-dark volume entitled *Four Americans in Paris*. A quartet of smiling Steins could be seen through four small portholes in the imitation morocco cover. It was a catalogue from a New York Museum of Modern Art exhibition and disclosed that, to keep her and Alice going, Stein had sold off Picasso still lifes with an ace of clubs, with a calling card, with a bottle of maraschino, and one with fruit, glass, knife, and newspaper, but admitted nothing about croissants.

Still, Wright observed, that's hardly conclusive evidence. You see, he told Henry, Picasso rarely titled a picture himself. He generally left that for his dealers, such as Kahnweiler and Rosenberg. It could be that a woman as original as Ms. Stein had one title for the painting and the artist's dealer at the time had another.

He suggested that the investigator pay a visit down the hall to the museum's excellent little library, where he'd find a copy of Christian Zervos's catalogue of Picasso's entire *oeuvre*. If it's reproduced there, you'll at least know it's a Picasso. Henry thanked him warmly for the advice. But the Zervos catalogue is not yet finished, Wright added, so if you don't find what you're looking for there, you can't say for certain that it's *not* a Picasso. All right, said Henry, but if it *is* there . . . ? Then, Wright had to agree, it's probably the real thing regardless of the title.

Henry looked depressed, confused, his methodical mind wearied battling against a quicksand of unexpected alternatives and sly expert qualifications. Only probably a Picasso? A sad, almost touching note crept into the curator's voice as he asked Henry if he knew how many paintings by Corot were hanging in the museums of the world. Henry did not. Three thousand, said the curator. Three thousand Corots spread pole to pole, and to the very best of our knowledge Corot only did two thousand paintings in his entire lifetime. My point, Mr. Tattersall, is this: Compared to the cottage industry in phony Corots, Picasso manufacturing is big business.

As a matter of fact, said Henry, glancing at the list of works and their dates in the back of the catalogue, he had found it hard to believe that so many early Picassos were still for sale and in one gallery. Not necessarily, cautioned Wright, and besides, the gallery may be operating as a middleman for private owners. Tattersall acknowledged that the dealer had said as much. He rose, thanked Wright again, and on the way out said, Ginseng root. The curator seemed puzzled. Henry said a Korean friend had recommended it for the hair. You could try. Maybe it'll do you some good.

LOS ANGELES, APRIL 5, 1966

MANDY MOORE

PREVIEW OF REMBRANDT

When news of Newton Ward's latest and greatest art coup was announced last month, Los Angeles art lovers hoped that they would soon get a glimpse of Rembrandt's fabulous "Jacob Wrestling with the Angel." Saturday night that hope became a reality at a glittering black-tie dinner at the Los Angeles County Museum of Art.

The painting's first V.I.P. preview was preceded by a champagne reception honoring Mr. Ward in the Ahmanson Gallery's atrium. LACMA's new director, Dr. J. Martin Donleavy, hosted the affair. The lavish dinner that followed was held in the Mr. and Mrs. Edwin Pauley Great Hall, decorated for the occasion by those floral wizards from Orzel Winslow. A wonderful Dutch treat for dessert called Limburgse Vla, better known hereabouts as fruit tart, was a masterpiece worthy of Rembrandt himself.

The museum trustees were out in force for the event. Mr. and Mrs. Howard Ahmanson could be seen congratulating Mr. Ward on his spectacular acquisition. Standing nearby and admiring the masterpiece were Mr. and Mrs. Norton Simon. No doubt Mr. Simon was wishing that he had it for his own collection. Mrs. Simon, recently returned from a European vacation, was looking smashing in a blue-tiered chiffon.

It was truly a spectacular gathering of the city's art elite, and even the bit of fisticuffs that occurred before the night was over couldn't ruin things. Dr. Donleavy called the incident "regrettable," and the less said about it the better. An ebullient Puffy Southworth summed up the evening as "inspired," and that's good enough for me. The stunning

Mrs. Southworth, by the way, was in a green and white print, and around her neck she wore the turquoise necklace lawyer-husband Bill gave her on their recent wedding anniversary.

Everyone agreed that the painting, soon to go on public exhibition, was *ravissant*. It is the artist at his most sublime. "But of course," said Jaime Cross of the Getty Museum to a group of the Master's awed worshipers, "he's Rembrandt. What more . . . ?"

—*Los Angeles Times*

LOS ANGELES, JUNE 16, 1976

The Zervos catalogue was bound in black and more than twenty volumes. The 1908 volume—the date given for the still life in the Marquis Gallery catalogue—contained works that were similar to the painting, but none was exactly the same. Always cautious, Henry examined some of the other volumes, stopping every now and again to savor a page. For example, 204.

How the naked sweethearts clung to one another in ecstasy and exhaustion! The slim young man grasping the soft curves of her thighs, and she with her head thrown back moaning her love. And not just one pair of lovers but pages of them, couple after couple in wreathed arrangements of legs forked and limp and writhing. A double-barreled toast by Picasso to the ingenuity of the human mind and the elasticity of the human torso.

The detective inspected the drawings not with the tunnel vision of lust but with the eye of curiosity, wonder, appreciation that somehow the trick had been brought off. Although Henry preferred not to talk about it, such sexual possibilities were not unknown to him. He knew something, too, about even more complicated combinations of three and four or more. It would have been impossible to live in the city of the swinging single and not be aware of the meat market polka and the group grope, but Henry dwelled on such excesses as rarely as he did on open heart surgery.

There was no *Still Life with Croissants* in Zervos. Before his talk with Gilbert Wright, Henry had hoped that he would be able to say no croissants, no Picasso, that he could establish with the curator's help that this unrecorded canvas was a fake and use that solid piece of information to squeeze the Rembrandt out of Hofstedler. But now he could only say that he still believed the Marquis Gallery painting (allegedly from the Stein collection) was either stolen or counterfeit, and nothing in Zervos had changed his mind. If anything, the string of his suspicion had been pitched a semitone higher by something he *had* seen there.

The reproduction in the Zervos catalogue was black and white and small, but it was the same amorous pastel he had admired in the gallery. The title was listed as *The Lovers*, exactly what he had been told. It was the identity of the owner printed below the title that surprised and puzzled him. Hofstedler had claimed that the collector was a private individual who insisted on complete anonymity, a wealthy and discreet client. Why, Henry asked himself, would the Jasper Middleton Gallery of London not wish to reveal that they owned the pastel when the Zervos catalogue made no secret of the fact? As soon as he got home, Henry planned to send a note to London expressing his interest in *The Lovers*, his desire to know the price of the drawing, and his intention of coming to England to see it.

The day had been a long one, a slow trudge in desert heat. Still and all, he had managed to pick up one or two provocatively shaped new pieces on his way to filling in the jigsaw puzzle of the missing *Jacob*. And he had done so without risking his life or committing a crime. Although Henry usually got the job done, he would never pretend that his investigative style was as colorful as that of some other West Coast private eyes. His wasn't the only way or necessarily the best way, but it was the honest, plodding, Tattersall way.

Since the museum was just a few blocks from Fairfax Avenue and the best bakery in the entire city, Henry decided to surprise Dorothy and buy a Jewish rye with seeds before going home. She loved well done, the crunch and crackle of the dark brown crust. Henry liked it too. He took number sixty-three from the holder on the bakery's counter and waited his turn amidst the buzzing crowd and confectionary smells. Hot rolls, fresh cookies, lemon frosting, a theatrical sense of urgency from dawn till dusk. Quietly biding his time, Tattersall enjoyed the drama of ethnic mingling.

Behind the counter a door swung open and from the back came the crystalline sound of Ornette Coleman's saxophone. Shouldering a tray of steaming egg bagels, a black man in white pants appeared, calling, One side, one side! The thin-faced redheaded saleswoman, whose curls looked as if they had been dipped in vinyl, boxed another pie and said to her customer, Yes, dear. Now, what else?

Near the cash register, her large co-worker was shouting and waving her flabby arms. She had been doing so for some time. Before Henry realized what had happened, she had breezed past several numbers and was serving sixty-five. Sixty-three, said Henry from the back of the crowd. Ringing up her sale, the redhead noshed on a cookie and called for sixty-six.

Here was a bakery, the best in L.A., that not only smelled good but was air conditioned. If not for the fact that he was tired, Henry might have passed an hour or two on the premises quite comfortably. But the longer he waited, the more melancholy he became. Easing his way gingerly up to the counter, he removed a bun from one of the small trays on top. It turned out to be cinnamon raisin and, he thought, really delicious.

The redheaded saleswoman, who prided herself on not missing much that went on in the store, caught him in the act. Coming over, she snapped, For your information we don't give those away. That's twenty-five cents.

Yes, of course, said Henry, thrusting a five-dollar bill across the counter. And a rye bread sliced.

PART V

OAKLAND, 1976

23. THE DARK CORRIDOR OF DON
JUAN MADOURA
New York, 1955
Paper, cigarette package fragment, celestial
navigation map, photograph of Rudolph
Valentino, colored sand, clock wheels,
springs on cardboard
Size: 9 x 12 inches
Coll. Museum of Modern Art

*The head of the Spanish don looms up out of the shadows. His
face—ending in a short pointed beard—is as thin as a blade. The
haunted, inward-looking eyes are a striking Gauloise blue. He
covers his ears with his hands to silence the mockery. On his ring
finger a gold wedding band.*

*In the dimly lit receding hallway behind him, some of the doors
are ajar. Men with cowled heads can be glimpsed, the flash of white
teeth in the murky doorways. Their laughter is merciless. Not one
of them feels the least sympathy for the tormented Madoura.*

There is a large window at the far end of the hall filled with moonlight. Outside, the night is ablaze with color. The lawn, smooth as a dance floor, shimmers with light. In the white gazebo, two figures are in each other's arms. The woman is blond, the man a Valentino. She surrenders to her darkly handsome lover, but he never forgets the formality of the occasion. Together, the two dancers whirl away the night, their feet seeming to spurn the ground, their feet actually floating on air. Above them the sky is a dizzying opera of wheeling stars and planets, chaste numbers and lines.

NEW YORK, FEBRUARY 13, 1958

The Levitzky dance company was rehearsing in a small theater on Second Avenue south of 14th Street. Years ago only Yiddish plays were put on there, plays with such titles as *My Mother's Tears* and *The Prince from Prague*, and it was called the Russian Art Theater of Second Avenue. Around the corner was Greenblatt's, which in Dan Asher's estimation based upon forty-two years of metropolitan experience was the best delicatessen in all of New York, and therefore the best in America, the finest in the world. He wondered if his new wife, Madeleine, with but ten years in the city, knew how close she was to unforgettable pastrami. They would take home a pound after the show.

The rehearsal had probably already begun. A blast of icy wind caught him as he dashed across to the east side of the avenue. He could feel his eyes tearing, his nose starting to run again. Behind his back, the long ends of the black-and-white woolen scarf that Madeleine had made for him streaked like the tail of a comet. Although Dan Asher had set the alarm clock in the studio to make sure not to be late, he had been busy arranging delicate mirrored slivers in a frame for one of his new hotel pieces and gotten caught up in his work. Coming toward him down the street, Seymour Bellamy and chum meant that he would be later.

Seymour was a sweet guy, a pleasure to meet under most circumstances, but he was a talker who adored gossip the way a pederast loves his lads. Seymour, as a matter of fact, was also a pederast. He was wearing his usual winter uniform of army surplus boots, suntans, a fur-collared khaki flight jacket. Some people assumed that he had served in the Korean War. The truth of the matter was that he bought his clothes in the Army-Navy store on Canal Street where Dan Asher, not too long ago, had run into him picking out a fatigue cap for one of his new boyfriends. Seymour was a poet, a good one whom Dan Asher admired, one who could mingle "wet nibbling lips" and "elephant balls" and somehow make the whole thing sound utterly convincing, witty, even urbane.

It occurred to Dan Asher that somewhere in a pile of letters at home on his desk was an invitation to a Bellamy poetry reading that he had missed. Shit, man, said the artist, wiping his tearing eyes and leaking nose on the frayed end of his black corduroy sleeve, sorry about your reading. I couldn't make it.

Although not usually given to modesty, Seymour was candid. It was not one of my better efforts, he admitted. The reviews, so to speak, were mixed. Unlike yours, I might add, in last Sunday's *Times*. I was pleased for you, Daniel. And oh, yes—his eyes twinkled like Christmas lights—that other matter . . .

Dan Asher said, Look Seymour—

The poet would have none of it. Don't think you can keep secrets from your friends. My warmest *félicitations*. I understand from Hans that she's a dancer. Do I know the lady?

Dan Asher didn't want to be rude, but he had no time for Seymour. He showed him only a cold, gap-toothed smile. A worn black corduroy suit. A thin, scruffy beard and wind-whipped winter cheeks the color of poinsettias. And said, No, no, I don't think so. Undaunted, Seymour introduced his friend Jimmy, a young actor of extraordinary talent with a future as boundless as outer space.

Jimmy took Dan Asher's hand incredulously. He said, *The* Daniel Asher, the artist, the one who shows at the Külicke-Reid? In the flesh, said Dan Asher. Impulsively, he pulled aside his blue woolen tie and yanked open his black flannel shirt. Here, he said, feel. Astonished, Jimmy stared at the exposed thick hairy swatch as if debating whether to probe. He stroked his chin, glanced up into the artist's noncommittal blue eyes, and smiled sheepishly. Seymour laughed at his young friend's confusion.

That's it, said Dan Asher, buttoning up. You had your chance. I'm freezing my sternum off. He raised a hand in farewell. Got to go. As he hurried away, Dan could hear Jimmy's mentor explaining that it was just as he had told him over lunch. New York has got it all, everything, the worst and the best. . . .

For Dan Asher, there had always been something deliciously decadent about entering a darkened theater in the afternoon. The unheated interior of this one was as cold and dank as the belly of a whale. He wiped his running nose and waited at the rear of the auditorium for his eyes to adjust to the darkness. There were only a handful of people in the audience, and he found a seat on the side away from them. Exhausted from years of resistance, the cushion flattened out under him soundlessly without a struggle, providing all the comfort of a leatherette pancake. Dan Asher's sneakers felt damp, his feet cold on the uncarpeted floor. Draping his legs over the seat in front of him, he lighted up a cigarette and settled back to enjoy the show.

At the moment the music was soft-pedaled boogie-woogie piano, a bass moaning steady and a pensive right hand picking out expressive clusters of treble. Memories of Meade Lux Lewis and Pinetop Smith, and the moving fragrance of Dan Asher's youth. Onstage, against a painted strawberry backdrop of heavily made-up women in short skirts holding beer steins on their laps and staring out at the paying customers, Madeleine was dancing what she called the part of her life.

She was not sorry that she had quit Graham to join Levitzky. Except for *Deaths and Entrances*, in which she danced one of the three battling sisters, Madeleine had had only minor roles with the Graham company and felt she was getting nowhere. Dammit, she told him, I'm already thirty-eight. She acknowledged that Graham was in her sixties and still dancing, but Graham was a genius. Although the Great One had rarely criticized her, Madeleine had never felt that she was satisfied with her work. Never.

New and flamboyant, the Levitzky company was out to make a name for itself with a sensational ballet adaptation of Josef von Sternberg's *Blue Angel.* The seductive Lola Lola had been transformed from a cabaret singer to a dancer, and Madeleine, in the role, looked naked on stage as she captivated a muscular young man wearing a derby hat, a tank top, and a jewel-studded jockstrap. My wife, marveled Dan Asher. She's gorgeous.

He watched, riveted by the dancer's beauty, her blond hair tied back with an innocent pink ribbon and her sumptuous curves apparent in a flesh-colored body stocking. The young man's passionate arm encircled her waist. Though her hips playfully caressed his, her upper body held back, arching away like a scythe.

Out from the wings came her husband, the professor. Academic frock tails flying, he seized her arm and attempted to pull her away. She repeatedly eluded the pathetic fool, staring with cool insolence at his bald head, his plastic bow tie. He cried, "You'd take the entire universe to bed with you, I think, just out of boredom, you lecherous, idle shrew!" Ignoring his words, she fell upon the young man, draping herself around his neck, and was lifted effortlessly into the air. Three dancers in Day-Glo orange and wide black patent leather belts surrounded the ranting cuckold, drawing him back.

"You," the old man shouted at his wife, "you need to keep your teeth sound, exercise your jaws, daily, for dinner, some new heart between your paws. Your eyes, all lighted up like shops, like public fairs, how insolent they are!" In her partner's arms, Lola Lola plummeted over and over, each time released and returning upon herself to climb up through his hands, behind his back, across his thighs, or clasped to his chest, and each time Dan Asher was dazzled as the two lovers, sculpturally fixed in space, were caught in a new intimacy.

The theater's musty thrift-shop smell that had initially depressed him was forgotten. His running nose no longer mattered. Lost in the dance, Dan Asher wondered at the amazing power of that body to seduce. He wondered at the pitiful degradation of the professor, who sat without hope, his shoulders hunched forward, his hands fallen between his knees as the three women pulled his bow tie askew and taunted him with their arms, their long scarves. In the end, Lola Lola, throwing a kiss to the old fool, was carried triumphantly offstage by her lover, and the curtain came down. Dan Asher's loud applause startled the near-empty house. Before anyone could see who it was, he had leaped into the aisle and was on his way backstage to congratulate the star.

The small smoke-filled greenroom off to the side was bubbling with the excited conversation of members of the company taking a break or waiting for the next number. He was surprised that there were so many of them. The dancer that he asked said, I think she's over there somewhere, and pointed vaguely to the corner. Unable to see her, Dan Asher telegraphed his heart in the general direction and eased his way through the crowd in pursuit, rubbing good-naturedly up against small hard asses and tiny tits—a seraglio of nimble wafer-thin creatures. With the exception of his wife, he had found that most serious dancers, by and large, were built on the wiry side. The gamy smell of damp armpits in the room was not unpleasant to him.

Dan Asher was apologizing effusively for stepping on an attractive young woman's shin when he looked over and spotted his wife from behind, her blond ponytail pressing against the professor's shoulder, her broad back being stroked by his hands. The two of them had obviously made up their differences. Confused, embarrassed, Dan Asher felt as if he had tactlessly intruded upon something that he was not supposed to see. His first thought was to get the hell out of there quick. He'd come back later, he told himself, when she was finished talking shop.

The professor had noticed the fellow glaring at him, and Madeleine, wiping the tears from her eyes, turned to see who it was. Dan, she called, Dan. Her wet haunted eyes glittering, she went after him, pushing her way through the crowd. She caught up with him and flung her arms about his neck.

Dan Asher took hold of his wife, a solid armful of sopping woman. Her sweating body was steaming like a thoroughbred after a morning workout. This big, healthy, midwestern beauty who had trained her flesh into muscle, this brilliant dancer, this woman whom he loved. He brushed away the perspiration from her damp forehead, smoothed back the matted strands of hair. What do you think? she asked him. Terrible, wasn't I? Her fingers flew to his lips. No, you don't have to say it. I know. Viewed close up, her heavy theatrical makeup gave her a grotesque, predatory look, and yet he was reminded of the expressive black-rimmed eyes of Byzantine painting. Bending over, he confided with a quiet intensity that told how sincerely he meant it, You were great. I mean *really* great.

That, declared the professor, who had come up from behind, is exactly what I've been trying to tell her. Offstage, he appeared to be a much younger man than the role he played, and no doubt there was a full head of hair hidden beneath his baldness. Madeleine introduced Anton Levitzky to her husband. Anton enthusiastically shook his hand, congratulating him on his good fortune to be married to such a richly talented woman. Dan Asher caught a flicker of irritation on his wife's face, as if she had little patience for such compliments.

Levitzky seemed to take pride in his handshake. He refused to let go. It was a boring endurance contest that Dan Asher could have done without and would have, if not for Madeleine. The head of the company had a strong grip, an ingratiating palm that was as smooth as a magazine cover. Drawing Madeleine in with his other hand, he suggested that they wait until the rest of the rehearsal was over and then all three of them would go next door for a glass of tea, a delicious corn beef sandwich.

Madeleine said, How about it, Dan? You like delicatessen. He shook his head emphatically. No, I'm not hungry. Besides, I've got to go and pick up Marissa. Why don't *you* go? Madeleine kissed Anton on the cheek and promised him another time. She wanted to get home right away and steep forever in a hot tub. A minute, she told her husband, and went to change into street clothes.

Without makeup, Madeleine's face when she returned appeared pale, vulnerable. Outside the theater in the thin gray afternoon light, her cold-creamed lips gleamed chastely. She was bundled up against the wind, a navy-blue pea coat buttoned to the neck, around her head a black-and-white scarf that, with the exception of the fringe, was identical to the one she had made for her husband. There was something regal in her walk, and when she took his arm Dan felt as if he were on parade.

A chill February gust caught them in the face as they headed crosstown toward Sixth Avenue. Having just gotten over a cold, he expected to hear from her about the handsome fur-lined coat that she had bought for him and he had ceremoniously hung in the front of his closet. It was a nice coat. If he ever wore a coat, he might have worn that one. Placing their arms around one another, the two tall figures leaned into the sharp, loudly gusting wind and Madeleine, turning to her husband said, What did you really think of me? What? cried Dan Asher.

BEL AIR, JUNE 17, 1976

Koontz lost his left arm in dense fog on the San Diego freeway just south of the Ventura turnoff. It was missing below the elbow. The police had found his wristwatch and gold wedding band on the center divider. They unbuckled the watch's black lizard strap, slipped the ring from his finger, and returned them to him in the hospital. As Koontz signed for his belongings, the officer described the five-car pile-up. Your vehicle, he noted, was sandwiched between vehicle number two and vehicle number four.

At the time, Koontz hoped that his missing arm might help him get back into pictures. Hollywood has a heart, swore the trades. If a star was down on his luck, there was always some industry giant like Roz or Frankie ready to lend him a hand off the record. Koontz had never been a star, but he had been a Nazi. Throughout the forties and fifties, he had swelled the noncommissioned ranks of Hitler's forces, fighting for all the major studios. Following his release from the hospital in 1965 —coincidentally, on the very day in January that the former English Prime Minister (his old, cigar-smoking, V-making celluloid nemesis) died of a stroke—Koontz saw himself as a U-boat commander with his sleeve pinned up or a Gestapo colonel. The studio where he had been working since 1961 as a security guard saw him as a security guard with an amputated arm and let him go.

Tattersall found Koontz on a bulletin board in a neighborhood supermarket. He was tacked up between an experienced baby-sitter and a three-speed Schwinn. The hand-printed sign read Private Chauffeur, Reasonable, Available Night and Day. Even though parts of Los Angeles were impossible to reach by public transportation, Tattersall wouldn't think of letting his wife drive him anywhere when he was on a case. He didn't mind sharing with Dorothy the broad outlines of his work, but he preferred to spare her the unrinsed details. When he couldn't get to where he was going by bus, Henry usually took the reasonable Koontz.

This sun-drenched Thursday morning, Henry was taking him up Camden Drive. Make a left at the next corner, the investigator instructed Koontz, and turn down the alley.

Koontz placed his stump under the wheel to steady it and powered the ancient, faded maroon Buick around the corner in a stately arc. He eased it into the alley behind the gallery. Despite the missing hand, he drove skillfully. But it was his smoothness that came as a surprise, given those elephant shoulders and his close-cropped steel-gray hair that looked like something that could tear up tank treads, mangle tires. Henry noted the parked Mercedes with the ART 2 plate. Satisfied, he leaned back against the musty, cracked, fake-leather upholstery and said,

Okay. Now we go to Bel Air, the east gate, St. Pierre Road.

The well-tended traffic island before the east gate held velvet clusters of pink, yellow, and violet pansies fluttering their petals in the ash-dry breeze. The Buick passed beneath the metal arch, passed the trim white building housing the Bel Air Patrol, and turned up St. Pierre Road. Any one of the huge houses, elegant estates, made Henry's comfortable two-bedrooms-plus-covered-lanai look like a stucco cheesebox. These places are really something! announced Koontz. You know, somebody told me that Charlton Heston lives around here? His tone suggested that he was hoping for confirmation from the back seat.

Slow down, said Henry. He consulted the address Ben Whitelaw had given him on the phone. Pull over here. This is close enough. As he opened the car door, Henry noticed that his seersucker pants needed a pressing, their soft crease having dissolved in the heat. It's goddamn hot, he complained, getting out. Swiveling halfway around, the driver reported a cooling trend on the way. Low pressure off the coast. But more smog, they say. I shouldn't be very long, said Henry. Koontz told him to take his time, and, opening a folded copy of the *Daily Variety* with its fresh spring-green border full of promise, he spread it out on the seat beside him.

The high chain-link fence alongside the road was covered with thick ivy, and vines hid the barbed wire at the top. Tattersall walked toward the entrance. Two square pillars of stone framed a driveway that was barred by the main gate, a hyperbolic black curve of metal spears tipped with gilded arrow heads. The sign posted on the pillar at the left said DANGER, ELECTRIC GATES, RING FOR ADMITTANCE. The smaller sign beneath it said GUARD DOG ON DUTY. Standing well away from the gate, the investigator squinted through the bars.

Those who know baseball say that the truly great hitters have great eyes. The great hitter can see the ball from the moment it leaves the pitcher's hand going one hundred miles an hour, see the rotation on it, see the printing on the horsehide, see the slanting stitch. Henry Tattersall was never much good at baseball, but he knew how to use his eyes. He could see that the driveway—bordered by a line of short clipped yew trees—ended in a brick courtyard. In the center of the courtyard was a small metal fountain that resembled a ball of twigs. It reminded Henry of the fountain in front of the Cal Fed building on Wilshire designed by Claire Falkenstein, but that was ten times the size. There were all sorts of ornamental trees that didn't look like California trees covering the property and screening most of the house from view. Espaliers spread themselves artificially against the side of the garage like great green candelabra. Parked in front of the garage, a gleaming cocoa-and-tan Rolls-Royce with the license plate ART 1. Henry had come to the right place. Although he couldn't see everything, he had seen enough to know that Mark Hofstedler would have to sell a hell of a lot of art to keep up such an establishment.

Very fancy, muttered Henry impassively. He felt no envy of such luxury. And what ordinarily might have gratified him seemed depressing. These grounds had been so fastidiously well tended, so unnaturally trimmed and tidied, pruned and pressed, that they had been turned into a botanical waxworks drained of life. Henry, who made no secret of the fact that he preferred things in their place, had to admit that here was something that could, like concentration camps, give order a bad name.

Tattersall had been standing outside the gates now for several minutes and had seen nothing of a guard dog. He wondered how long Hofstedler had been living here. The posted signs were certainly not new. He considered the possibility that the art dealer had acquired the signs when he bought the property and had not bothered to take them down. He had no desire to test the electric gates to find out. The button announcing visitors was on a bronze plate bolted to the inside of the stone pillar bearing the warnings, but rather than push it he turned and crossed the road to the house on the other side.

It was a two-story white colonial mansion with thin white columns supporting a simple pediment. There were no gates here, and Henry walked directly across an expanse of manicured lawn and up the low front steps. Chimes echoed through the house in response to his ring, and he could hear someone approaching. Yes? inquired the middle-aged maid through a crack in the doorway. She had the large, intelligent, watery eyes of a horse. No sooner had Henry mentioned the name Hofstedler and begun to explain than a shrill voice behind her called, Is that them? Is that them? I'll handle this, Martha. And the maid was brushed aside, to be replaced by a wiry gamecock in a wine-colored vest. Thin, freckled, leathery, his face was the same color as his vest. Henry glanced at his balding right temple, where the bulging vein hinted of stroke.

It's about time, snapped the man. What's the matter with you people? I've called your office a dozen times already, and all I get from you is a kiss-off. Some little pink-tonsiled voice on the line, saying, Sorry, sir, but he does have a permit and we'll send someone around to investigate just as soon as we can. That was four months ago, for cryin' out loud! Four months! How the hell am I supposed to work in my own house with all that goddamn racket going on? I need my peace, my quiet. I'm a writer.

That's interesting, said Henry. I wonder if I've read any of your books?

The thin-faced man bared his teeth in a sour look of contempt. I don't write *books*, he said sharply. I write routines. Some of the biggest comedy acts in Las Vegas. Headliners. The tops! And I can't do a damn thing now with those shrieks coming from across the street at all hours. In the middle of the night, hyenas, jackals, baboons. They belong in a jungle, not in Bel Air. Since that nut moved in, living here has been like a safari. What kind of screwball keeps wild animals in the city? All right, a duck, a squirrel. I'm no Mussolini. But that asshole has vultures, snakes. Look, what are you going to do about it?

Tattersall didn't think there was anything he could do. He scratched his cheek with a clean fingernail and gave a weak smile. It was suddenly plain that here was somebody who had nothing to do with the city's Animal Regulation Department. Then, asked the livid homeowner, his voice pitched to the frequency of urban emergencies, who the hell are you?

Henry Tattersall introduced himself and an explanation came forth, sober, businesslike, one unhurried step after another serenely balanced above a canyon of disbelief. There had been a misunderstanding. He was not in animal control. Henry Tattersall was in validation. Producing his wallet, he flashed a small white card that whispered *private investigator*. Today he was working for the Western Auto Insurance Company of Bellflower, a routine confidential report on one of their new applicants, his neighbor Hofstedler, Mark W. And how long has he been living across the way? asked the investigator, his ballpoint poised coercively over his pad. About a year now, but it seems like twenty. It always amazed Henry how rarely they refused to answer. Who doesn't relish the compliment of an attentive ear?

After that, Western Auto Insurance wanted to know everything about Hofstedler. Did he drink, smoke, dope, give wild parties? He's got a girlfriend, if that's what you mean. Perhaps, Tattersall suggested, she's a member of the family. The writer's neck puffed up like a purple bagpipe. He let out a shrill hoot that shook his windowpanes, flattened his grass. Never! Not *her*! Not Lola. A broad in a million.

Tattersall was curious how he knew her name. The answer was simple. Every time the missus—a smart-looking number with a short cut of French-frosted hair and silk scarves—left the premises in the Rolls, up would roll South-of-the-Border in a red convertible Alfa Romeo with the top down. One day after tooling in she comes running out wearing a bikini that's nothing more than two raisins and a shoelace. She's waving something over her head like she knows I'm watching from behind the curtain and is signaling. Hofstedler is after her. He's naked as a white ass in a picture window. He's shouting, *Lola*, Lola, goddammit, give me back my bathing suit. There is a whole lot of rage, laughter, and passionate grappling.

The two of them are so busy with each other that no one but me sees the Rolls tiptoeing back up St. Pierre, the missus at the wheel with murder in her heart. By the time Hofstedler sees her it's too late. His penis is pointing at the girlfriend like an accusing finger. Snatching his trunks from her, he places both his legs in the same hole and stumbles. Lola's laugh is like little bells. The missus gives him daggers as he straightens things out.

I ought to kill you, she screams. Hofstedler glances across at my curtain and then turns to his wife. Shut up, he says, and, grabbing each of the women by an arm, tosses them both into the back of the Rolls and zooms off up the driveway behind the gate. Once or twice after that Lola would show up when the missus was home, but she hasn't been around for a long time.

Henry nodded sympathetically. He supposed the residents didn't care for that sort of thing in Bel Air. The writer said, I don't give a crap about that. A nice social life is a good thing as long as there are no rock bands with amplifiers. Live and let live. But—his hands knotted up into two little freckled walnuts —we've got to zone out the zoos.

Lola was definitely a new development. The story of the art dealer caught with his trunks down was odd enough to be true in Los Angeles. Then again, thought Henry, maybe it was merely a fresh Las Vegas routine in the works. He was on his way to learn more about it from Mrs. Hofstedler when, some twenty yards from the main gate, a section of the ivy-covered fence began to open.

LOS ANGELES, JUNE 17, 1976

CBS-TV PLANNING
Blockbuster WW II
Vidpic for New Season

CBS-TV is mapping a major war telefilm for next season with a budget of $1.2 million, according to Malcolm Schreiber, vidpix veepee for the network.

The longie is called "Wings Over Munich" and will videbut Jeff Barry and Diana Diehl. Worldwide Associates is producing and Frederick Stone will be in the cockpit. The vehicle rolls in early August in Europe.

"Wings" is the story of a captured German pilot who falls

for an American nurse. It was scripted by Terrence Hubley and is a first for him. Schreiber says, "It's part of my philosophy to encourage new talent."

The whole cast is not yet set.

—*Daily Variety*

SAN FERNANDO VALLEY, JUNE 22, 1967

The red World War I biplane looked like a toy in the light-blue early evening sky. It circled lazily above Roscoe Boulevard, making a wooden knocking sound as if it were on a string being dragged by a child.

Lacey Griggs looked up. He had just locked the loading platform of Baxter Paper and Box for the night. It had been a perfect bitch of a day. First, they had lost the Lowry Laboratory account because the stupid greaser who drove a truck for them couldn't understand plain English. Next, they had accidentally short-counted Standard Pump over fifty custom boxes and very nearly lost them too. And then, on top of all that, his son-of-a-bitch boss had been on his tail like a boil since nine that morning. The only thing Lacey wanted now was a cool, quiet beer.

As the plane floated over him, a festive orange cloud exploded directly beneath it. Was somebody in Canoga Park trying to shoot the thing down? Lacey, who had served in Korea, knew better. Hollywood, he sensed at once, and then seeing the orange leaflets fluttering down realized that it was something else. A dozen or more leaflets drifted into his driveway, and Lacey went over and picked one up. It said, "Stand up and protest. Get out of Vietnam now. Join the march tomorrow at Century City. Tell the President what you think of his war."

Lacey's face became small and vicious. The President was his friend. He crushed the sheet between his hands, ripped it into silence. Then he went after the others. He attacked them as if he wanted to tear each one limb from limb. Come on, damn you, he cried as a gust of wind blew one away from him. Give me a chance.

BEL AIR, JUNE 17, 1976

The leaves shivered and the vines stretched as a chain-link door in the ivy-covered fence began to open. A green plastic trash can appeared in the arms of a woman wearing a brown apron that looped around her neck. She was a short dark mestiza with high cheekbones and straight black hair balled into a chignon at the nape of her neck. That looks about right for the cook, thought Henry.

The trash can was full and, as she set it down near the curb, a few of the empty jars and tins fell out onto the grass. Hurrying over, Tattersall picked them up. One of the jars had once held Iranian caviar. The label on a flat oval can told of Fancy Cherry Wood Petite Smoked Oysters. Idly turning the empty tin in his hand, Tattersall mused, He lives well, and tossed it on the pile. The cook silently gave him the once-over. It was clear that she did not care to have squint-eyed strangers messing with her trash.

Tattersall identified himself and said, I'm looking for Lola. The words had barely been spoken when there was an explosive roar and rush from the gate, a concussion of sound that came thundering down, leaving him face to face with the white-hot mouth of a furnace. It belonged to a Doberman pinscher. The animal was rampant and breathing fire, at the end of his tether and straining to close the gap between their two noses. Henry was so amazed, so frightened, that he couldn't move, afraid to turn his back on the animal, afraid to do anything. From the house across the street, an onlooker, unable to see that the muscles in the investigator's face had lost all their elasticity, might have mistaken Henry's behavior for a foolhardy act of bravado.

Down, Hump, down! cried the cook, and the Doberman dropped down on all fours in an on-guard position. You better be careful of that dog, she warned Tattersall. He got trained to attack. He only go forward, period. She pulled back the animal's lips, showing his powerful teeth. You know how far something like that sink in?

Henry stared at the dog mesmerized. The black of its muzzle was a dirge, its brown paws four rusty spades, its teeth as clean as coffin nails.

All the way, she said and smiled. She couldn't have been prouder if the teeth were her own. Then she added, I don't know no Lola. This here's the Hofstedler house.

Shifting his gaze from the animal to her, Henry felt a wonderful surge of relief mingled with a great weariness. He moistened his lips and asked, Is Mr. Hofstedler in? The cook, a curious expression of pensive cunning on her face, wanted to know if he had an appointment. Henry said no. Then he ain't in. How about Mrs. Hofstedler? inquired the investigator. Busy, she shot back, and seemed to dare him to challenge her.

The woman was bluffing and Henry knew it. He tried a little of the same. That's all right, he said casually. We're old friends. I can wait. He turned and headed for the gate, but she stopped him before he had gone two steps. Her attitude was conciliatory. Look, she reasoned, why trouble the lady? Lola don't work for Meester Hofstedler no more. Henry said he knew, and that was why he was trying to get in touch with her. He ran an art gallery himself. If she was Lola's friend, he was sure she'd want to help. I might have something to offer her, he said.

The cook wiped her hands on the edge of her apron while considering the likelihood. She looked old and worried and made whimpering automotive noises clearing her throat. Okay, she said. Her brother owns a music store down on Broadway and Fifth. You can try there. Tattersall thanked her for the information. The cook told him to beat it. The meester, she said, he don't care for surprises. That's how come Hump. She seized the dog by the collar and raised him snarling into the air as if to remind Henry that his own somewhat short but generally dependable legs were only a whistle away from becoming ground beef. Now you get out of here and don't come back.

The cook had not wanted him to see Mrs. Hofstedler and open old wounds. Whoever this Lola was, thought Henry, people seemed to like her.

VENICE, JANUARY 10, 1966

Miles Dorfman tried Rose Street but couldn't find a place to park. He left his car two blocks away, locking the door and then tugging on it just to make sure. There were all sorts of stories about Venice. He dreaded the thought of his beautiful golden Volvo alone in the Venetian night being picked as clean as a piano key by the local junkies.

Walking back, he moved quickly. The sound of his own bootheels thumped in his ears. Lurking about in the darkness were the neighborhood's small, ugly, stucco bungalows, with here and there the excitement of a lewd orange light in an unshaded window. He superimposed fleeting Pigalle images on the bare frames—luscious, full-lipped, languorous creatures who bathed irregularly. At the corner of Rose, he turned. The only light on the beach block came from the small red and white bulbs that formed a cross of letters above the Holy Unity Mission door. Jesus Saves.

Umu was next to Jesus, Irving Carp had told him when he called. But the front door of Umatsu's studio was locked. Miles went around to the back of the small factory building, and the sound of voices grew louder, more animated. Groups of people were standing about in the alley with drinks in their hands. The warm light from the open door revealed heads bobbing like buoys on a moonlit sea, and some familiar faces amidst the shadows. It was a summery January night after a Santa Ana day, and inside the studio an overflow crowd. Miles elbowed his way in, acknowledging friends with a nod, a kiss, a hug, a great wave of his amiable arm that semaphored love.

After almost two years as curator of modern painting at the County Museum, Miles was well liked in the art community. Oh, of course there were some who wished that he would take more risks. A few complained of his compromises, but his friends argued that everyone makes compromises. Miles had a gift for making friends. Secretly he would have preferred if it had been for painting. Unable to be an artist, he had chosen the next best thing and become a curator. It was as if he lived somewhere between his upwardly mobile blue pinstripe suit and the romance of the cowboy boots that he wore for his evening at Umu's.

Stacked to the rafters of the noisy studio were large blue metal drums on which warnings were written in white stenciled letters. The containers held the resin polymers that Umatsu used for his massive wedge-shaped sculpture. People were leaning against them, against the yellow forklift nearby, against the white-washed walls. The long, loose belt that turned the exhaust fan above the door snapped and shivered, then flapped convulsively, and each completed revolution ended with a grinding death rattle.

The ache, Max Roth shouted above the noise. It passes from one peasant to the next. The story is from Russian folk tales, a big megillah about a firebird that even I, frankly, don't understand one hundred percent. Ah, Miles, my friend! Having spotted the curator, Max pulled him into his embrace. You look like a million. Make that two. Four. How are you?

Miles couldn't imagine himself wearing a safari bush jacket, but, casually unbuttoned, it looked good on the handsome Roth. The tan belt dangled with flair. He shook hands with the art dealer, shook hands with Carlton Lang, the wealthy collector to whom Roth had been talking about Stravinsky.

Egg, said Lang. You mean egg, don't you, Max? Yes of course. An ache, said Max. With his hands he shaped a huge one out of air. You know, from the chicken.

As Max rattled on, Miles left them and went to look for Mona. She had told him that she would definitely be there that evening. She planned to visit Dan early and then come directly from the hospital. Miles found her in a leather skirt the size of a tobacco pouch. It was, he noted with pleasure, much shorter than anything she had ever worn to work. She was surrounded by admirers. Although he had great respect for his assistant, regarded her as a clever girl thoroughly professional in her job, a terrific co-worker and a pal, Miles scoured her smooth glistening luscious naked upper leg with his eyes.

The small man talking and waving his arms in Mona's face was Irving Carp. His long hair was a stiff blond haystack that reached no higher than her eyebrows. Whenever anybody in the crowd pushed past him, the stack swayed from side to side. Carp, a mediocre painter, was outstanding in causes, petitions, leaflets, and round-table discussions. He always sounded emphatic, his voice muscular. He was often quoted in the underground press. When asked by a reporter for the *L.A. Free Press* about his painting *The Policemen's Ball on Crenshaw*, he said, I paint 'em as I see 'em. The subject was last summer's Watts riot, the action three cops bashing in the head of a crippled black woman with a baby cradled in her bloody arms. The critic for *People's Art* praised the work as an important political statement and called it "Hobbesian."

Miles called it a crummy painting. Carp wheeled around and let out a whoop that shivered his hair. Dorfman himself! he shouted, and slapped a soul shake on Miles. The more biggies here the better. Maybe this time for once the L.A. art community will get off its collective ass and do something.

The curator winked at Mona, who returned him a radiant smile. Spreading his legs stiffly, Miles surveyed the crowd. His straight, blond, neatly combed hair glowed with health, youth, enviable prospects. Quite a turnout, Irving, he shouted approvingly.

As she watched him, Mona was reminded of something Dan had said after their first meeting. I like him, said Dan, but do you see the wooden way he holds himself? He's like a piece of folk sculpture. Perhaps it was true that Miles did sometimes hold himself a little stiffly, but Mona could find nothing unappealing about it. On the whole, she got along well with her young and ambitious boss. Okay, cried Carp, it's time to get this fuckin' show on the road.

No sooner did Carp leave than his place was taken by a man in a hawk shirt. Beneath the word HAWK roosted a picture of a bird. It was more or less a crow with talons. Parkinson was the guy's name. Everyone called him Hawk because he rarely changed his tee shirt. Hawk called himself a conceptual artist, but no one had ever seen anything he had conceived. Miles tagged him a phony and a pest.

How's Dan? the Hawk asked Mona. A little depressed, she reported. He's afraid that everything will be changed now, but he's got his color back. The nurses tell me they think he's cute. A good sign, he said.

What? asked Mona. Hawk had to shout to be heard above the exhaust fan and the shrill of metal grinding against metal. *A good sign!* He turned to Miles and yelled, How much do you have? I need some cash.

Never better, replied the curator. Miles had long ago ceased to be amused by this creep who was always trying to squeeze money out of him. *Cash!* screamed Hawk. *Fork over, tight wallet.* Miles asked Mona if she cared for a beer, some wine, an ice cube. Not so fast, Dorfman. This is even bigger than what I did with Wong's Stolen Rembrandt. He quickly summed up his plans for a monumental new work. A cemetery of maimed and martyred pieces of furniture. Missing legs, missing arms. Tiny American flags beside every victim and fresh flowers every day. It's going to cost a pretty penny, he predicted, and held out his hand to the curator palm up. Miles shook it vigorously and wished him all the best. *You cheap mackinaw,* screamed the Hawk. You're not pro-war, are you?

With Mona looking on, Hawk was an embarrassment that

Miles, generous by nature, could do without. Having patiently heard him out, he leaned forward and whispered, Fuck off. Not even *one* lousy buck? whined Hawk. Nothing, swore Miles.

It was apparent even after Hawk had left that the curator had been upset by the situation. You're much too nice to him, Miles, Mona said to her boss. Everyone knows that he's a ripoff artist. Miles shrugged modestly and said, What the hell, basking in her praise, her surveillance.

The knocking had been going on for some time, but now it grew louder, more insistent, and people looked up to see where it was coming from. Pint-sized Irving Carp was angrily striking the wall with a ball peen hammer. He stood on top of Umu's worktable in order to be seen. Thank you, thank you, he said when he had gotten everyone's attention. The exhaust fan let out a piercing scream, its metal shaft grinding in agony. Turn that damn thing off, shouted Carp, and, the plug pulled, the loose fan belt shivered, flapped hysterically, and fell silent.

Carp promised that if it got too hot he'd turn the fan back on. He scanned the packed studio. I've got mixed feelings about this, Carp let it be known at the top of his commanding baritone. I'm glad, he said, glad to see you all, but I think it's a goddamn shame that in L.A. it takes something like a war in Vietnam to get us all together.

A roar of agreement went up from the crowd. We're all so isolated here, he went on. Maybe we ought to take our art to the streets. Bring it out where the people are. Somebody shouted, Forget it, ain't nobody out there. Laughter spilled over the stifling room.

Billy Correy, one of the Drum Gallery's brightest stars, yelled something, but his voice came out shrill and pinched. He tried again. Pushing his Mexican peasant's straw hat to the back of his head, he cleared his throat and shouted, If you really want to do something about the fighting, let's close down the County Museum. It's your art-loving trustees who are waging the war in Vietnam. All those rich hypocritical bastards. Let's just not let them exhibit any more of our work. Shut the fuckers down.

134

That's easy for you to say, Billy. You've already got it made. It was Eva Beck, a frail young woman in a thin purple dress, cheap Japanese sandals. But if Newton Ward wants me, she swore, I'm his. Why not Ward? Billy whispered to his pal Delman Thorp, another Drum Gallery artist. Everyone else has had her. Thorp snickered from behind dark glasses and guessed aloud that she probably didn't give a shit about the war.

Eva was furious. It's a goddamn lousy war and everyone knows it and every real artist knows it and is against it and so screw you. Eva's middle finger shot high into the air, where it met with cheers, whistles, and general applause.

Irving Carp recognized Mona. She began by explaining why she didn't think closing down the museum was a good idea. As she spoke, Delman Thorp saw Eva turning away and moving through the crowd. Sure, Eva, he called mockingly, you're so much against the goddamn war you're leaving. Worming her way along, Eva reached the makeshift closet that served as Umatsu's lavatory and yanked open the door. Can't I even take a pee in this place without it becoming war and peace? The freestanding walls heaved in shock as she slammed the door behind her.

Hardly anyone noticed. Mona was holding forth and Mona was a tornado, whipping them up with her possibilities, her conviction. You mustn't, she pleaded. Don't give up on our institutions. Change them. Make them relevant. The best place to turn the museum around is in the museum itself. That's what I'm trying to do. Together we can put artists on the Board of Trustees in decision-making positions. But if we close down the museum now, the only people who are going to get hurt are working people and students and minorities and the artists themselves. The Establishment isn't going to get hurt. Don't you see? Thick damp curls jiggled on her forehead, and, as she gazed about at the surrounding faces, her bright eyes burned with an idealism so resolute, so pure, it could have shaved diamonds into jeweled threads. Mona's suggestion was a La Cienega Peace Walk. Some Monday night when the galleries were open late, artists and critics and dealers and collectors marching shoulder to shoulder along Gallery Row with candles flickering and black armbands.

Miles thought she was wonderful. He didn't care to tamper with the trustees himself, but he could understand why, under the circumstances, she had to say what she did. Bending to her warm curls, her shimmering golden hoop, he whispered, Wonderful, Mona. I mean really terrific!

After Mona had finished, everyone wanted to talk at once. Irving banged for order, silence, he couldn't hear a thing. When he gave the floor to Ross Rappaport, the figurative painter spoke of the need for money to fight the warmongers and came up with the idea for an auction. Artworks would be donated and sold to the highest bidder.

Peter Knight said, That's good, that's very good, I like that. Wadding up his handkerchief, he dabbed at his sweaty receding hairline. He himself was willing to contact East Coast artists and ask them to contribute works too. Ad Reinhardt and Jack Levine and Esteban Vicente. But of course, he pointed out, we'll need a committee to organize everything.

It was Max Roth who suggested that the auction be held outdoors. Right in the center of the public eyeball, recommended Max. Let the world know, he declared, exactly where we are located. There was a lot on Sunset Boulevard that a friend of his owned. A piece of property worth hundreds of thousands with nothing on it currently but empty bags of Fritos and wilted crabgrass. Max said, Let me ask.

If the land could be gotten, the sculptor Mark di Suvero volunteered to put a Peace Tower on it that would soar sixty feet into the air and split the sky like a siren. It was a grand prospect, a stunning sound that stirred all hearts and filled every inch of the large studio; it segued into a shrill aeronautical whistle and dribbled off to a plosive suck. Irving Carp glared at the lavatory door. Having flushed, out came Eva to join the throng. Okay, cried Irving, let's stay the hell out of there until this is over. And that means you, Phil, he shouted at the fellow with the long sideburns about to go in. Give me, said Umatsu and, reaching up, took the hammer from Irving's hand.

The time had come for nominations to the auction organizing committee. The gentle Leland Sonderman, his great bearded face hovering benignly above the crowd, hoped that they would not forget Mona when choosing a committee. Do I hear a second? yelled Irving. Umu, though short, had a powerful upper body, and his thick arm was a blur as he drilled the nails like bullets into the lavatory door. *Bam, bam, bam, bam.* In a twinkling, what was once a noisy toilet had become a sealed crate. Hey, what the hell! shouted a voice from within. Who's playing tricks? Let me out of here, you goddamn stupid mackinaws. Let me out!

Clasping his hands comfortably behind his back, Miles glanced up at Irving, and the expression on the curator's shining face was that of someone who had just unbuckled his belt after a sumptuous dinner. Second, Miles sang out brightly. Second.

VENICE, FEBRUARY 12, 1966

Perhaps he had misjudged the bastard. He decided that he had misjudged him. Still, he would never have put his fingertip in the hole if he didn't need the money. Roth's ring was a chainsaw. The voice itself was suede.

No, don't tell me, said Roth, let me guess. Dan Asher tried to explain. Ah, the rakish Bloodstone, is that you, my friend? Dan Asher could hear music in the background, the bewitching laughter of women with exposed navels. Dan, he repeated, Dan Asher. Even through the receiver, he could whiff the expensive alcohol on the dealer's breath.

Dan *who*? Roth was incredulous. Let me check my calendar. Is this some great national holiday involving pranks and shmucks? You're talking on my private line, phone fellow. Such service costs extra. I don't expect to find just anybody at my ear when I pick up this thing.

Cut the shit, Max. You said call. Okay, here I am. Daniel-

Daniel-Daniel-Daniel-Daniel, chanted Max. What took you so long? Mona tells me that you're mending wonderfully. How are you, my friend? Dan Asher made no bones about it. He had to pay for his heart. There were big medical bills and only ten bucks a month to spare. When you came to the hospital, Max, you mentioned money, a show. He slyly blurred the difference, refusing to open a five-year-old gash by demanding the money Roth still rightfully owed him for pieces sold. I've started to work again, he pointed out. Something new. I'd really like you to see what I'm doing, Max. I think you'll like it.

Yes, yes, I'm sure. . . . Roth's voice seemed to tire, fade as if he had momentarily shrunk or turned away from the phone to look at somebody in the room displaying a private part. But—he was back—that's not what I had in mind right now. Forgive me, Daniel, there are guests, a small soiree, so allow me to make this short and plain. Mona, of course, has informed you about our Peace Tower. I, too, am on that committee. We are asking artists from here, New York, around the world, to donate a work to protest the war in Vietnam. A worthy cause, *nicht wahr*?

Sure, he agreed, but you know I don't do political art. No matter, no matter, the dealer assured him. Does Ad Reinhardt do political art? The esteemed Motherwell? Bobby Rauschenberg? Jap Johns? What counts is to stand up and be counted. And in the end everything will be auctioned off to help the cause of peace. How can you say no, Daniel?

Dan said okay. He said, Drop by the studio tomorrow and I'll let you pick what you want from the new work. You're going to like it, Max. No more of the old blackness sostenuto. I've gotten involved with world's fairs now. The imagery is completely different and the colors— He could hear himself selling and didn't care for the sound. Well, he said, you'll see. But then his enthusiasm got the better of him, and he wanted to know if Roth remembered the Heinz pickle at the 1939 World's Fair. A souvenir pin in the shape of a small green plastic gherkin.

Interesting, soothed Max. Nevertheless, I suggest something earlier, not so fresh. Perhaps from your New York days, a "Waiting Room" or "Great Hotel" that you still have lying around on the couch gathering dust would be more heartwarming to your admirers. New work on such an occasion only dirties the waters. You understand, my friend, we need fourteen-carat gold. We must raise thousands to end this ugly madness.

It's your auction, Dan Asher conceded wearily. Come early and we'll check the couch. I'll see you tomorrow. Impossible, Roth informed him. His desk calendar groaned with appointments, responsibilities. I'll leave it to you, Daniel. Give us something truly choice.

Thwarted, Dan Asher felt mean as barbed wire, jagged as broken glass. Listen to me, Max. I need cash. You'll get the piece you want for the auction, but what about one for yourself? A kind and beautiful thought, praised the dealer. *Malheureusement* my funds at the moment are all tied up. But who can tell of the future? It was good of you to remember your old friend, Daniel. Truly touching. Don't think I am not grateful.

They flee from me that sometime did me seek, thought Dan Asher. He sliced Roth's suntanned windpipe to the accompaniment of poetry, cutting the smile out. Once a bastard, always. There was a chorus of loud snickering at the party. The soloist a vaguely familiar female giggler, her sharp staccato redolent of pearls bouncing on parquet. One thing, he called. Did Mona put you up to this?

The dealer admitted that it had been Mona's idea. She had not wanted Dan to feel obligated to donate a work to the cause solely as a favor to her. She's a wonderfully sensitive young person, Max reported. And stupendous legs too! You're a lucky mensch, Daniel. Now I really must go. My guests cry out for me.

Have a good party, said Dan Asher, and hung up the phone. He listened to his pulse and heard nothing. Death came as no surprise. He might have lived if only there had been even a trace of irony in his voice as he said goodbye, a Parthian shot to save his self-respect. He didn't know which disgusted him more, appealing to Roth for help or failing to get it. When all you want to do is get on with your work, why is it that instead you've got to waste your time sucking after money and catering to creeps?

He should have known better than to call Roth. How could he

have fallen so low? He felt so sullied, so humiliated, that he could have ripped off his clothes, his coffee-stained jockey shorts, and right then and there in the middle of winter plunged bare-ass into the lonely Pacific and come out as wholesome as milk. And would have, too, but the thought of an ocean of ice water smalled his balls.

LOS ANGELES, JUNE 17, 1976

Henry had taken the bus downtown. There was no need of Koontz and his Buick, and anyhow he was unavailable. The chauffeur had been excited about some new acting opportunity that had suddenly developed, but he couldn't say anything about it just yet. Henry had not been curious. He had been considering Hofstedler's lavish life-style.

Following the death of his old man, young Mark takes over the family's moderately successful gallery, and a year later he's living in a Bel Air mansion surrounded by barbed wire with a Rolls-Royce, a Mercedes-Benz, a zoo, charge accounts at the best stores, and a taste for smoked oysters. Not to mention the fact that he now has a mistress with a weakness for expensive red convertibles who, a neighbor says, is capable of snatching away his last stitch. Would Hofstedler steal for Lola? Henry was anxious to see her and decide for himself. He wondered if he, Henry Tattersall, would be capable of committing a crime for a woman. Probably not, he had to admit, but the idea of such a passion was sexually stimulating.

It had been years since Tattersall had been in this neighborhood. Broadway had changed. Now it was the way he imagined Tijuana must be. The sidewalk crowded with people and trinket stands and signs in Spanish and English. Brassy mariachi music rang out above the brakes and horns of traffic. Stores were selling tacos, enchiladas. Stacks of chicken and shrimp deep fried and slick as poker chips were in the windows.

Out on the pavement, racks of clothes took the sunshine. Henry followed the mariachi music. It was blaring from an amplifier above the entrance to a store called Toscano's. To judge by the windows, Toscano's sold more than music. It was a Japanese colony of binoculars, tape decks, transistor radios, pocket calculators, and cameras.

Inside, the saleslady looked more like a file cabinet than a Lola. She was talking animatedly in Spanish to a customer. A thin dark man sagged dimly behind the cash register. Henry approached him and asked if Lola was around. Dropping his eyes, the man sank further behind the counter. Two, he said, and raised a pair of skinny nicotine-stained fingers as if not convinced that the English word alone was enough to convey his message. Henry glanced at his watch. There was almost an hour to kill, and he knew exactly where to kill it. Only a few blocks away on South Broadway, the Central Public Market contained dozens of stalls piled high with inexpensively priced, exquisitely ripe fruits and vegetables rapidly rotting under one roof. If you could consume eight or ten pounds of peaches overnight, the potential savings were enormous. Once upon a time, Tattersall, owner of a short-lived restaurant, had bought all his produce there. The market was hot in the afternoon, a noisy steambath crowded with bargain-hunting housewives and kids. The big commercial buyers always shopped in the early hours of the morning.

After a nostalgic cup of coffee at a sandwich bar, Henry spent the next half hour wandering the littered aisles and remembering, but no one seemed to remember him. It had, after all, been more than ten years since he'd last been here. The taste was bittersweet, like thumbing through an old family album where the pictures had faded and relationships blurred. Ten years, he told himself. Time enough for culinary dreams to die and for the Tattersall face to sag in the morning mirror. Henry found it hard to believe that it had been so long. He fingered the tomatoes. Their skin was smooth, taut, the unequivocal red of stoplights. At two pounds for thirty-nine cents, here was a bargain he couldn't pass up.

Behind the stand stood a long-necked woman in a blue denim housecoat, her sleeves rolled back and her fingers covered with Indian rings of turquoise and coral. She had the jaws of a steam shovel, but the raven shadows beneath her eyes and in the small hollows of her cheeks told of jittery sleepless nights. Hello, Flo, he said quietly.

Flo looked at him, and ten years flew in the window. A long time, she said. You're looking good. Is the hair your own? Henry chalked it up to the neighborhood. There seemed to be a lot of local interest in wigs, false eyelashes. She admired his narrow tie, his white shirt, his summer suit. He had done well for himself. Do you still have the restaurant? she asked. Henry told her no. I'm in the investigative line. She said her daughter was studying to be an anthropologist at Cal State Northridge. How about some tomatoes? she asked. He took two pounds, paid for them, and left. Don't be a stranger, she called after him. They had once fucked in the back of her trailer, their bellies grinding down differences, her rings clicking and clacking like castanets. She doesn't remember my name, thought Henry, putting on his dark glasses as he came out into the sun.

At two o'clock in the afternoon, Mexico, heavy with siesta drowsiness, closes up shop. On Broadway at two, everything was wide open, and the bright mariachi music coming from Toscano's never missed a beat. The same dark, taciturn clerk was still lurking behind the register when Tattersall entered the music store. Except for a couple of customers browsing through records, he was the only one there. Henry asked for Lola. Had she come in?

The cashier replied by emphatically flicking two fingers three times in the investigator's face. Did he mean six o'clock or buzz off? Two, said Tattersall coldly. You told me she'd be here at two. The cashier directed his attention to the large wall clock overhead on which was written *Sanyo* 8-Track. Henry was surprised to see that there were seven minutes remaining before the hour and said he'd be back.

Across the street from the store, he took up a position near a parking lot. He slumped casually against the side of a building, blending into the white brick wall as if he were mortar. By two-thirty there was still no sign of anybody who might be Lola. The heat rose from the sidewalk into the air, squeezing Broadway between two sheets of steel. It was a dull, tedious vigil. Henry regarded the boredom as part of the business and didn't let it bother him. His legs were another matter. His aching calves longed for a pillow, a kind stroke.

An elderly white-haired woman carrying an open green parasol walked toward the group of three outdoor telephones against the side of the building. Then she noticed Tattersall slouching nearby and, with a look of mild disapproval, marched past. A half-hour more, decided Henry, and he'd take his tomatoes home.

He began to pick out the runaways in the passing crowd. A thirteen-year-old kid with a khaki knapsack on her back and peek-a-boo hair that hid her eyes. Another of about the same age but shorter and with hips, sporting an Irish nose, a blond natural, and a beat-up suitcase with a blue Dodger sticker. If the pimps didn't get them, the pushers would. Occasionally Henry took on a runaway, but he didn't care for the work. Although it was generally easier to locate a missing kid than lost art, the success was more ambiguous. No one runs away from a good thing, least of all kids. You can't change the world, Dorothy had pointed out, trying to cheer him up after one of his returned teenies had gobbled up a can of Drāno. Henry had not been cheered.

The old lady with the green umbrella was back. This time she didn't look at him at all, her eyes searching the ground for a lost key or a dropped earring, her slow step meandering. She arrived at the telephones vaguely, as if by chance, and with a deft, practiced motion hooked her index finger in and out of the three empty coin-return slots, frowned, and shuffled away down the street.

One of her regular stops, Henry guessed. She kept herself neat, which was important, but it was hard for old people like that living on fixed incomes in these inflationary times. He sometimes worried what he would do when his legs became too old for surveillance. He was worrying about it once again when a red convertible with the top down came roaring up onto the sidewalk and into the parking lot.

The engine was still running as the young woman behind the wheel—her long, straight black hair tied back smartly with a leather thong—got out, waved to the attendant, shouted something, and slammed the car door closed. As she crossed the street, Henry observed the tan high-heeled sandals, the gold ankle bracelet twinkling in the sunlight. She moved decisively, every step a tan hammer. Her knee-length skirt was a rich chocolate, her blouse was mocha-creme. Although more tastefully dressed than the Lola described to him by Hofstedler's neighbor, she breezed into Toscano's as if her brother owned the place. Before crossing over himself, Henry plucked a quarter out of his pocket and slipped it into one of the telephone coin returns. He had no illusions that the old woman would actually get the money, but at least it was worth a shot.

OAKLAND, 1976

DANIEL ASHER: Collages 1943–1967.
The Oakland Museum, 1976.
Introduction by Mordecai Bell.

If, as I believe, he is a modern romantic, then surely Asher's romanticism is nowhere more evident than in the exotic musical instruments he chooses to represent in his work, instruments more customarily associated with past centuries than our own. Matisse, Braque, and Picasso, for all their artistic innovation, were musically content, by and large, with the prosaic percussions and strings—the drum, piano, and guitar. Only Asher in the twentieth century had the recherché imagination to give us the tambourin, melodeon (cat. no. 35), panpipe (cat. no. 89), and Jew's harp (cat. nos. 15, 17). His use of old sheet music fragments in his series devoted to the great hotels of the world (cat. no. 31) lends a fugitive delicacy and aura of nostalgia to materials that otherwise would be frankly erotic.

LOS ANGELES, JUNE 17, 1976

She had taken over behind the cash register at Toscano's music store and was exchanging a few words in Spanish with the dark fellow before he went off duty. Walking up to the counter, Tattersall interrupted them. Are you Lola? he asked. She looked at him through wide, suspicious eyes fringed by long mascaraed lashes—angling black hooks on which to snag a heart. They were the longest lashes that he had ever seen. Her lips and fingernails were an identical flaming red. I am Lola Toscano, she said. She was Lola of the false eyelashes and the smooth olive skin and the dark, rich voice that nuzzled the ear, and oh, yes, he thought, men would steal for *her*, all right.

Are you the Lola Toscano who worked at the Marquis Gallery in Beverly Hills? It was a good guess. Her lashes quivering, her eyes narrowed and drilled him to the floor. Who are *you*? she demanded. Henry told her precisely who he was and of his many close friends on the L.A.P.D. with whom he often worked cheek to cheek. Ms. Toscano was in trouble. Big trouble. The police at that very minute were building a case against her former boss, closing in on him, and there would be no fooling around. The more she revealed about the Hofstedler operation, the easier it would go for her. Anybody withholding information was, of course, an accessory and liable to prosecution to the fullest extent of the law. Do you understand what that means, Ms. Toscano? Henry could see that he had made an impression. Feeling the moment had come to squeeze, he said, Okay, Lola, let's have it all.

Sweet Jesus! Her voice shot into the air like a startled bird. What the hell do you want? Beat it! Get out! From behind the counter, Lola ran at him, screaming, Get out of here, I don't have to tell you nothing. Henry told her to calm down. He appealed to her dour co-worker to reason with her. The fellow looked at Henry as if he were a torn poster announcing something important.

From the back of the store, a thickset man in starched shirt sleeves came rushing toward Tattersall shouting in Spanish. He was breathing smoke, belching fire, his long red knit tie a fearful alarm. Wrapping the investigator in a vicious bear hug and crushing their chests together, he clumsily pushed him backward, stumbling toward the front door. Henry found it difficult to breathe, the man's odor overwhelming. The smell was disturbingly complex, a pungent, suffocating, alien aroma, and yet not completely unpleasant.

Shit! gasped Henry, unable to recall a single word in Spanish that would help. Hold on! The words had an immediate and stunning effect on the thug. He stopped his unintelligible raving and, releasing his hold on Henry's ribs, seized him by the throat. The bear hug and the stranglehold were close-cresting waves, between which Henry had gulped just enough air to clear his mind and permit him to resolve on a course of action. With all his might, he kicked the bastard in his gray sharkskin shank. The fingers clamping his throat twitched thrillingly and then tightened with an irresistible enthusiasm.

No, Manuel! cried Lola, pushing him away from the detective. You're making a mistake. *¡Bastante!* And she hastily explained something to him in Spanish. As he wiped the perspiration from his glistening square jaw, he looked Tattersall over. He had the same smooth olive skin as his sister. Finally he shrugged, and with no more of an apology than an earthquake or a volcano, Manuel Toscano said in perfect English, I am going out, and left.

Are you okay? asked an anxious Lola. Henry ran his fingertips gingerly over the welts on his neck and wondered if he wasn't getting too old for this sort of thing. Here, she said, returning his sunglasses and the bag of tomatoes that she had picked up from the floor. And only two of them squashed! A silver lining. Did he think I was Hofstedler? asked Henry. No, said Lola. He thought you were from the Immigration. That's my cousin Julio, over there behind the register. He's from Cuernavaca.

Henry nodded in his direction and told her that as far as he was concerned, Julio could stay in the U.S. as long as he wanted. Forever. Longer if necessary. Wetbacks weren't any of his business. But he advised her to do something about her brother's temper before he got his teeth kicked in, because the Immigration officials might not be as understanding as he was. For the moment, Henry could see no useful purpose served by filing assault and battery charges against the man. Now, he said to the sister of Manuel Toscano, how are you going to help *me*?

Lola pleaded, But I don't work for the Marquis Gallery anymore.

I know, said Henry.

No, you don't. You don't understand. Mark and I are through. Finished. I quit as soon as I found out what was going on. Honest, she swore.

What *was* going on? asked Henry. Lola looked at him imploringly, searching his face for a single shred of pity, her lashes fluttering helplessly, her arms limp. It reminded him of *Gone With the Wind* and Scarlett O'Hara laboring busily to wind Rhett around her little finger. She was a man-eater, all right. Henry was on guard. He trusted her about as much as he trusted Hofstedler's dog.

Even Lola could see her wheedling was a waste of time. Okay, she said. Motioning to her cousin to mind the store, she led the investigator to a hot, cramped, windowless office in the rear and locked the door. On the desk was a pink plastic record holder crammed with correspondence. Henry observed several envelopes bearing Mexican postmarks as he walked behind the desk and slumped down on the only chair in the room. Sitting was tactically wrong, he knew, but Henry was bushed, his throbbing calves a sig-alert of twisted nerves and muscles. Lola, her arms folded across her chest, stood before him as if *she* were about to ask the questions and he was the guilty party.

She began by saying, I only work here part time to help out. I go to school now. I go to LACC. You can check if you like. I'm studying art history. In four years I have my degree and become a teacher. That's my plan. Not bad, eh? Her fingers plucked nervously at her mocha-creme sleeves.

She didn't look like any schoolteacher Henry had ever seen. He spoke softly, trying to calm her down. Tell me about Hofstedler, he said.

If I do—she took a deep breath—do you swear you won't tell him it was me? She seemed genuinely frightened, her chest heaving as if the room were suddenly drained of air.

Henry promised and waited. Her toes curled uneasily in her sandals, the nails painted the same flaming red that she wore on her fingers and lips.

Staring at the closed door, Lola slowly shook her head and said, Why not. She turned to Henry, who sat deadpan, motionless, the iron peg in a game of horseshoes waiting for the ringer. You guessed it, she told him. He's a crook. He sells paintings sent to him on consignment for maybe twice, three times as much as he tells the owners and keeps the rest for himself. Sometimes he sells paintings and returns nothing. He's even sold things loaned to him for an exhibition and not for sale. And there's something else, she said. Her voice was barely audible. His biggest swindle is—

Henry was on the edge of his seat. What's that? he said.

His biggest swindle, repeated Lola. I don't really understand it all myself, but one day Mark told me business was looking up and he was going to make millions. I do know that he got a lot of money from a Century City lawyer by the name of Nachman or something and Ted Leonard—you know, the TV producer —and some big real estate developer from Palos Verdes called Sterling. I know because I made out invoices for paintings that we bought and sold for them. The only thing is—the thought caused her to shift her weight, and a raven eyebrow rose meaningfully—all the invoices that I made out were for the same paintings, and I never saw a single one of them in the gallery.

Interesting, said Henry. He noted with satisfaction how tan the back of his hand looked in contrast to the blue-green fly strutting around on top of it. He flicked the fly away. Did any of the buyers ever come in and ask for their paintings? No, said Lola, that was the funny thing. Suddenly it occurred to her that perhaps one of them finally did come in. Is that what happened? Is that how the cops found out? Could be, replied their self-proclaimed pal evasively. A curious, puzzled expression flickered across Lola's attractive face. Are you working for Nachman or one of the others?

Henry explained that he was not at liberty to say. He apologized. His clients expected absolute privacy, and that's what the Tattersall Service provided. He had a pretty good idea of the service Hofstedler provided but said nothing about it to the young woman. It was a classic Ponzi scheme. First the mark with his money in search of an investment and a quick buck, then the nonexistent masterpieces, the phony invoices, the occasional profit to sweeten the scam, and all the time Hofstedler wheeling and dealing and gambling that his money will double before his bluff is called. Tattersall's brother-in-law, Fletcher, the sociology professor at Berkeley, was fond of telling him that when you sit down to play poker and you don't see a sucker at the table, you're it. Too damn fond, thought Henry.

Anyhow, said Lola, that's all I know. Everything. Now you won't forget your promise, will you? As far as Mark is concerned, you've never met Lola Toscano. Never! Henry was by no means satisfied that she had told him everything she knew. But what about the *stolen* artwork? he asked. The hot stuff. He's a fence, right? And what about the forgeries he markets? All Lola knew, she said, was what she had told him. The one thing she might not have mentioned was the threat. Mark had sworn that if she ever went to the police he'd kill her. That was why she thought she'd wait until they came to her. I'm not such a good Catholic, she said, that I can afford to die.

Where does he keep the Rembrandt? The tone was lightheartedly casual so as not to alarm, Henry scanning her face like the scene of the crime. Lola said, What Rembrandt? The Marquis Gallery specialized in *modern* European painting. The School of Paris. She had no idea what he was talking about. *Jacob*

149

Wrestling with the Angel, snapped Henry, the Rembrandt lifted from the County Museum in 1967 without a trace. Lola dimly recalled hearing something about it, but that was almost ten years ago. *Madre mia*, ten years! She was still in pigtails then.

Henry saw her galloping recklessly through East Los Angeles in fallen anklets, her thin skirts lapping about her ears, and the lonely, grizzled old men who loafed in front of the Brooklyn Avenue bodegas eyeing her salmon-pink wrinkled drawers with tears in their eyes.

The Rembrandt, said the investigator hoarsely, and cleared his throat. Hofstedler keeps it in the storeroom at the back of the gallery, doesn't he? Lola shrugged. She didn't think so but acknowledged that it was possible. She hadn't worked there in more than six months. All kinds of dirty things might have happened since then. When she took the job at the Marquis Gallery, she had no idea what sort of man her new boss would turn out to be. How should I know? she said. He liked me and was nice to me, and that's all I cared about.

He gave you presents, said Tattersall. The young woman bristled. Sure. So what? A few little odds and ends, there's nothing wrong with that. Mark could be very generous. Henry wondered if she had been given the Alfa Romeo to keep her quiet.

Don't be dumb, said Lola. I can see what you're thinking, and you're dead wrong. Mark didn't steal to buy me diamonds and rubies and gold ankle bracelets. He stole because he's a thief. He likes to steal, to get something for nothing. Stealing turns him on. Believe me, he is one *malo* creep.

Tattersall didn't think that was good enough. Human beings didn't operate that way. They stole for gain or because of compulsive chromosomes or unwholesome chums or to realize political dreams, like the Symbionese crew of recent memory who had gone up in smoke only a few miles south of where he was sitting, but not as a game. And she was wrong about the Rembrandt too. Now more than ever he was certain that it would be found exactly where Harris said it was. Everything was falling neatly into place, the Old Testament battlers coming more sharply into view with each new piece of information he collected.

I've got to get to work, announced Lola. I'm in the clear now, right? Henry was looking at the wall calendar. A jagged shred of May still dangled from it, the old month dispatched with a fury that seemed to be Toscano's trademark. In the June boxes, the graceful notations with their elegantly curling letters—Villareal, *sobres, papeles*, Scotch; Puig, Small Claims Court, 8:30; Cupido —seemed as if they could scarcely have been written by the same man. His hand should have been brass knuckles, sticks of dynamite.

June, said the calendar. June called for roses and pearls. Hofstedler would probably have come up with them, too, had she hung around longer. Henry smiled to himself and then at the gorgeous Lola, who, hand to cheek to dark brown iris flecked by the fire from her nails, had been watching him, mesmerized by his shifting expressions. Pushing himself up out of the chair, he thanked her for the help and said so long. His hand was on the doorknob and turning when she stopped him.

You ought to hire a detective, she advised. You could use somebody to keep an eye on these. She handed him his bag of tomatoes and unlocked the door. Lola had a sense of humor. Maybe that was what the Hofstedler cook had liked about her. It wasn't hard to see what Hofstedler had liked. Be careful, she warned. He's dangerous. It was later while he was standing at the bus stop waiting for the Number 83 to take him home—the crepe soles of his shoes frying on the late afternoon pavement and his legs beat—that Tattersall suddenly realized how elated he was that a young woman who looked like Lola Toscano didn't want anything unpleasant to happen to him.

VENICE, SEPTEMBER 10, 1965

Dan Asher trod a line of dry seaweed and small shells. Marlene Dietrich trotted alongside him. Walking the beach through the dwindling late-afternoon light, he tried to measure the horizon against a middle-ground sailboat luffing home to Marina del Rey and a background sun sliding into the Pacific. He had no watch but guessed that it must be around six, a lonely hour, with sea gulls replacing people on the beach and here and there a jogger scurrying away from death, a surfer hugging his board. The one thing he hated about Los Angeles was the enormous spaces between people. The thought of Mona helped him shrug off the fleeting melancholy of the moment. Bending over, Dan Asher stroked the overweight dog's long black ears and watched the animal's expression turn introspective. Come on, honey, he said, I'll race you home. Even though Mona usually worked late at the museum on Fridays, he thought there was just a chance she might be back by now.

Galloping off the beach and onto Market Street, and sure enough her gray Volkswagen was parked down the block. He charged up the front steps at Marlene's heels and, lungs heaving, burst through the door. His mouth pushing out salt air, his nose sucked up the fragrance of frying onions. Mona, in the kitchen, was holding the end of a long-handled wooden spoon to her lips and intently studying a recipe Scotch-taped to the wall. She looked so young to him, so childishly absorbed, that she might have been playing house. Sauté onion and green pepper until tender, instructed the recipe for Eggplant à la Creole. It was another inexpensive low-calorie suggestion from the *L.A. Times* and promised six mouth-watering servings.

Wrapping his arms around her waist from behind, Dan Asher nuzzled the brown curls, nuzzled her warm young neck. Who, he panted, who's coming to dinner? Come on, Dan, cut it out, she complained, making an effort to pull away. I'm trying to read this thing. He told her that it smelled great. Me or the onions? she wanted to know. The onions, he said.

She turned back and gave him a searching green-eyed look. Well at least you're not a liar, she had to admit, even if you are an old man. Taking two handfuls of apron, he squeezed her breasts and confided that he had missed her all afternoon, his kisses falling on her right cheek as lightly as apple blossoms. Okay, she said, okay. Very sweet. Bending over, she pushed him away with her backside. Now—she was all business as she stirred the pan—look up there and tell me what comes next before this burns. Dan looked, and what came next were flour and salt, tomatoes and bay leaf.

Beneath her apron and protected by it, Mona was wearing the loose shirt made in Morocco that he had bought for her, a low-cut tan overblouse with intricate green stitching around tiny circles of blue glass. She loved what she called its Siamese cats' eyes. In her hair bloomed a yellow paper flower, one of a bouquet of flowers that he had made for her. Mona was dressed for company, and he wanted to know who. Peter Knight, she replied carelessly, as if the name would mean nothing to him. Peter Knight and his wife, Joan. She glanced up at Dan, and her cool expression dissolved into a rose blush of amusement. I called to tell you, but you must have been out walking Marlene.

Goddamn! he said, flashing a gap-toothed smile. He shook his head in amazement and repeated softly, Goddamn. Leaning down, he kissed her and stroked her cheek with adoring fingertips. You rascal, he whispered. How soon will they be here? Soon, she said. Now get out of here and stop bothering me.

Peter Knight was the editor of *Artworld*, the Los Angeles–based monthly that since its inception only a few years ago had become the leading avant-garde art magazine on the West Coast. Mona knew Peter well, having met him initially at the museum, and they would run into each other frequently at parties and in the galleries on La Cienega. It wasn't hard for her to get him to come to dinner. The trick would be to sell him on Dan's recent work, which she herself had reservations about. Prior to that morning, Mona had been reluctant even to try, but now, regardless of whether or not Peter finally decided to run an article on the gloomy series of collages, she knew that she had done the right thing after seeing Dan's reaction. His foolish, excited smile was like a finger on her heart.

She hadn't realized how guilty she had felt in ignoring his hints to speak to Miles about his work. But there wasn't a chance in the world that her boss would have given Dan a museum show. Having just opened its doors at the end of March, the new museum was the center of national media attention, and it was obvious to her that the attractive, energetic Miles was out to make a reputation for himself. He was after prime-time television interviews, lines of visitors three-deep along Wilshire and around the block. Miles would have dismissed Dan's small grim dreams as marginal. As for Mona, she found the pieces wonderfully well made but, iconographically speaking, irrelevant. Why, she wondered, why didn't he care about Watts or poverty or Indochina?

From inside the bedroom, Dan called, Where's Marissa? He untied his hair, pulled the yellow broken-toothed comb once through the long brown tangle, flicked at his mustache, and, satisfied, tossed the comb on top of his bureau. The freshly shaved face in the bureau mirror looked back at him curiously, without smiling. There were too many of the gray ones now to bother yanking them out. He shrugged off the grays as fatherhood and signs of the times. What the hell! he told himself, and checked out the clothes. His body-hugging blue-striped shirt was open at the neck, a cluster of tiny burn holes from hot cigarette ashes forming an interesting random pattern on the right side. He wore fine tight black leather pants, black boots. Early Zorro, he said, and whistled in admiration. I like your style, Asher. Since Mona moved in with him nine months ago, Dan had never been happier. He started to hum. As he came back into the kitchen, he was humming a few bouncy bars from the new Simon and Garfunkel album that his daughter had just bought and was playing night and day. Where's Marissa? he asked.

Marissa was spending the night with her friend Doreen. I told her that it would be okay, said Mona. You don't mind, do you? The way Mona had fit so completely into their lives delighted Dan, and his daughter loved her as much as he did. What's the matter? he asked. Mona was scowling at the two plates she held in her hands, one with a smoke-blue border of fleurs-de-lis, the other throbbing with a bold brown Aztec pattern. On the nearby table were a gray-white pair, the only two dishes in the house that were alike.

They don't match, she complained. The depth of the dismay in her voice surprised him. Is that so important? he asked. The need for matching china was something that would never have occurred to him. No, she said and sighed, and a small fragile smile touched the corners of her mouth. Not terribly, I suppose. Good, said Dan. Trying to cheer her up with a hug, he pointed out that identical plates were invisible plates. Ours have personalities, high visibility, presence, class. And, Mona added, a hell of a lot of cracks and chips! Of course, said Dan, that's what makes them special. Like people. Take me for instance—

Mona burst out laughing, her perfect teeth a dazzling reward for his effort. Come and help, she ordered, and together they finished setting the table for their guests.

The Knights arrived like a Bedouin family hunting for a place to make camp. She carried the baby and two large plastic bags strapped to her shoulder containing disposable diapers, bottles, nipples, brushes, Q-tips, oil, Vaseline, rattles, paper fish, and a spare pacifier in case the one plugged into the infant's mouth should become dislodged and lost. He carried her leather shoulder bag and the baby's portable cradle.

Don't bother, Peter Knight insisted as Mona hurriedly tossed the pillows off the broken-down couch with its lumps of stuffing, clearing it for the cradle. No need at all. None at all. This will do nicely. He placed the powder-blue plastic cradle on the floor. Fine, fine, fine, fine, he said as his wife eased the baby into it. Ah, there we are. Splendid! Knight was a Columbus, one of those conquerors who plant flags and claim rights solely by reason of their presence. Dan Asher knew the type. In the interest of harmony, he decided to give up his house without a struggle.

An Australian by birth, Peter Knight spoke in brassy, clipped syllables. He held himself ramrod straight. The deep affection that he expressed for the sunny, laid-back ways of L.A. appeared to be genuine. Although younger than Dan Asher by about fifteen years, the editor of *Artworld* was balding and bearded and looked older. A Berkeley education had been unable to rid him of his fondness for houndstooth sport coats, but it had ripped the tie from his neck, unbuttoned his collar, and given him an American wife, a pair of blue track shoes with yellow stripes, and a revolutionary commitment to the very latest wrinkles in art.

One round of martinis and Peter began to tell jokes. A second and he was Dan's pal, eager to share local art-world gossip. He told maliciously funny anecdotes about the Drum Gallery artists and why they rode motorcycles, about Newton Ward's fondness for English actresses with big tits, about the widow of a well-known collector and her protégé. As Dan listened, he was anxiously considering whether or not there was enough gin left in the kitchen to refill his guest's empty glass when Mona announced that dinner was served.

It's delicious, declared Joan Knight, after swallowing her first steaming mouthful of baked eggplant. Her long, straight, blond hair, parted carefully in the middle, dipped forward as she forked up another sample. Joan had a flat face, tranquil eyes, and an expression as bland as junket. Oh, absolutely! called Peter in agreement, interrupting what he was saying to Dan Asher. First rate, Mona. He leaned over and flirtatiously stroked her cheek. Lovely. Joan ignored him. Alcohol brought out the John Wayne in her husband, his secret longing to be a native-born American full of manly rectitude and sexual promise. She wasn't worried, but she *was* just a little embarrassed for him.

It's not one of my specialties, said Mona, but it's not bad, is it? Dan could see that she was pleased with Peter's approval, and she positively glowed when Joan, lifting the fussing baby up onto her lap and unbuttoning her blouse, asked for the recipe.

Dan thought of madonnas. The Northern Renaissance ones by Jacquemart and Jean Fouquet that had the same aloofness from the child, the same inward eye. But there was nothing spiritual about this pair. Theirs was a commensal arrangement. They were exclusively a food chain that stretched from eggplant to Joan to Junior. The ravenous little fellow's name, as it turned out, was actually Hillary.

Removing the child from her breast, Joan placed him on her shoulder and gently patted his back. Hillary David Knight, revealed the proud mother. Mona said, I like the name. You might have done worse. We almost did, Joan reported. When Nehru had his heart attack last year, I thought we might wind up with something terrible like Jawahawa. Peter, you see, has this incredible Indian thing. I have to sprinkle curry on practically everything. Jawaharlal, corrected Peter, Ja-wa-har-*lal*! Do *you* like curry? Joan asked her. It was clear from the tone of her voice where she stood on the matter. Here, said Mona, let me take Hillary.

What is it about women, Dan Asher wondered, that brings out this mothering instinct in them? They all had it. Even Marissa at thirteen with her stuffed animals and asparagus plant. And then he thought of Marissa's mother, who had run out on the two of them and couldn't have cared less, and had to reconsider. The baby nestled in Mona's arms as if he were home, gazing up wide-eyed at that sweet face framed by curls bending over him, perhaps dazzled by the glint of the gold rings in her ears. Dan titled the picture *Mona with Child*. He was pressing it into his memory album when Joan said to her, Why don't you have one of your own, Mona? You'd have an adorable baby.

Some day, replied Mona vaguely. Some day, she said, but she knew that right now she hadn't the slightest intention of providing cannon fodder for the Pentagon in order to protect U.S. rubber interests in Vietnam.

WEST LOS ANGELES, JUNE 23, 1967

The pilot of the large charcoal-green military helicopter was named Gary Cooper, and the lanky young lieutenant even looked dimly like the actor. The President took a shine to him at once. He sat next to Cooper on the short flight from the airfield to the hotel. Never been to Texas! he howled, enjoying himself immensely, exaggerating his astonishment. Well, we'll just have to see about getting you down to the ranch on your next leave. Won't we, Lynda? he called to his daughter, who sat beside the Secret Service agent behind him. What's that, Daddy? the young woman shouted above the noise of the engine.

The President gazed down at the stream of cars on the freeway below him and smiled. His two dimples were deep cracks, and his big face had more lines than a smashed windshield. He was in excellent spirits. After dinner, they had promised him Jack Benny and the Supremes. He loved the Supremes. The thought of Earl Warren and Thurgood and Abe and the rest of them singing together in their long black judicial robes made him laugh. He didn't suppose there was one of them who could carry a tune worth a damn. He wiped his giddy chuckles into his jumbo hand. Hell, he'd been up since five that morning. It had been a long day, and it was still far from over.

Palm trees! Watching them race by beneath him like giraffes, the President was delighted. Will you just look at those damn things! Yes, sir, Mr. President, the pilot said proudly. That's Southern California for you.

And only a few hours ago I was in New Jersey talking with Kosygin. . . . The President's brown eyes narrowed as if he were striding into a stiff headwind. He's a reasonable man, Cooper. Don't believe what you've heard to the contrary. Surprised the hell out of me. They don't want a third world war any more than we do. The buoyant President rubbed his palms together in eager anticipation of his next meeting with the Russian premier on Sunday. If I were a gambling man, Lieutenant, I'd bet that we're going to be able to work something out with those people. That's wonderful, sir, said Cooper, and reduced his airspeed. The Century Plaza was dead ahead.

The President was curious. What's that over there? he inquired with interest. The reply turned his face as white as his dinner jacket. Brushing aside the objections of his Secret Service agents, he insisted on flying over the demonstrators. Look at that! Look at all of them! Who needs this sort of crap? He thought fondly of last month's Loyalty Day Parade in New York —a tremendous turnout, they told him—thousands of fine men and women led by Mayor Lindsay and Cardinal Spellman. . . .

Students, he said. All at once his voice sounded thick, husky, like the morning after. They've turned against me, Cooper. I don't know why. I'm their President. I'm working hard for them. It's no picnic, believe me. And every day more of them are leaving the universities, taking to the streets, chanting that horrible song. Don't they realize I'm really one of them? I always hated cops myself when I was a kid. It hurts, Cooper. It really hurts. The pilot nodded sympathetically. Shall I land now, sir? he asked.

Goddammit! bellowed the President, why should I listen to all these student peaceniks? What do they know about the world? They were barely in their cradles when China fell. They wouldn't know a Communist if they tripped over one. Take it from me, Cooper, you can't get peace by acting nice.

Mr. President. . . . The Secret Service agent directly behind him placed a gentle hand on his shoulder.

I've read about Lincoln, announced the President. I know about all the troubles he had fighting the Civil War. Yet he persevered and history honors him for it. No matter what anyone says, Lieutenant, I know that the vast majority of Americans out there love me a great deal. Deep down I know—I simply know—that they love me. After all that I've done for them . . . given to them. . . .

Please, Mr. President, repeated the Secret Service agent. They're expecting us down there on the parking lot. It's getting late.

You're right, cried the President, and instructed the pilot to set it down.

At exactly 7:51 P.M., the President stepped out of his helicopter, appearing to have been refreshed by the ride. He held himself erect. Six foot three, he towered over the members of the Party welcoming committee who had come out to greet him. Exuding a calm dignity, he shook hands warmly all around, determination in his grip, but as they hurried him toward the rear of the hotel, he said, Hold on. What the hell is this back-door shit? Lyndon Johnson was not someone who slipped in side entrances or back doors.

It's in the interest of your safety, sir, explained one of his hosts. The President took pains to inform him that he had walked with Mrs. Johnson through an angry and dangerous mob into the main lobby of the Adolphus Hotel in Dallas in 1960, and he would be damned if he'd do less in California in 1967.

There have been death threats, Mr. President, said a Secret Service agent. We just can't take any chances. The President visibly shrunk up into a smaller target and nodded. Would he never forget that bloody head falling over onto the pink suit? Turning to his tall daughter, who looked radiant in a white evening gown and teardrop earrings, he whispered, Is my tie straight? She patted it. Perfect, Daddy. Just perfect. Entering the back door, he was glad that Bird wasn't there to see him.

VENICE, SEPTEMBER 10, 1965

It had been a fine dinner with enjoyable guests. Dan Asher had been completely charmed by Joan's innocence, her placidity, and found Peter to be surprisingly funny. Mona had been the ideal hostess, and he saw himself as smooth as an egg. In fact, everything had been perfect until Peter, in the midst of telling them about Merle Oberon's remarkable performance in *Wuther-*

ing Heights, happened to mention the name of her seaside mansion in Acapulco.

It's called "Ghalal," he revealed. Mona wanted to know what that meant. Patting her hand, caressing each finger individually, he gazed deep into her unwavering green eyes and said, *That*, my dear, is the Indian word for love. The silence that followed was as brittle as dead wood.

Dan Asher glanced uncomfortably at Knight's wife. Joan was sitting on the couch with Hillary and idly looking up at an old poster that announced Asher at the Galerie Lapautre, à partir du 28 Octobre 1955. She couldn't have cared less. Dan, on the other hand, was suffocating. What the fuck was this son of a bitch trying to do with his girl? What was Knight after? Beverly Glen, said Peter. You really must come and visit. Stroking and patting the flesh off her hands. You *must*. He thrust his high gleaming forehead in Mona's direction like a welcome mat and his baritone voice promised soft music, dim lights. And of course, he said, of course, Dan, too.

Turning to Dan, Peter explained that they had been living in the Glen for two years now. He loved the place with its easy life-style, its freedom and privacy, the incredible variety of flowers, and the wonderful mixture of kooks and stewardesses, of actors and artists and health-food store owners. The only two things about living in the canyon that they didn't like were snakes and fires. Mona reassured him that even in Eden there was a snake or two.

Exactly, exactly, said Peter. It *is* a sort of Paradise. Except, of course, for the rent—he smiled—but what the hell. It's the same all over L.A.

Dan Asher prodded the lone lettuce leaf left on his plate with his index finger and said quietly, I understand there's a woman in the Glen who specializes in killing rattlers. Rattlers! Peter gasped. His face fell. Rattlers? You're joking! Of course he is, said Mona. Dan Asher, however, was quite serious. They call her the Dragon Lady, he confided. She has black boots like these—he pushed his chair away from the table and extended his legs for Peter to see—and they say she goes after them with two six-shooters strapped to her hips and a shotgun in her hands.

Knight deserved more than that, the bastard. Much more. Up your canyon, sweetheart! Dan wanted to give him snakes in the trees, snakes in the grass. Eight feet of glittering diamonds slithering down the hillside into the Knights's back yard where precious little Hillary lay dreamily soaking up sunbeams in his carriage, and then the rattler's eyes rising up at the edge of the patio, two scraps of milky blue sky floating serenely above the emerald grass and the tongue alive and twitching and as delicate as the filament in a light bulb.

Staring thoughtfully down at his boots, Dan Asher mumbled, And she's always on the go, they say. Mona bristled. Cut it out, Dan. Why don't you show Peter your new series of collages? I think they're really terrific, Peter.

It was a wonderful suggestion, but as far as Dan was concerned it had, alas, come too late. He was already beginning to tell Peter of a sign on a telephone pole that he had seen announcing an antiwar rally in Beverly Glen at which it was promised that draft cards would be burned, flags incinerated, fireworks exploded—the sky a molten shower of hot flashes and fiery sparks. Dan was amazed. He couldn't believe the strange things that were coming out of his mouth. Peter Knight had come to his house as a well-meaning and welcome guest with nothing but good intentions and the usual amount of male lechery. Whose side was Dan Asher on? Unable to contain himself, he abruptly got up. Mona thought he looked pale. Are you feeling all right, Dan? Where was he going? Can I show Peter your work? she called after him. Suit yourself, Dan said, and left.

Peter Knight was prepared to make allowances for artists. He regarded this one as an odd but colorful type. The sort of intense, moody, unpredictable fellow that some women, he supposed, found attractive. What did such women care about a few gray hairs? Ignoring them or perhaps even finding the gray attractive, as they did baldness in other men—more than once during that evening he had caught Mona glancing at his scalp—or dismissing the gray as premature. But Peter knew that Asher had been around on the art scene for a long, long time. True, his work had a certain curiosity value, but for Peter it was associated with something that had happened forty years ago in Europe and, as far as art was concerned, ancient history.

Under the bright lights and spread across the table before him were eight small collages. Peter noted the same old surrealist influence with odd imagery and strange goings-on. Once years ago this sort of thing might have had some validity but, frankly, it bored the shit out of him. The title of the series was "Pompes Funèbres." You know, explained Mona, like things associated with death. I think *that* one over there is particularly strong.

She pointed to a work that depicted what looked to be a laboratory of some sort. Gowned figures in gauze masks stood about in a twilight room, absorbed in their work. On the shelves lining the wall behind them, row upon row of jars sat like the chorus of angels in Giotto's *Last Judgment*. Each jar held some dark object in solution, a sepia organ or twisted face that might have been cut out of an ancient medical textbook. There was an operating table in the foreground. Protruding from beneath the lumpy sheet was a smiling Harlequin in a pointed hat, his face covered with broken glass and red metal shavings.

Peter stroked his lower lip. Very small. He works very small, doesn't he? Mona didn't care for his tone. Surely, she said, that comes as no surprise to you. He's always worked on this scale. Oh, yes, acknowledged Peter. Quite. But one always hopes for change in an artist. Growth. Discoveries. That sort of thing.

Mona was happy to be able to supply him with change. Four years ago in Dan's Museum of Crime series there had been no doubt about what was going on and who was responsible. It was a logical if dangerous world. Now something truly terrible seemed to be happening, but it was almost impossible to determine exactly what it was and who was to blame. Given her reservations, Mona wondered if Dan fully appreciated what she was doing for him.

Precisely, cried Peter. That was precisely what he objected to. The lack of clarity and openness in these new works. They were stylistically too closed, too dense, too hermetic, too lacking in color and dependent on a narrow range of dark and light accents. Peter detected the Abstract Expressionist influence here as even more deadly than that of surrealism. His friend Clement Greenberg believed that any contemporary work of art that failed to define itself in opposition to what Clem called "Painterly Abstraction" was nothing more than an imitation of the past.

And dammit, he's right, you know! Clem is one hundred percent correct. Peter lowered his voice in deference to his host. There is only one perfectly logical style in art at any one given historical moment. And for our time, *this*—he dismissed the work on the table with a wave of his hand—isn't it.

Bullshit! shouted Mona. Her flushed cheeks were the color of jelly apples. She could imagine a half dozen wildly diverse styles—a dozen!—democratically coexisting as happily as vegetables in a gumbo. You know, Peter, sometimes—her voice throbbed with emotion—sometimes you and those writers of yours in *Artworld* sound as if you're all a bunch of art fascists.

Oh! oh no, oh no, not that. He was more excited than offended. How can you do that, Mona? How can you? Peter absolutely refused to discuss aesthetic issues with political rhetoric. Au-then-tic-i-ty. He cracked the syllables like a whip. It's simply a matter of evolutionary authenticity. Pop art, assemblage, there are all sorts of bastard offshoots of modernism, but the only logically correct style for right now is Post-Painterly Abstraction.

Talk about political rhetoric, fumed Mona. My God! All you'd need is a shoe in your hand and you'd pass for Khrushchev. It occurred to Peter that somehow he had become the enemy. Perhaps he *had* been too dogmatic. There was no doubt in his mind that he preferred to have this gorgeous young woman's good opinion.

Suddenly, aesthetic virtues sprouted in her boyfriend's work like mushrooms after a hard rain. Peter praised the colored glass, the maps, the unquenchable fire, this and that. He nodded his head a few times in approval and made friendly chewing noises. Although hesitant to look at her, he could sense that

Mona was relenting a little. He waited for her to say something, hoping to catch the sound of forgiveness in her voice, a hint of music.

Dan Asher had heard their argument from inside. Looking out his bedroom window at the blue-black sky, he brooded on his genes. The oil pump in the back yard softly rattled the pane until he placed the warm palm of his hand on it. His mother had had the same effect on their family. Her apron of calm unrolled in his memory. A quiet, gentle woman totally lacking in ambition and with no more adrenaline in her than a place mat. She had always been an intensely private person, her life centering around her family, her plants, her postcard collection. Certainly she wasn't to blame for her son, for this demon Asher who at fifty was still raving uncontrollably and as horny as any high school kid.

His old man wasn't responsible either. Not Big Julie, the perfect salesman. Ah, *there* was a smoothie! He could get along with anybody. The firm handshake, the eye to eye, a smile to warm your wallet, the nip and tuck at the shoulders and waist, a look of approval that could squeeze a size 44 into a 40, everything measured and under control. Daddy, his sister Marion said, could charm the dust off the floor. Dan Asher remembered that the old boy could even get along with his son on occasion.

Why then was he, Daniel Asher, the only volcano in the family? He never ceased to be astonished by these outbursts of his, the dumb passions that bubbled through his heart. One day telling a complete stranger on the beach that her ass was a valentine. On another ripping off a book that he had come in to buy, simply because the saleslady said can't you wait a minute and froze him with her chilly eyeballs. Cut off by another car on San Vicente, he chased furiously after it and very nearly got himself killed when, cutting back in front, the MG was hit. Whatever the root of this rashness, Dan swore to himself that from now on he would do better. He returned from the bedroom with his secret life all buttoned up inside and a handful of joints. He was eager to make amends.

Peter Knight saw him coming and squirmed. He hoped that

his compliments had been as audible as his complaints. Yes, yes, he announced brightly, I like them.

Despite everything that Dan Asher had overheard, he even now wanted very much to believe him. It wasn't easy. Have a joint, he offered. First-rate Columbian grass. Although drugs played a very small part in Asher's life, he did appreciate a quality item. He could tell from the look on the editor's face that Knight also valued good merchandise.

Peter said, Love to, yes indeed, and took the joint. The baby, said Joan. That was all she said, the baby, but Peter knew instantly what she meant, and the innocent joy on his face disappeared under a mountain of disappointment. It was time to go.

Already! cried Mona, who by now had written the entire evening off as a disaster. With blazing speed, she gathered all of the baby's things together for them. A drag, declared Peter. We really must do this again. He shrugged helplessly and surrendered the joint of fine Columbian grass to his host. Keep it, Dan told him, and gave him another for Joan. A grateful Peter began telling a long story about Frank Stella playing soccer in Hanover, New Hampshire. Dan advised him to stash the joints. With their presents wrapped in a clean diaper, the beaming Knights strapped on their belongings and broke camp.

After they had gone, Dan noticed that his collages were still out on the worktable. The six of them looked smaller to him now, more vulnerable. He put them tenderly away and turned off the spotlights. Mona wasn't saying anything, but it was obvious to him that she was seething as she snatched up the dirty dishes from the table and tossed them clattering into the sink. Finally she said, did you hear that? Did you hear that asshole going on about au-then-tic-i-ty? She was a good mimic. Dan said that he hadn't.

There was something curious about her expression. Anger was there somewhere, but skepticism at his response had tamed it. Perhaps rather than skepticism it was her sense of humor. Converting the anger into muted forms—her hand rubbing the weary back of her arm, a brightness of the eye. She said, I guess it was nothing really. Just what you'd expect from him. Peter riding his Greenberg hobby horse at full gallop.

Dan felt so proud of the way that she had stood up to Peter. The spiritedness of this blissfully young creature! He adored her. Whatever disappointment there was for him in Knight's reaction to the new work, and of course there had been disappointment, was forgotten by Dan in his wonder at her loyalty, her pluck. He couldn't understand his incredible good fortune. Under the kitchen light, the blue glass on her blouse sent out enticing messages, the glass twinkling like sapphire lamps seen at a great distance in the sweet jasmine-scented Los Angeles night.

Near the sink was a container of coffee ice cream that had been packaged in small print to resemble an insurance policy. Guaranteed only natural ingredients. Dan Asher picked up the carton and the lid came off effortlessly in his hand. Inside was coffee soup. Licking his fingers clean, he said, You forgot the dessert, and handed the container to Mona. Her look of annoyance with its heavy weight of self-absorption held his heart. As far as she was concerned, Peter didn't deserve any. The only thing she forgot was to put it in the refrigerator when she came home.

Mona took out a couple of spoons from the drawer, plunked herself down at the table, and said, Come on. Have some dessert. But Dan had no desire for ice cream. He leaned toward her across the table. I want you, he whispered. First ice cream, said Mona. She licked her spoon clean with childish enthusiasm, her pink tongue burnishing the silver. Then me.

NEW YORK, JUNE 30, 1959

Since their marriage a year ago, they had been living on Sixth Avenue, between 9th Street and 10th. Dan Asher loved the Village. Small bronze plaques on the sides of buildings revealed that Mark Twain had once been a neighbor and Bret Harte and

Henry James over where the NYU cafeteria was now located. The surrounding streets held history like some fabulous beast that Madeleine, born and raised in Minneapolis, had half believed prowled only in books.

But Dan Asher needed no historical marker to tell him that the site of what was formerly Stieglitz's 291—the gallery in which America first discovered Rousseau, Picasso, Matisse, and Picabia—was within easy walking distance up Fifth Avenue. A few blocks away on University Place, a tacky awning over the front door was enough to identify the already legendary Cedar Street Tavern where Abstract Expressionism drank. The Club was on Eighth Street. Matta's studio on Ninth. And right around the corner at 28 West 10th lived the notorious seventy-two-year-old rebel who had once proposed the use of a Rembrandt painting as an ironing board, the recently naturalized citizen who considered himself as American as mouthwash and Dan Asher considered to be among the most important artists alive, his old friend Duchamp.

They had initially met at the Art of This Century Gallery in 1943 when Kurt Seligmann had introduced them. The Frenchman had been generous, praising his first two publicly exhibited collages as courageous. Definitely, he said, the most courageous work in the show. Over the years the two artists had become friends, and Dan Asher had even assisted him in assembling one of his *Boxes in a Valise.*

A few weeks before leaving for a summer in Europe, Duchamp invited Dan over for a game of chess. Asher preferred not to go for two reasons. First, Marcel was a very good chess player, and second, his own image of himself was not that of a congenital loser. Still, he liked the man and went anyway. They played with wooden pieces designed by Max Ernst, the pawns resembling squat saltshakers, the bishops in cleft miters. After twenty-one moves, Dan Asher as usual was in serious difficulty. Twenty-five, and his condition was critical. Pondering the apparent hopelessness of the situation, he angrily shoved a Camel into his mouth. Cigarette? he offered. Smiling, Duchamp held up the Blackstone cigar that he had been smoking since the game began and, leaning back in his blue easy chair and closing his eyes, puffed on it contentedly. Wisps of smoke laureled his head.

Okay, said Dan at last, your move. Duchamp leaned his long, thin face forward over the board. Suddenly he looked puzzled. The bags under his eyes darkened, the large knuckles of his hands bulged. Then he realized what his friend Daniel had done, and a wry smile creased the side of his mouth. The black knight forking his rook and bishop had cunningly moved one more space than the rules allowed. *J'adoube,* he announced, returning the piece to where it belonged. Asher's forces retreated ignominiously. A lightning thrust by his opponent's queen, and it was all over.

Dan Asher surveyed the damage. I'm afraid, he observed, that my game is much too dangerous for you. Every goddamn time you checkmate me you're becoming more smug. Grabbing the sides of the board, he cried *J'adoube!* and poured the pieces onto his friend's startled lap. Duchamp exploded in laughter, tears streaming down his cheeks. It was the last time that Dan Asher saw him before both of them left town for the summer, and, as it turned out, the last time ever.

That year it seemed as if everyone he talked to was fleeing the city for July and August. Duchamp went to Cadaqués on the Costa Brava. The card he sent back said, "Very crowded here. Stay where you are." At Madeleine's urging, Dan Asher rented a house for the three of them in East Hampton and, Marissa having just finished her term at school, they were packing to leave the next day.

Dan Asher was not eager to go to Long Island. Grass bored him, sand stuck in his crotch. Swimming was for fish. He was a city boy who really didn't mind the heat at all, enjoyed being alone in a crowd, and hated to have to leave his splendid studio for some makeshift arrangement at the beach. But his wife, sounding more like a Jewish mother than a Catholic stepmother, insisted that Marissa needed a change, some color in her cheeks.

Fuck the color in her cheeks, complained Asher. It was a last gasp, a lost cause. Secretly delighted with her concern for his kid, he couldn't say no.

Lights burned and packing was going on all over the once run-down duplex apartment that they had renovated elegantly. Since his appearance five years ago in the Venice Biennale, Dan Asher had buyers for his work in Europe as well as America and, though he was hardly a millionaire, there was more money now than ever before.

Simply furnished, their apartment had an assortment of tastefully amusing details that revealed the artist's hand. Instead of a banister to the second floor, there was a three-ply hemp cable. The kitchen door was divided horizontally in two, each half distinguished by an antique wrought-iron bolt. The Dutch door and tesselated floor might have been lifted whole from a Vermeer painting. Upstairs, he had mirrored the walls and put in a barre, dedicating the entire floor to a practice studio for Madeleine. Downstairs, he had torn down a wall between two rooms and set up his own studio. Now, sitting on the wooden studio floor, Dan carefully finished loading a small carton labeled Burry's Girl Scout Cookies with nineteenth-century engravings of old inns and hotels and Kodachrome vistas of newer ones. He was sponging a piece of gum tape to seal the box when Madeleine came in.

She was wearing one of his old shirts tied at the bottom and exposing a midriff that looked as sleek as if it had been modeled by Arp. The blond hair knotted loosely on top of her head spilled light into the room. In her hand she clutched a piece of paper. Did you get to the post office today? she wanted to know, and when he reported that he had filed the temporary change of address, she scratched it off her list. One less thing to do before leaving.

Let me have that, he said, pointing to her pencil. On the side of the sealed carton he wrote *Hotel Prints* and stacked the box on top of the others that he had piled near the door. He was about to return the pencil when he noticed that it was all chewed up, the brutalized yellow surface scarred with pocks. Nervous? he asked. A little, she admitted. There's still a helluva lot to do. But the pencil belongs to Marissa, if that's what you mean.

Dan Asher yelled for his daughter, and she came running —saucer eyes set in a thin, pale face, and small teeth with a childish space waiting for incisors. He warned her about chewing on pencils. Splinters, he warned. Lead poisoning. Crooked teeth. Daddy—she reached up toward his mouth—did you chew on pencils when you were my age? Never, declared her exemplary father. He ran a finger over the gap in his front teeth. Not everyone is born lucky, baby. You're the tooth fairy's dream girl. Take care of what you've got. He lifted her up and, nuzzling the tender flesh, gave her a kiss that whistled and popped against her cheek, reducing the child to a puddle of giggles. Now beat it, he ordered, and go to bed. We're leaving *early* tomorrow morning. Scram.

When Madeleine returned from putting the excited child to bed, she found him bent over the bureau in their bedroom, angrily pulling out clothes and launching them into the air like flares. Where's my shorts? he demanded. Madeleine had no idea what he was after at first, and then she recalled the split seat on the faded, torn dungarees from which he had chopped off the legs.

Those old ones? She was incredulous. I threw them away long ago. Asher shook his head. You couldn't have, you didn't. Don't be silly, Dan. You couldn't possibly have worn those things anymore. I tossed them into the rag bag. Asher flew to the hall closet and was back in a flash, triumphantly waving his tattered shorts, on his face a blissful smile as soft as a moonbeam. Idiot, said the amused Madeleine affectionately and kissed him. You're such a baby.

The expensive leather valise open on the high, canopied bed had been packed with exquisite care. It was loaded as discretely as the drawer of a cash register. While Madeleine watched, he gathered up one of his sweaters from the floor and folded it meticulously. I forgot to tell you—she handed him a plastic bag for the sweater—there were some phone calls. Your mother is feeling much better and sent love. I gave her our number out in

East Hampton and said you'd be in touch as soon as we're settled. Who else? he asked. Mordecai Bell called. He plans to drop by tomorrow to say bon voyage. Dan looked up. I hope you told him that we're leaving at the crack of dawn. I told him, said Madeleine, that you'd be leaving about ten.

He means well, Dan supposed, but he's such a royal pain in the ass. Ever since he dreamed up that idea of someday doing my biography, he's been trailing after me like the CIA. Did I tell you that last week when I was in Woolworth's getting some of those straight pins with the colored heads I caught him watching me from behind the Orange Crush machine? He was about as inconspicuous as a Clydesdale. Normally, of course, I would have said hello, but I didn't want to offend him. Madeleine, cross-legged on the floor, was not paying any attention. What did you mean—suddenly realizing what she had said—what did you mean by *I'd* be leaving? What's that supposed to mean?

Madeleine didn't answer. Her bent head remained motionless, the rolled sleeves exposing her tightly locked elbows, her palms flat on the bare studio floor. And not a word. It was as if her mind had dropped down a rabbit hole. The one thing in their young marriage that Asher couldn't take were these silences of hers. They had come as a surprise. He felt utterly left out, helpless, guilty of unspeakable crimes with no hope of reprieve or even conjugal visitation.

When at last she spoke, she did so without lifting her head. I can't go with you tomorrow morning. It's the new ballet for next season, she explained. It's not going too well. Anton wants to work on it with me one more day before I leave. He's talking about making changes. I couldn't say no.

Dan Asher was relieved that it was nothing more serious. She might have said, I'm all wrong for the part. How many times had she said that before? And then he would say, You're perfect for it; and she, No, I'm too old, or, It needs someone smaller, lighter, more ethereal, or, God how I hate my big-hipped, big-breasted, childbearing body.

Okay, he said agreeably, we'll wait until you're through rehearsing. There's no hurry. But Madeleine wouldn't hear of it.

No—she was up in one fluid movement and confronting him —that won't do at all. Marissa would be heartbroken. She's expecting to be playing on the beach tomorrow. We couldn't do that to her, Dan, could we? She'll survive, he said. Madeleine didn't think so, and finally Madeleine prevailed. She promised to be out in East Hampton on one of the early evening trains.

The next morning as if to prove a point Dan Asher was up at six, but by the time the car was loaded and they were ready to go, it was well after nine. Despite the girl's noisy objections, Madeleine had insisted that she wear her best red pinafore and then spent a quarter of an hour patiently braiding the squirming child's hair. His wife seemed to have some funny ideas about how Marissa should dress to begin a vacation. Rather than risk an argument on a wobbly, early morning stomach, Dan Asher said nothing. He took the kid downstairs, settling her in the front seat of the convertible—a handsome old Riley with the top down and its landau irons gleaming in the morning sun—and hurried back up to say goodbye. They kissed, and the warm taste of coffee in her mouth made him want to stay. You'll leave just as soon as the rehearsal is over, he reminded her, and she swore that she would. From a hook in the front closet, he yanked down his favorite traveling hat, a checkered deerstalker, tearing the rear peak in his haste. Shhhit! he groaned, surveying the damage and, slapping the hat on his head, ran out.

Daddy, cried the alarmed Marissa as he got into the car, look what you did to your hat! He leaned toward her, his smile a poor weak shrunken thing without zest. Do you like it? he asked hopefully. She made him her spinach face. That's what I thought, he said, poking his ticklish daughter under the arm. He turned on the ignition, and the rocket roar of the Riley's engine drowned out her giggles.

Looking down from the window in her bathrobe, Madeleine answered his farewell wave with a kiss. The night before she had polished the brass buttons on the child's pinafore, and they glowed like six tiny moons in a red sky. As a child, she herself had once owned a dress with brass buttons, a blue party dress that she loved. She wondered if there was anything left of it now.

A shoe rag, a plume of Minnesota smoke. Dan was waving, smiling his silly gap-toothed smile, and the winter white of bare knees hanging out from his shorts squeezed the tears from her eyes.

Then she caught sight of Mordecai Bell. He was far down the block in a rumpled white suit with his leather briefcase clutched two-handed under his bulky arm as if it were alive and might leap away at the first stumble. She had never seen the art critic without his case. A sturdy antique affair with flaps and straps that seemed to be as much a part of him as his chubby face, his round wire-rimmed glasses, and the wispy strands of hair that covered his scalp like the strings of a guitar.

Bell glimpsed the Riley. He began to shuffle more quickly, shouting and beating the air with his briefcase in an attempt to catch Dan's attention. A clanging delivery elevator erupted out of the sidewalk, momentarily blocking his way. She supposed she could have called to Dan, told him to wait, meddled in his fate, but she didn't. Turning away from the window and its complications, Madeleine felt a tremendous sense of relief.

When the doorbell rang, she was sitting upstairs on the spotless floor of her studio contemplating Marissa's teethmarks on the yellow number-two. The sleeping pills had gone down as smoothly as jelly beans. Already nothing is happening to me, she thought. No more years or jobs or pains or flaws. No more humiliations of the limbs and mind. Yesterday Anton had taken the part away from her, and she had quit him on the spot. At forty, she had had enough of dancing and failure. The wailing sirens of Sixth Avenue dropped on her through the open skylight, disasters in search of a name. She hoped the two of them would be careful. She hoped that Dan, who was not a fast driver but easily provoked, would do nothing foolish. She tried to see his face and saw only the back of his head, the torn and dangling peak of his hat jiggling away from her forever. One last flap goodbye.

She looked into the mirrored walls and stared at the staring woman in the plum-colored robe. Her hair was a mess, straggling down her shoulders in dejected strands. She couldn't see the tears but could feel them dripping inside her like internal bleeding. Again the doorbell. It rang on and on, an electric summons that stopped at her heart. Bending over the paper on the floor, she smoothed it out and wrote, *My Dearest* . . .

OAKLAND, 1976

DANIEL ASHER: Collages 1943–1967.
The Oakland Museum, 1976.
Introduction by Mordecai Bell.

Whereas earlier he had seemed to enjoy experimenting with diverse themes, Asher began now to take single subjects and thoroughly explore them. This method became typical of his mature work. Seized by an idea, he would have to exhaust the impulse completely by doing countless variations on the theme before he could be free of it. His first such series, begun in 1955, he called "Waiting Rooms and Dark Corridors."

The Dark Corridor of Don Juan Madoura (cat. no. 23) is an exquisite sample of his work of this period. We see here his associative mind in action as it restlessly searches for the secret relationships among things. Through pinpoints of lights in the crepuscular corridor, Asher subtly links the laughter of the Don's cowled tormentors with the gold wedding ring he wears. From the most prosaic of materials—sand, a photo, map fragments —he succeeds in creating a powerful drama of jealousy and romance. His tiny clock wheels and springs hover in the sky like planets or beating hearts or eternity. It would be foolish to select but one of these meanings when we sense the richness and rightness of all. The Museum of Modern Art purchased this collage shortly after it was completed.

Perhaps the most hauntingly lyrical period in Asher's career began in 1958, and it coincided, not surprisingly, with his second marriage. His new wife was the gifted dancer Madeleine Benedict. The works in the new series, "The Great Hotels of the

World," are the artist's most sensuous, but always we find a note of introspection; always there is impeccable restraint. Of special interest here—in addition to his effective use of sheet music as mentioned previously—are the bits of mirror to be found in the evocative *Hotel California*.

In 1914, Juan Gris, whom Asher greatly admired, was perhaps the first to use pieces of broken mirror in his collage entitled *The Marble Pier Table*. Gris said at the time that "a painted surface can be translated onto a canvas, a volume can be interpreted on it. For a mirror, though—a changing surface that reflects the viewer himself—one can only glue on such a piece of looking glass."

The decade of the fifties had brought recognition to Daniel Asher, but it also brought him great personal tragedy. At its beginning in 1950, his sister had died. His first wife left him in 1954. Then in 1959, at the close of the decade, his second wife committed suicide. Devastated, Asher decided to leave New York with its heartbreaking memories and, together with his seven-year-old daughter, go west.

LOS ANGELES, APRIL 2, 1966

Dan Asher didn't want to go. There was a chance the bastard might be there, and Dan didn't want to go. But Mona had insisted, said that he'd been working too hard on the new series and needed a change. She couldn't force him to follow Felstein's advice and exercise if he didn't want to, but this was something else.

Since the auction, she pointed out, he hadn't even been outside the house. You could use an airing, she said. Dan's face softened into a schoolboy grin. Besides, she added, I've got to be at the gala for Ward and I'll be damned if I'll go to that stuffy thing alone. Her insistence surprised him, and because Mona rarely asked Dan to do anything, he wanted very much to oblige. Even if Max did show up, he thought, there needn't be any bloodshed. Dan was, after all, old enough to keep his flayed and raving sense of outrage at injustice in its cage. He would stay cool. He would look the other way. For her, he would even put on shoes. Her arms flew about his neck as Mona kissed him, enveloped him in her lilac mist. Do I have to wear a tie? he asked skeptically.

They drove east down Wilshire to the museum, the sun setting red-eyed in his rearview mirror. Having gotten him out, Mona did all she could to amuse him with cracks about the people in the other cars. Look-look-quick! she would say and lean her bare shoulders toward him and captivatingly muffle a giggle on the faded and unfashionably narrow remnant from another age that was his tie. She was delicious, practically naked in an Empire-style, high-waisted slippery thing held up by two straps no thicker than cross hairs.

On the radio, a new San Francisco group called the Jefferson Airplane was singing, *Cause you're so much younger than I am, come up the years, come up the years and love me.* Mona gave him an affectionate squeeze. The evening air seemed to be doing Dan a world of good already. It was while he was engaged in nibbling on Mona's divine neck and digging the music and trying to guide the powerful MG—despite wheels dangerously out of alignment and tires slick as soap—that the museum showed up. Dan wrenched the car into a U turn and roared to the front gate. It was closed. Oh, said Mona, glancing up. Not here. Around the corner. The Ogden Avenue entrance.

Strange pulsating sounds floated on the nocturnal air of L.A., and a right turn onto Ogden made them louder, more exotic. The uniformed guard at the kiosk recognized Mona and waved them through into the small parking lot. It was jammed. To Dan Asher, looking about for a spot, it appeared as if they were permitting only expensive imported cars to park there that evening.

And quite right, too, he informed Mona. Keep the riffraff in their place. Filthy domestic upstarts. She laughed, tickled by his deadpan knuckling of his mustache. That was more like him, she thought, pleased with herself for having insisted that he come. Dan shoehorned his battered English treasure between a gleaming Mercedes 230 SL and a spotless Rolls Silver Cloud and got out. Hey, what about me? yelled Mona, unable to open her door.

Coming around to the passenger side of the convertible, Dan Asher leaned in and grabbed her under the arms. She giggled. Stop, she said, no. She was laughing and squirming, and then she became serious. No! she said, and then all at once there was a frightened look on her face as she felt this invalid only two months out of the hospital actually lifting her up. No, Dan, no! she cried, and suddenly she was out of the car and in his arms. Dan kissed her. Still strong as an ox, he swore, and set her down. You're sweet, said Mona, slipping her slim arm into his, but you're also a Grade A, first-class, prime chuckleheaded idiot. Dan had to admit that as usual there was some merit in what she said.

Between the parking lot and the museum's side entrance was a group of about thirty dancing and singing Hare Krishnas, and in the gathering shadows the Krishnas blocked their way. Dan Asher felt his jaw go rigid, his hands become fists. He should have known the minute he first heard that rhythm, that mindless sound.

In the center of the circle the men wore sandals and baggy peach pants and orange sweaters, and the long-fringed, woven purses that hung from their shoulders swung with abandon. At the outer edges were young women with shawls covering their heads, and their loose saffron gowns ballooned as they danced. And they all chanted, the lot of them blissfully hopping and skipping and jigging and chanting Hare Rama, Hare Rama, Rama Rama, Hare Hare.

Merely a coincidence, he reasoned, nothing more than a coincidence. Somehow they had gotten word of the party that night—big money on the premises. Why would they want to follow him? Then a very different thought occurred to Dan. Was it, he wondered, even remotely possible that he was pursuing them? Dan Asher trying to solve the disappearance of his dear sister Marion, his old man, Julie, the puzzling Elbert. Dan Asher running after death. Nonsense. It was a ridiculous idea that he promptly dismissed. Come on, he called to Mona, and began angrily to push his way through the dancers.

The smell was dense, suffocating, a weird mixture of sweat and incense—lotus blossoms in the locker room—as the dancers shuffled about in ecstasy. Dan could feel their thin, slithery arms twine about him, their hands seeming to want to draw him into the dance. They were small soft hands with pale white palms the color of fish that live their entire lives at great depths. Tiny cold fingers touched his back, stroked his neck, seemed to slip beneath his clothes, in and out of his pockets. Dan Asher felt as if he had fallen into an Alexandrian house of pleasure serviced by little girls between the ages of nine and eleven. Their deathly cold lips seemed to seal his lips, cold fingers pinned his hands. Was this then to be his final waltz, he asked himself, Asher's last kiss? He tried to tell Mona, but she wasn't there.

Mona, back where he had left her, was listening intently to a woman who wore draped over her head a white shawl with pink and purple bands. There was a child with her in a worn stroller. As the woman talked, she rolled the stroller back and forth; despite the racket, the child was slumped over sound asleep. Mona opened a small purse and handed her a few coins. You're so good, praised the grateful member of the order, so kind, so loving— Hey! cried Mona in annoyance as Dan Asher yanked her away before she could take the woman's pamphlet.

She wondered what the hell this was all about. All of a sudden he was awfully eager to get to the party. Then she saw his face and knew it was something else. Are you feeling all right? she asked anxiously. He said, Fine, thrusting the word home like a butcher knife. Mona pressed the bell at the side door and tried to think of something uncomplicated to talk about. Did you know they were vegetarians? she asked.

The sound that came over the intercom was garbled, stentorian. Mona identified them. The steel door buzzed and clicked open. Dan Asher quickly slammed it behind them, cutting off the Krishnas and eliminating all trace of their music as effectively as if he had lifted the needle from a record.

The quiet of the loading area was soothing, the stationary crates and boxes on the ramp rested his eyes. He relaxed in the rationality of their footsteps on the asphalt and the cheerful warmth of Mona's arm in his. As they came up to the metal turnstile and the glassed-in security booth beside it, Dan said something to show her that he was really okay and make her smile, and she did.

Evening, Miz Block. The good-looking black man in the cocoa-brown uniform greeted her from behind the glass. He said, I see they got you working overtime. He approved of her party dress, called it outasight. Mona said, Thanks, Dewayne. He had the bushiest head of hair Dan Asher had ever seen, an Afro that formed a jet aureole around his head. Dan liked it. Dewayne Taylor, the guard, could not say the same for Dan's ponytail. Raising his clipboard, he ran down the guest list and put a warm check of approval next to his pal Mona's name. Then coolly he turned to the hippie as if he were leftover Brussels sprouts. Mona explained that the limp collar and stained tie belonged to Dan Asher. Sign here, ordered the immaculate guard, and through the open glass wicket he thrust out his clipboard as if it were a summons.

While Dan signed, Mona informed Dewayne that the museum owned one of her friend's collages. It was called *Palisades Pileup*. That's right, said Dan Asher, as if he had forgotten. He returned the clipboard and, speaking in a quietly convincing manner, added, It *is* mine, and I'm here to liberate it. The guard's eyes opened wide, his lower lip sagged like an empty shopping bag. Taking her lover's hand, Mona mumbled, Very funny, and tried to pull him away. Wait, said Dan Asher. What's going on there?

He stared through the glass at the bank of nine closed-circuit television screens that formed a part of the museum's security system. There was no sound, or if there was any it was impossible to hear outside the booth. The pictures were black and white, the light a pathological ice blue. Only number three, the one covering the atrium in the Ahmanson Gallery, had any action. Dan Asher pointed to it. *There,* he said.

Just then the Ogden Avenue doorbell shook the booth and Dewayne Taylor, turning smartly to the intercom, demanded to know who it was. From his voice, it was clear that he had had enough nonsense for one night. *That,* said Mona, is where we're going. Come on.

The sounds coming from the Ahmanson Gallery were loud but not uncivilized, a tastefully animated blend of well-bred voices and wise laughter. On the colorfully glazed tiles of the atrium floor, the distinguished guests stood sipping champagne and enjoying each other's company. They all seemed to know one another, as if Los Angeles were no bigger than a putting green. They spoke the same language. Their maids shopped together at Jurgenson's, their cooks exchanged tips on abalone. They were used to sunny days and a smooth fast track.

A few of them Dan Asher had met. Others he had seen pictures of in the *Times,* receiving awards or returning from Europe or donating money to the museum. Their fortunes— mostly first or second generation—had come primarily from oil, steel, food, real estate, communications, savings and loan companies. It was art that gave their cash visibility and class. The great names were Ahmanson and Ward and Carter and Chandler and Hammer and Taper and Simon and . . . son of a bitch! Dan Asher swore in amazement as he checked out the glittering assembly. Were they *all* here tonight?

Mona, oh, Mona. . . . It was Trisha Wiley. Thank heavens! she cried. Come quick, come quick. The excitable Trisha was in charge of public information for the museum. A redheaded woman with skin so transparently fair that her nerve endings were almost to be seen twitching just beneath the surface, Trisha had been looking everywhere for Miles. The French Consul, Monsieur Husson, wanted to hear all about the plans for the big Man Ray show in the fall, and she could answer only a few of his questions. You absolutely *must* rescue me, she pleaded.

Mona turned to Dan to see if he would mind. Her eyes with

their astonishing blue shadows startled him once again. He wasn't accustomed to the eye makeup. The effect was sinfully decadent and a most agreeable surprise. He smiled and assured her that he'd be fine. Go ahead.

Reminding him that dinner would be served in Pauley Hall on the plaza level—one flight up at the top of the white marble staircase—Mona arranged to meet him there. Affectionately touched his cheek. All right, Trisha, she announced, but the impatient redhead had bolted and was already halfway across the floor.

No sooner did Mona leave than Dan Asher felt the crowd begin to oppress him. He was not going to allow that to happen, he was not going to ruin his sweetheart's evening. An attentive white-coated waiter approached with a tray. Lifting a glass of champagne, the artist decided that a mild sedative was just what the doctor ordered and downed it in a gulp. Graceful bubbles soothed his frayed edges and danced their way to his heart. He stretched for a second glass, bummed a cigarette from a woman with a pack in her hand and a high forehead like Merle Oberon's, and then asked if she had a match. He inhaled, exhaled, sipped. This was definitely more like it.

The woman was tall, elegant, engulfed in a cloud of pale green chiffon. She wore open-toed shoes from which her cruel, thick big toes protruded. There was a sour expression on her face. The little guy in the red velvet jacket and black bow tie with whom she had been talking turned and negligently acknowledged his presence. Hello there, Asher, he said, the voice so languid, so frail that it seemed like a confidence one had to strain to share. Madame Husson, allow me to present the artist Daniel Asher.

The little guy was Chris Bates, an art dealer who in a relatively short time had become enormously successful. In addition to possessing an instinct for trends, he was a clever businessman who got along well with people who counted. Dan Asher summed him up as an affected jerk who at some point had probably been influenced by Vollard's *Recollections*. Unable to become a sleeping bear like Vollard, Bates had been content to fashion himself into a lackadaisical hamster.

Madame Husson looked the artist over from top to toe and

scowled. A lovely dress, he complimented her. Madame Husson blushed and looked at him again. It was as if she had bitten into a lemon and the taste proved to be jam.

People were starting to go up to dinner and, noticing them, Dan Asher offered her his arm. Shall we go, Véronique? Bates suggested, and the two of them left arm in arm. If the twerp had had a more expressive face, Dan Asher might have called what he saw there a smirk.

The small plaque above the door said that he was entering the Mr. and Mrs. Edwin Pauley Great Hall. Gazing up at the ponderous columns, the useless wall of glass, a ceiling that was practically out of town, Dan Asher judged the room a lousy place to hang a collage. In fact, he thought, it reeked. The woman in the beaded bolero jacket in front of him wheeled around to see who had said that and her escort did the same, two alarmed faces that upon seeing him slowly filled with disgust. Dan smiled, winked, shrugged his shoulders. It does, he repeated, and boldly brushed past them, a little surprised at his inability to keep a secret. Champagne after weeks of abstinence was the diagnosis; the prescription, not to worry.

The hall was furnished with large circular tables for this special occasion, each table decorated with green candles and sunbursts of daffodils. Silverware gleamed like a hundred mirrored strips, and goblets twinkled amidst the snow-white napery. Dan had just spotted Newton Ward down at the end of the hall when the flashbulb went off, catching the proud owner standing beside his Rembrandt. He was surrounded by onlookers, admirers who had that animal sense of who has the power. While not necessarily number one in this realm of money and art, Ward was sure as hell no lower than two. Even Dan Asher felt compelled to take a few steps toward him.

The relaxed Ward seemed at home here in the Great Hall and much less formal than most of the men around him. He wore the blue jacket of his well-cut business suit casually unbuttoned. He was, Dan noted, losing his hair. The few faithful gray wisps around his ears had been indulged, and they had lengthened into scruffiness. Although a lifelong Republican, the industrialist was apparently much impressed by the Kennedy style. This was a dry, bony man, and Dan Asher regarded his forehead—grooved by at least sixty years of erosion—as a natural wonder. Ward lowered his thick eyebrows. He glanced down at the waxed parquet and gloomily listened, running his tongue over his teeth, as the new director of the museum, J. Martin Donleavy, tried to tell him something.

Dan Asher could imagine the conversation. The oleaginous Donleavy oozing with enthusiasm over the breathtaking new acquisition and stroking Ward up and down like a buffing machine. With your collection, Mr. Ward, LACMA will become one of the great museums of the world. We will rival the Met, the Prado, the Louvre, the Uffizi. People from every country on earth will know of your great . . . And the collector listening, listening, his ears open and his mouth mum. The man didn't have an impetuous bone in his body. It looked to Dan Asher as if the only risks Ward ever took were calculated ones. Why can't I be a little more like that? he wondered vaguely. Just a little.

Behind Ward and the museum director, hovering in the background like a serviceable afterthought, was the curator Miles Dorfman. Dressed quite fashionably and talking to two silky, gray-haired ladies and meeting with their approval. He was entertaining Newton Ward's wife and sister-in-law, amusing them with his chic stories, his funny gestures. Their eyes glittered as they listened attentively to the young man, dazzled by his charm.

Dan Asher had to give him credit. The guy really had it, that ability to suck up to people effortlessly. At Princeton there had been kids like that, and at the time he had thought there was something unnatural about such behavior, embarrassing. Now he had come to realize that it was either in the blood like perfect pitch or congenital like a harelip.

Complicated? said the tall man standing before the Rembrandt to his tall companion. Not at all. He explained that at Sotheby's they know that when Newton sits down he is bidding. When he stands up he is not bidding. When he sits down again he is not bidding until he strokes his chin. He raises one finger to place a bid. Simplicity itself. Dan moved around the two tall viewers and leaned forward to get a better look at the spotlighted painting.

Please sir, the rope. Dan wondered what the guy wanted. The rope, sir, said the guard, pointing to the velvet rope that had been set up to keep admirers at a safe distance. You're leaning on it. Right, said Dan Asher, and straightened up.

His initial reaction to the painting was a sinking sensation and . . . oh, my God. More than two million bucks for *that!* A fraction of the amount would have cleared up his debts for a lifetime. It was signed RHL van Rijn in the lower right corner and must have been authenticated or else the cautious Ward and his advisers wouldn't have touched it, but Dan Asher couldn't get over the work's obvious weaknesses. The murkiness of the setting for the battle, the angel's limp right hand that resembled a suede glove. It was not one of Rembrandt's finest.

The Jacob wasn't bad, though. His legs planted solidly on the ground like two windmills and his dark, curly head bent forward watching his opponent's feet, looking for an opening, ready to go in on him instantly for the takedown. And then—*whammo!* Angel sucked in by fireman's carry. Two points Jacob!

The idea of a Jewish wrestler appealed to Dan Asher. There weren't any in college that he could remember. The sole wrestling Jew from that long-ago time was the great one, the New York cop who went to the Olympics and won gold. Dan had thought he would never forget his name. *Sic transit gloria mundi.*

Nevertheless, there were still the exploits, the images. A young man in a crewcut with a bull neck who held himself like a cocked pistol. Everyone once knew that he did thousands of pushups on his fingertips, hung by his nails from the tops of doors. You might in those days run into him anywhere in the city doing handstands on mailboxes, pressing heavy garbage cans hundreds of times over his head. Some said that he could make his body as stiff as an ironing board and hold it at right angles to no-parking poles, hanging out there for hours like a railroad semaphore. And always he was wrestling, night and day perfecting his wonderful man-eating traps called guillotines and cradles and Oklahoma whizzers with which he could put a man on his back in the blink of an eye.

But Jacob was no Olympic hero. He had neither the muscle of Michelangelo, nor the mythic size of Rubens. That, for Dan Asher, was the beauty of it. Rembrandt had taken some ordinary guy who was just strolling along minding his own business and came face to face with this blond heavyweight with wings. No matter how come the fight. The Jew was set upon and showed the bully his human stuff. Taking blondie unawares and the angel's eyes ablaze with the sudden realization that mortality is not synonymous with chump.

Whether in the work of others or his own, Dan Asher was somebody who relished remarkable things happening matter-of-factly in art. Angels showing up on the doorstep like the morning paper. Lads in ringlets and ruffles cranking melodeons amidst a Venetian holocaust. It seemed to him that life was always turning up new marvels. An old man and a young woman, says the *I Ching*. The wonder is their coming together. Dan at fifty regarded himself as hardly more than slightly used middle age, but Mona's love was still a miracle.

He looked for her in the hall and, not finding her, searched the tables for a place card. The names on the ecru cards read like a society column. What was he doing here among so many strangers when he might have been home working? He began to feel oppressed again. He finally located Mona's card on a table at the end of the room farthest from the Rembrandt, but even here in the cheap seats there was no place set aside for Asher. Of course, he reassured himself, who knew he was coming? Snatching up the card to the right of his love, he slipped Jerome Greenspan into his pocket and sat down. There was no room in Dan Asher's life for self-pity.

He helped himself to a glass of red wine and listened to the big guy on the other side of the table holding forth on the Watts Towers. He had strong white teeth, a Palm Springs tan, and his name was Abelson. He was an art collector. Dan had met him once a long time ago. Abelson wiped the corners of his lips and added, But I haven't been down to Watts to see them in a while. Then he noticed the gray-haired black man at the table and explained, Not since, you know, that business there last summer. The black man stroked his bow tie. I know, he said diplomatically.

Dan poured himself another glass of red and said, Hello, Mrs. Abelson. The quiet woman seated nearby looked at him with no sign of recognition. Oh, she said, hello. He was surprised it came out English. Clothes like that were worn by the wives of concentration camp doctors, Gestapo colonels. Dan Asher, he reminded her; we met at Max Roth's house. Yes, of course, she said, not caring to contest the fact, and replugged her cigarette holder into her mouth.

The sculptor Ed Harvey was waving to Chris Bates at the other end of the hall, Bates's red jacket vibrant with energy, his raised hand drooping at the wrist. Dan Asher liked Harvey's work. He asked him if he was still with the Bates Gallery. Absolutely, said Harvey. Chris doesn't try to fuck artists the way some dealers do. Sell things and don't pay. Tell you they've lost your art or something. Chris is probably as good as the top four or five dealers in New York. Reaching for an olive, Harvey asked, And who are you with now?

Excuse me. The short, white-haired man peered down between them at the place cards. There was a daisy in his buttonhole. A gold-capped bicuspid flashed when he said, I can't seem to find . . . Coming up from behind, Mona asked, Can I help? He blushed, his cheeks embarrassed at the fuss he was causing. No matter, no matter, my dear. He kissed her hand extensively. Forgive an old man. Relinquishing her delightfully soft hand, he sighed, apologized yet once more, and, making small, black, herringbone steps, wandered off.

Mona thought he was cute. Dan Asher said he was a disgusting old lecher taking advantage of an innocent young girl. Another one? said Mona, sitting down next to Dan and leaning provocatively close. All the men at the table seemed overjoyed to see her and vied for Mona's attention. Abelson told her an amusing joke. Flaring the candlelight, Mona's laughter was generosity itself.

Mrs. Abelson sucked on her cigarette holder and said nothing. Dan felt genuinely sorry for her, this pathetic woman in her tight white suit, her narrow tinted glasses, her funny beretlike hat, the skimpy chignon wrapped in a gray snood, the heavy shoes, the jeweled cigarette holder.

He saw her motion to her husband, trying in vain to get his attention. Turning to a waiter, he borrowed a pack of matches and lit her cigarette. Mrs. Abelson puffed on it and studied the artist's sympathetic blue eyes through her rose-tinted lenses. Dan Asher, she said. You make collages, don't you? I like your work. Tell me about it. Sure, he said, and gave her a gap-toothed smile that was as natural as sunrise. What would you like to know?

The dinner had progressed beyond the artichoke hearts vinaigrette to the coupe à l'oignon gratinée when Max Roth made his appearance. He was incredibly handsome, his dinner jacket gleaming like a tray of black olives, the white ruffles on his shirt front crisp as new money, the tip of a black silk scarf where a bow tie would ordinarily have been expected. The clothes Max wore and the cocksure way he wore them made those of the other men in the room seem to be out of focus.

Mrs. Abelson was quite fond of the dealer and valued him as a glorious soldier of fortune in the art world. He's a remarkable individual, she said. A romantic buccaneer of sorts, a man who truly enjoys life. Dan Asher turned to see who it was. Had Mona, who had been laughing at Abelson's description of a scene from the new Antonioni movie, seen the expression on her lover's face at that moment, she might have grabbed him and gone home.

Dan Asher sank down in his seat and raised his spoon with care from beneath the hot cheese surface of his soup. He sipped inconspicuously. If he just sat tight, there wasn't a reason in the world that among so many people in a hall this size they would ever have to come face to face.

The arm that swept around Mrs. Abelson's shoulders was as

exciting to her as finding an unopened envelope with her name on it in some rarely used drawer. Darlink, cried Max Roth, you look *schener* every time I put eyes on you. Tell the husband over there that you're through with the old boat. Abelson looked up and called cheerily, Hi, Max.

It was then that Roth noticed him. Daniel, Daniel my friend. There wasn't the slightest twinge in his voice. No trace of discomfort anywhere. He was a smoothie, all right. Good news! I have wonderful news for you, I think. He revealed that the possibility of a major retrospective exhibition of the work of Daniel Asher loomed on the horizon, that he had spoken to young Phillips, the director of the Municipal Art Gallery, that Phillips was eager to make the public exhibition space something more than a showcase for prizewinning elementary school posters and ethnic crafts, that he had practically promised to see what he could do. And what did Max Roth expect in return for all of this? Roth blew out his cheeks and went *poof.* A handshake, a smile, no more.

Dan Asher jumped to his feet. His chair tipped over backward and slammed to the floor. You crooked bastard, he called him. One would have had to have been standing very close to have heard what he said in that large hall filled with the lively sounds of people enjoying themselves over dinner. Max Roth heard and went white.

It was *you* who bought my *Hotel California,* accused the artist. You gave that creep the money and he fronted for you, and you got it for peanuts. And even the goddamn peanuts you probably take off your income tax as a charitable donation.

Calm yourself, advised Max. Regaining his composure, he said, Calm yourself. Naturally I bought it. Who else would buy it? Some big spender for fifty dollars. Maybe you'd like to see your prices fall through the floor? Drop like iron bagels? No, thank you. I happen to own a few Ashers myself. Max placed a paternal palm on Dan Asher's shoulder. He softened his tone and said, Look, boychik, I only tried to do you a kindness. After all, your stuff right now is not exactly selling like fireworks on the Fourth of—

It was a good punch, not your usual Saturday-night-brawl amateur swipe. Dan Asher threw it straight, straight from the shoulder, and followed through. Surprisingly, he never blinked, never closed his eyes, but kept them fixed like radar on the dealer's face. He caught Max on the left cheek just below the eye, and he went down.

The silence that followed was that of a great orchestra, a Berlioz *Requiem* orchestra with three massed choruses and a two-beat rest. Max, stunned, sat on the floor shaking his head. You dumb bastard! It was Abelson out of his seat and rushing to Max's side. He helped him to his feet. Look what you did, you hit him. Without a shred of remorse, Dan Asher said, That's right. Abelson was outraged. He cried, Slug him, Max. The dealer gingerly touched his fingertips to his left cheekbone and, gazing at Asher, shook his head. You're a sick man, he said. You might drop dead at any minute. I can't hit you.

Mona was tugging at Dan's arm. Come on, she urged, but Dan stood there catatonically and refused to budge. He was looking at his knuckles, at the brown smudge on his knuckles, and grinning. Mrs. Abelson's romantic buccaneer wore pancake makeup. What's the matter with you? Mona whispered. Are you crazy? I would never have told you if I . . . There were times, he had to admit, when he thought of himself as a Woyzeck rushing through life like an open razor. He wondered if perhaps he really was as crazy as some of the evidence seemed to suggest.

Dear Mona. Her eyes rarely showed such uneasiness as they did now, and the mascara only heightened it. He wanted to stroke her curls, tell her everything was going to be just fine. He could see that he had embarrassed her, perhaps even endangered her job. The trustees demanding to know who brought the clown? How did he get in here? And, of course, professionally speaking, he hadn't done himself a damn bit of good either. The whole thing from start to finish had been wrong. And yet, despite all that, why was it that he could hear nothing bad from his heart?

WEST HOLLYWOOD, MAY 7, 1967

Ouch! . . . The magazine section of the Sunday paper was open on the dinette table, propped up on half a loaf of Wheat Berry bread. A two-page spread displayed lilac-tinged vistas of the good life as lived by Ray Bradbury. . . . Ouch, dammit! Dorothy had drawn blood. A tiny ruby bead shimmered on the top of her left index finger. Placing the finger in her mouth, she sucked. A Asbury dozen light to dry eater, she announced.

Huh? said Henry. Proud Clarion had done it in the rain at Churchill Downs. At 30 to 1, Proud Clarion had ripped through the mud like a bayonet to win the run for the roses, horse racing's greatest plum, and not even two bucks on his muddy nose from Tattersall. Henry, who didn't ordinarily gamble, had decided only a few minutes earlier to place his bet on a long shot named "Rembrandt." Huh? said Henry, glancing up from the sports page.

You know, said his wife, the science-fiction writer. He reminds me of you. He doesn't like to drive either. There was always something about Ray Bradbury in the paper. His humble beginnings, his lemonade stand, his lack of formal education, his good marriage, his countless daughters, his reaction to the likelihood of a lunar landing before 1970, to Corman's *The War of the Satellites*, to *Star Trek*. This was the first time that Henry had ever heard anything about the famous writer that interested him. What's wrong with your finger? he asked.

Dorothy had been doing two things at once, reading the paper and pricking herself with a needle. Where are your glasses? he wanted to know. His farsighted wife hated to wear them. Her eyes were attractive, the clear pale green of watercolor. On the dresser in the bedroom, she said, but don't bother. I'm almost finished. Henry found the plaid eyeglass case on top of the dresser next to Jumbo. The small, gray, fuzzy dust gatherer with tusks had been her good-luck charm since college days. Henry brought the case into the sunny breakfast room and placed it before her on the table.

Wait a minute, she said. She bit off the thread and put the needle back in her sewing box. How does this look? Standing up, Dorothy removed her housecoat and pulled on the light-blue cotton skirt. The length? she asked. She slowly turned, pivoting in bare feet. Is it even all around?

She still has great-looking legs, thought Henry. No children, no varicose veins. And he probably wouldn't have made much of a father anyhow. He had always liked kids, but it was hard for him to imagine what there was to say of mutual interest to somebody under six.

Well, she demanded, what do you think? You have nice legs, said Henry. Dorothy came over and playfully mussed up his hair. Then she smoothed it back into place and said, Come on, silly. Is the hem straight or not? Henry looked down again and reported that it was.

It seemed to Dorothy that during the past year or so every time she turned around she had to be shortening her skirts because they always felt too long to her. Until now, she said, and turned to show him what she meant, they barely cover my backside. All Henry could see were the blue-shaded hollows behind her lovely knees. That's the way they're wearing them, he reassured her. Dorothy was pleased. She went inside, checked the length with sandals and heels in front of the bedroom mirror, and then hung up her skirt and returned to read the parts of the paper that he had finished.

Henry enjoyed the dinette. It was a cozy, pleasant room in which to wile away a Sunday morning. The round gold-rim eyeglasses his wife wore made her look like a Berkeley hippie. On top of the heavy Spanish sideboard, a large cherrywood saltcellar and pepper mill were the only mementoes left to him from his bankrupt past in the restaurant business. A tall glass cabinet in the corner displayed elaborately hand-painted porcelain cups and saucers. The money for her collection had come from a small inheritance left by her father, who had been in wholesale flowers. She could do what she wanted with it. Henry was satisfied that the Tattersall Service paid the bills that counted.

Good Lord! she called out. Here's another one. Somebody else against the war has burned himself to death. The forebodingly close-cropped photo on the front page showed a smooth-cheeked dull-looking young man with his collar open. She wondered if he was sane. But if he was . . . To believe so completely in something that you sacrificed your life for it. The names that occurred to her at the moment were Joan of Arc and Julius and Ethel Rosenberg. It was frightening. Dorothy was against the war in Vietnam too, but she couldn't bear the thought of the kerosene fumes and the flaming match and the billowing smoke blackening her eyes. She asked her husband, Why couldn't the boy have just sent a letter to his congressman or carried a protest sign? That's a terrible way to die. Henry briefly considered whether or not there was a good way, but it was a depressing thought and something else was on his mind. Draining his second cup of coffee, he brushed the crumbs from his bathrobe and went into the living room to use the phone.

A short time later, when he came back, Dorothy was beckoning to him excitedly. Henry, she cried, did you see this? The story was on the bottom of the front page. Somebody had stolen Newton Ward's new Rembrandt. The one we just saw this past winter at the museum. That beautiful Jacob and the Angel. It's worth two and a half million dollars, Henry! They say it was taken Friday. "The police," she read to him aloud, "indicate that they have few leads in the case and, as of now, no suspects have been named."

Dorothy showed him the paper. It's a wonderful opportunity, darling. She was sure they would need his help. Henry was not so sure. I don't know, he said. In a case this big they could bring in somebody from one of the large New York agencies. Dorothy was confident. Everybody in Los Angeles knew her husband's reputation as a specialist in recovering lost art objects. Hadn't his name been mentioned in the paper when he found the Terborch painting buried in a tin box under the porch of a house in Pasadena? Henry didn't appreciate his own abilities. All he needed was a little support. I bet the insurance company is trying to get in touch with you at this very minute, she said encouragingly. Go ahead, dear. Call your answering service. You'll see. I just did, Henry reported. There was nothing. Don't worry, dear, soothed Dorothy, kissing him on the cheek. They will.

The next morning the paper carried a follow-up story, but there were few new details. An accompanying photograph bore the caption: STOLEN PAINTING—Newton Ward stands beside Rembrandt's "Jacob Wrestling with the Angel" at last April's museum gala honoring the collector's purchase. Henry had never met Ward, only seen photographs of the man, who appeared to be a nondescript and balding sixty, your basic industrial multimillionaire. Nothing much, as far as he could see, with the possible exception of the eyebrows. Thick, black, philosophical masses, they pressed down on the outside corners of his eyes, giving him a haunted look; even on the happy occasion of the gala event he seemed to detect disaster. And he was right, mused Henry, folding his paper and trying, as he stepped out into the aisle of the bus, not to trample the large, bare, grimy feet of the blond teenager with the beach towel draped around his neck who had been sitting beside him. Beverly Glen was the next stop.

Tattersall had made up his mind that as soon as he got to the office he would make a few inquiries. If Ward's collection was covered by one of the local companies, there was a chance. He had done work for all of those that specialized in the fine arts: Aetna, Dutton, the Southwestern Group, Van Cott. They all knew that this was his sort of case.

Henry was not one of those salaried hacks working for a large detective agency which took on every prospective client who came to the door. Others could corner philandering husbands and missing parakeets. To pay the bills, Tattersall located debt skippers, vanished jewelry, senile grandparents, mixed-up kids, embezzled stocks, and occasionally handled a health disability investigation, an accident claim, industrial espionage, a juggling of the books, but his heart wasn't really in any of them. Art, for him, had the permanence of time, the dignity of museums. He thought longingly of the Rembrandt. The painting that he conjured up was in mint condition, and he tucked it away in his mind for reference.

Henry had picked up his mail and was climbing the stairs when he heard the telephone ringing in his office. Leaping two steps at a time, he managed to get to it before his answering service. Lennox Chandler here, Henry. The tenor voice was cultivated, bored. I imagine you know what this is all about. Henry said no. What's on your mind, Mr. Chandler? The Rembrandt painting stolen from the County Museum of Art, of course. Newton Ward happens to be one of our clients, explained the Vice President of Dutton Insurance. We'd like to avail ourselves of your services, Henry.

The private investigator indicated that he would take the case, and from the other side of the line came an audible sigh of relief. Very good, Chandler said. Excellent. And I assume our financial arrangement will be the same as in the past? By and large, agreed Henry, but there's been one change. To the usual per diem plus expenses, he was now adding a surcharge of a dollar a day for health insurance. As a self-employed worker, Tattersall was not eligible for any of the low-cost group plans.

Is that okay? he asked. Chandler said that it was. But I should think, he added, that given the hazards in your line of work no company would be particularly eager to offer you coverage. Henry said nothing. He rather enjoyed the romance of the dangers of detection, and no one would believe the truth anyhow.

The last thing that Lennox Chandler told him before hanging up was a Russian proverb. Remember, Henry, better the live hen than the dead fox. Go gently, he advised. As you know, we're prepared to deal. It was understood that Dutton would prefer to settle with the thief rather than capture him. A ransom was a hell of a lot cheaper for the company to pay than the full value of a policy. I'll be in touch, promised Henry. He was well acquainted with the rules of the game.

PART VI

OAKLAND, 1976

77. THE DEATH OF THE HORN
PLAYER
Los Angeles, 1965
Paper, pins, match, seashell fragments,
cloth on cardboard
Size: 8½ × 11 inches
Coll. Miss Marissa Asher

*On the stage, the bare bulb glares like a flaring match and casts
shadows into the devastated theater. The balconies are blacker than
burned fat. Piles of large jagged fragments of plaster fallen from the
ceiling cover the empty orchestra seats. Abandoned coats, bags,
shoes litter the wake of the fleeing audience. Can it be possible that
there has been only one victim?*

*The French horn player is dead. His body lies stretched out in
formal dress on the floor of the orchestra pit. Sewn on his chest is
the number 1. The candles at his head and feet are twin pinpricks of
light in the gloom. With his beard immaculately combed and his*

face in repose under dark glasses, he seems merely to be resting during intermission. He cradles his horn in his arms.

Two women, in gowns of philharmonic black, embrace and attempt to console one another. On her knees, a music lover from the audience gazes adoringly at his face. Many other women have also refused to leave the theater. They hover about the body with hands outstretched in grief or covering their faces. It is as if Liszt had died. Caruso. The members of the orchestra encircle the mourners like the black rim of a volcano.

Standing with the musicians is another French horn player. Sewn on his chest is the number 2. He wears dark glasses and also has a beard. Perhaps this is a fashion among horn players, or the two men are related. In the dangerously crumbling building, there would hardly be a question as to the cause of death if not for number 2's expression. The secret of my art, it seems to say, is spite, self-pity, and revenge.

VENICE, JANUARY 17, 1967

Marissa and her friend Doreen had discovered the Holy Unity Mission on Rose Street, only a few blocks away from Market. More specifically, they had discovered the Reverend Bruce Valentine. Bruce was tall, slim, blond—a Viking sea captain with sky-blue eyes, fair skin, a manner so inspirational that even oarsmen with blistered palms would have beat the sea white for him. At twenty-nine, Bruce had decided that he could do more with his life than cut wood in an Oregon lumberyard. He had come to California to see what else there was and three years ago opened the Holy Unity Mission in Venice. It was devoted to Jesus as a revolutionary teacher and to good works in the community.

The two idealistic young girls believed in good deeds. They hosed down the sidewalk in front of Bruce's mission, put in flower boxes near his door. The prostitutes who worked in the rooming house across the street complimented them on the geraniums. But not too much water, one of them had cautioned. My mother's died from too much water. Together with Bruce, they had cleaned out the rubble in the adjacent lot, hauling away bags of empty wine bottles and garbage. A California jay shrieked on the telephone line above them, his blue frock tail twitching, his gray vest swelling with alarms. Bruce kicked at a clump of weeds, and the cat went scurrying. He worked bare to the waist, humming Good day sunshine, good day sunshine, and when he happened to glance up and saw Marissa watching him attentively, he said goof-off and laughed.

She was fifteen now. Her straight hair golden like her mother's, a heartstopping plunge of sunlight. The hoop earrings had been given to her on her fourteenth birthday by Mona. She had always seemed older than she was because of her self-assurance, but it was not until the past year that her short skirts revealed legs that were more than transportation. Reverend Valentine had noticed. He asked her about herself, her family.

Marissa boasted of her father, whose work was in the Museum of Modern Art in New York and who, the year before last, had taught at UCLA. Bruce had never heard of him. Dan's a good artist—she jumped to his defense—but he never got the breaks. He could've been really big. Like Picasso or Goya. What was that last name? he asked. Marissa was relieved. Bruce was wonderful, but he didn't know anything about art.

Here, Doreen said to him the minute they opened the arched wooden door of the mission. Another Help Our Neighbor campaign was under way, this time a Mexican-American family whose shack on Cabrillo had burned down. Doreen handed him the folded patchwork quilt. She wasn't claiming that she made it all by herself, but she wasn't denying it either. Marissa informed Bruce that they had worked on it together every chance they could. Do you like it? she asked.

In the background, the muttering of George, the caretaker, grew richer, more conspiratorial. He waved his finger menacingly at the broken chair he was trying to repair. You got to be straight, he shouted. You got to be straight with Him or else. You cannot fool around with God. George! called Reverend

Valentine, and George, as if awakened from a deep restful sleep, went innocently back to work. Sick but harmless was the popular diagnosis. I don't want to go to a nuthouse, he told the Reverend, and the Reverend had taken him in.

The patchwork quilt was made of red, brown, tan, and gray squares, some of which had been sewn on crookedly. Bruce ran his fingers over the squares. He had lost the tips of the middle and index fingers of his right hand to a circular saw in a lumberyard accident. Nailless, they were sealed at the ends like sausages. The amount of work that had gone into the making of the quilt was impressive, and he thanked them both. Returning it to Doreen, he told her to give it to George.

Bruce asked Marissa how they had made it and she explained. As the late-afternoon sun poured through the Rose Street window of the mission and hot flakes of scarlet and gold reflected in his eyes, he listened to every word. When she was finished, he took her hand. Thank you, he said gently, and Marissa was thrilled by his stumps in her palm.

WEST HOLLYWOOD, FEBRUARY 26, 1966

Dan Asher wore a light woolen ultramarine sweater, stuffed his hands in his pockets. He was as much interested in holding his parts together, in not banging into anyone in the crowd, as he was in warding off the mild breeze. His deep blue sweater was torn at the elbows and seemed large on him, droopy at the bottom. In the two months since his heart attack, he had lost weight, the sideburns were definitely grayer now, and there was weariness beneath the eyes. Arnold Skolnick, a young photographer who had visited his studio on several occasions, told Dan that he looked better than ever. There were, thought Dan, easier ways to improve one's looks. He smiled wanly, winked, thanked Arnold for his kindness anyhow, and resumed his inspection of the Peace Tower.

Di Suvero's sculpture was made of tubular steel that formed the skeleton of two intersecting diamonds, a wide one at the base and a long one aloft that appeared to shoot skyward. Dan Asher rather liked the soaring effect. Max's friend, Webber, had provided the Tower's high-visibility location. His lot was on Sunset near the point at which La Cienega—the main street of L.A. art galleries—rises up toward the Hollywood Hills to intersect with the Strip.

A political liberal, Webber was happy to let them use his property for their peace demonstration. He was also a good businessman. The painters Bill Copley and Bob Rauschenberg advanced the rent money. Dan Asher applauded their generosity. Shaking his denim pockets, he heard the thin, sheepish clink of pennies. They could afford to be generous, he thought wistfully. That year they were selling like Zig Zag papers in head shops, like short skirts.

Although Dan wanted to end the mindless, escalating war even as much as Mona did, he didn't care to see one of his older works auctioned off to do it. He had too few of them left as it was, and he badly needed the bucks himself. The Santa Monica Hospital's bookkeeping department had recently broken out in a rash of dunning letters and phone calls to him, perhaps suddenly fearful that they were dealing with permanent red ink. Dan Asher knew that someday these early works would once again be worth a great deal of money. His insurance policy for Marissa, he called them. Gloomy thoughts under the mask of comfort.

Sad, too, was the sight of the small, delicately blue-tinted window of the *Hotel California* crushed between the other works twice its size that were to be auctioned. Displayed on the huge wooden billboards behind the Tower were paintings of death and doves and mushroom clouds. A dollar bill bore a portrait of Ho Chi Minh. Again and again the words STOP and PEACE and FEAR and WAR appeared, the letters in blood red, bone white.

Posters, he sneered. They were merely posters disguised as paintings. That life's transient political surface occasionally produced great art was no doubt true. He could think of Daumier, of Goya's *Third of May, 1808,* of Picasso's *Guernica,* but for his own work all that mattered was what went on beneath the surface in the basement of the human heart.

He had completed the *Hotel California* in 1958, the year before Madeleine's death. Of course the naked adolescent girl gazing out at the world from the hotel window wasn't Madeleine, but there was that same curious combination of toughness and vulnerability he had loved in her. Flashing in the sunlight, the tiny pieces of cracked mirror in the collage cheered him up. It was a good piece of work to have done, and, despite the chill of the scissors of Atropos recently nuzzling his string, he was still alive to do more. He congratulated himself on his durability. Champagne for everyone in the house!

Irving Carp handled the bidding, and it opened briskly. The Ho Chi Minh dollar bill was knocked down for over six hundred dollars. A collage with the headline LBJ WAR TRIP and the word "canceled" stenciled across it sold for almost as much. Works were going quickly and for good prices. Dan Asher watched as the art dealer Bunelli, intent on the proceedings, took a pack of cigarettes from the pocket of his black suit. He watched him light up and, carelessly flipping the match to the ground, lip the end of his cigarette, drag on it, let the smoke loll from his pink tongue, then blow it away. The hell, thought Dan, no one lives forever.

Sure, Dan, sure, replied Bunelli, handing him the pack. Help yourself. It wasn't a Gauloise, but the comforting sensation of the paper tube between his fingers and the familiar acrid taste in his mouth made him feel less anxious. With any luck, he figured, the *Hotel California* could earn as much as a thousand bucks for the peace movement. Even seven fifty wouldn't be too shabby. But five hundred was definitely rock bottom. Below that he'd sooner pull his piece out of there. Dan took another drag on his cigarette, a deep one this time that made him feel woozy. He knew there was absolutely no way that he could withdraw now without looking like a fink.

On Sunset, the traffic crawled past, with drivers rubbernecking to see the crowd that had gathered and what they were up to.

Dan spotted the Toyota pickup and a chill, fluttering black wing touched a corner of his heart.

In the open back of the small truck was a full load of Hare Krishnas. Their shining heads swung around to look in his direction. Their gaunt, stocking-mask faces appeared resolute.

Where did you get that? It was Mona, her gleaming velour blouse an emerald jewel box. She had no intention of telling him what to do. Just surprised, she said. If Dan wanted to go back to smoking, that was his business. She pulled the hair away from her eyes the way she always did when she was angry. Dan was touched. He felt guilty, too, and tried to be honest with her. He explained that he was a little upset, a little worried. It was just then that the dramatic baritone of Irving Carp announced, Dan Asher and his *Hotel California*.

The bidding began at fifty dollars. Then sixty. Sixty-five. Irving Carp was incredulous. Dan Asher, he reminded them. *Dan Asher,* for crying out loud! This is good people and great art. One of America's most original makers of collage. Come on, friends, what do you say for peace? Two hundred, called out the guy in the soiled tee shirt with the hawk emblem. Well, *that's* more like it, approved Irving. Now who'll make it three?

Not long afterward, Dan Asher's *Hotel California* was reluctantly hammered away for two hundred dollars. It's a steal, fumed Mona. A lousy out-and-out steal! And did you see who got it? Dan tried to lift the weight from his chest, breathe evenly, show her—Bunelli—the lot of them that he could still roll with the punches. Hawk, she cried, and raised her eyebrows in disbelief. He can't afford any two hundred dollars. He can't even afford to change his shirt. You know how he's always broke, always bumming money from anyone he thinks is a soft touch.

Only two hundred. Dan felt crushed. He pulled nervously on one of the torn woolen threads at the elbow of his sweater. That's why, he thought, trying to cheer himself up. It was different from the others. There was nothing there about the war in Vietnam. It contained no message of outrage or hope. In fact, no message at all.

Maybe he's been doing acid, said Mona, or sniffing glue. Dan Asher slowly shook his head. No—he slipped his hands back into his pockets—no, he must be fronting for somebody. Mona looked surprised. She hadn't thought of that possibility. Dan wondered who it was. Don't worry, said a confident Mona, intrigued by the idea. I'll find out.

SANTA MONICA, JANUARY 5, 1967

The air on the Santa Monica Pier was hot and damp, the January night tropical. Dan and Mona stood near the closed fish-and-tackle shop at the far end and leaned over the metal railing. Below, out of the darkness, the waves unrolled like sliding snow. Loosening her shawl, Mona agreed that they would not stay late at the party. He wanted to get back to work early the next morning, and for her there was still Friday to go at the museum. Miles's idea for a Twelfth Night party was great, but unfortunately it fell on a Thursday. Typically, her boss had been weak on details.

They walked back past the seafood restaurant, through whose large porthole window they could see empty tables and a small, quiet group of drinkers bent over the bar, past the pinball arcade, past the snack stands that sold snow cones and candy apples and hot dogs on a stick, past the shooting gallery where a teenage Chicano squeezed off a round at Donald Duck as his three companions cheered. Donald, hit, whirled like a bobbin. *Hey!* All *right, vato!* shouted one of his friends. You dreeel that *pato* right up the ass.

The merry-go-round was at the very beginning of the pier, a sprawling, ramshackle, two-story, mustard-colored building dating from the turn of the century with fresh red trim around all its doors and windows. On the second floor circling the carousel were three or four unusual apartments. Miles Dorfman had one of them. Unable to live elegantly on his museum salary, the curator had chosen to be original. The shrill whistling sound of the organ drifted across the wooden planks and faded innocently into the night. Dan Asher wondered how he managed to put up with the noise. Compared to this, his back-yard oil pump was Harpo Marx.

This way, said Mona, pulling him down the alley between the entrance to the merry-go-round and a closed store that sold plastic statues. On the side of the mustard-colored building, the wooden stairway leading to the upstairs apartments had high risers and narrow treads. It seemed to ascend endlessly, forebodingly. Dan Asher stopped to catch his breath. On the landing above him, Mona opened the door, and a blast of "Great Balls of Fire" exploded, Jerry Lee Lewis wailing lewdly out of control. *You shake my nerves and you rattle my brain. Too much love drives a man insane. . . .* Come on, Mona called to him. This looks like fun.

The music was deafening when he stepped through the door, and the narrow room rocked with twisting bodies, dancing feet. Dan felt the wooden floor sway beneath him as if it were a temblor. Instantly, he checked the hanging plants. He had experienced dozens of earthquakes since moving to Southern California in '59—the big frightening ones roaring down on him like the D train to the Bronx of his childhood, the mild ones registering a mere three or four on the Richter scale that were nothing more than a gentle nudge—but, large or small, each one had the uncanny knack of catching him with his defenses out to lunch. As usual, he was well prepared when it was nothing. The plants hung motionless.

Miles, surrounded by a small circle of his guests, was greeting Mona on both cheeks. He had recently returned from Paris. Amused, Dan Asher watched him place each kiss like an official wreath. Although Mona thought well of her boss and he seemed nice enough, Dan found it hard to believe that there were some who regarded this young kid as Mr. Suave.

Dan! Dan! came the excited cry. The young woman pounced jubilantly on him as if she knew he would be there and had been lying in wait. It's Florence, she told him. You remember me, don't you? Of course he remembered her. She had been a student in the one class he taught at UCLA before he was canned.

She reported that she had left school and had a studio of her own now, and she had taken his advice about scale. It was curious, he thought. No matter how much his students had insisted on doing things their own way, on the unique value of their own youthful vision, they still treated every word that came out of his mouth as if he were Jesus Christ.

She asked if he liked the music, if he liked to dance. I've been sick, he explained. Writing down the address of her studio, she gave it to him and he promised to visit and meant it, but somehow he didn't think that he ever would.

Some people he knew were talking about backpacking, and he joined them. Billy Correy had just returned from hiking in Death Valley and was telling about going into an outhouse at a ranger station near the Nevada border. No sooner did I drop my pants and squat, he said, than I saw it coiled in the corner, just flicken its rattles and licken its chops.

The painter John Altoon, who had a handlebar mustache almost as long as his own, introduced him to a stubby, middle-aged man with short blond hair and the look of a decadent colonial administrator. He had had something to do with the making of the terrific Alec Guinness movie *Kind Hearts and Coronets*. Uh-uh, the man blandly corrected him, his index finger a wobbly metronome. *Man in the White Suit.* He was wearing a beige suit himself and a tie that hung dissolutely to one side.

I didn't get the name, said Dan Asher. The man's mouth opened and closed like a fish. It's Nancy Marmer! shouted Altoon over the music. A striking young woman with long, glistening corkscrew curls turned around to see who it was, her right eyebrow cocked superciliously. She wore a short blue-and-white-checked dress with a high mandarin collar and, though Dan Asher had never met the West Coast correspondent for *Art International,* he thought her dimpled knees adorable. Altoon kissed her, told her how much her review had meant to him, and added quite sincerely that she was the only critic who seemed to understand what he was doing.

208

Wow! It was the fellow standing next to Dan Asher. His name was Richard Webber or Weaver, but it was hard to think of him as having a last name. Dan recalled somebody having mentioned that he was a printmaker. His clothes were one long tourniquet squeezing his body from head to toe. Art critics! Richard said in disgust, and emphatically threw his hip forward. That really does put a pall on things. Removing the silver comb from his shirt pocket, he ran it through his shoulder-length hair and, wheeling about in the opposite direction, marched off.

Candiece, Billy Correy's girlfriend, leaned toward Dan and slipped her arm around his. Max Roth, she whispered. Her bad breath was still the same. He didn't really find it unpleasant, just surprising given that childishly sweet voice. He assumed that she wanted to turn him on and find out the real story behind what had happened at the County Museum party, and he had no wish to perform for her. Candiece was into vegetables and pure water and good dope and, best of all, she loved a conspiracy.

After mumbling something impossible to understand, he asked her about Jack Ruby. Oswald's killer had died only two days before of cancer. Oh, sure, cancer! Candiece laughed derisively. Sure that's what they said it was, cancer, a natural death, but do you have any idea *where* he died? Dan knew, but it turned out to be a rhetorical question. Her theory was that the doctors at Parkland Memorial had murdered Ruby to keep his mouth shut. And you know about the changes that they made in the Kennedy autopsy report, don't you? Although amused at her predictability, Dan was maybe a little annoyed at how pantingly eager she was to perform herself.

Mona rescued him. She came over and wanted to dance the slow number. The Beatles sang of changing my life with a wave of her hand. Marissa, he knew, would have approved. It seemed as if it had been ages since he had last danced. His sneakers, luckily, were so worn on the bottoms that he could glide. Mona danced with her eyes closed and he held her close, his fingers spread wide across the graceful small of her back. She moved easily, following his every twist and turn as if they were pasted together. She was humming along with the music.

The room was warm, all the windows wide open and gaping for air. When the dance was over, Mona suggested going upstairs to cool off. She led him up a small flight of stairs to the top of one of the building's four corner towers where, from a lighthouse of windows, it was possible to see in all directions. The flat band of beach, the undulant white line of waves, the black slab of ocean on this moon-dark night. There was a door that opened out onto the roof, and she held it open for him. How many times, he wondered, how many times had she been here before?

That such a thought should have occurred to him made her lover feel like a peeping Tom. What business was it of his how many times she had been here before? Of late, he had noted an increasing frequency in these shameful soap-opera attacks of jealousy about Mona. That's it, he warned himself. No more.

The smell of the salt water was pleasant out on the roof, but even here the air was heavy, still, close. Above them only a few stars were visible—pinpricks of light in a black wool sky. The music that filtered up from below was a muted mixture of the Beach Boys singing "I Get Around" and the carousel organ playing *um-pa-pa, um-pa-pa.* In the darkness, a couple danced to their own music. Walking across the roof with Mona, he nearly tripped over another couple stretched out making love. Sorry about that, he apologized, and stepped more gingerly.

You can't see it tonight, she said, but Catalina is right over there. And back up this way is Point Dume and— I can see *you,* he said. His husky voice sounded like that of a stranger. He placed his hands around her damp young body and drew her toward him, smelling the perfumed soap she used, the powder. You're quite beautiful, you know. Mona had been trying to show him something, and she didn't care to be interrupted. Come on, Dan. She gently pushed him away.

Neither one of them realized how close to the edge they had been standing. Off balance, he took a step backward, and when he placed his foot down there was nothing there. Dan! she screamed. *Dan!* Catching her hand, he just managed to pull himself back. He could feel her cold fingers trembling in his grasp.

You know, he said—he leaned back over the edge and looked down at the nearly empty parking lot behind the merry-go-round, a sheer three-story drop—somebody could get killed up here. Idiot! shouted Mona. You idiot! He was touched by her anger, touched by the look of concern he saw in her face and by her sudden passion to get him off the roof and back down on the dance floor.

Downstairs, Mona said she preferred to wait for the next slow number, but Dan wouldn't hear of it, refusing to be handicapped by a damaged heart. He enjoyed dancing and was still pretty good at it. What he didn't know, he would make up as he went along. Mona, familiar with most of the latest steps, was a terrific dancer, her movements flashy and commanding. Dan tracked the beat like a cardiogram. He tried to set the patterns, anticipate her moves, keep in step. She spun around in her thigh-high skirt and he spun too, they stomped, shuffled, and together snapped their fingers one, two, and on three the music stopped. It was wonderful. Dan's chest hurt him, his ankles ached, and he thought that he had better find a place to sit before he fell down. He squeezed Mona's hand and gasped, wonderful. . . .

He sat by an open window, his weary legs stretched before him, and with a crumpled tissue dried his forehead and was wiping his chin when the little guy came over. Hey, you're not giving up already? You're *good,* man. Dan Asher felt a warm glow that someone had noticed. I bet, said the little guy, there was a time when you could really jitterbug.

The artist took in the runt with the shag-rug vest. This was pure admiration but nobody he knew. The fellow gazed on him as if he were a relic from one of the heroic periods in the history of the dance, shook his head in wonder, and, turning to Mona, seized her firmly by the elbow. Let's dance, he said. Give the old champ a breather. Mona said all right. Removing her shawl, she left it with her boyfriend.

Giving up? mulled Dan. Old champ? He decided that he had better keep an eye on this little bastard.

"Good golly, Miss Molly," shouted Little Richard, electrifying the room with sexual urgency, and Mona and the runt leaped into the music. Dan Asher could tell immediately that he was good, very good, and together they were something special. This was dancing that went beyond keeping time to the music, beyond precision. They moved effortlessly in a linked chain of dizzying ins and outs, somehow knowing without looking exactly where the other was as if they had danced together for years. They appeared simply to give themselves up to the rhythm, letting it take them wherever it would, with no necessity to think about the next step because they each seemed to know that it would be there and that it would be right. Smiling. The two of them smiling as if in wonder at themselves and what was happening to them and Mona's face aglow with a patina of sweat and pleasure.

For the moment, Dan Asher lost sight of the little creep in the hairy barbarian vest. Watching the dance unfold, he thought of how sometimes when he was working on a collage things would fall into place that way and his hands would be guided by some wonderful inevitability beyond the rudiments of composition and the discipline of form, a whispered secret from all the artists who had ever lived (prodding him to check the corners of his studio to see who else was there), a gift of magic that made him want to jump up, kick his heels, and clap his hands.

The clapping hands, however, were not his. They belonged to some of the Hollywood crowd. Two sinuous young men whose hair had obviously been styled by the same barber—no sideburns and shaped to resemble a hubcap—were encouraging one of their friends. She was doing a solo. The dancer, a medium-size chubby, looked thirty and was probably seven or eight years younger, but it was hard to tell given what she was wearing. A large floppy straw hat, a brown checked shirt that hung out over a baggy and poisonous pair of purple terry-cloth shorts, magenta knee socks and, strapped to her feet, gray Mary Janes that were flat as flagstones. It was sartorial bad taste that almost achieved

212

the level of art but, falling short, struck him as pathetically vulgar. The woman minced about in a circle before her clapping admirers, arms outstretched like a glider soaring on a thermal high, totally mellow. She didn't seem to have any idea that she was making a goddamn fool of herself. Unwilling to take any more of this travesty and unable any longer to watch the perfection of the little pro and Mona dancing together without wanting to cut in—cleaving his head with a meat ax—the artist went to get a drink.

The conversation was about art. Irving Carp arguing excitedly with Billy Correy while their host looked on noncommittally, and Dan was thinking that maybe it was time to go home. Ain't politics, Correy had said, and it ain't religion. Art in L.A. is the cool school. He had spoken negligently as if the point were self-evident, and Irving had choked on it.

Small but tough, Carp was a street fighter who knew where to kick the Drum Gallery stud. Fag art, he insisted with a twisted smile, only fag art turned its back on society. The muscular Correy studied him narrowly, rolling the cigar around in his mouth, and seemed to be considering if this was a nervous breakdown. When Correy turned to Dan Asher for his opinion, Dan said, I was just leaving.

Dan gave the approaching Mona her shawl. He could see that she was exhilarated from the dancing, bubbling over with words, laughter. She took his wineglass and finished what was left in it. Resting her lips on the rim of the empty glass, she was still lost in the music. She beat time to it with her sandaled foot, tapping out the exciting promise that she might soon return to the dance floor with one of her admirers. Miles obviously thought it was a wonderful idea, but before he could volunteer, Correy had her by the shoulders and was laying out a view of art from the Drum Gallery window. He was the sort of speaker who anchored his listeners with his hands to prevent any drifting away. Mona erased the tiny diaphanous beads of moisture from her upper lip and, having heard him out, suggested that there was some work by L.A. artists that she regarded as *too* cool, *too* plastic, *too* removed from what was happening in the real world. Vietnam. Racism. Irving beamed his approval.

Dan Asher said, Crap. With neither bitterness nor edge, his composed voice was fit for a shrine. The artist's job—he was talking only to her now—is to make worlds, not change them. He waited for her to say it, to tell him once again of the irrelevancy of his small gaudy fairs in an unhappy universe. Upset though he was, he knew perfectly well that his disagreement with her had nothing to do with art.

They stared at one another in silence. Her soft green eyes had turned rock hard—precise jade targets flecked with steel. Dan Asher felt such an immense wave of rejection sweep over him, crush him, that his chest heaved for air. The upbeat music in the background smashed him in the ears, poured down the walls like blood, congealed in his heart. Hey, you two, said their host with forced joviality as he took them both around, remember this is a party.

Mona's dancing partner was back for more. He fluffed up his vest like a preening rooster. Dizzy with desire, he asked her, How about it? His voice, his entire manner presumed the intimacy of a long, close relationship. She looked at Dan Asher and said, Will you hold this? He might have been a cloakroom attendant, her tone gave him so little. It was nevertheless something, and he took the shawl, folded it carefully, then, dissatisfied, unfolded it and tried again. The shrimp tapped his thick boot heels rhythmically on the wooden floor. Grinning at Mona from ear to ear in anticipation, he led her away, saying, Can't can't can't, just can't get enough. . . .

Miles hurriedly began to talk about Paris. He described the delightful little-known hotel in the sixth where he had stayed that had chamber music in the lobby plus fresh chrysanthemums every day, the terrific restaurant that he had discovered, the best way to go from the Louvre to the Marmottan by metro. He talked quickly, enthusiastically, full of his subject, making many colorful observations, subtle distinctions, his eyes closing on the choicest recollected pleasures. Bored, Billy Correy left. The shawl folded in Dan's arms held most of his attention. Like a flag given to the family of the deceased at a military funeral, it was all he had left of his love. He decided that it was time to get the rest of her.

Mona bloomed before him on the dance floor, an elusive Fragonard blur of soft blues, soft greens, and her lips, her cheeks the warmest pinks in the spectrum. It's getting late, he pointed out to her. Let's go. Breathlessly, she said, Not now. She was enjoying herself and didn't want to leave. He recalled other times he had seen the pulse in her neck throb excitedly as it was throbbing now.

I'm going, he said. Laughing as she whirled about, Mona seemed perfectly willing to dispense with him. He fleetingly toyed with the idea of telling her that he wasn't feeling well, but he had too much pride for that. Aren't you coming? he asked, his heart caught by the light in her bouncing curls. Don't be a drag, she said. If you want to leave, go ahead. I'm in no hurry. I can get back by myself, you know. Stomping and whirling as he brushed by Dan, Mona's partner cried, One side, champ.

At the door, Dan Asher looked down and found that he was still holding her shawl. He pushed past the back of somebody in a tight striped shirt outside on the landing. The voice was sincere and trembling with eagerness. You really must—it was Richard, the printmaker—you really *must* come. Dan noticed that he was talking to Nancy Marmer. He took the stairs to the roof two at a time. Throwing open the door and rushing to the edge of the roof, he hurled the shawl away as if launching a rainbow, a glowing emerald and amber and orange javelin to pierce the heart of the night. Nobody paid any attention to him.

He was tired, drained, and as he came downstairs his legs felt stiff, leaden. The party had spilled out of Miles's apartment and taken over the merry-go-round, drunks and potheads racing one another draped across the charging wooden horses. Stark white, glistening black, salmon pink, the animals lunged forward with their frenzied eyes, their mouths asthmatically agape. The sign above the ticket booth said HAPPINESS IS A RIDE ON THE MERRY*GO*ROUND.

Glumly, Dan Asher stood there looking at them carrying on, his mind elsewhere. He was remembering another carousel and the man who ran it, whose mouth was an alien, exotic, long-ago land fragrant with garlic and wine. The crank man. He was the engine that made it turn. On the back of a truck near the park of his childhood was the wire mesh cage that he climbed into and the circling horse that he sat on like a throne as his sister watched anxiously from the curb, and shouting, waving, tried and failed to catch his eye. That was a time, it seemed to him, when everything wheeled in. The coziness of cages and strong leather straps that snugly buckled you in place. Now his life was threatening to spin off into the void.

At first, he thought the shrieks were coming from inside the building. A keening sound. It shot up above the organ whistle like a frightened bird. There were shouts overhead. Footsteps thundered down the stairs. The roof, someone yelled, she's fallen from the roof! Dan reached into his pocket and found a dime. Outside at the public telephone, he discovered that the phone book had been ripped off. He called information, got the number, and then spoke to the Santa Monica Hospital, told them to send an ambulance.

Although he had a lot of faith in the hospital that had saved his life, he pictured the drop from the roof to the asphalt parking lot below and figured not a chance, no way. Whoever it was that had fallen from up there was finished. Suddenly he knew beyond a shadow of a doubt that it was Mona. Up on the roof with the punk as soon as he was gone. His body went from hot to cold and back again, his hands broke out in sweats. A madman was at the controls, playing hysterically with his thermostat.

He raced between the buildings down the alley, forgetful of his weary legs, his sneakers thudding *dead dead dead*. The dim parking-lot lights cast blue shadows over the group huddled around the body. Those closest to it seemed to hold their breaths as if guarding a secret.

One of her feet lay shoeless, motionless, twisted beside a crushed candy-striped straw, a shriveled corncob, an empty bag of Fritos. Nearby he found the shoe and picked it up by the strap, turned it in his hands, a Mary Jane. From the middle of the crowd, a shout went up, She's alive! She's still alive. Somebody call an ambulance.

Fortunately, the woman in the purple shorts had suffered only a broken leg, a broken arm, a few cuts and bruises. Had she not been loaded and loose, thought Dan Asher on the way home that night, the ambulance attendants would have had to collect her with an eyedropper. She was lucky. She had been insulated for survival.

But once home, he himself had no desire to be similarly insulated—numbed out of his heart. In the kitchen over a cup of tea, he sat and waited to see her come in the door, to feel her tight within the circle of his arms. He was sorry about the shawl but he would go back tomorrow, check the parking lot, look under the pier. If it didn't turn up, he'd get her a new one. Glancing at the wall clock—a plastic cherry-red coffeepot with a missing spout more interesting than its presence would have been—he made small bets with her, swearing not to be pissed off if she showed up within the next fifteen minutes . . . the next thirty. His anger, in fact, had long ago burned itself out.

A little after five in the morning, he was awakened by the sound of talking. He was still sitting in the same place, still dressed the same way, his chest nailed to the kitchen table, his elbow bent beneath a wet cheek. He raised his head and looked expectantly toward the front door, but the sound was coming from his daughter's room. Marissa was talking in her sleep. She had been doing that recently. And Mona still not back. Oh, he knew that she could take care of herself, but he was worried about her. He hoped that she wasn't alone. He got up, took a drink of water, and walked around the house feeling very much like a stranger, like some prospective buyer who peered into corners looking for flaws. Except for Marissa's room, he turned on every light in the place, and then, having done that, went back in the kitchen to wait.

(from the Dutton/Ward folder in the
files of Henry Tattersall)

Interviewed: Dewayne Taylor
Place: Security Control Room (LACMA)
Date: May 9, 1967
Comments: Taylor is 32, married, no children.
Has worked for museum security since new
buildings opened in '65. Well respected,
though called somewhat of a loner by other
guards. Good on-the-job record. A smooth Sid-
ney Poitier type, but appeared edgy at the
interview as if he had something on his mind.

1. Sure. Like you, Tattersall, just doing my
job, just earning my bread and butter. May
number 5, Friday P.M., I was right here where
we are now, which is where I was on Thursday
and Wednesday and Tuesday and . . . Sorry, man,
I'm getting just a little frayed. A little
tired of all these bullshit questions everybody's laying on me. The cops and the people
upstairs in the big hats putting a lot of
heavy pressure on, a lot of nasty stuff coming down. I just tell the story like it happened. Like I'm telling it to you. And you're
right about alone. This is a one-man operation in here, and last Friday afternoon I was
your man.
2. It works like so. Nobody comes through the
Ogden Avenue door without talking to the box
and getting buzzed in from here. Once in, the
party got to pass this window and this gate.
The gate stays shut until we know who's who
and what's what and there's clearance from
upstairs. See this sheet. All five columns
have to be filled out. No one leaves the SC
room without signing in and setting down the
time they arrive and who they going to see
about what. And no one sees nothing without
wearing one of our official-visitor badges
like the one you got on. *But no one!* Which is
what I don't understand, and believe me I been
bustin' my head over this thing. How the hell
could some guy slip in that door, float by me
like a cloud in sneakers, come out haul-

ing three feet of oil painting, and get clean away without my seeing him? Now you tell me that.

3. The sheet says 4:38 and the sheet don't lie. Mr. Dorfman was leaving for the day, and he had a visitor by the name of Asher with him. When they get here and are signing out, this Asher remembers that he left his umbrella back in the office. Mr. Dorfman tells him sure, go ahead, the door is open. Mr. D and I have what you call rapport—both being Libras—so he waits here with me and tips me to some one-hundred-to-one sure thing he's backing in the Derby. Dewayne, he says, would you believe a gold mine? I don't care for the horses, but I like Mr. D, so I listen politely and don't let him see what's tickin' inside my head. Less than two minutes go by and Asher's back with his umbrella. Frankly, I don't like the man. First time I seen him the night of the big party for Mr. Ward we had a little run-in. I file him away as a wise-ass, blue-eyed joker, so when the man goes by I look him over hard from cap to can. He was clean, Tattersall, clean as a mint.

4. That's because of the packers. They still down the end of the hall in their workshop hammerin' up the crate. Ten minutes later and it's done. Then they go to pick up the picture in Mr. D's office and it's out to lunch. After that, man, all hell breaks loose down here.

5. No, they don't. Not his or any of the offices. The TV covers all the public galleries on the fourth level and the third level and the plaza level and the first. And you can see up there on screen number four how good they are. Some things you won't believe. Look at that old man in the corner of Prints and Drawings polishing his zipper. But down in this area where you get mostly your private offices, the cameras monitor just the main corridor and the members' lounge and that's it.

6. They're from Cal-Cool. They fixing over our central air conditioning. Yeah, they were

here last Friday, the three of them, working
out in the hall. Leave? Let me see. The sheet
says they knocked off work at five-o-seven
that day and the sheet don't—Sure I checked
their toolboxes on the way out. Man, you
don't think I'm that dumb, do you?
7. Me? You got to be joking. I never budged
from this place. That's my job, Tattersall,
to guard the family jewels, and that's just
what I was doing. . . . Why you lookin' at me
that way? It's the truth, man. Look here.
Here's the Friday sheet, and from Dorfman and
Asher through Crespi at five there's someone
signed out every two minutes. How the hell
could I have moved anywhere even if I wanted to?
8. What about Mr. Dorfman? Okay, that's it.
I've had it with you, Tattersall, You know,
man, I'm only human. I make mistakes just
like white people do. I'm no robot. So before
I go and mess up again, my advice to you is
pack in the questions, because I got to tell
you I'm worried. Right now it looks to me
like your karma ain't worth a fuck.

OAKLAND, 1976

DANIEL ASHER: Collages 1943–1967.
The Oakland Museum, 1976.
Introduction by Mordecai Bell.

Arriving in Southern California, Asher settled in Venice. He
liked its permissive atmosphere, the other artists who lived in
the neighborhood, and especially the cheap rent. For the forty-
three-year-old New Yorker, California was a revelation. "This is
it!" he wrote back to his dealer, Hans Külicke, soon after moving
west. "The place where the sun goes when it disappears behind
the Crisco sign on the other side of the Hudson. I love it!"

A darker response to his new life can be found in the artist's
work of this period, which became increasingly violent. The

220

collages in his series "Major Disasters" are replete with scenes from California newspapers of fires, explosions, mud slides, earthquakes, and freeway pileups. Undoubtedly, their grimness owes much to Asher's recent personal tragedy. What they owe specifically to California is their imagery.

If we encounter incongruity in these collages, it is never there for easy, startling effects. If—despite their violence—we are moved by the works in this series, it may be because the artist himself is moved. Asher reveals a deep compassion in *7.6 on the Richter* (cat. no. 39) for the woman sitting in the middle of the deserted street on a dining room chair, her stockings fallen, her legs limp, her face red with tears. He shows genuine affection for his vulnerable little white birds in *Boy on Venice Blvd.* (cat. no. 35). When in 1960 the "Major Disasters" were first exhibited at the Maxwell Roth Gallery in Los Angeles, they were received by knowledgeable West Coast people with enthusiasm.

I regard the artist's next series as central to an understanding of his vision. Furthermore, "The Museum of Crime" contains some of his most disquieting and compelling images. Terror is rolled in a carpet or hidden under a seaside pier. And nowhere is the menacing power of silence made more explicit. Evil exists, Asher assures us, just beneath the pedestrian surface of things.

VENICE, MAY 12, 1967

The house next to the old church that Asher lived in was a pink stucco shack with a cracked porthole in the front door. Someone inside was playing a trumpet. Tattersall thought it was the sweetest trumpet that he had ever heard. The sound floating out was seamless perfection, a miracle from which hung crepe streamers above the Hollywood High School gymnasium floor. Nostalgia had offered up her lovely young face, and Henry kissed it flush on the lips. Gone was the rubble of Market Street, gone the squashed cans, the garbage, the broken bottles of Ripple and sauterne. Harry James was playing "You Made Me

Love You," blowing that big, open, craving tone that could break your heart if you didn't have Mary Lou Fuller in your arms at the sock hop, and sheer enchantment if you did. On the sidelines, Henry held his breath and watched adoringly as this luscious ghost from his past performed a no-nonsense fox trot with Johnny Di Rico, the class hood, who always wore black socks.

He waited until the music was over and then knocked. He had to knock several times before anyone came to the door. Sneering out at him, an unshaven face filled the porthole window, the cracked glass villainously scarring the man's double chin. The name on the mailbox was Robert Sloan. Henry was about to try Bob when the door was thrown open.

The man with the trumpet in his hands was short, burly. He wore a torn grease-stained undershirt that held his paunch like a membrane. Except for his shorts, he might have been a sanitation worker or a fireman. It was obvious to the trained eye of Tattersall that the long, baggy, grayish-blue Bermudas he wore belonged to the post office. Was that you playing? inquired Henry.

You, the man said disdainfully. You disturbed my practice session. You realize that, I hope. He was not at all happy about being interrupted. Are you Bob Sloan? asked the poised investigator.

I may be unknown, but that doesn't give you the right to barge in like this. Who do you think you are, Governor Reagan? What sort of right-wing, power-mad, barbarous age do we live in? The world's greatest trumpeter torn from his work. Mark my words, my cheeky friend, one day Sloan will be known.

Henry told him that he liked the music. I see, said Sloan. You're not a complete blockhead after all. "You Made Me Love You"? Henry wondered aloud, hoping to hold his interest. No, no, the musician quickly corrected him, and in a voice as true and sweet as his trumpet sang, If I fa-all in love, it will be for-ever. . . . The Lettermen cut that goldie for Decca. Mid-fifties. Now, what the hell do you want? And make it quick.

Henry revealed that he wished to ask a few questions. One of your neighbors wants auto insurance from us—Western Auto of Glendale. Merely a routine check. It will only take a few minutes. He opened his memo pad to a fresh white page.

A few minutes! cried Sloan. Don't you realize that in a few minutes Armstrong and Condoli and Davis could be gaining on me? Ha! But they'll never catch up. They've got plastic lips like on dolls. Toneless bunglers, the lot of them. Henry said that he was sure Bob wanted to help his neighbor, and equally certain that Mr. Asher would be grateful for any assistance Bob might give him. Asher? said the surprised Sloan. Asher. Why didn't you say so? Shoot.

Tattersall handled the interview that followed with his usual skill. Throughout he kept the tone of his voice mechanically flat, never tipping his hand, never pursuing a question to the point of alarm, never showing the slightest surprise at an answer. By the time the interview was over, Sloan actually seemed to be almost enjoying himself. His neighbor Asher had so many solid qualities.

Unfortunately Asher was a head, a dope fiend, a hopeless hasher and drag-racing degenerate with an inexplicable way with the ladies. But they wise up, he said, expatiating pleasurably on the theme. I suppose you know that the gorgeous young woman he was living with walked out on him. And then his own daughter. But naturally since his heart attack last year he's become a new man. Oh, yes, I'd say he's a wonderful risk. I heartily endorse his application.

A woman in a yellow bikini suddenly appeared behind Sloan. What is it? she said. No doubt she had just stepped in from the back yard where she had been sunning herself. The tan she had was incredibly deep, radiant, total. Her body seemed to glow from the inside out. What is it? she asked Sloan. What does he want?

A mistake. Wrong number, he said, pushing Tattersall away from the door and slamming it after him.

Henry was surprised. He bent over and picked up his pad from the sidewalk, tucked it away, then straightened his jacket. He had no idea what was going on. He had been thrown out of better places than the Sloan house, so that didn't especially bother him. It was something else. Why, Henry asked himself, why had the world's greatest trumpeter been bullshitting him?

Hello? That you, Dan? . . . Yeah, right. Look, I thought you should know. The FBI was nosing around here a little while ago asking questions about you. Just what the hell have you been up to lately? . . . Ho, ho, nasty, nasty. Vicious. . . . Sorry, old swinger, but the truth is it's your auto insurance. Some putrid cockroach from the company was asking if you were reliable. Reliable? I said. Shit, he's the Bank of America. That okay, Dan? Did I do all right? . . . What do you mean am I sure he wasn't from someplace else? Hey, look, the lip's getting cold. I've got to get back to my horn. . . . Sure, anytime. You know how we artists have to stick together. Keep middle-class scum in the bag. . . . Brenda? Oh, yeah, he said, unconsciously adopting the flat, noncommittal tone of the professional investigator, I'll do that.

VENICE, FEBRUARY 22, 1967

Brenda Sloan was an athletic-looking woman in her late thirties who took care of her body as if it were a limousine: washing, creaming, polishing. Every night brushing her short, honey-blond hair hundreds of strokes. Every day out in the sun.

She was most comfortable wearing a bikini, and Brenda seemed to have a different one for each day of the month. They came in metallic shades of copper, silver, bronze, and gold, in dark coffee and bright lime, in tiger stripes and leopard spots, in prints, solids, and iridescent rainbows. When dressed to go shopping, Brenda always seemed to have a gaping zipper, a seam that had sprung open, a button missing or undone. She was the sort of woman who kept popping out of her garments as if she couldn't wait a second to expose her skin to the sun. Inadvertently, she also showed it to the entire neighborhood.

Living next door, Dan Asher could hardly not have noticed. She was stretched out in the adjoining back yard practically all day, every day, even in the frailest of sunbeams baking her parts. Turning her body slowly, voluptuously, this way and that, she toasted every inch of her flesh like a modern St. Lawrence. Dan concluded that she was indifferent to skin cancer, to prying eyes, to boredom. Occasionally she would raise her head, eyes half closed, and catch him watching her from behind his kitchen window. Clutching her open bra so it didn't fall off, she would wave. Her tan was exquisite the year round.

Not having any children of her own, Brenda had grown fond of Marissa. Marissa, on her part, was no more than lukewarm. The young girl had over the years dropped by the Sloan house to trick or treat, to collect for hearts or lungs or hungry children, to search for lost tennis balls. In general, Brenda never had much to say to her on these occasions and almost nothing when sunbathing, as if she were too busy concentrating on the rays.

I don't know what to talk about with kids, she one day confided to Dan Asher. I'm a body person. Her husband, Bob, could talk to them forever. But then he's a trumpet person, she said, and they're more outgoing. That was Sloan, all right! In a neighborly way, Dan Asher had once praised his schmaltzy rendition of "I Can't Get Started," and Sloan had pumped his hand until it was numb, wrapped him in a hug. Outgoing, said Brenda, but basically insecure. That's why he's in the post office. You know how hard it is to be a serious artist today. It was never easy, thought Dan Asher, but it was not the sort of thing he cared to discuss.

He also had nothing to say about Mona. Mourning her loss, he turned the lights off in his studio where he had been working all night and stepped out into the sunny back yard. Brenda wanted to know where Mona was and hoped she wasn't sick. No, not sick, was all he would tell her. Brenda looked at his tired, unhappy face. Here—she handed him a plastic bottle—rub my back.

Although her self-involvement was staggering, the pleasure she took in her body was not uncontagious. Turning over, she revealed the high breasts so prized by writers of historical romance, small boyish hips, a childishly immature chin. Her pale gray eyes looked as if they had been bleached by the sun. She whispered, Bob doesn't get home until four. Dan Asher suggested that they go inside. Only on rainy days, she said.

Brenda believed in the outdoors, and that's where they made love. Whether they were on the beach or in her back yard, she insisted on being massaged first. She might have been a world-class athlete receiving a preludial rubdown before competition. He felt like her trainer. She fucked as if records were involved, medals to be awarded. What's that supposed to mean? she wanted to know when he asked for an autograph.

After massaging Brenda for two solid weeks, Dan was beginning to feel even lonelier than he had when Mona first left. Brenda was so self-absorbed. Together they heard the radio's warm, sunny forecast for Thursday, the twenty-third, and Brenda casually mentioned that tomorrow he would find her on the beach. That is—she stroked the blond hairs on her dark forearm and stretched—if you're still interested. By now he was familiar with her laid-back California ways. There was no reason to think that she had any idea how he felt.

It was a little after one the next day that he finished work, and putting on his faded blue boxer shorts—the only bathing suit he owned—he headed for the beach. A neighbor, Mrs. Zimmer, stood in front of her house in slippers and a housecoat as big as her house. A gray plastic bag covered a head full of pink curlers. She was holding a broom, wielding it viciously, mowing down everything in her way: the front path, the sidewalk, her neighbor's bare feet.

Careful! said Dan Asher. She gave him a sour look and reported, *Mrs.* Sloan is on the beach, if that's who you're after. He thanked her and walked on. Nosy bitch, he muttered.

The beach was more crowded than he expected for a school-day in the middle of February. A few yards from the water, he found the bikini he was looking for. It was strawberry this time with Brenda barely inside, her eyes closed, her limbs dead as driftwood. He dropped down on the blanket beside her. Once again, he was immediately struck by the pathos of his whiteness against her mahogany. She raised one eyelid and then lowered it. Hi, she said and, handing him the plastic bottle, turned over onto her stomach.

They soaked up sunbeams all afternoon and finally went into the water. He was reluctant at first but she coaxed him, swore that it wasn't cold at all. Then why are there so few people in? he wanted to know. She splashed him, pulled him by the arms. It really wasn't so bad once he got wet and they had wrestled a bit, thrashing about like seals. Playfully, he grabbed her between the legs and discovered that she had removed the bottom of her bathing suit. He removed his own. There was no one near them in the deep water, only a few distant surfers off to the right where there was no sandbar. He stroked her ass, ran feathery fingers over the warm folds between her legs. Bobbing up and down in the choppy waves, their bodies brushed tantalizingly up against one another. He tried to hold her still and slip inside, but it was impossible. Threading a needle in the dark would have been easier. How about the sandbar, he suggested, and she agreed.

They swam out until they could feel the sand under their feet. Dan Asher sat down in the shallow water and Brenda, facing the shore, sat on his lap as if in the driver's seat. She squirmed about, and suddenly he was hard as a board and thrusting inside her. Brenda went *ah!* She moved heavily up and down, a slow tidal motion. Dan could feel his body responding to her thick, sluggish, heaving sensuality.

But Mona . . . Mona in his arms had been quicksilver, as graceful as smoke. Her lovely legs wrapped around his or sprawled in abandon. The wild joy of her beauty showering him with its youthful glories, its tender strokes. Her laughter, arpeggios of delight filling their room. The whole world had been in his arms then, in his bed. Oh! cried Brenda, caught off guard by his passionate rhythm. More!

Was this mental detour a betrayal of Brenda? Of course it was.

He pleaded innocent. A human being addicted to memory. And furthermore there was no evidence that Brenda minded at all. In fact, she seemed quite happy. She cried More, more, more! her arms churning the air gaily—Brenda signaling the sky okay. Glancing up, he spotted the gulls flocking home to the sea as they did every evening at cocktail time. It was later than he thought.

What the hell are you doing? he asked in amazement. She cried Don't-don't-don't stop. That's it! Ooooooo! She oozed down on him like a mud slide, and it was all over. Dan wondered if she remembered that there was somebody in the back seat. They really had so little in common—an alley between houses, a mutual admiration for her tan. By way of reminding her that he was still around, he asked ironically, Who were you waving at? My husband, said Brenda. He's there on the beach. I've got to go.

Dan Asher gazed beachward and sure enough, there he was in his long shorts, his collarless blue-gray short-sleeve shirt, his double chin, his paunch. So what if I'm in the same ocean as his wife, he thought. It's a big place. There's enough water for everybody. Brenda said, Don't be silly. What are you doing? He was sticking his head in the water. Come on, Dan, he's seen you. You're no ostrich. Shut up, he told her, and help me find my bathing suit. He found it and put it on.

As they came out of the water, Brenda waved to her husband and called innocently, What time is it anyhow? Sloan didn't appear to see her. He had a blank look on his face as people sometimes do in front of an ocean.

VENICE, MARCH 4, 1967

Bruce asked her to come live with him, and Marissa, in love, said yes. He didn't seem too old to her at all. She was sure that once she explained the situation to Dan there'd be no problem. She would tell him all about Bruce, make him know Bruce the way she did—his positiveness, his sincerity, his always having something good to say about people, his efforts to turn things around in the world, his kindness—make him understand. Don't worry, she told Bruce. I know how to talk to him. He's not a bourgeois father. He's an artist.

It was important to Bruce that Mr. Asher see that he wasn't a pimp or a pusher or a religious fanatic. Bruce said he'd do his own talking. Marissa didn't think that would be such a good idea. She said, He doesn't like to be bothered when he's working.

When isn't he working? Bruce wanted to know. Marissa could think of no stories that she had ever read in which a messenger was put to death for bearing good news, but she knew as if the future had been slipped to her like the correct answer to an examination question that his going was a mistake. Okay, he said. Come on.

Dan Asher had found a chunk of cheddar in the refrigerator and, cutting off the white mold, made himself a sandwich. This was breakfast at half past three in the afternoon. He had had a backache Friday evening, not been able to get to sleep until sometime early Saturday morning and only just now gotten up. He thought he was feeling wonderful, but it was still too soon to tell. The Dijon mustard tasted better than the cheese. His legs crossed, he sat barefoot at the kitchen table, in a shrunken tee shirt and blue track shorts that had turned gray with age, and munched, absentmindedly rubbing the callus on the heel of his foot. Sandals. He was thinking that he had to do something about the bottom of his sandals when Marissa came home accompanied by a tall blond guy with beads. His first impression was a Swedish masseur who specialized in Beverly Hills house calls for aging stars.

This is Bruce, she said. Bruce Valentine. Dan Asher reached for the proffered hand and it went through his fingers like a ribbon. The guy was big, but he had nothing to do with muscles. Dan Asher wondered who this Valentine was and how he knew his daughter. Marissa hadn't wanted to complicate the matter just yet by mentioning Bruce's title. Although her father spoke well of the religious impulse in art, she knew that he regarded organized religion as the worst. Group virtue, she had heard him say, being even duller than group vice. That coffee smells good, she told him. Going to the stove, Dan offered them both a cup.

Bruce emptied his ceramic mug in silence, put it down, and declared himself minister of the Holy Unity Mission on Rose Street. We run the thrift shop on Speedway. In the near future, we hope to open a free clinic for the entire Venice community. I wanted to tell you about this so that there'd be no misunderstanding. I love your daughter and she wants to come to live with me. Dan Asher calmly said, I had no idea. Despite the love beads and the huaraches, the guy was old enough to be her high school principal. Isn't she a bit young for you? he inquired.

Marissa didn't give him a chance to answer. Look how much older you were than Mona, she reminded him. Her father's eyes narrowed in warning. The difference should have been obvious even to a C− in mathematics. Mona, when they met, was in her twenties and on her own. Marissa was still on the green side of sixteen. He felt sullied at the thought of having to go through this in the presence of a stranger, wearied to have to defend himself at all. That was different, he told her. She demanded to know what was different about it. Dan Asher had never spanked his daughter, wouldn't dream of it, but occasionally he had a strong urge—as he did now—to boot her in the can.

With a wave of his hand, Bruce swept away the question of age like crumbs from a table. The only thing that mattered was that they loved one another. Her father agreed that was important. Remember, Asher, he told himself, no ultimatums. She'd never stand for that now with him here to beat her offended heart into a frenzy. His best bet was to manipulate the creep, stall for time. Above all, keep cool. He mustn't lose his head, or he would undoubtedly lose his daughter.

What else do we do at the mission besides sell old clothes? Amused rather than put out by the breezy tone of the question, Bruce repeated it good-naturedly. The issues themselves, however, were no joking matter, and his strong commitment to them deepened his voice as if he were entering a combat zone. First of all, he began, we're working to eliminate the harassment of aliens by the thugs from the Immigration Service. Then there's our counseling. We advise young people on draft resistance. Marissa—he glanced at her proudly—would like to start a small nursery for the children of working mothers.

It seemed to Dan Asher that his daughter was hardly more than a child herself. Perhaps she had caught it from Mona, this love of causes. We've got a problem here—he cleverly hinted at an alliance. You realize, of course, that Marissa being under legal age presents certain difficulties. The police, the courts. . . . Valentine said, There'll be no hassle with the fuzz as long as she has your approval. Dan gave his daughter a tender look. Oh, he said, she has that all right. I love Marissa. I don't own her. But how can I let her go? I promised her mother that she'd finish high school first. It was all that occurred to him, but fortunately he could lie with feeling, on his face the conviction of a psychopath.

Marissa couldn't believe her ears. You never told me. . . . She closed in on Dan. Gretchen never—

Hold on, interrupted Valentine. That's no sweat. Stepping between them, he took his girlfriend by the shoulders. You don't have to live here to finish high school, he pointed out to her. She can do that anywhere, he told her father. He had dispatched the problem the way a bear solves a beehive. Dan Asher hated the possessive way he held her, despised his smugness, the tutorial tone, the ugliness of those blunted fingers which for the first time he noticed, and he understood then the glancing handshake.

Let her talk, he insisted angrily. With the approval of Marissa's eyes, the Reverend Valentine declared that he was speaking for both of them. You—Dan tapped him on the back and, predictably, Valentine turned—you've said about enough. If he hadn't felt so mean, so greedy for destruction, he would never have done what he did. It was a sucker punch. He went for a roundhouse right, total devastation, a Big Bertha that would splatter him across the kitchen walls like hot fat. Seeing what was coming, Valentine brushed it aside like a windblown lilac branch. He was surprisingly quick. The thought flashed through Dan's mind that this Valentine was in outstanding shape for a man of the cloth. It was his last thought before a wicked left hook–right cross combination dropped him to the kitchen floor.

He sat there feeling dazed and a little sorry for himself. He had scraped his bare knees, his jaw ached, and there was the taste of blood in his mouth. Valentine seemed to want to help him to his feet, and he pushed his hands away. The clergyman was trying to apologize to him for losing his temper, for not turning the other cheek, no doubt afraid that the injured party might report him to Jesus. There'll be no forgiveness for you, Valentine. Dan Asher had already filed his black star. The Reverend's image of himself as a good-deed guy had apparently been tarnished and, unable to bear the scene of his crime, he told Marissa that he'd wait for her outside.

Are you all right, Dan? Marissa was bending over him, stroking his head. He moaned bravely and kept his mouth shut, hoping for the best. Perhaps now she'd see that this paladin she planned to move in with was nothing more than a sadistic gorilla. I'll be right back, she said. He regarded that as a good sign. He anticipated a cold compress and two aspirins.

The sounds from inside, however, were ambiguous. Why was she rummaging about in her bedroom? Then he remembered the elastic bandage that she kept there for bike riding. Would it, he wondered, stretch long enough to cover all of his internal injuries if she should actually leave him? Out of the blue came a vision of Valentine that was unexpectedly comforting, the impatient gorilla cooling his heels at the curb suddenly pinned beneath a sanitation truck that had lost its brakes. It hurt Dan Asher's face when he smiled.

When Marissa returned, she was lugging her small overnight suitcase with two hands, her back bent like a bow. She put the suitcase down as carefully as she could and it shook the floor. Pulling out a piece of paper and a pencil from her shoulder bag, she wrote something down and placed it on the kitchen table. I'm leaving a number where I can be reached, she told him. Then she kissed him and said, Goodbye, Daddy. Lifting her suitcase, she shuffled toward the front door.

You're not really going? His question was a thread of glass that hung between them, binding them momentarily together. Then it snapped. You'll forgive me, she said. You love me, and I know you will. Wait! he called to her, but by the time he had pushed himself up and gotten unsteadily to his feet, she was gone.

He took the phone number from the table. Wanting to tear it to bits, he nevertheless folded it carefully and put it away in his pocket. The pencil stub she had left behind was all chewed up, completely dented with half-moons and craters. She had never gotten over that nasty habit. How like his perverse daughter that she should have a mouthful of beautiful teeth. In her bedroom, the only things that Marissa seemed to have taken were her records, her bikinis, and Oscar, the stuffed poodle that Madeleine had brought back from Montreal where she had been performing.

Dan went into the bathroom to try to get the taste of blood out of his mouth. The inside of his cheek felt as if it was badly cut. He rinsed his mouth with warm water and, straightening up, glanced at himself in the mirror above the basin. Externally there didn't seem to be too much wrong with him other than a large bruise on his left cheek that would shortly turn black and blue. It was nothing serious, but it was enough to tip the balance. Suddenly big tears began to roll down his cheeks, and his face cracked into a million pieces.

WEST LOS ANGELES, MAY 12, 1967

It was late afternoon by the time Tattersall got back to the office from Venice. Sullen, smog-filtered sunlight claimed the L-shaped room, mocking Monet's luminous effervescence in the poster on the wall. Henry, feeling hungry, pulled open the refreshment drawer of his desk. The only thing he could find there to eat was an old box of Armenian cracker bread. The crackers had probably lost their snap after a year, but the sesame seeds still looked okay. Popping a cracker in his mouth, Henry lifted his feet up on the desk, leaned back, and glumly munched a dry Armenian wad as he thought over the situation.

A week had gone by since the disappearance of the Rembrandt, and as yet there had been no ransom attempt. No anonymously muffled phone call, no sealed envelope containing secret instructions, no dull-witted go-between—not even a false alarm. Whoever the thief was, he had made good his escape without dropping a button or losing a thread. The prints the police found on the frame in Dorfman's office had turned out to be either those of the curator himself or smudged. Having gotten away undetected, the fellow was plainly not now going to be rushed into error. Tattersall acknowledged his adversary's patience, loathed his good luck.

The time had come for his own luck to take a turn for the better. It wasn't some booming, loud-mouthed voice deep inside that swore to him, You're next, Henry, but a modest recognition that he could use all the breaks he could get. Even the now-famous Van Cliburn, he had read, while preparing to go out to play the "Rhapsody on a Theme by Paganini" in the finals of the Tchaikovsky piano competition in Moscow, had the soothing sensation that he was being helped on with his coat by a beaming Rachmaninoff. Henry sifted through what he had just learned from Sloan. Buried beneath that mound of steaming bullshit, was there some cool nugget of pure gold that he had missed?

For instance, what about Asher's heart attack? Perhaps that at least was true. On a hunch, Henry pulled out the telephone directory for the Western part of the city and made a list of hospitals from the yellow pages. There were ten in the area. Playing percentages, he began with the ones closest to Venice. Saint John's was first. Saint John's told him they had no record of an Asher. Next was Santa Monica Hospital, and on only his second try, he hit the jackpot.

That's right, he said into the phone. Dr. Henry Tattersall. He had awarded himself an honorary degree. He liked the official, matter-of-fact, money-making sound of it, and so did the woman in billing. Oh, yes, doctor, she snapped, up on her hind legs and wagging her tail.

I have a patient, Henry explained, a Daniel Asher. The man had a coronary episode last year and was in your hospital, but he can't recall the name of the attending cardiologist. I'm trying to get in touch with him about the case. It was one final errand of mercy in bone-tired tones at the close of another grueling day in the life and death business.

Of course, doctor, said Billing. And the patient's name again? He gave her the name and the address on Market Street. In seconds her computer had discovered the man, exposing him in one swift, soundless green line after another. That's Daniel No-Middle-Name Asher at 24 Market Street in Venice zip 90291 Attending physician Dr. Morton Felstein, that's F-E-L-S-T-E-I-N, Santa Monica. And by the way, doctor, the next time you see Mr. Asher we'd be grateful if you'd ask him when he intends to pay his bill.

The alert investigator dove through the telephone and pounced upon the news as if it were the stolen painting itself. Henry said, What?

His bill, doctor. He still owes $2,910 for the twenty-two days he spent with us in January of last year. I see eight in our coronary unit at $210 per day and two weeks in a semiprivate room at $90 per day. Doesn't he have any health insurance? asked Henry. Dorothy had assured him that nowadays everyone had health insurance.

No health insurance, she reported, and since he's 12-29-16, which means under sixty-five, and not on welfare and not blind or disabled, he's not eligible for the new Medi-Cal program either. It looks here as if we did receive ten dollars a month from him for the first three months following his release. At that rate—Henry could hear her mumbled lightning calculations —he'll be finished paying us in 1990. That is if he's still alive. We've turned the case over to a collection agency. I'd keep my eyes open, doctor, she warned him before hanging up. I think he's a deadbeat.

Henry hoped so. Money made sense to him. At this relatively

early point in his investigation, he was still operating under the good-natured assumption that the party who took the Rembrandt was sane. Should the thief be a nut it might take years for the painting to surface, if at all. Henry dreaded to dwell on how many glorious one-of-a-kind works of art had been sadistically ravaged, turned into pen wipers and shoe rags since the dawn of time. Even the *Mona Lisa* had been taken by a crackpot. Its rescue unscathed in December of 1913 in Florence was comforting, but it was saved only by the merest chance. The painting had been pinched in 1911 by an Italian housepainter, the mad Vincenzo Peruggia, who spent the next two years in bed with the enigmatic woman arguing violently. The frightened neighbors said that there were times when it sounded as if he were about to cut somebody's throat.

All ancient recorded history, but only five years after that theft in 1911 came Asher. Tattersall had not thought of him as fifty. For some reason he had assumed a younger man from what Sloan had said about Asher and women. In a way he felt sorry for the fellow. Henry had had only the vaguest idea of how expensive it was to get sick in America these days. And Santa Monica hadn't even included Felstein's fee in the $2,910 bill. A debt that size was no easy thing to be burdened with, even for a young man with lungs like a whale and a heart like a valentine, let alone a middle-aged invalid. No doubt it weighed on his mind terribly. Here was no maniac, but an ordinary guy desperately in need of instant cash. If Asher was the one who took the painting, there wasn't a thing to worry about. Very soon now he was either going to try to sell it to a private party or attempt to arrange a museum buy-back. It could happen tomorrow. The next day.

As it turned out, Henry had a week more to wait, but the call finally came.

PART VII

OAKLAND, 1976

54. RAIN ON DON ZAREMBO
(The Museum of Crime)

Los Angeles, 1961
Paper, cloth, string, hair, thread on card-
board
Size: 4⅛ x 5⅛ inches
Coll. Mr. Leland Sonderman, Los Angeles

*The horse-drawn carriage waits at the curb. It is raining on Don
Zarembo Street, gray threads of water slanting in the cold wind.
The driver huddles on the box, head down and shoulders hunched
against the rain. His shabby bowler shields his face. The horse
stands dripping in the street like an old awning, his head lowered
submissively. The door of the coach is open, the driver ready for
instant departure.*

*Across the way, a woman in a dark coat hurries along, her head
buried in her umbrella. There are no other passersby. The buildings
on this quiet residential street are two- and three-story red-brick
structures in the Georgian style. No one seems to be home. The*

trees that line the sidewalks are winter bare, their hairlike rain-blackened branches making a delicate tracery against the gray sky.

A hulking figure comes down the stairs toward the carriage. He carries the heavy rolled rug on his shoulder as if it were a bolt of dimity. A black rain cape covers his body. A black trilby hides his face. There are gloves on his huge hands. He has tied the long brown cylinder in the middle to keep it from unrolling. The blond head of a man can be seen inside. It is impossible to glimpse his face, impossible to tell if he is alive or dead. Behind the fleeing figure's back, the door of the house is locked, the windows closed, the shades all drawn. There are no witnesses.

LOS ANGELES, MAY 5, 1967

It was on an impulse that he went in. He had passed the museum more than once since the night of the party at Miles's place. He had been sure that he would run into her and had even gone to a couple of openings on La Cienega that he thought she might be at, but she never turned up. When he called the museum, she spoke to him—the faraway voice in the telephone receiver making counterfeit dream sounds that might have been hers if he didn't know any better—but she wasn't interested. Romantic unpredictability had lost its charm. Gone out of fashion. She called it neurosis and a bore. Past tense, said Mona. Forget it.

He left the car downstairs in the May Company parking lot so that the inside wouldn't get any wetter than it was. The worn canvas top of the MG was a semipermeable membrane. Crossing the street to the museum, he saw himself as a Whistler study in gray and black, the loneliness of a single figure with a battered umbrella against the flat sheet of rain. Somebody had forgotten to shut off the fountains in the reflecting pools out front, and the blowing spray from them filled the gaps between raindrops. By the time he got inside, he was soaked.

Dan Asher wrung out the bottoms of his dungarees, ran a hand across his face, through his hair. Mona Block, he told the security officer, as if it were the most natural thing in the world. The black guy inside the glass booth seemed to place him like a toothache. Dan, said Asher, Dan Asher, and the guard grimly picked up the phone and dialed. She wasn't in. Dan pulled out a blue pack of Gauloises, popped one into his mouth, and lighted up. A vision of disaster had become so vivid to him that it was almost a relief to have another chance. Oh, by the way, he said to the guard. It was a casual request from an old friend for Mona's home telephone number. He straightened out his sweatshirt and tried to make a good impression. Dewayne Taylor said no. It was against museum rules, and that—turning his back —was that.

Apparently driven from his office by the noise of the workmen in the hallway, the curator came storming out. Three guys in white coveralls emblazoned Cal-Cool lounged on top of their ladders and tried to make time with the secretaries passing below. Cooing like pigeons. Dropping screws. Their dirty laughter flagrantly blue collar. Miles made a sour face and asked them to *please* keep it down, people were working. They said sure thing.

When he heard Dan Asher call and saw who it was, Miles seemed not to recognize him at first—a heartbeat of indecision —and then hurried over. Dan, he cried, what are *you* doing here? Good to see you again. Jesus, you're soaked! It must be pouring out there. I've got some paper towels in my office. Come on, we'll get you dry. Dan Asher looked in vain for a Red Cross sticker pasted to his forehead. He was overwhelmed by Dorfman's geniality. Hold on, ordered the security guard, and before the visitor could get away, he was badged.

Miles led the way past the crates, around the ladders, the file cabinets, the desks, the pyramids of rolled posters with their colorful rubber bands. Watch your step, he called, and explained that on top of everything else that day, they were moving their public information people from one office to another. How's it going, Trish?

Hands on her hips, the redheaded Trisha Wiley stood in the doorway surveying her new quarters. Chaos, she groaned, absolute chaos. Then she saw Dan Asher behind him. Oh, hello. . . . The icicles hung from her words as if painted by Lichtenstein. He guessed that she didn't approve of his slugging Max at her gala. It didn't go with the flowers, the dessert. When she arrived at his place the weekend after Dorfman's party to pick up Mona's things—her clothes, her dog, her mail, her books, her radio alarm clock—Trisha Wiley seemed overjoyed to have her friend out of there. But Mona wasn't entirely gone. Every so often something would turn up, a recipe taped to the inside of a cabinet door, a cork from a champagne bottle, the box from Alvarado Street that had held her twenty-fifth birthday shawl—precious fallout from the comet that had raced through his life.

You can leave your wet umbrella over there. Miles indicated the stack of acoustical tiles in the corner of his office that had been peeled from the ceiling by the men working on the air ducts. Sit down, sit down, he said. Don't mind the mess. It's not always like this. He apologized with a laugh and gave Dan Asher the paper towels he had promised.

Wiping himself off, the artist wadded up the used towels and tossed the ball at the wastepaper basket beside the desk. Miles said, I want to ask your advice. Bending over, he picked up the paper towels and placed them in the basket. That's what I want to ask about, he said, seeing Dan Asher studying the Rembrandt. It inclined against the wall and seemed much larger to Dan here than it had upstairs the night of the gala. He hadn't noticed then that dark rock in the shadows with its diamond glint of light.

Miles explained that *Jacob Wrestling with the Angel* was on its way to the Art Institute in Chicago for a big Rembrandt exhibition. They were making a special crate for it down the hall. The advice Miles sought was about the article he was doing for *Art International* concerning the influence of Rembrandt on certain contemporary painters. He described what he had in mind.

Dan thought it was a good idea. You can't leave Rembrandt out of the picture, he said generously. Miles was pleased to hear it . . . very pleased. He respected Dan Asher's opinion.

The artist got up. There was a small photograph on the wall, and he went to have a closer look at it. No bigger than wallet size, a single rose in a thin vase, the edges of the image soft as a child's slipper, the muted surface a taupe veil. The diminutive silvery-sad world of the photograph spoke to him of his departed daughter in whispers and tears. Miles revealed that it was a platinum print by Outerbridge. An ex-New Yorker like you, he said, who settled here in Laguna Beach and kept pretty much to himself, too.

The *too* came out like a concealed weapon, annoying Dan Asher and making him squirm. He lit up another cigarette and tossed the match into the air. The incredulous curator tracked its glowing downward arc, pinpointing the gray corpse on the carpet out of the corner of his eye. Controlling his irritation, Miles asked, Are you familiar with his work? Of course Dan was. Outerbridge's photograph of the Ide shirt collar on a chess board had for years hung in the studio of his friend Duchamp. That's right, said Miles. You've known Duchamp for a long time, haven't you? I keep forgetting how old you are. Dan wondered what it was that was troubling Dorfman, warping his charm, mangling their relationship.

The curator had more to tell about Outerbridge, and Dan Asher listened to him without comment, at ease in the comfortable leather chair, glad to be smoking again so that he didn't have to say anything. When Dorfman mentioned Dan's own work, the artist was instantly on guard. How's it going? the curator wanted to know.

Presented with an opportunity to discuss his new collages, he ordinarily would have grabbed it by the throat, but here and now he wasn't sure. Fine, he said. It was a clipped *fine,* an impersonal *fine,* a single word razored out of a newspaper, giving away nothing while at the same time promising something of value that was being withheld. The artist was rather pleased with his self-restraint.

Mona told me that you were no longer doing abstract things. Dan Asher thought he detected a genuine interest in his work. Dorfman spoke of Dan's earlier, more figurative periods, and his specific knowledge revealed the possibility of an enthusiast. Perhaps he was sincerely interested.

It was almost, Dan confided to him, almost as though I could do too much too easily. With only abstract forms, things became too simple, too geometric, the texture too smooth, and finally for me there was never enough to work against, to confront. Right now my world's fairs supply what I need, the figures, the colors—He broke off. It wasn't that there was any indication the curator had lost interest, but suddenly he came to the conclusion that he had said too much, exposed too many secrets. Miles expressed the hope that he would be able to come by the studio after he returned from New York and see the new work for himself. Dan Asher hoped that he would, too, but didn't believe it, and refusing to believe it was ashamed of himself for the pathetic way that he nevertheless desperately clung to the possibility.

I was looking for Mona. The artist couldn't have sounded more guilty if he had been confessing to a crime. It was ridiculous. He tried to sound indifferent. Will she be back this afternoon? Miles said that Mona wasn't coming back. Poor kid, she's exhausted. He explained that she had been helping to set up the big Century Plaza protest demonstration on the twenty-third of next month, and the Angry Arts candlelight march the night before, and—he chuckled—doing a few small things for me on the side. Together they were putting together what he believed would be the most important retrospective exhibition yet held of drawings, paintings, sculpture, everything, of the man who during the '40s and '50s probably influenced art in L.A. more than any other single individual, Rico Lebrun.

Rico Lebrun! The very name attacked Dan Asher like the bite of a tsetse fly causing a drowsy numbness to seep through his limbs. The museum trustees loved Lebrun. They were nuts about real human suffering in a style so glib that it was painless.

I told her to take the day off, said Miles. She's home.

Hesitating to seem too eager, Dan Asher waited for Miles to reveal where home was, drop some clue, but he didn't. They looked at one another, the repressed question a long, polished dining-room table with the two of them seated at opposite ends. And that's not a bad idea, he said, getting his raincoat from behind the door and straightening one of its many English flaps. I'm going home too. There was little chance of getting any more work done on his essay that afternoon with all the noise in the hallway, and he would be leaving for the airport in a few hours anyhow.

Hold on a minute, he suggested to Dan, and we can leave together. He went outside to tell his secretary that he was going home. Dan Asher zipped up his soggy gray sweatshirt and took one last look at the photograph of the rose. When Miles came back, he said, Should I tell Mona to call you when I get home? He was matter-of-fact about it, but there was no doubt in the artist's mind that Dorfman did not mean that he intended to leave a message with her answering service or write a note to a mutual friend. He was going home to Mona. Dan was hurt, confused; his hands drifted into the pockets of his sweatshirt like ashes.

His expression really surprised Miles. You knew that she was living with me, he said, didn't you? Dan said sure . . . sure. He knew, he said. As they went out into the corridor, Miles promised that the three of them would definitely have to get together for dinner when he returned from the East. He didn't mind in the least telling Dan that his trip had to do with the Lebrun exhibition, but as if he had been pressed for that information, he held up his umbrella to wave away any other questions. Dan Asher couldn't have cared less. He had no interest in the museum's Lebrun show, or anything that had to do with it. Except Mona.

Didn't you have an umbrella? asked Dorfman, as they came to the end of the corridor. Distracted, Dan Asher glanced down. The front of his sweatshirt bulged farcically with his pocketed hands. He said, Oh . . . oh, yeah. I'll be right back. The door's open, Miles called after him. I'll wait for you here at Security.

245

Dewayne Taylor handed the curator the sign-out sheet with his usual pearly smile of anticipation. He liked to crack a joke with the man, shoot the shit. I see you getting a running jump on the weekend, Mr. D, he said, his irony a rubber dagger. I bet you got something heavy on tonight.

The knob turned under Dan Asher's hand, but the office door refused to budge. He slapped at it angrily, the palm of his hand striking out at all his frustrations, and it sprang open. Dan slipped inside, and the door swung closed behind him. His umbrella was just where he had put it in the corner near the stacked tiles. Reaching down for it, he scraped the back of his hand on the edge of a metal toolbox that one of the workmen had left open on the floor. A nasty white gash turned red as he watched, but there was hardly any bleeding. The stab of pain was out of all proportion to his injury. He felt such a sense of outrage at the injustice of Dorfman having everything that Dan Asher wanted that he was shaking inside.

The scrape had given him the occasion to feel his fury and the closed door the privacy to indulge it. Rage flooded his veins at dizzying speed as if something had broken. In the hallway, the sound of an argument and a provokingly loud banging door—an act of defiance that came out of his childhood. How long? he wondered guiltily. How long before someone barged in on him? Turning his back to the door, he considered Dorfman's Rembrandt. A huge hand came down on his shoulder, stern fingers clamped him to the spot as if he were not allowed to have such strong, dangerous emotions.

Have I ever lied to you, Dewayne? said the curator, turning his palm up like the past. Take my word for it, if they get rain at Churchill Downs tomorrow the way it's raining here today, it'll be Proud Clarion at thirty to one. A gold mine! This horse goes through mud the way you go through money. Dewayne liked that and was about to give Mr. D his pink-gum ho-ho-ho award when he spotted the slob in the sweatshirt coming back with his umbrella. The guard stopped him and said, I'll take that.

Unpinning the badge from his sweatshirt, Dan Asher returned it and signed out.

Miles's parting piece of advice to Dewayne was Proud Clarion winning in the slop going away. As they walked off together, he was telling Dan Asher about the horse when the guard came out of his glass booth. Just a minute, he said to the visitor.

Although he made light of it, Taylor asked him to open his umbrella. Dan seemed puzzled and said no. The guard insisted, saying he just wanted to make sure there was nothing liberated inside. Miles Dorfman frowned at Taylor, not knowing what to make of his behavior. A look of cold recognition came into Dan Asher's eyes as he returned the black man's steady gaze. It's bad luck, he wanted him to know and tossed him the umbrella. *You* open it.

WEST LOS ANGELES, MAY 22, 1967

The call had come on the previous day. Someone asking to speak to Newton Ward. The museum official who answered the phone replied that it was Sunday and impossible. I may be able to help Ward get back his painting, was the message. That is if he's still interested. Naturally Mr. Ward was interested, and the price was set at one million dollars.

Explaining all this to Tattersall, Lennox Chandler of Dutton Insurance had informed the detective that he wanted him to handle the exchange. The money, he said, will be delivered to your office in a canvas flight bag at seven o'clock tomorrow morning, and a caller will then notify you where to take it. Do be careful, Henry. No slip-ups. One million dollars is a great deal of money. The usually blasé Chandler sounded nervous, as taut as a tie rod, and when he rolled the *r* in "great," the tie rod shook. Henry had been impressed.

On Monday at seven, he was at his office. The money came two hours later. He was standing at the window, peering discreetly through the half-closed Venetian blind, when a gleaming silver-colored Brink's armored truck rumbled up to the NO PARKING ANY TIME sign in front of 766½ Little Santa Monica Boulevard. Security since 1859, pledged the truck. What the hell's going on here! Henry had given Chandler credit for at least a Volkswagen or Toyota in black with battered fenders, bad rubber, and no hubs. Why didn't the idiot take out ads in the paper if he wanted to draw a crowd? Henry didn't relish the prospect of having to defend a million cash against every early-rising amateur and semi-pro thug in the neighborhood.

Sign here, said the Brink's guard after checking Tattersall's identification. He had a jumbo, mean-looking .38 Smith and Wesson strapped to his waist that made Henry's pearl-handled .22 seem like a lady's compact. Henry lifted the heavy blue canvas flight bag and looked inside. It smelled stuffy. There were packets of twenties, fifties, hundred-dollar bills. Henry saw himself carefully counting from one to a million while the armored truck on his doorstep raised eyebrows. Where do I sign? he asked. Here, right here, said the peevish Brink's and, snatching away the signed receipt, left. Did the slammed door on the way out mean he expected a tip? Henry had never before received a million dollars.

Unfortunately, it proved to be one of those mornings when the phone kept ringing. A recent immigrant by the name of Karlinsky was being followed by two Russian secret agents. Tattersall expressed sympathy and took the case, suspecting his tails were the FBI. Apple called from the store below to complain that his lights were flickering. Had Tattersall hooked up any unusual appliances? Every time the damn thing went off, Henry felt his hands jump, his mind twitch, but with the discipline of an old pro, he allowed himself the insouciance of a second ring.

The call that mattered came at 10:07. Two rings and the receiver was at his ear. You got the money? the man asked. Yes, said Henry, do you have the painting? I'll call you back at eleven tonight with instructions where I want you to go. I don't have a car, Henry informed him. Will I need a car?

That's eleven sharp, said the caller. If you're not there by the

248

phone at eleven, the deal is off. It was a statement of fact rather than an ultimatum. His voice was composed, without melodrama. Wait, said Henry. Hold on. How will I recognize you? He knew the longer he kept him talking the better his chances for success. Can you hear me? called Henry, but the line had gone dead.

The thin white crescents that were his cuticles rose and fell as he slowly tapped the desk. There was a smudge on his wedding band. Henry wiped it away with a moist fingertip and wondered what was so special about eleven. He guessed that Soft Tonsils was a go-between, someone who needed time to lay his hands on the painting. It made no difference to Tattersall how many crooks were involved with Asher in the caper so long as the exchange was carried out without a slip. He took some precautions to insure that it was. When Koontz came to the phone, he said sure he was available, but night work cost a little extra. Park downstairs just around the corner, Henry instructed him. That's ten sharp, and be there. I don't want any fuckups.

All that day Henry remained in the office trying to ignore the clock. The long afternoon was solitary confinement with no calls, no knocks on the door. He riffled through the packets of money like Charlie Chaplin in *Monsieur Verdoux* but kept losing count and having to start again. Finally he gave up. He knew that all he was really doing with the money was killing time. He put it away under his desk. Whoever delivered the painting wasn't about to call the whole thing off because the bag was light a couple of bucks.

Seen through his office windows, the western sky over Santa Monica went from milk-fed veal to rare lamb chops to a ruby sunset of glowing barbecue coals. Henry had had nothing to eat since breakfast. He considered Chicken Vindaloo, the curry sauce as hot as Madras in August. He tormented himself with Cuisses de Grenouille and the tenderest of shallots, the freshest of parsley. He settled for Pizza Guy across from the Mormon Temple because he had their phone number handy on the Rolodex and they delivered.

Pizza Guy, said the pimply high-pitched voice that answered.

What flavor? Tattersall said that he wanted a pizza. Yeah, well we got cheese sausage onion mushrooms green peppers meat balls pepperoni olives anchovies combinations and the house special. Whadduhyuh want? What's the house special? asked Henry. Everything together. The whole ball of wax. Whadduh-yuh want?

Henry thought over the possibilities and said, I'll take a cheese. Small medium large? Henry said medium. That's small, cautioned Pizza Guy. Only fourteen inches. Figure maybe a slice bigger than an LP, that's all. You buy large and for a few cents extra you get two full inches more all around. I know, said Henry, but I'm not hungry. Name and address, demanded Pizza Guy and refused to make any promises about how soon he would eat.

An hour and a half later, a lukewarm fourteen-inch pizza arrived from down the block. The crust was extra thick the way Henry liked it. He boiled some water on a hot plate and prepared himself a cup of instant coffee, putting in three teaspoons of Yuban to make it demitasse strong and adding the water to the coffee as directed for best results. It still tasted like hot powdered water to him, but it was cheap and quick. Henry sipped his brown water and watched the minutes soundlessly slip by on the desk clock.

At ten, he went to the window. Two of the maroon Buick's four decorative fender vents—huge chrome eyelets—peered out from around the corner. Koontz was right on time, ready to take him wherever the money had to be delivered. So far everything seemed to be going according to schedule. Henry noted the facade of the neighboring two-story apartment complex streaked by red and amber and green spotlights like so many other small apartment houses in Los Angeles. It might have been a ride at a rundown amusement park with only a few threadbare thrills. The big cactus plants in front of the building looked to be lethal clusters of green bayonets. In daylight, Henry knew them to be melancholy dog-eared things covered with dust. Calm down, Tattersall, he told himself.

At 10:56 the detective straightened his note pad, uncapped his pen. At 10:59 he drew the phone closer to him and took a deep breath. The desk clock showed 11:00. He went to his wristwatch for a hurried consultation, and it was eleven sharp. At 11:05 Henry wondered if he had heard wrong and was making a mistake about the time. At 11:30 he toyed with the idea that the caller had chickened out. The telephone rang a little after midnight, screaming in shock. Henry snatched up the receiver and softly said hello.

Is that you, darling? Dorothy sounded upset. I was getting worried about you. Is everything all right? Henry said, Of course it's me. Look, Dorothy, get off the line. I'm waiting for an important call. She thought he'd be all through by now, she told him. It's after midnight. Did you have any dinner?

Henry kept his voice low, the message terse as if he feared their conversation was being overheard. Dorothy, he said, hang up. Dorothy informed him that when he got home he'd find some delicious tuna salad mixed for him in the refrigerator and some fresh sliced— Goddammit, dear, rasped a tight-lipped Tattersall, will you please hang up the fuckin' phone? Without another word, his wife shot the receiver into its cradle like an iron bolt. Fortunately, Henry, having counted on her low threshold for profanity, had been holding the instrument well away from his ear.

Opening his collar and loosening his striped tie, he prepared to wait as long as it would take for the next ring. It was a wearying vigil. The sounds of traffic on Little Santa Monica dwindled to a low intermittent hum, the Doppler fade of homeward-bound pleasure. Henry rested his head on the desk, his black hair an enameled island floating in an orange pool of lamplight. He would have to wake her up when he got home and straighten things out. Throw ashes on his head. Kisses all around. Married long enough to know that without a handshake the night before, the morning after was connubial hell. A frosty wasteland of Siberian monosyllables and cold shoulders. Into which glided the feather duster of a dreamy footstep and the great Fred

Astaire, first class from white tie to tails, soft-shoeing his way to her heart. Somebody had come in off the street and was climbing the stairway to the second floor.

The detective's head shot up from the desk. Running a hand over his face and feeling the reality of thick stubble, he cleared his eyes, collected his wits, marshaled his forces. The footsteps grew louder, inevitably homing in on their target. They stopped just outside his office as if someone were reading the name on the door. Henry steeled himself and waited for the knock. Peering beyond his desk lamp into the shadows, he saw the doorknob turn, the door crack open.

A yellow hard hat flashed into the room like a sunburst, the headgear masculine as a steam engine, sleek as a tooth. Gold-rim dark glasses hid the visitor's eyes. His body was sheathed in a blue pin-striped coverall, the kind usually worn by employees of the Los Angeles Department of Water and Power. His heavy western boots had a wide ornamental leather strap across the instep. At that early hour of the morning, he was the most glamorous thing that Tattersall had ever seen in his office.

Hard hat seemed nervous, jumpy, kept to the shadows. His head thrashed from side to side as he scanned the corners of the room, apparently on the lookout for uniformed cops, plain-clothesmen. He wore blue latex gloves and clutched in his hands a narrow cardboard cylinder that Henry estimated to be about three feet long. It was the sort of container that might have held a poster of the sullen James Dean in tee shirt and cowboy hat, or the Sgt. Pepper Beatles dressed as pastel-colored circus bands-men with frogs and epaulets, or the inimitable Marilyn stretched out in the altogether, her hair streaming breathtakingly above her like a blond parachute that had failed to open, or it might (on the other hand) hold a stolen Rembrandt. The money, he said, you got it?

Tattersall recognized the voice from the telephone. The cheap-skate had decided to save a dime and come in person. The aroma was also familiar. When the visitor opened his mouth to speak, it smelled like the Paradise Bar on 2nd and Spring. I'm waiting, he grumbled. Yes or no? Henry nodded slowly. It's down here, he said, bending under the desk.

Catching sight of the heavy canvas flight bag, hard hat leaped forward—his face a ghoulish mask above the lamp—and seized it by the shoulder strap. Tattersall's fingers clamped down on his wrist. Uh-uh, he said. First show me the painting. Hard hat shoved the cylinder in his face. Scooping up the bag, he raced toward the open door, his boot heels tearing holes in the silence.

Hold it, called Tattersall, pulling out his gun. Stop or I'll shoot! The word "shoot" had hardly left his lips when the gun exploded, producing a deadly spondee. On the floor, the round shaggy mat gave a balletic little jump as if it had been drilled dead center. Simultaneously, a loud ping came from the doorway. In its downward trajectory, the small-caliber bullet had splintered the edge of Henry's desk and sent a tiny wooden fragment shooting across the room, striking the fugitive's metal helmet. A freak accident. Hard hat wheeled around in his flight and glared at him. It was a complicated look, part condemnation for bad sportsmanship, part recognition that he had nothing to fear from Tattersall but carelessness. A second later the doorway was empty and hard hat banging down the stairs.

Henry appeared as pale as boiled potatoes, as unsettled as Vietnam. He was astonished at his itchy trigger finger. How could he have allowed himself to be such a victim of chance, so lacking in self-control? Didn't he have any goddamn safety rules? Why, he might have killed the jerk! Taken a real human being who once liked to steal a little bit and drink booze and wear funny hats and turned him into dust. Some trick. He tore away the masking tape, removed the tin cap from the top of the cylinder, and found it empty as expected.

Where was Koontz? Throwing up the window, he stuck his head out, hoping to find Koontz gone, off in hot pursuit of the fleeing crook, but the Buick was still anchored around the corner, motionless, lights out, waiting for orders. If a gunshot hadn't awakened him, shouting wasn't likely to do the job. It was too late now anyhow. The bag-grabbing bastard had got clean away. Let him go, thought Henry. He would probably have turned out to be a dead end regardless, some free-lance opportunist leading nowhere, a solitary rip-off artist trying to cash in on another's crime.

Tattersall looked east toward the twinkling lights of the Hollywood Hills, toward the white neon rimming the top of the new Century Plaza Hotel. Somewhere out there under the crystalline stars, hard hat was lugging his heavy canvas bundle through the nighttime city like a hippie Santa, his bag crammed full of phone numbers clipped from the Los Angeles Yellow Pages for everything from abdominal supports to zoological gardens. Henry almost felt sorry for the guy. There was no question about a crime having been committed, but shit, he reasoned, you don't kill a man for a canvas bag.

The million-dollar container was still under his desk exactly where Henry had left it. He would have to spend the rest of the night holed up in his office and return the money to Chandler as soon as Dutton opened in the morning. He didn't like to wake Dorothy but thought it best to call, explain the situation, put her mind at rest, apologize for what had happened earlier in the evening. And after that he'd send Koontz home to bed. The phone rang five, six times before his wife finally picked up the receiver. Hello, she said. Her sleepy voice was small and furtive, a guarded stranger waiting for bad news.

WEST LOS ANGELES, JUNE 23, 1967

The KPFK reporter slapped a new cassette into his tape recorder.

I heard no warning, he went on. There has been no warning. The police are charging into the crowd without any warning. Here they come. You can hear the screams of the crowd. It's like somebody pressed the panic button. All around me people are pushing, people shoving. The monitors are great. The monitors are shouting "Walk slowly, walk slowly," trying to maintain order and keep things from getting out of hand, but there's not much they can do. The police are coming in waves, attacking the crowd in waves. They're pushing them back out of the street, but there's nowhere for them to go. Good Lord, people are falling over one another! Old people and children! The police are using the tips of their nightsticks, pushing the demonstrators back. People are cursing at them. A rock just missed me. I hope you can hear this. The noise here is deafening. Oh, my God! She's fallen. A young girl right in front of me has fallen and is being trampled on by people being pushed by the police. Help her up! Help her up! That's it, help her up. I just can't understand this. The police are hitting everything in sight for no apparent reason. There's a fire over there. It's a fire. Somebody's started a fire near the reflecting pool in the middle of the road. The flames are shooting straight up into the air maybe ten feet high. A policeman has someone, he's caught someone, a young man with a mustache. I can see a flag upside down on his tee shirt. They're struggling. Other cops are running to help. Three of them are beating on the young man with their nightsticks, hitting him over the head, the shoulders. Oh . . . oh, he's bleeding terribly. His whole face is covered with blood. They're dragging him away. My God, I think he's dead! This is horrible. People are holding their heads and screaming in fright, hysterical. It's a riot. I've never seen anything so horrible in my life. Ladies and gentlemen, I never thought I'd see such things in L.A. . . . But I'm a reporter, officer. Okay, okay, I'm moving. Take it easy, will you? Stop it! Stop—

OAKLAND, 1976

DANIEL ASHER: Collages 1943–1967.
The Oakland Museum, 1976.
Introduction by Mordecai Bell.

Fifteen collages from "The Museum of Crime" suite were first shown in 1961 at the Roth Gallery. The public seemed to have been unprepared for the strength of these works with their dark view of human nature. This Los Angeles exhibition proved to be the final one Asher would have prior to his death.

For the last six years of his life the artist continued to make his collages with a selfless, singleminded, yes, even heroic devotion, despite the decline of interest in his work and increasing financial difficulties. His "Pompes Funèbres" series of 1964–65 was clearly not designed to curry favor in the marketplace. These are stark, uningratiating, enigmatic works. They guard their mystery the way a fruit holds its pit. There is, for example, a gloomy, ominous atmospheric veil shrouding *Harlequin in Twilight* (cat. no. 78). It is reminiscent of Seurat's *Side Show,* a painting Asher greatly admired.

The lone article written on his Stygian work of this period is entitled "Asher's Black Theater" and appeared in the December 1965 issue of *Artworld.* It is a well-meaning but misguided trifle that tries (and, of course, fails dismally) to make a case for Asher as an American Surrealist. Let us hope now, with the Oakland exhibition and the unusual opportunity that it provides to see the full range of Asher's achievement, that this sort of blunder will not be repeated.

BEVERLY HILLS, JUNE 18, 1976

The blistering Santa Ana was over. Low clouds had come into L.A. the night before and were still there when Henry left his office on that cool gray morning. By eleven thirty, when he got off the bus at Camden Drive, the sun had just begun to burn through. Although he couldn't put his finger on exactly what it was, Henry was filled with distrust. It was as if he had bent down to retrieve Dorothy's fallen program at the Music Center, and when he looked up again somebody had switched the backdrop, the lighting, the flats, the props. Everything whisked away to make room for the next scene without leaving a shred of evidence.

Then he realized that it wasn't only the weather that was different. A new Polynesian restaurant had opened on Camden, spreading itself out like a painted fan, and there had been a change on the corner of Brighton Way as well. The white flower cart and the old guy with the cigar in his mouth were gone. Henry looked to see if it was the right block, looked to make certain that the Marquis Gallery hadn't turned into a liquor store overnight. It hadn't, but the adjoining shoe store had become The Garment Bag. Around here, thought Henry, they come and go like hives. Walking up to the gallery entrance, he pushed on the heavy black door and, when it failed to yield, pushed harder.

The lights were on inside, the Picassos still thick on the walls, the gallery empty except for the flashy blonde who worked there. As he came in, she looked up from her desk at the rear, and Henry could hear the music-box tinkle of her bracelets. It wasn't until he came close that she recognized him. You were the man who wanted a Chagall, weren't you? She might be nearsighted, but there was nothing wrong with her memory. He asked if her boss was in. Henry Tattersall was calling.

She disappeared into the inner office and he heard the whispering, the sound of urgent give-and-take. There was a subtle sleepy smile on her face when she returned. In a little while, she promised. Been to the beach? He touched his nose tentatively, and she nodded. Henry had forgotten about that. Hofstedler would see the flaking bits and pieces, the ribbons of dead skin, and laugh in his face. It was no snap to make crooks quiver with a peeling beak. Brushing the loose stuff off his nose, he felt better. Where's the old man across the street? She looked at him. The flower guy, he said. All at once, her eyes misted over. Oh, poor poor Bernie! He died. Right there on the corner yesterday afternoon. It was horrible. He was such a wonderful human being.

Out of delicacy, Henry averted his eyes as she fumbled in her bag and drew out a tissue. He gazed in the direction of the storeroom. Everything from Harris's tip to Lola's confession fit together beautifully. The Rembrandt was in that room. After nine years of dead ends and silence, it was almost within his grasp. How the painting got in there Henry had no idea, but Hofstedler was a shark. What difference would it make to him if it were stolen as long as he could turn a profit? You can go in now, she told him. Henry thanked her. Stroke, she said. He stopped and looked back at her. It was a stroke, she explained, and he shook his head sympathetically as if she were the widow.

OAKLAND, 1976

DANIEL ASHER: Collages 1943–1967.
The Oakland Museum, 1976.
Introduction by Mordecai Bell.

Asher's brief fling with abstraction at the very beginning of 1966 was a curious and unlooked-for development in his work. *Giant White Dancing* (cat. no. 83) is one of the few collages that exist to document this transitory phase. There is a hint of Cubism in the flatness of its space. There is a suggestion of Precisionism in the geometry of the butterfly. There is the artist's characteristic meticulous construction.

Finally, however, abstraction was alien to Asher's sensibility. His was an art too firmly grounded in the texture and shape of things ever to become totally abstract. In his work at its best, the human voice speaks to us and the human face shines through.

Asher had suffered a heart attack in January of 1966, and this may explain the unnatural direction that his work briefly took. Fortunately, he was soon able to once again find himself. Displaying great personal strength and courage, he turned his creative energies decisively away from abstraction, and in the final year of his life produced his most joyous work.

BEVERLY HILLS, JUNE 18, 1976

It's amazing! cried the affable Mark Hofstedler when Henry entered his elegant office with its thickly carpeted floor. I was just looking for your phone number. I think I may have a wonderful Chagall for you. Look out, Henry, he warned himself, you're dog paddling in shark-infested waters. The informal young dealer appeared innocent enough in his sporty blue pinstriped shirt with its clerically white collar casually opened at the neck, but Henry was on guard. Lola had called him dangerous, and anybody who kept wild animals in his house was no creampuff.

As usual, Tattersall's gun was back at the office. If you weren't an ex-cop, it was practically impossible to get a concealed weapons permit in L.A. County. But there was no law against lumpiness, and before leaving his office he had taken the precaution of putting on his bulletproof vest. There were dark forces loose in the world—evil that even a private investigator who had seen more than his share of it couldn't imagine. Henry accepted his limitations. He was no fool.

You understand, cautioned Hofstedler, that nothing's definite yet. But if I get the Chagall I'm after, Mr. Tattersall, you're going to be a *very* lucky man. Forget Chagall, said Henry abruptly. I've changed my mind. I'm looking for a Rembrandt now.

But, but, sir—the baffled dealer held out the palm of his hand as if the names of his gallery's artists were inscribed on it—we don't have any Rembrandts. I thought you knew. We specialize in the moderns here, not Old Masters.

Tattersall watched him like radar. The Rembrandt I'm after, he said, is called *Jacob Wrestling with the Angel.* Hofstedler stared at him. Slowly, he began to laugh. It was a cold, hard, mirthless sound, the monotone staccato of a firing squad. That painting was stolen years ago from the County Museum. Don't you know that? I know, said Henry. He also knew that right now it was under a sheet in Hofstedler's back room. Through clenched teeth, the dealer hissed, You're nuts. Get out of here.

The game's up, Hofstedler. Henry told him that it was all over. He knew exactly what was going on in the Marquis Gallery. The young dealer rounding up suckers whose primary interest in art is money and paying them off out of their own investment and calling it profit. It's a Ponzi scheme, charged Henry. You're running a classic Ponzi. Hofstedler sat back in amazement. You're absolutely out of your mind. What are you, some sort of swindler? A blackmailer?

Tattersall didn't care for that at all, the disease calling the patient sick. He had more than paid his dues as a legitimate private investigator: the long apprentice hours, the exam, the security clearance, the spotless record. Pulling out his wallet, he flashed his California investigator's license. Hofstedler examined it but was not impressed. Okay, so you're Herny Tattersall, private eye. So what?

Give me that, said the investigator, snatching his new 1976 card back and studying it closely. He was annoyed with himself for not having noticed. That should be *Henry,* he explained. Somebody made a mistake. Hofstedler agreed with him. Somebody did make a mistake, and I think it's you. At this point, Henry knew that all he had to say to rattle the young man was Lola Toscano, but he had promised her that he wouldn't, and Henry liked to keep his promises.

You're bluffing! cried Hofstedler, seeing him hesitate. It sounded like a pretty good suggestion, and Henry decided to try. He informed him that the painting hanging outside in the gallery entitled *Still Life with Croissants,* which the dealer claimed once belonged to Gertrude Stein, never belonged to Gertrude Stein. Not only isn't it listed as part of her estate, but it's nowhere to be found in the Zervos Catalogue of Picasso's work. It's an imitation, an invented painting in the style of the artist. In short, Mr. Hofstedler, a forgery. The selling of forged work is just one of your many art crimes. Striving to sound as definitive as death, Henry hoped that Gilbert Wright, the museum curator, was nowhere in the vicinity with his deflating expert testimony.

Getting up from his desk, Hofstedler went by Henry, who caught a whiff of the jungle, of rare, sweet, tropical plants, as he passed. Why don't you go to lunch, Audrey? he suggested. She asked if Mark wanted her to bring him back anything. He said no, and as soon as she left locked the door. It was an odd thing to do in the middle of the day, a disturbing thing that made Henry feel as vulnerable as a delicate fabric in hot water. Motioning to him, Hofstedler called, Come with me.

He led the way to the storeroom and switched on the light. The suspicious investigator hung back slightly and watched. Hofstedler went right to the rack where the Rembrandt had been. Henry relaxed. He didn't think there'd be any trouble now. There it was on top in the corner, exactly the same place he had spotted the shrouded painting three days ago.

The tall Hofstedler had no difficulty pulling it down, but the dust made him sneeze. Placing the canvas on the floor, he brushed the dust off the wrapping with such style, such grace, such practiced care that it would have made whatever he was selling almost worth the price. Henry drew closer. He could hear himself breathing heavily. *Et voilà*, said Hofstedler, taking hold of the sheet and undraping the canvas. Your *Jacob Wrestling with the Angel*.

The Rembrandt at last! Henry gaped. His arches suddenly collapsed under the weight they were carrying, his pulse slowed to a trickle. Here was an angel, a wrestler—the cast of characters absolutely correct as Harris had promised—but these poor people looked as if they had drowned and been underwater for years, their heads all swollen out of shape, their eyes glassy, their color drained.

Magnanimous in victory, Hofstedler seemed to take pity on the unhappy little fellow. As you can see, he said, it's only a bad imitation. I bought this copy nine years ago as a joke when the original was stolen. I thought I'd sell it to someone here in Beverly Hills. You know, as a sort of amusing conversation piece. But now almost everyone has forgotten about the theft of the Rembrandt. Even me, for that matter. I completely forgot this was up there in the corner. Funny-looking thing, isn't it?

Henry sighed. Well, he thought, that's that. Another dead end. He tried not to feel too sorry for himself. As they walked back to his office, Hofstedler told the investigator that people can forget all sorts of things. For instance, there's something else I forgot. Back in a minute, he said, and hurrying out into the gallery, he returned with the amorous pastel by Picasso that Henry had so admired.

You seemed to take a fancy to it when you were last here. I'd like you to have it. Please— He handed it to Henry. Take it. As a favor to me. Tattersall stared at him incredulously. No, the dealer insisted, it's not too much at all. He smiled ingratiatingly. And about those other matters you mentioned. You *will* forget about them, won't you?

Holding the pastel with cautious fingers, Henry was tickled to be able to examine its earthiness up close. Okay, he muttered after weighing the offer, I'll take it. But on one condition. I want you to make out a sales slip to me. The dealer's eyebrows bent with surprised amusement. A sales slip! For a gift? Henry told him, I wouldn't want you to accuse me of walking out of here with your property.

Although Hofstedler was irritated, he tried not to show it and looked at the plain little fellow with a new respect. You're a careful man, Tattersall, he acknowledged. He went behind his desk and considered the top drawer as if there was nothing inside he really wanted.

Henry prided himself on being streetwise about danger and being able to avoid it. He had a sixth sense about that sort of thing. He didn't trust what was in that drawer any more than he would a blade at his heart. He said, On second thought—but it was too late. Hofstedler already had the drawer open. Squinting, Henry tried to see what was inside and nearly swallowed his chewing gum.

The snub-nosed revolver was a mean-looking, blunt bastard. The fluorescent overhead light in the office gleamed viciously on its angular cartridge chamber. Its handle was brown, the barrel black. Henry groaned. The same colors as his damn dog. It looked to be a .38, and if the gun was loaded with shot shells, Hofstedler could be as blind as Helen Keller and still blast Henry's cheap bulletproof vest into a shower of bloody cotton balls. There was a loud thump on the floor at his feet. Henry looked down. It was his tombstone, and chiseled in immortal granite the words: Devoted Husband, Reckless Schmuck.

Gun in hand, the dealer stood opposite him. He had noted the grim expression on Tattersall's face and, picking up the weapon said, Oh, this. Don't be silly. I have a license for it. There've been so many art thefts recently one has to take measures. Only last month in Paris a Picasso was stolen in broad daylight from the front window of the Gobelins Gallery. You can't be too careful in this business, he assured his visitor quite seriously, and put away the gun. The sales slip that he wrote out was undated. Henry brought that to his attention. Oh, said Hofstedler apologetically. He shook his head in a small gesture of annoyance with himself. Henry rated the performance C−.

On the way back to his office with the wrapped Picasso bouncing on his lap and the dated receipt in his pocket, Tattersall was completely disgusted. Mark Hofstedler was a clever, attractive pathological liar and crook whose estimate of human nature was lower than Death Valley. Did he really think he could bribe Henry? Imposing not only on his integrity but his intelligence as well. Giving away what only a few days ago, he said, belonged to a private party who preferred to remain nameless. Henry intended to nail this louse, and he had the evidence to do it too. There was really only one thing that worried him. A few more public-spirited nonprofit detours like this one, and the Tattersall Service would be out of business.

PART VIII

OAKLAND, 1976

92. LA GRANDE ROUE (1900)

Los Angeles, 1967
Paper, cloth, shells, beads, glitter (diamond
dust) on cardboard
Size: 12 × 15½ inches
Coll. The Oakland Museum

*It is a rare autumn day at the fair. The Paris sky is luminous as if
dusted with diamonds, and flags flying above the immense main
archway flutter and dab the air with tricolor. A wedding party
stands stiffly before the great gate. Joined by an African flutist in an
orange toga and a booted Russian cossack, they freeze for their
photograph. Only the angelic young newlyweds smile.*

  *The bride is dressed in a magnificent white beaded gown with
bows and bustle and flounces falling in taffeta tiers to the ground.
Holding a pink and white bouquet of baby's breath, she leans
coquettishly on the arm of her new husband. The smooth-cheeked
groom wears black. He wears high black stockings, satin breeches
that buckle at the knee, a soft black velvet hat with upturned brim.*

267

The bride's gown billows, the groom's cape swirls in the breeze.

Beyond the archway (designed by the celebrated architect Binet), the fairgrounds are as crowded as a medieval city. The colorful flags of a dozen nations stream from the tops of dome, steeple, and parapet. Far in the distance can be glimpsed the roof of the remote Gallery of Machines in which Henry Adams sits by the hour pondering the mammoth Hélios dynamos. High above all rises the giant golden Ferris wheel.

What young person could resist the excitement of such a ride? Seated in their chair, she clings to his arm and the happy newlyweds wait to be whisked aloft. A seemingly indistinguishable bride and groom sit in the chair above them. More astonishing still is that identical siblings are to be seen in every chair but one. At the top of the wheel, pinnacled above flags and turrets, the young bride leans coquettishly on the groom's black satin sleeve. Dressed exactly as her husband, the old man smiles broadly through his trim white beard and rests his hand on her breast.

OAKLAND, DECEMBER 24, 1976

On top of Big Dad's Deseret Bar-B-Cue and Broasted, an American flag pink with age snapped in the gusting wind. Off to the left, the ocean rippled itself white. Near Pismo Beach, Henry caught a glimpse of something fluttering in the sky. It was bigger than a bird, smaller than a Piper Cub, and purple.

He had seen pictures of hang gliders in the *Times*, but this was the first time he had seen the real thing. The huge purple wings—indifferent to the daring arms and legs that dangled beneath—soared lazily above the highway, circled twice, and then dropped into the sea.

VENICE, JUNE 23, 1967

At the end of Market Street near the ocean, in an empty sun-bleached lot amidst broken glass and shriveled weeds, two middle-aged black men with Afros sat opposite one another on cardboard boxes and used an upended metal garbage can as a card table. The one with the white headband was known to Welfare as unemployable, Hard-Core Unemployable Eames —HCE to his friends. The other was named Crawford.

Everybody say Crawford a dummy, said Crawford, picking up the six of hearts and slipping it between the five and seven of hearts he already had. Everybody say Crawford a slowboat, Crawford a tool. He laid his hand out face up on the bottom of the can. That's gin, baby. The big G. Read 'em and weep.

Scanning the cards, the loser's face was a stone. He ran his tongue over his teeth, cleared his throat with a Last Judgment rumble, and said, Brother, how much I owe you now? The bill came to nineteen dollars and thirty-five cents. HCE threw in his cards as if he thought it might be time to go. Catching sight of the heavyset teenage girl coming down the street, he checked her out: the fine-looking blond hair, the bare feet, the beads, the shirttail flapping carelessly over the tight dungarees, her fat white face.

Hey there, mama, he called. What time you got? Caught off guard, the girl looked at him bemused, anxious, unable to handle the question. I don't know, she had to admit. That's all right, mama, he reassured her. That's all right. Gotta split, man, he informed Crawford, getting up. I see you still got an eye for the ladies, said Crawford. Brother, said HCE, these eyes ain't old enough they don't see fine young women no more.

She said, I don't believe in it. The teenage girl had stopped not far from the crowded benches near the edge of the beach and had turned back to tell him You know, time, she shouted over the music. I don't believe in it. She gave him a smile that could turn a pocket inside out and floated off toward two teenage boys who had their transistor radio blowing maximum bass. Hold on, cried Crawford. What about my loot? HCE adjusted his dapper white headband. On the bill, brother, he said as he strode away toward the beach, toward the limp net and his first love, volleyball. Put me on the bill.

They didn't say anything, not wanting to lose the music, but the two boys were glad to see her. She sat cross-legged on the sand beside them, and the one holding the joint gave her a drag. He had long red hair, a beaded Indian necklace, a brown boy scout shirt from which the sleeves had been cut away. The three of them sat mute like fish and listened to the Doors belting out "Light My Fire." The disc jockey cut in even before the final chord, his mouth in the speaker crying Oh yes, oh yes, fell-ahs and gals, who else but the Doors and the number-one song in the Southland this glo-ree-us twenty-third day of June. The weather hazy sunshine and a predicted high of 81 degrees.

Then came the news: urgent electronic beeps followed by flat vocal tones straight from the shoulder and no crapping around. President Johnson and Soviet Premier Alexei Kosygin met for more than five hours this morning on the campus of Glassboro State College in New Jersey to discuss arms limitation, the Vietnam War, and the Middle East. Following their talk, the two leaders were smiling broadly. President Johnson had this to say as they came out: *This meeting today was a very good and very useful meeting.* The two world leaders announced their intention to return to Glassboro on Sunday afternoon to continue their deliberations. According to White House Press Secretary George Christian, the President is going back to Washington immediately and will be leaving from there for Los Angeles. The thousand-dollar-a-couple Democratic fund raiser that he will be attending here this evening in the Century Plaza is scheduled to begin at seven thirty. Spokesmen for Twentieth Century–Fox, located near the hotel, have indicated that it would be possible for the presidential helicopter to land on their lot but say they have no idea whether the President actually will. Security precautions are extremely tight because of the planned demonstration by antiwar groups. In Vietnam today—

That's where they belong, said an angry Sam, rocking back and forth on the edge of the bench. The tip of his cane struck at the ground like hailstones. Send all of them to Vietnam, the lot. Kill 'em all. Calm yourself, Sam, soothed the man sitting beside him in the stiff Panama hat, take it easy.

How can I? How can I take it easy? Sam wanted to know. Don't you see that that Senator Ribicoff knew what he was talking about? Right now Los Angeles don't stand for a damn thing. Look around you, Nathan, look, look at this place. Fifteen, twenty years ago you had a paradise. Now all you see is drug fiends and niggers and spics and dog shit. Tell me what kind of Great Society do you call that?

Such talk was not typical of his good-hearted friend, but Nathan understood. Three days ago Sam's twin brother, Larry, had been sliced open by a junkie looking for cash. It was Sam himself who had gone to Larry's room up the block at the Hotel Edgewater and found the body, a pile of rags in a pool of blood. A tragedy, said Bertha, who sat listening at the other end of the bench. A tragedy, she moaned, and the two glum channels from the corners of her lips lengthened with pain. The elderly man next to her unfolded a wrinkled tissue and wiped his glasses. They had thick cataract lenses. His hat was black. His worn black double-breasted suit—looking as if it had traveled half a century and thousands of miles from Poland—still had every black button anchored smartly in place, though not all were matching in size. These things happen, he philosophically observed, settling his glasses on the high bridge of his nose and turning a jumbled blur into the jeweled froth of Pacific waves.

As for me—he considered what was to follow like a high diver perched on his narrow platform—for me death has always had a very different meaning than it does for many people. I'm not afraid of it. I do not consider death to be my enemy. If it's an eternal sleep, I'll rest. If it's not, I may go on up to a higher sphere. What do I care? I'll have plenty of company.

Bertha said, I once saw a moving picture about an explorer who was frozen to death, and they brought him back to life maybe a thousand years later by heating him up in Reynold's Wrap like a baked potato. Bertha was interested in stories like that. She believed in science. Her companion knew that she carried a special card in her handbag at all times and had donated her body to the UCLA Medical School. He regarded her as an interesting girl, very-up-to-date in her thinking. He ran his bony fingers over his thighs and enjoyed the sea breeze. I love to look at the ocean, he told her, to watch the ships, to communicate with the waves. I don't know what lonesome means. Ask me, said Bertha, I'll give you an earful.

Meyerhoff, a tall man wearing a crew cap patterned with beer labels, stood before Sam, commiserating. I was in the first World War, he said. I fought at Ypres in Flanders. I'm more terrified now living here at the beach than I ever was there. Sam banged his cane into the ground as if it were the enemy. A woman in sneakers with a thin rose scarf over her white hair came along. Bending over, the stranger peered through the lower half of her bifocals and asked, Is that you, Larry? No, no, he said, I'm Sam. I'm afraid, Nathan gently explained, that you'll never see Larry again. The woman stared at him incredulously, her hand on her chest and her chest heaving.

We looked a lot alike, Sam said aloud to no one in particular. But Larry was all sunshine and good news. I'm not like that. I'm a brooder. Larry loved to sing, to dance. Tap dance, shuffle, waltz, the South-American stuff, you name it. He was a guy who was always kidding. A guy who loved his fun. He was seventy-nine and looked like fifty and had all of his marbles too. All of his lovely marbles— Sam's voice cracked, his eyes misted over. The woman tried to comfort him. She said, We still have our memories, he's still alive there. Dead is dead, snapped Sam. You don't come back from dead.

On the back of the adjacent bench, Mount Sinai advertised their mortuary, their cemetery, and urged heads of households to Consider Your Family Now. Leaning his narrow shoulders, his blue windbreaker against the sign, the frail Isidore Siegel barely covered the word "Now." Siegel—a mangled paperback copy of *Murder in the Garden* open on his lap—was reading aloud with remarkable concentration. Beside him, his ailing brother, Mo, sat slumped in a wheelchair, Mo's head fallen to one side, his numb fingers stiff as thorns. As the sun broke through the early afternoon haze, Siegel stopped to pull down the peak of his white cap, the cap that bore the circular patch of the Bay City Rollers on its crown.

He was about to resume reading when he saw that his brother was sound asleep, had been perhaps for some time. He glanced accusingly at the fellow wearing what he took to be a black toupee who was seated beside him on the bench poaching on Mo's story. The look said, Why didn't you tell me he had dropped off, moocher? Siegel tenderly straightened Mo's bent arm, then eased him back in his wheelchair, and as he did so the paperback mystery fell from his lap. Bending to pick it up, he keeled over on the ground.

Tattersall, who had been enjoying the story and was anxious to discover what happened next, instantly lifted the reader and set him back on the bench, brushing the sand from his windbreaker. Siegel shook his head. Dizzy and flustered, he rose unsteadily to his feet. The investigator didn't like what he saw in the thin man's red and twitchy eyes. You sure you're okay? he inquired. Okay, okay, mumbled the woozy Siegel. Taking the book from Tattersall and shuffling behind his brother's chair, he propelled it waveringly in the general direction of the Hotel Edgewater, the run-down rooming house where the two of them shared one room plus kitchenette for eighty-five dollars a month.

Beyond the Edgewater and halfway up the block, the space in which Asher's car had been parked only minutes before was empty. Tattersall shielded his eyes against the afternoon glare, but he had made no mistake. The little red MG was gone. Ineluctably, the Rembrandt trail kept drawing Henry back to Market Street. Police and museum officials with whom he had spoken were in agreement that the painting was nowhere in the museum, which meant that somebody had devised an ingenious way to somehow get it past the guards—a plan that frankly had him stumped. At the moment his prime suspect for that somebody was the debt-ridden Asher. And if not for cash, then for revenge on the guy his girlfriend was now living with. Or perhaps both. Henry had for the last three days been staking out the artist's ramshackle old house, watching the comings and goings to see what large parcels went in or out, and waiting for his opportunity.

Across the street from the Asher house, two men in overalls were removing linoleum tiles from a vacant store and loading them onto a rusty pickup truck, plodding back and forth with the slow survival rhythm of work animals. They knew nothing about the red car, they told Tattersall. Hadn't seen a thing.

The brick-faced drunk stretched out in the empty storefront three doors up, on the other hand, claimed he could tell him everything that he wanted to know. Cradled on his stomach was an open bottle swaddled in a brown paper bag. Henry decided that he'd risk a buck and see.

I don't want your lousy money, the man snarled at Henry, and grabbed the bill. But in my condition I've got no choice. He said he saw a guy come out of the gray house over there, get into the red car, and drive off. Looking real comical in a funny hat and a tee shirt with this great big American flag upside down and peace signs and flowers painted on the front of his pants and the stars and stripes sewed on his backside. Plus a few feathers, a couple of beads, you know all that peace shit. And, let me see . . . oh, yeah . . .

Whoever the clown in the peace suit was, he didn't sound like Asher. The man Henry had under surveillance wore somber, dirty blues and blacks.

. . . carrying some sort of package in his hands. What sort of package? The drunk said a package, a package. What's the matter, you don't know a package? Tattersall was growing increasingly irritated with his dollar's worth. All right, the drunk conceded, like a telescope. What size telescope, demanded Henry, Mount Wilson? Oh, about yay big, replied the drunk blandly, spreading his hands maybe a foot apart, and as he did so the bottle rolling off his chest onto the sidewalk. Too small, thought Henry, too small, out of the question. He picked up the wine-soaked bag and looked inside to see if the bottle had broken, but it was okay. Here, he said, returning it. The drunk took the wet bag and cried Goddammit, goddammit, see what you made me do? Look how much I spilled. It's your fault, you jerk. Henry, with commendable restraint, suggested that he suck the paper and left.

The son-of-a-bitch narc. Tattersall had suspected something when the bastard sold out for a buck with no bargaining. Then there were his shoes. The unworn leather heels. But the wine gave him away. No heavy-drinking stumblebum is brown-bagging Pinot Chardonnay. The creep was an undercover operator, a wise-ass narc doing a bit of method acting while waiting for sundown to nail the potheads on the beach for smoking grass and pushing a little hash and coke after dark.

Crossing the street, Henry climbed the stairs and knocked on the high front door that rose ecclesiastically to an ogive. If Asher shows, Henry blows, he kept telling himself while waiting. But he was sure he would think of something sensible in a pinch. It was a risk Henry had to take. To the best of his knowledge, there had been no one else inside the place but the artist. Despite the far-fetched description, the guy who drove off in Asher's car had to be Asher.

Tattersall knocked again and considered the possibility that the theft of the Rembrandt might have something to do with the movement. There were the car's bumper stickers, of course, the BRING THEM HOME NOW and MAKE LOVE NOT WAR and the others, but his investigation had led him to believe that it was the ex-girlfriend who was the peacenik. Besides, he reasoned, if the theft had been a politically motivated act, there should have been a public proclamation, some telephoned message that capitalism was dead. Henry did his seldom used knee buckle, and as he fell into the door, he turned the knob. It was locked.

Around at the back of the house a working oil pump whined down and up. The thing was an eyesore and probably cut a few dollars from Asher's monthly rent. Whatever royalty the oil company was paying, the money was being collected by an organization called the Bright Way Missionary Baptist Church, Inc. Henry had discovered the name of the owner on the tax rolls of the county assessor's office in Culver City. A lightning glance into one of the rear windows—a kitchen—and he saw no one. He tried a bedroom with the same result. Although to have forced either window would have been child's play for him, Tattersall had no desire to be collared for breaking and entering. He had no desire to be caught at all. If possible, he preferred not to commit a crime.

At times like this it was difficult for Henry not to think of the Christmas catalogue of the Morton L. Rodderbush Company of Englewood Cliffs, New Jersey. Rodderbush—"since 1959 helping the professional gather information without conspicuity" —specialized in sophisticated electronic equipment for surveillance at a distance. Not your old-fashioned crapper tappers and alligator clips but the latest microwave intercepts and such advanced items as the hookswitch bypass, the silver box, the harmonica bug. But even if Henry could afford that stuff, he felt that there was something unethical about it, something mechanical and impersonal and cold that robbed his work of its human drama. Who doesn't enjoy people and a small thrill every now and again?

The small thrill provided by the back door was that it was unlocked. It was as if Asher had sent him an invitation, insisted that he drop in. Stepping inside, Henry softly closed the door behind him and stopped dead in his tracks when he heard the trumpet strut into the opening bars of "I Can't Get Started." Motionless, he listened. Flashing through his mind came Sloan. The world's greatest trumpeter home early from work. Henry could breathe again and did, winking at himself for the passing flutter, and then he heard the reeds, the rhythm section. If that wasn't the post office marching band practicing next door, he knew he was in trouble.

Henry inched his way into the house, his feet gliding down the hallway like falling shadows. The bare floorboards crepitated. The music grew louder. It was coming from the kitchen up ahead. Rather than wait to be shot for trespassing, he called out, Mr. Asher? Are you there, Mr. Asher?

A radio was playing on the kitchen table, but there was nobody there. He hurriedly went through every room in the place. If Henry hadn't turned up, the trumpeter's final chorus, with its searing, poignant, ear-tingling high C, would have been played to an empty house. Obviously Asher has been in a hurry when he left. Though sorely tempted to turn the radio off and eliminate waste, Tattersall realized that there was nothing he could do about it and immediately began his search.

Working swiftly, he examined every likely hiding place for the painting. The artist's cluttered bedroom was a reluctant witness and he showed it no mercy, yanking out drawers, pushing cartons around on the floor, wrenching open the warped door of the closet, peering under the bureau, the bed. The place was littered with dust-covered books and cigarette butts. In the girl's room it looked as if the kid was still living there, though Tattersall had located her a few blocks away, shacked up with a guru named Valentine. The poster of the long-haired baby-faced Beatles hanging over the bed was signed "Great to have you with us." Under the bed, Henry discovered a pair of sandals and a brassiere. The bureau held nothing but a few neatly folded clothes. Although the painting wasn't in the room, there was stuff scattered all over the place, and even the kid's jewelry had been left behind, her phonograph. What struck him as odd was that there were no records. It could mean that she didn't have any. Henry guessed it meant that she wasn't coming back.

The entire front of the building was Asher's studio, and the white walls were covered with fascinating things that Tattersall had no time to enjoy. He might have been a surgeon engaged in an exploratory operation, cutting here, probing there. Nothing behind the piles of magazines, nothing behind the makeshift bookcases of bricks and boards, nothing in the two long cabinets but trays of funny odds and ends such as buttons and bits of broken glass. He threw open a large wicker basket that contained old, yellowing newspapers and sneezed violently, almost knocking over a full ashtray on a nearby table. No sooner does the guy get over a heart attack—Henry wiped his nose and put away his handkerchief—then he begins working on lung cancer.

There was a peculiar smell in the room that he had noticed when he first came in, a strange, pungent, dizzying aroma that reminded him of ether. Now he discovered the source on Asher's worktable, where a large bottle of rubber cement was open. Alongside the bottle was a small unfinished collage with tiny flags framing a bright yellow Ferris wheel. How could the man making that, he wondered, be the same one who ripped off the Rembrandt? Henry, whose respect for artists and writers was enormous, never ceased to be amazed at the failings of accomplished people, their lacks, their blind spots. With all these books of his, these magazines, this art, hadn't he learned anything?

Somewhere in the house there was a stolen Rembrandt painting, and Henry, glancing about in helpless frustration, didn't know where to look next. He had already been in there much too long. Asher might be back at any minute. Despite the vocal fireworks in antiphonal bursts coming from the group singing in the kitchen, he tried to think hard, to concentrate. Where might a canvas that size be hidden that he hadn't already searched? Then it came to him.

Although most of these old beach places had no basements, many of them did have crawl spaces underneath big enough to store a steamer trunk or a packing case or a rug. Why not? he speculated. While envisioning somewhere beneath the floor-boards a worthless tattered carpet with scrunched piles rolled about a fabulous core, Henry suddenly became aware that a minor irritant had disappeared. Something caught in his teeth had been flossed out, a sty had shrunk to nothing. It was the music. The radio had stopped.

Not to worry, was the investigator's advice. Level-headed possibilities filled his mind like life preservers. In all likelihood the radio's condenser tube had blown, or it could be that the station was having transmission problems and would be back on the air in a matter of minutes, perhaps the Department of Water and Power had pulled the plug on a delinquent account, or possibly an electrical storm in the San Gabriel Mountains had caused transformers to blow, circuits to overload, cut-off switches to come smashing down, and the entire Los Angeles metropolitan area from the ocean to the foothills was as dark as death. Please stand by.

But what if Asher had come back? Or what if someone else was in the house looking for the same thing that he was after and would stop at nothing to get it? Henry held his breath and strained his ears for a footfall.

WEST LOS ANGELES, JUNE 23, 1967

The crowd had started to gather in the early afternoon. There had been fog and a little local drizzle overnight, but the morning sun cheered things up, drying out the grass in Cheviot Hills Park, and with the temperature in the high 70s the Peace Action Council—organizers of the march—were looking forward to a really big turnout.

Young people were stretched out on blankets laughing, or played guitar and sang, and it felt like a neighborhood picnic. An elderly blond woman opened her aluminum beach chair and sat down. She had just returned from having her hair retouched at the beauty parlor, eager to look her best for the President. There were dogs barking and babies with balloons and college kids throwing Frisbees that hung in the air as if in no hurry to come back down to earth. A long-haired guy wearing a tee shirt labeled CONTRABAND said, Check this nail delay, and the long-haired girl with a necklace that had been artlessly fashioned out of red bottle brush watched as the Frisbee spun around on his index finger, as fixed in its whirling course as a planet.

By five o'clock the park was beginning to swarm with marchers. Maybe ten thousand already and two hours yet to go. The baseball diamond was covered with flags, posters, painted banners, signs that said Suppose They Gave a War & Nobody

279

Came, and No Draft for Vietnam, and Get Out of Vietnam Now, and Stop the War Now, and Bring Them Home Now. A bedsheet stretched across home plate identified the Women's Strike for Peace. Coming straight from work on this Friday evening, men in business suits joined their wives and babies and mingled with the kids in buckskin and overalls and headbands, feathers and beads.

Dan Asher, while generally preferring people in the singular, rather enjoyed this beautiful, motley mob. What he distrusted were their halos. The self-righteousness of the protestors made him feel very old and cynical. Like Humphrey Bogart, he was suspicious of causes—even the good ones—because they usually got you into trouble, and if he wasn't certain that Mona would be among the marchers, he would have been back home at that moment working in his studio. Wandering through the crowd in search of her, he had no doubt that he was on the side of the good guys, but what worried him were the flags, the streamers, the medieval bravery that suggested Richmond's camp at Bosworth Field on the eve of battle.

The speeches were to begin at six thirty, but before the speeches came the songs. Tuning up his guitar, folksinger Phil Ochs sang an antiwar number about not marching anymore. It was hard to hear all the words with the police and TV helicopters chugging overhead, but his voice—young, pure, burning with conviction—was an acetylene torch that welded his listeners together. United, Ochs promised, they might even end a war. There were thunderous cheers, horns, cowbells, signs on sticks bobbing up and down, and the crowd chanting Hell no, we won't go! Hell no, we won't go!

Donald Kalish, a UCLA philosophy professor who was one of the leaders of the march, read a telegram. Joan Baez was sorry that she couldn't make it. Keep up the fight, she urged, and the crowd went wild. Then he introduced Dr. Spock. All Dan Asher could see from deep center field was the sun reflecting off a distant pair of glasses, a balding head. Dan's first wife had hated the doctor's sensible, nondidactic book. A new mother, Gretchen craved orders, finality. Once, ages ago it seemed now, a hint from that man had sent him racing into the night for suppositories for their howling infant daughter. Had he, the world, ever really been that young? he wondered.

Excuse me. The enthusiastic big guy wearing the World War I helmet apologized for stomping on his foot. It was a polite crowd, thought Dan Asher. What did Spock say? he asked him. Dr. Spock said no young man has to go to Vietnam unless accompanied by his parents. Dan Asher thanked him for the information. Muhammad Ali! somebody cried, and a smiling black face appeared. The cheers drowned the helicopters out of the skies.

We ain't for no violence, said Muhammad Ali, 'cause violence is wrong. We don't believe in violence. We believe in peace, that's what we believe in, and if anyone starts somethin' it won't be this group. He opened his lips and gave them a heavyweight smile. I guess, he said slyly, the *po*-leece will have to start it! The crowd loved him, roared its approval.

It became more and more difficult for Dan Asher to make his way through the excited mass of people. Rumors shook them like earth tremors, and all around him they were talking about Johnson. That he had decided not to come because of threats against his life. That he would be late. That he had actually arrived and was already inside the hotel where the Democratic fund-raising dinner and dance were to be held. The bearded, gloomy face of Leland Sonderman loomed over the crowd like an Old Testament prophet, and Dan Asher, lifting the paper cylinder in his hand, waved. But not until he was almost at his side did his friend notice him. It was obvious that Sonderman couldn't believe his eyes. Decked out as he was, Dan Asher realized just how foolish he must look to him. He felt dumb, embarrassed, too burdened to explain, a victim of circumstances beyond his control. Sonderman said, You brought something after all.

Earlier that week, Leland had called to tell him that a number of artists were going to burn their work during the march. It was to be a ritualistic destruction of art in sympathy for the terrible destruction of life in Vietnam. Dan Asher had no intention of destroying his work for any reason, but then Leland mentioned Mona. Mona was in charge of the burning. Over there, Leland shouted above the noise of a circling helicopter, and pointed toward the entrance to the park.

Recently, Dan Asher had become fascinated by the idea that having lost Mona on top of one emotional peak the night of Dorfman's party, he would be most likely to find her again on top of another. The occasion of the Peace March had struck him as promising. Seeing her now totally absorbed in talking to a small group in the parking lot, however, he wondered if he had miscalculated. He was reminded of an oil painting of a radiant, larger-than-life Lenin triumphantly addressing the first Council of People's Commissars. His second vision was more hopeful—a Rossetti drawing of the sensuous, full-lipped Elizabeth Siddal surrounded by a dazzling nimbus. He tried again, and there was Mona looking lovelier than ever, her uncombed hair seeming to hold all the light in the sky. She was earnest, exhilarated, triumphant, a flaming sword. Dan! she cried in astonishment.

Open-mouthed, Mona stared at his getup. Fastened to the cuff of his knit cap like a third blue eye was a large pin that said Free All Political Prisoners. He had sewn an American flag upside down on his tee shirt. Stars and stripes were patched on his seat. For her, he had willingly turned himself into a cartoon, a grotesque poster. That was one of the curious things Dan Asher had learned about love. Unless you were willing to make the few trivial sacrifices that it demanded, love wasn't likely to hang around.

He had come to her dressed as an offering, and, while her friends looked on, he waited to see if the offering would be accepted. The wry expression on her face warned him that he might have made a mistake. At least she wasn't laughing at him, he thought. Finally Mona said, Even *you* here. She held out her arms to him. Now I know we can't lose! Lifting her off the ground, he squeezed her tightly and kissed the air out of her sweet mouth. Although he knew that he had missed her, he had no idea until that moment how very much. At last, he was through sucking on the bones of an old grief. The bad times were all over now.

Here, he said.

The bearded Dobbs handed his wife the card. It was unlike anything that his London firm had made previously. Their other valentines were collages, too, with fringes of paper lace and gilt-edged borders. But this was 1845 and there were no cupids and no hearts. There was instead a barometer surrounded by pastel-colored flowers that had been pasted on by hand. The indicator was poised between FAIR WEATHER ("Never to be separated") and SUNNY ("Within the sunshine of your smile"). The degrees of the thermometer rose from "esteem" and "friendship" to the feverish highs of "rapture," "unity," and "bliss."

"I call it 'The Barometer of Love,' in keeping with the scientific spirit of the age," he announced with pride. Nervously, Dobbs fingered the braided gold watch chain that hung from his lapel and hovered over his wife as she examined the card.

"Well?" he asked, unable to contain himself. "What do you think?"

WEST LOS ANGELES, JUNE 23, 1967

Trying to sound casual, trying not to think about what he was doing, he said, Here, I brought you something for the fire. It was his *Carousel in Brussels* from the World's Fair suite. A small price to pay for a happy ending.

Mona gave it to a bearded pyromaniac with a shopping bag full of art, and Dan Asher found it hard to watch as his collage was stuffed inside. Dan loudly advised him to burn it quick. It was almost seven o'clock. In a few minutes the rally was going to break up and the march begin. Pulling Dan's head down, Mona whispered, Fuzz. The park was crawling with them. Wherever she looked she saw uniformed rangers, plainclothes cops, secret service agents, and FBI finks eager to learn what they were up to. She explained that she had no intention of burning his or any of the other artists' work here in the park where it would be wasted preaching to the already converted. The strategy was to set the bag ablaze right in front of the main entrance to the hotel where Lyndon could see it. Tell him to go back to Texas and call upon the prime-time TV audience to get us a President in the White House we can trust.

She thrust a stick in Dan Asher's hand with a sign nailed to the other end that said LIAR! Borrowing a thermos jug decorated with daisies from a pinched-faced chum wearing wire-rimmed glasses, she unscrewed the top and handed it to him. It was still hot in the crowded park despite the setting sun, and he welcomed a cool drink before the march. Bending lips to jug, he was overwhelmed by the fumes. And nobody—Mona snatched back the kerosene and screwed on the top—but nobody is going to stop us. Let's go.

Dan Asher thought of those who in futile efforts to end the war had doused themselves with kerosene and gone up in smoke. Fiery exclamation points at the end of anguished cries that were never heard. Poor forgotten human torches. Hey, he cautioned her, be careful with that stuff. We're through being careful, said a grim Mona.

The time for talking was over and the speeches had all been made. Now it was time for action. The Los Angeles Police Commission had granted them a permit to conduct their march as long as they didn't stop in front of the Century Plaza hotel where the President was going to be. Dan Asher could imagine thousands of angry, chanting, determined-looking protestors passing legally under Lyndon's nose and perhaps a handful of activists stopping to tweak it while the cops, with guns drawn, closed in on the six or seven desperadoes. Of course his spirited girlfriend would be among the half-dozen civil disobedients and—he shrugged in resignation—there by her side, he supposed, the jerk who never again was going to let her out of his sight.

He held Mona's arm tightly, and the artist Eva Beck held his and kissed him on the cheek and said, Careful, don't step on my feet. He looked down and she was barefoot. Watch the fucken sign, complained Irving Carp after it had mashed his blond haystack, rapped his back, and then he saw who was holding it and cried, Danny, baby. Goddammit, everybody's here! I love it, I love it. He was right. Everybody *was* there, with maybe one minor exception, which could only mean that Mona had washed her hands of the curator. Definitely. Dan Asher's guess was that the trustees had reminded Dorfman the museum received federal funds, that in his position it would be unwise to join the antiwar demonstration, and he was too chicken to buck them.

Mona's repentant lover had planned to tell her at once about what had happened that day at the museum when he came to find her and the curator first told him they were living together. Start again with a clean slate. He was sure she'd understand and be able to straighten things out without a fuss, but he just couldn't bring himself to say the words. Not here . . . not now. After all, what if she didn't understand? He was too desperately afraid to lose her. He stroked Mona's arm and she smiled at him ravishingly.

There was a bit of pushing and shoving as the scraggly lines formed up, but once the crowd began to move out of the park it became a parade. Young and old marching twenty or twenty-five abreast. Kids in strollers comforting themselves with their thumbs while their mothers cried *Peace!* and *Now!* at the top of their lungs in response to the shouted call for what was wanted and when. Dan Asher could feel the tremendous sense of excitement among the marchers, their exhilaration. Most of them had probably never protested anything before in their lives, and somehow they had all come together here—good people with a common cause and a constitutional right to do what they were doing. Strangers became instant friends. Doctors arm in arm with chiropractors, truant officers and absentees.

Although the warm, chummy camaraderie of linked arms appealed to Dan Asher, he didn't deceive himself into thinking that Johnson was the enemy. The only enemy he knew was chaos, which he found impossible to eliminate from life and just barely manageable to outwit in art, where the rules at least seemed clearer to him, the odds less frightening.

The march route was to take them down Motor Avenue to Pico to the Avenue of the Stars, passing right in front of the hotel. As they came out of the park onto Motor, a clean-cut academic-looking type in suntans and a white shirt, on which he wore a monitor's armband, kept saying, Don't stop, that's it, keep it tight, keep it tight. He was light on his feet and incredibly happy. Too old to be a dancer, he might have been a choreographer who felt privileged to work with a great chorus line. Spotting the huge yellow police bus bearing down on them like a runaway moving van, he shouted, Look out! and Dan Asher yanked Mona back. The cop driver slammed on his brakes and smiled. It was nothing more than a playful warning, a hint of what was in store for them.

Lining the west side of Motor Avenue like a blue picket fence were hundreds of policemen dressed identically in white helmets and gleaming plastic visors, and busloads more of them arriving every minute. They seemed to go on forever, as if in facing mirrors. Forgetting what their batons meant—and he did momentarily—Dan Asher thought the cops looked great. They were a static somber grid for the marchers' flamboyant motley to play upon. Or, it suddenly occurred to him, vice versa, and he reconsidered their long, dark, wicked-looking clubs with a shudder.

He tried to pull Mona along, to move faster, but up ahead the line seemed to be slowing down. He decided that he really didn't like the looks of these cops at all. They were just too personally interested in what was going on and appeared to disapprove of everything. One after the other, they bore an uncanny resemblance to Ronald Reagan, the new governor. These were the brutal fringe-boys, he suspected, the free-lance privateers who operated far from the center of town and might rough up a Sanchez or cream a Washington just for kicks.

Dan Asher was well aware that whatever illicit protest actions had been planned would occur in front of the Century Plaza, but there was nothing heroic in his eagerness to get there. What he also knew was that Reddin, the police chief, would post his very best men there, the cool professional ones with heavy thighs and tinted glasses who ordinarily never stepped out of their patrol cars except to grab a taco. These cops wanted everything to run smoothly, and that was where Dan Asher figured he and Mona had their best chance of survival. A quick, sensible arrest for the public burning of art, release without bail, and home sweet home. He had it all worked out.

The gentle giant, Leland Sonderman, was marking time in front of him when Dan Asher walked into his back and apologized. Mona wanted to know why they had stopped. What's going on? she asked. The rumor was that the police had objected to a pickup truck with a loudspeaker on the back, blaring Hey! Hey! L.B.J., how many kids have you killed today? On Pico, the truck had tried to get to the head of the march, and the cops went after it like a demolition derby. They took the thing apart until all that was left of it was a bent ashtray. Mona became furious. She shouted at the cops nearby, Hey! Hey! L.B.J. . . . and, as the monitors had them moving again, everyone around her picked up the chant like a challenge.

A thrilling moment! Dan hugged Mona, squeezed her arm, but when he reached for Eva's, he found a stump. Unnoticed in the excitement, she had slipped away and been replaced by the next in line. One of Hitler's ex-henchmen. No doubt he had fought on the eastern front and left his arm at Stalingrad. Dan hoped he wasn't a born loser. A bad omen. As they turned onto Pico and passed the main gate to the Twentieth Century–Fox studios, the man said, I used to work there. Good, said the artist, that's swell. The man explained, I'm an actor. Swell, swell, said Dan Asher, anxiously watching the group of hard hats on the curb behind the police lines.

They were yelling, Look at that one with the flag on his shirt. We ought to give him a haircut down to his balls. Go back to Russia, you long-haired commie creep. The split-fingered V of the marchers infuriated them. Everything they believed in was being threatened, violated. You goddamn bastards! they screamed, livid with rage.

A sharp left-hand turn, and the demonstrators were marching down the Avenue of the Stars. The final lap. On the other side of the wide center divider that separated the six lanes, there was no traffic and more and more cops stationed ever closer together. Dr. Felstein would be proud of you, Mona called to him. He gave her a puzzled look. Getting all this exercise and fresh air, she shouted. He said, Very funny. Any minute—he had a sudden ugly premonition—I'm expecting tear gas. Don't be silly, she said. They'd never do anything like that. Not with the President here. He realized that it was useless to argue about it. They'd find out soon enough.

A bottleneck had developed in front of the hotel, and the marchers pouring into the area began to flood it. Some people had sat down in the middle of the blacktop. The monitors tried to open things up, move the demonstrators northwest of the building to Constellation Boulevard, but without success. Dan Asher and Mona were squeezed up against the side of the long reflecting pool that formed the road's center divider before the hotel. He wondered if the fountains had been turned off to give the sharpshooters peering through their telescopic sights better visibility. He could see them up on the rooftop in their dark baseball caps silhouetted against the sky's fading magenta. Directly above them, the wheeling helicopters chopped up the air.

Mona shouted something to him, but he couldn't hear. The noise was deafening. There were cheers, howls, horns, and handclapping chants of Get out, get out, get all the way out! Demonstrators called to the guests watching safely from the balconies that covered the concave front of the slab building. They taunted them, challenged them to come down and join the protest. Gazing across the pool at the thousand helmets, the thousand grim faces beneath them that stood between him and the hotel's glass front door with its metal canopy inscribed in neat white letters CENTURY PLAZA, Dan Asher felt pains in his chest. These cops might be pros, but they had obviously never seen anything like this before. Perhaps they were a little frightened too. Dan Asher saw a smiling girl with eye-catching blond hair that resembled Marissa's try to give one of them a flower, and he knocked it out of her hand. Had it been possible at that moment, he would have grabbed Mona and beat it.

This is Sergeant . . . The voice coming through the bullhorn was tinny and shrill: This is Sergeant . . . —there was a sharp whistling sound similar to a warning blast prior to a detonation— . . . state of California and city of Los Angeles. . . . Dan Asher watched a contingent of cops being assembled into three platoons, their visors down, their clubs at port arms. It was plain to him what was about to happen. The bullhorn shrilled: . . . awful assembly.

Pigs! shouted someone, they're coming, and the cry went up, Here they come!

Hurry! It was Mona's voice. She was holding the bag of artworks on the ledge of the pool as the fellow with the wire-rimmed glasses doused it with kerosene. She lit a match, threw it. Dan saw it hit the bag like dynamite. There was a flash, a roar, an instant rush of flames, a hissing snapping six-foot column of fire that shot blazing scarlet flakes into the air. If the burning bag happened to fall over the wrong way, he and Mona and everyone around them would be fried.

Under the impression that there were some demonstrators who in the confusion were plotting to charge the hotel, break inside, confront the President, even harm him, the police put their emergency dispersal plan into operation. Just beyond the reflecting pool there was an opening in the center divider and six helmeted cops on motorcycles drove into the gap, wedging their machines through the crowd and turning it into a mob. Marchers screamed, pushed, fell over one another trying to get out of the way, but there was no place to go. It was almost impossible to move. Then came the foot cops, one wave after the other charging into the mob to clear a path. Their plan called for them to split the demonstrators into two groups, rolling one down to Constellation Boulevard and the other back to Olympic. Chief Reddin labeled it a beautiful plan, and it worked.

Having tripped and fallen on Dan Asher, Mona's bearded friend was crushing him, and the artist jabbed him hard in the back with his elbow, straightening him up. This was not Dan's idea of fun. He reached for Mona, grabbed her wrist, and yelled, Come on. Let's get out of here. Although he didn't know where he was going, he sure as hell wasn't going to stay there and be trampled to death. Mona shook his hand off her wrist like a bread crumb, her face radiant in the firelight. We're not budging, she screamed. You said it, he heartily agreed, absolutely, and resigned them both to the scrap heap.

A kid standing nearby had been shouting *Sieg Heil! Sieg Heil!* and a cop corporal—two chevrons on a short-sleeve shirt—hit him in the gut. Holding his club like a Louisville Slugger with two hands, the corporal positioned himself, comfortably spreading his legs, and Dan Asher watched him whack away as if swinging for the fences. The kid doubled up and sat down. No, he thought, this is not a game like baseball or football where, though somebody might accidentally get hurt, what wins are the runs scored, the points tallied. The goal here is to bash everything in sight, everything that for them is taunting, contemptible, alien, un-American, and nasty.

Nazis! shrieked a heavyset middle-aged woman who had also seen what had happened to the boy. Coming up from behind, a cop pulled the necklace she was wearing tight and slammed her across the back with his club. Move it, beads, he commanded, shut up and move it. Another cop came toward Dan Asher. Using his nightstick he toppled the burning bag into the pool, where the fire fizzled out.

All right, officer, Dan told him, you got us. We did it. We give up. The sooner the two of them were arrested, he figured, the sooner they'd be safe. You! said the cop, pointing up at Leland Sonderman. I want you. Not *him,* shouted Dan Asher. He had nothing to do with it. Didn't you hear what I said?

Spreading his arms out above the stampeding marchers, the

pursuing police, the general panic, a rueful Leland demanded to know, Who gave you the order to do this? The cop grinned at him. The chief. Is that good enough for you? he inquired sardonically. But where do you want us to go? The cop replied that the others were going down the embankment to Olympic, but *you*, you're coming with me. Leland was confused. Just turn around and march, he ordered. Leland turned around, and the cop rammed the end of his club into his right kidney. Why did you do that? he asked. I'm not resisting. Oh, good, said the cop, and cracked him on the side of the head. Dazed, Leland grabbed his head, but he did not go down. Why did you hit me? he asked.

Fall down, fall down, thought Dan Asher. The big dope didn't even know enough to fall down. Dan wanted to smash this son of a bitch who was tormenting his friend and realized that he had dropped his sign. Stop it, Mona screamed at the cop, stop it, you sadistic bastard! She spat at him, kicked him in the legs. Wheeling around, the cop struck out at her with his club. Dan Asher caught it before it hit Mona and yanked the club out of his hands. He was surprised at how easily it came away. He thought how curious that he wasn't in the least afraid. He was, in fact, quite calm.

The split second before the first club hit him, he noticed that the cop wielding it had a small crescent-shaped mustache. The blow caught him right above the bridge of his nose. It came out of nowhere like a playground fence-pole while you were racing after a fly ball. He could feel his eyes watering, filling up with tears. It infuriated him. Somebody grabbed the back of his hair, tore at it. The blow in the stomach emptied the air out of him like a balloon and knocked him down.

Opening his eyes. Rolling his head to one side—his cheek on the warm tarmac—he saw the blood. If it was his, he was leaking Chinese red. *More* colorful stains by Asher. He hoped that Mona had gotten away, that Leland was all right. The President probably didn't even know that they had tried to tell him something. Maybe—he suddenly began to ache all over—Johnson had never come. He looked up and hovering over him were the blank stares of the hotel's picture windows, the grinning gray mouths of its balcony railings. They had thrown him to the lions and seemed to enjoy the sweaty business. Go ahead, he thought, laugh at me. I deserve it in this costume. He could hardly remember what he once looked like. Even the body he wore was a crippled stranger. Ordinarily he never had headaches, but his head hurt him terribly now. It pounded with the violent irregularity of loose shutters banging in a storm. All that was left of him were his blue eyes and, closing them tight, he felt himself disappear entirely from the face of this awful world.

VENICE, JANUARY 6, 1967

Nothing that has been said meets our case, thought Dan Asher. Yes . . . yes, that was absolutely so, and he reread the passage. "Behold then, the blue madonna streaked with tears. This is my funeral service. We have no ceremonies, only private dirges, and no conclusions, only violent sensations, each separate. Nothing that has been said meets our case."

VENICE, JUNE 25, 1967

He reached for the ringing telephone and, with an effort, lifted the receiver and held it near his ear. It was Mona. She had been trying to get him since yesterday. Her low voice, her warm breath in his ear. His wounds dried to scabs and fell off. I just got back, he explained. They kept me in the hospital for observation. She wanted to know, Are you all right? I'm all right, he said, fine. But, she said, you were bleeding so badly.

There was a catch in her voice that touched him deeply, interfered with his breathing. He wasn't used to such concern

292

from her. Making light of his injuries, he reported a few stitches here, a few there, nothing to get excited about. And actually I think the stitching gives me a new, rugged, outdoor look. Have you ever seen a face like a snowshoe?

Mona told him to quit kidding and asked if he was in pain. It wasn't a problem. These pains he could live with. The pain that he dreaded was the rapier thrust in the chest and, despite the beating he had taken, his sternum was the one area of the Asher anatomy that was free and clear. Truly a complete recovery. Wonderful! None to speak of, he told her.

She felt in a way that she was responsible for what had happened to him. She thanked him for what he did, for trying to protect her. It was brave of him. She couldn't get over the fact that the bastards hadn't even booked him for resisting arrest. He said, I guess they figured they had done enough to me for one night.

She wanted to know if he had seen any of the papers. Outrageous, she informed him. Estimating less than ten thousand there when everybody knows it was probably closer to twenty. Claiming the marchers violated their permit by stopping in front of the hotel when the truth is that even if they wanted to they couldn't move. Reporting only a few minor injuries when I myself saw more than a dozen bloody heads. Describing the cops as acting with restraint under great provocation and quoting city officials falling all over themselves praising what they did. That asshole mayor of ours called it a superb job of security. Can you beat that? It makes me want to puke.

Dan Asher hadn't seen any of the papers. In the hospital he had heard something on the radio, but he hadn't seen any of the papers. When are you coming back? he asked. Mona said, What? He longed to hold her in his arms, stroke her hair, tell her how terribly he had missed her, missed their lovemaking, missed the jubilant laughter that followed it—the two of them confounding that ancient nonsense about everyone being sad afterward except the cock who crows. I want to see you, he told her in an urgent, steamy, unambiguous voice. When are you coming back? I'm not, she said. What gave you that idea?

He shifted his weight in the chair and suffered a relapse, all of his wounds instantly declaring themselves—each wound a mouth and each mouth full of caries. I'm a sick man, thought Dan Asher. What do you mean you're not? he asked.

Mona was living with Miles and had been for months. You knew that, she insisted. Still . . . but . . . he fumbled for words. You two split, didn't you? You're through with him now. No, Dan, she said unequivocally. You're wrong. The pause that followed spread through him like an ink stain, permanent black. At last, Mona said gently, Dan . . . She said, I really don't want to hurt you, Dan, but I'm not going to lie and say maybe. We're through. I'll admit it was never dull, but it's over.

He wondered if marriage was what she wanted. Maybe that would interest her. Perhaps to a girl as young as that, marriage was still important, still meant something. A sign, a ritual to pass through, a public declaration of commitment. She certainly wasn't going to be tempted by first dibs on all his worldly possessions. As for himself, he wouldn't ordinarily have dreamed of marriage. Given his track record, it could be the kiss of death. And yet, if that's what it took to bring her back—

Look, Mona, he said, I've got to see you. I have something important to tell you. He waited, listening for her okay. Had she forgotten his name already? She was so quiet. I'm glad, she said, I'm glad you're not hurt, and hung up.

THE WHITE HOUSE, MARCH 31, 1968

". . . With American sons in the fields far away, with America's future under challenge right here at home, with our hopes and the world's hopes for peace in the balance every day, I do not believe that I should devote an hour or a day of my time to any personal partisan causes or to any duties other than the awesome duties of this office—the Presidency of your country.

"Accordingly, I shall not seek, and I will not accept, the

nomination of my party for another term as your President. But let men everywhere know, however, that a strong and a confident and a vigilant America stands ready tonight to seek an honorable peace, and stands ready tonight to defend an honored cause, whatever the price, whatever the burden, whatever the sacrifice that duty may require.

"Thank you for listening. Good night and God bless all of you."

VENICE, JULY 4, 1967

When the phone rang at five thirty in the morning, it leaped at his sleeping throat, threw him out of bed. Marissa, is that you? It was a bad connection. The woman at the other end reported that his mother was dying. Dan Asher told her he'd be there as soon as he could. Hanging up, he said thank you, as if a waitress had just handed him a clean fork.

Although he hated to leave his work and uproot himself, he hated even more to think of his mother dying among strangers in a nursing home in the Bronx. Leland Sonderman loaned him the money for the trip. Because of the holiday, it was hard to get a reservation, but he was finally able to make one on a TWA flight to New York that evening. Only Leland knew he was leaving town. It seemed to him that there was no one else to tell, no one else who might be interested. At twenty, he had read about the loneliness of the human soul being unendurable and not known what it meant. At fifty-one, he had some idea. Gloom weighed him down like a dead animal, and a gloomy Dan Asher, he decided, would be of no use to anyone. Pulling out a small leather overnight bag, gray with dust, from under a pile of boxes in the bedroom closet, he got ready to go.

He packed and dressed quickly and then suffered the waiting until nightfall as if wedged inside a crushed automobile. The day was warm, with the sun a smear and the light a glare and even the birds sounding tired and irritable and perhaps wondering if it was worth the effort to sing on such a day. It was better when the sun went down. It was better until the firecrackers blasted potholes in his frayed nerves. Dan Asher had a troubling premonition, and the last thing he did before leaving for the airport was call his mother.

I don't think we have anybody here by that name, said the woman who answered the phone. Dan Asher explained that it was his mother. She was very ill. They had called that morning from the nursing home to tell him. Just a minute please, said the woman at the other end. Hold on.

Another voice got on and said, She's gone. Dan Asher demanded to know what she meant. I think, said the woman evasively, she was discharged. How the hell could she have been discharged, he shouted, when only a few hours ago she was dying? He insisted on speaking to Mrs. Taggart. The director of the nursing home got on and was as smooth as cream. We have a little problem getting the right sort, she apologized for her staff. Your mother is expecting you.

LOS ANGELES, JULY 4, 1967

Lennox Chandler lived way up on Mulholland Drive near Benedict Canyon. Tattersall had never been to his house before. I know it's a holiday, he had said on the phone. I'm sorry to bother you, but something's come up. I've got to go to New York.

The Vice President of Dutton Insurance became extraordinarily excited. Henry! his cry a rusty-hinge squealing falsetto, you've found the painting. No, it wasn't that, but he was getting very close. Oh, said the disappointed Lennox Chandler, unconvinced, barely interested. The investigator explained what it was he wanted and, when he was through, Chandler gave him his address on Mulholland Drive. Why? asked a puzzled Tattersall. Come ahead, Henry. I'll be waiting for you.

It was a damn nuisance. To get there by bus was hopeless, and Koontz was unavailable, stretched out in bed on a board with a wrenched back. He had been at the Century Plaza riot. He had tripped running away from the cops. Henry had to call a cab. It would eventually go down on the bill to Chandler, but right now he needed all the cash he had for New York.

The taxi driver went up the narrow canyon, turned onto winding Mulholland Drive, and found the address. A high wooden gate blocked the driveway. Henry Tattersall, said Henry into the speaker, and the gate slid aside like a secret panel. The steep driveway ended at a garage in which was parked a black Lincoln Continental. After obtaining a receipt from the driver, Henry got out. It was a white, one-story, Bauhaus-sleek, flat-roofed structure with huge glass windows. Henry ran his comb through his hair and rang the front doorbell.

The maid who showed up looked as if she had formerly been a bouncer in an East German beer hall. Not tall, but thick as cement. She had blond bangs, bulging calves, forearms the size of fire hoses. This was no one to fuck around with. I called about an hour ago, Henry quickly explained after identifying himself. He's expecting me.

You will go straight ahead, she informed him. You will not make any turns. You will then go out the screen door to the patio. You will find Mr. Chandler by the pool. Is that clear? Thanks, said Henry, and tried not to make any mistakes. He could see her watching after him as if she were worried about the silver.

In the back yard there were tall cool-looking cypresses, and despite the beige layer of smog that covered the Valley, the view below was spectacular. It looked to Henry like a giant grill of straight boulevards and straight streets that intersected at right angles, a simple layout for barbecuing the natives on a sizzling cloudless day. Lennox Chandler, wearing a skimpy French bathing suit, was stretched out in a deck chair beside the pool.

At the sound of footsteps, he opened his eyes and raised a hand to shield them from the sun. It wasn't so much the absence of clothes but the missing glasses that made him look unfamiliar to Henry.

Chandler greeted him, apologizing for not shaking hands. He was covered with suntan lotion and gleamed like an oily sardine. Listen to that, he said. Henry listened to the pleasant splash of water as it trickled down the rustic fountain of piled rocks at the far end of the pool. He was surprised that there wasn't more noise from the traffic on Mulholland. Do you hear all the birds? Henry heard a few birds. It's going to rain, said Chandler. They always sing that way before it rains. Henry glanced up at the tranquil blue sky. You've got a nice place here, he complimented his client.

Chandler invited him to pull up a chair. He had something to tell Henry. He had already agreed over the phone to cover his plane fare to New York, so it wasn't that. First, began Chandler, I'd like a report. Tell me about your progress.

Henry told him everything that he had been able to find out about that rainy Friday afternoon at the museum. He told him about Dewayne Taylor, about Trisha Wiley, about the maintenance workers who were helping her move, about the three guys from Cal-Cool repairing the air conditioning, about the two packers who discovered the Rembrandt missing. He described his early suspicions of Dorfman.

I still haven't completely written off the curator as a suspect, Henry went on, but at this point I feel that it didn't have to be an inside job at all, and probably wasn't. In fact, I'm pretty well convinced now that our thief is an amateur with no previous criminal record. He's an artist living in Venice by the name of Asher whose discovery of the unguarded Rembrandt in Dorfman's office was merely a matter of luck. Good for him, bad for us.

Chandler thought it over for a minute. Could you be on the wrong track, Henry? he asked tentatively. I've spoken to the FBI, and they think it's a professional job. Henry said they were wrong. Fearing that he had stepped on the little detective's toes,

Chandler wondered if Tattersall was even aware that the FBI was in on the case. Of course he knew. When the loss is greater than fifty thousand dollars, they enter almost automatically. Mason's good, Henry acknowledged, but he's the only agent they've got on art. Chandler pointed out the obvious, that Henry was also a lone investigator. That's right, but the Tattersall Service doesn't stop at nine to five, said the detective, showing him how much Dutton was getting for its money. As an afterthought, Henry said, I don't stop at all.

Lennox Chandler smiled. Have you spoken to this Asher? Henry said no. Why not? he demanded. Tattersall preferred to go about things his own way. I know who he is, and he doesn't know me, and that's an advantage. But the police have questioned him, and I've spoken to them. Growing slightly impatient, the insurance executive said, All right, all right, fine, now why do you think he has our painting?

Two reasons, replied Henry. He had the motive—he was heavily in debt with large medical bills following a heart attack. And he had the opportunity—he was the last one to see the painting. Chandler asked, But how did he get it out of the museum? Sitting in the direct sun, Henry felt as if he were being grilled under a probing light and forced to come clean. He wanted to open his shirt, loosen his tie, put on a bathing suit. He took out a folded handkerchief and dabbed at his neck, his face. I don't know the answer to that yet, he admitted. Maybe under his clothes, rolled up in an umbrella, I don't know.

That there had been no serious attempt to ransom the painting since its disappearance on May 5—only the one crackpot—was, according to Tattersall, significant. That the theft was not a political act by a member of some extremist group hungry for publicity was also important. He claimed that both facts supported his conclusion. The longer the silence, explained Henry, the more likely that the painting is to be sold privately, and my hunch is that it's going to happen now in New York.

Why New York? Chandler's curiosity was piqued. Henry reasoned that there were only a limited number of places in the world where you could fence a work as well known as the

Rembrandt. New York, Zurich, Paris, London, Rome. Maybe Vienna. Given Asher's New York background, he had to know people there, and even if they themselves didn't want the painting, people in New York knew people everywhere. I put my money on New York, said Henry. I gave his name to a friend who works airport security at LAX. A few hours ago, he called to tell me that a Daniel Asher had booked a last-minute reservation on TWA's seven o'clock flight to New York this evening. It fits in, Mr. Chandler. It all fits in.

Do you think he'll be carrying the painting with him? asked Chandler, with new interest. Henry thought that was a definite possibility. But there are other ways he could move it. We'll see. . . . He stood up. Don't worry, Mr. Chandler. There's an old saying in my business that the hotter the item, the harder it is to unload. We'll get Mr. Ward's painting back. I expect answers at the other end of this flight to New York.

Lennox Chandler said, So do we, Henry. I think you should know that we've been getting pressure from Mr. Ward's lawyers to settle his policy. If this trip of yours proves to be a blind alley, we're going to have to conclude your investigation and pay Ward. Tattersall's expression—melancholy even in its most halcyon moments—became positively funereal. He had figured Chandler had something like that on his mind. Good luck, Henry. Don't miss your plane.

Inside the house, Henry found a telephone in the living room and dialed for a cab. Waiting for somebody to answer, he glanced across toward the hallway and saw the maid silently watching him from the shadows with her thick forearms folded. It's local, he explained, and decided to wait for a drink of water until he got home.

LOS ANGELES, JULY 4, 1967

At the airport with an hour to kill, Dan Asher fell asleep, exhausted. A final boarding call snapped up his head. It was a flight to Kansas City leaving from gate twelve. He still had fifty-five minutes to go. The next time Dan woke up he was in Italy. Completely surrounded by Mediterranean mothers, fathers, grandmothers, kids in shorts, fat-cheeked bambinos—a huge family excitedly waving their hands in Italian and laughing. They looked at him and he smiled like one of the family, but the light in his eyes felt terrible. If they had expected his black suit to speak Italian, they were in for a disappointment. The suit was a Santa Monica Thrift Shop bargain, and the one thing he owned that didn't show stains.

Walking toward the boarding gate, he glanced back. They were all shouting now, leaping frantically up and down, pounding one another, hugging anything that cried, all except one distant uncle, a small, quiet guy with gangster hair squinting after him from their midst.

Dan Asher hurried down the gangway and, without thinking, planted his right boot in the plane. He was amused when he realized what he had done. Appropriately enough, it had been his mother's doing. Always the right foot out the door on trips, the right foot into cars. Since his childhood, her wisdom had absolutely guaranteed his safe journeys. Dan Asher was not superstitious, but he was rather tickled by this tiny bit of the medieval world safeguarding the jet age.

His seat was on the aisle, and when he sank heavily into it, he could still feel the cops' clubs mauling his kidneys, bruising his back. He reached behind him and rubbed. He was rubbing as Jane Mansfield came down the aisle. He watched fascinated. Considering that he had read of the actress's death in an automobile accident earlier that week, she looked wonderful. Her shoes, her bag, her skirt, her blouse, everything matched.

She paused, stopped, glanced down at him with a puzzled

look, her eyes as shiny as blue silk and her arms full of coats. Could he be so lucky? Of course, he said, jumping up so that she could slip into the vacant seat beside him. She smiled and shook the gold out of her bleached hair. No, hers was directly across the aisle. Dan Asher thought he had never seen such beautiful small teeth.

He helped her place her pea coat, raincoat, and fur coat in the overhead rack. That's very kind, she said. It was a trained voice, but soft and with a hint of the Confederacy. If it belonged to Jane Mansfield, the rest of her, when viewed close up, belonged to someone else. She was shorter, slimmer, younger than the dead actress. He pointed to the coats and, teasing, asked, Are you expecting snow in New York? Eventually, she said and, sitting down, buckled her seat belt.

The plane taxied to the end of the runway past deep blue lights that floated like tropical fish at the bottom of a tank. The seat next to him was still empty and the dark, rumpled man nearest the window didn't block his view at all. Clutching the armrests, the anxious fellow was leaning back stiffly as if at the dentist. The four jet engines roared and the 707 leaped forward, raced thumping down the runway, and, wings shivering in anticipation, sprang into the sky. It still took Dan's breath away. All this steel and glass and aluminum hammered together with rivets and stitched with wires, this whole gigantic junk pile hurtling through space like smoke in a high wind.

Leaning over, he gazed down at Los Angeles, an open jewel box. He had come to love the brilliant nighttime city almost as much as Mona did. She had taught him that. It was difficult for him to believe that never again would they share its promises together. The lights below—row upon glittering row of rubies, emeralds, diamonds—royal gems, he thought, crown jewels at the Crystal Palace.

He imagined a nineteenth-century English crowd staring at them, their backs to the foreground making a somber silhouette of bonnets and top hats. In the great exhibition case on a cloth of midnight blue, the blazing colors of the coronets and tiaras, crowns, scepters, and orbs dotted with ceramic buttons and glass eyes. Hearing the pilot's electronic signal, Dan Asher noted the No Smoking light had been turned off and reached for his Gauloises. The collage idea fit right in with his fairs. It excited him. He was eager to see what could be done with it as soon as he got back.

Spotting the cigarettes, his blond neighbor asked him for a match. Absolutely, he said, pleased that she hadn't lost interest, and going through his pockets, he was annoyed to discover that he didn't have any. There was a toothpick in a paper wrapper on which was printed The Crow's Nest, Malibu—the restaurant up the coast where Mona had taken him on his birthday—a ticket from the parking lot near the airport where he had left his car, some change, an opened package of Tums, the blank postcard that he planned to mail from Kennedy as soon as the plane landed. And not one lousy match. Hold on, he told her with a smile and turned to the individual near the window. What? said the startled fellow, his left eye twitching. Oh, no, no, sorry, he said.

Dan Asher asked the passenger reading *Time* in the seat behind her. Slowly putting down his magazine, the small man with the black gangster hair studied the artist, squinting at him as if he were some unfamiliar vegetable on his plate. Dan wondered what had become of all his Italian relatives. He repeated his request for matches but without much hope, for the guy was chewing gum.

I think so, said Henry Tattersall, and produced a pack. Although he no longer smoked, Henry generally carried matches as part of his job the way a waiter might. They were useful for reading names on mailboxes in dark hallways, handy for license plate numbers on unlighted streets. He told Dan Asher to keep them. I've got others, he said.

It was Elijah whose mission it was to straighten things out in Israel and, having tidied up the mess, departed spectacularly in a chariot of fire in a whirlwind. The best Henry Tattersall could imagine for himself was a TWA jet with four sputtering engines dropping into Jamaica Bay. Henry hated to fly. It wasn't a phobia, but he figured that everyone had just so many chances in life, and each time you went up and came down whole, there was one less. Not to mention the rubber food, which he also wasn't nuts about. He tossed aside the menu with its hollow French promises. Henry had been in the business. He knew. He pulled down the tray in front of him and told the stewardess scotch and soda.

From behind the magazine, the detective observed Asher trying to make time with the flashy blonde seated on the aisle. That guy never quits, Henry marveled. He was waiting for him to get up and go for a walk, take a pee. As far as Henry could tell, the only piece of luggage that Asher was carrying with him to New York was the suitcase under his seat. It was small, but not impossible. The width of the missing canvas was twenty inches and the painting could have been rolled as tight as a towel. And if not in the suitcase, he might have sent it on some other way. Perhaps it was being held for his arrival at the front desk of some hotel or a post office General Delivery window. He was an artist, a clever guy, probably much cleverer—Henry was not ashamed to acknowledge—than Henry Tattersall.

The tap on his knee startled him and went to the bone. Henry lowered his magazine and saw who it was. I've been spotted, he thought. Do you happen to have a match? asked Dan Asher. Having seen the names of the injured in the newspaper, Henry was not surprised by the purple bruise on Asher's temple, the two-inch zipper above his eyebrow. The cops must have given him a good going over at the Century Plaza. But what had he been doing there dressed in a peace suit? It didn't fit in.

The detective observed a dark, shadowy patch of stubble beneath his lower lip. Asher had not shaved well that morning. It was a good sign. He was on edge, careless, all ready to make a mistake.

Keep them, said Henry. I've got others.

Now I mean no disrespect to the recently departed, but honestly—she pointed to the open top of her attractive salmon-colored blouse—do I look like that cow? Her name was Penny Rushton, and she was indeed an actress. She was, however, through with Hollywood. The major studios had never really given her a break. They all thought she looked too much like Jane Mansfield. Not a bit, said Dan Asher. Penny liked that. The threads of smoke from their cigarettes braided in the air.

Penny confided that she was going back East to work in the theater, her first love. I never should have left, she said. The East has people, seasons, time. Dan Asher saw a long-gone photograph of a snow-suited Marissa—age three—in her stroller, a tiny pink astronaut floating stiffly in January. He thought of his mother. She had visited them once about three years ago in California. How old she had become. The eyelids had fallen down at the corners, and all that was left of her once lovely neck were two strings, the flimsy life-support system of arteries that still kept her alive. Be careful, he warned Penny, time makes you old. That's normal, she said, for she was young enough not to care. All there is out here in the West is space, and you can get lost in space.

She was right about getting lost, but he wasn't frightened of it any more than he was of dying. Recently, he had been looking at the paintings of Ingres and the mirrors in the paintings through which can be seen a gray, tranquil world of great distances. Death, he thought, must be like that. No solutions, but the mysteries no longer disturb. Dan saw himself falling into those mirrors and lamented all the collages he would never make.

Plainly his mother's condition had gotten him down. But for some indefinable reason, he suddenly felt light as an eyelash and sure she'd pull through. It was as if a scorching Santa Ana had given way to a sea breeze. The first thing to be done was to mail the card to the museum. Then, as soon as that was taken care of and his mother was on the mend—as soon as they were both, in a sense, out of danger—he'd go back. He had a world of plans. He was going to see Marissa and her boyfriend, talk the situation over with them quietly . . . sensibly, invite them to dinner, patch things up. He was going to finish his fairs, work harder than he had ever worked before. He was going to find a part-time teaching job at Otis or Chouinard or one of the other local art schools. He was going to forget about Mona. He was going to really try to do that. The future was an emphatic knock on the door, and viewed through this peephole of possibilities it looked okay.

Dan Asher called for a split of champagne to celebrate. The stewardess was happy to oblige. She popped the cork, tipped the bottle, and poured it into his lap. Oh, my! Oh, my! She said she was sorry but seemed pissed off that he had made extra work for her. She found the napkins on her serving cart and began to rub at his jacket. He took her hand, moved it aside, and damply stood up. Thanks, he dismissed her. I'll survive. He wanted to have as little to do with this fumbler as possible.

In the lavatory, he dropped his pants and rubbed them inside and out with paper towels. Pulling them up, he felt only a slight chill, a few goose bumps. His glance fell on the mirror, and he was unprepared for how grim and gray that fellow with the mustache had become, but he could still flash a childish, gap-toothed grin and smile him away. He made his way back down the aisle and nearly passed his seat. On the floor, the little Italian guy was on hands and knees pushing around his bag.

Anything wrong? asked Dan Asher. Henry Tattersall froze. He turned his head. He looked and saw who it was. Henry held up the tiny one-shot empty bottle of Johnny Walker as if it were a prize from the bottom of the sea. I dropped it, he explained, and returned to his seat. Dan guessed he was somebody who sold something. There was nothing flashy about him to suggest used cars, so maybe hardware or groceries. The worried expression said that whatever he sold, business was bad.

A stewardess was at his elbow, a different one this time. She seemed a little nervous. Watchful. She must have been warned about him. Would you care for chicken or steak? she asked tentatively. The menu had promised romance, rhapsodizing over tournedos forestière and poulade châtelaine. Chicken, he told her, not to be difficult, and saw even that reduced to a c on her order sheet. Thank you, she said and, relieved, smiled. Moon-faced, pink-cheeked, she hadn't yet been around long enough to become plastic.

He liked her and would have said something pleasant if not for the white-hot coal that was burning its way through his chest at the moment. Although the dinner was still to come, Dan diagnosed indigestion. His stomach had been upset all that day, and he had been taking Tums. It was understandable. He took one more, and then another, but it was like trying to drench burning chaparral with an eyedropper.

Are you okay? asked Penny. He was fine, a little indigestion, that's all. She thought it was too bad that they were going to miss the fireworks. *The New Yorker* on her lap was full of them. Her favorite was the fiery pinwheel that spins around and hisses. He recognized the very one that was frying his insides. The pressure just above his stomach, the intense pain, made him feel as if he couldn't bear chatting with this stunning young woman another second, and that really scared the hell out of him. Maybe it was something serious. No, he didn't think so. He had glanced around the cabin at the other passengers, and there wasn't a single Krishna aboard.

This is your captain speaking. They were cruising at thirty-seven thousand feet, there was fair weather in New York, and they would be arriving on time. Dan leaned back and tried to breathe normally. Unless the pilot— A chill froze his hands and feet; his damp suit turned to cardboard. Either someone had turned up the air conditioning or the plane had sprung a leak. His windpipe seemed no wider than a straw.

This wasn't like his first heart attack at all. Then it was one smash and down he went. This time it was fire and ice. This time it was the pneumatic sleeve slipped around the heart, the unseen hand closed on the rubber bulb, the unexpectedly slow pumping. He stayed calm, tried not to panic. He recalled that his hospital roommate, Elbert Thomas, had lived through four of these things.

The stewardess was back, so flustered that she could barely look at him. She had forgotten to jot down his beverage. She asked, What did you say you wanted? He knew damn well, but even though he liked her, he wasn't about to tell her. Or anyone else for that matter. What I wanted—once again confronting the old failure head on like a wrestler—what I wanted was to have known myself better than a stranger. Not to have been constantly surprised by this visitor, this madman bearing my name who leaped out and did what he pleased, who acted in ways I wanted nothing to do with and had to justify with lies.

She leaned over him. Is there something wrong, sir? You don't look too good. Can I get you a glass of water? He peered up into her face. Those healthy pink cheeks, those moist, frightened eyes the color of whole wheat. Yes, of course she could be trusted. Listen! he said. There was something he had to tell her. There might not be time enough for the anonymous postcard after all. He hated the thought of unfinished business, ugly loose ends dangling disagreeably into the future.

He would explain that there had been a toolbox, but say nothing to her about the gash on the back of his hand, the anger, the bleakness of loss. There was no way to tell her the why of it, only the how. Inside the box was a screwdriver with a yellow plastic handle, a roll of electrician's tape. He knew then what he was going to do as if it had been months in the planning. He pried the painting from its frame, rolled it up, jumped onto Dorfman's desk. There in the ceiling where the acoustical tiles had been stripped away to reveal the secret world above our heads, he shoved it in among the cloud-gray pipes, the thin copper tubes, the silver conduit, and taped it to the top of the rectangular air duct covered with insulation that resembled fleece. It was as invisible as the dark side of the moon. The whole thing had taken him less time to do than would the telling of it.

He said, Listen . . . He tried to form the words clearly so that she would understand. He tried to say them quickly so that everything would be said. She bent closer. There was a pimple on her chin. She was young. Too many sweets. Her mouth opened and closed excitedly. She was saying something to him. She shook her head up and down as if she had grasped exactly what the situation was and would take care of everything. She seemed to want him to know that there was nothing to worry about. Dan wasn't worried. He could see Penny—her mouth in a state of shock, her hands strangling one another—standing over him shining with tragic beauty as one stewardess slipped a pillow beneath his head and another held a glass gently to his lips. They were back mothering him again. He didn't mind. In fact, it felt good.

Henry sank down in his seat and fingered the little scotch bottle he had rolled across the aisle. Having squeezed Asher's bag and pressed on it, he had gotten his answer. There wasn't very much inside and nothing as solid as a tightly rolled canvas. But that didn't bother Henry. It merely eliminated one empty possibility and simplified his work. In fact, the closer the plane got to New York, the more excited he became, the more convinced that the solution to the mystery lay there, the more confident that if he stuck with Asher the missing Rembrandt was surely within his grasp.

The ruminating detective pounded his sugarless spearmint gum to shreds, and green pieces stuck to his teeth, his gums. He pulled them out in gooey, adhesive strands and hid them away in a tissue. Seated beside him, the woman in the white pleated skirt had seen enough. Excuse me, she commanded, and before Henry could get out of her way, she stomped on his toes and was gone.

Tattersall rubbed his right foot and watched the three of them hovering over Asher as if he were a forbidden treat. Although the artist had trouble holding his women, he certainly knew how to attract them. And Mona Block, who had apparently lived with

Asher for a couple of years, Henry regarded as a remarkably fine-looking kid. How the hell does he do it? wondered Henry. We're nearly the same age, for crying out loud!

He had been mulling that over when the cockpit people were back on the intercom. This is your captain speaking. This time it was an emergency, but the voice was as matter-of-fact as if, once again, reporting fair skies in New York. There was need of a doctor. We have, said the captain, a passenger who isn't . . .

OAKLAND, 1976

DANIEL ASHER: Collages 1943–1967.
The Oakland Museum, 1976.
Introduction by Mordecai Bell.

A second heart attack occurred in 1967, resulting in Daniel Asher's death. But prior to that, and following the attack and subsequent depression he suffered the previous year, the artist was to enjoy his most productive period and complete his most appealing work. Selecting the theme of world's fairs for his diminutive collages, as if he now wanted to celebrate all of life and cram it into a thimble, Asher created the romantically festive series that climaxed his career. If we miss in these fairs the richness of his "Dark Corridors" or "Great Hotels," we are nevertheless charmed by their simplicity and freshness. They look at us like smiling faces. Though Asher was considered something of a recluse during the last year of his life, it is impossible—after viewing the work that he did then—to think of him as that tiresomely familiar figure of modern fiction, the alienated artist.

There is a wonderful energy and exhilaration in these scenes of weddings, births, banquets, dances, revelations. Invariably, the atmosphere is saturated with a warm light and brilliant color. The mood is lyrical and, in some instances, even rhapsodic. I am sorry to say that nowhere was the small, hurriedly assembled posthumous show put on in 1968 by Carpenter Phillips at the Los Angeles Municipal Gallery more woefully inadequate than in its representation of the artist's work of this period.

La Grande Roue (cat. no. 92) is a joyous epithalamium and an outstanding example of the buoyant last phase of Asher's *oeuvre*. The wedding scene depicted is washed in sunlight. The very air appears to shimmer. Amidst the gaiety, there remains an aura of artifice and romance that we have seen in his earlier works. (The habits of a lifetime are not easily discarded.) The motif of the man's hand on the woman's breast may remind some of Holbein's *Jacob and Rachel* or Rembrandt's *The Jewish Bride*. But at the most, we sense no more than a tiny echo. There are few echoes, however, in the sudden inexplicable appearance of the bearded white-haired man in groom's clothing. For me that is pure Asher.

At the time of the artist's death, the painter Leland Sonderman made the statement that "In any generation there are only a handful of artists who really matter. In mine, Asher was one of them." It is sad that Asher's reputation has so declined in recent years that relatively few people have had an opportunity to share his work. These ninety-two collages—a number of them never before publicly exhibited—contain some of his finest achievements. The visitor to the Oakland Museum can feel confident that he is seeing Asher at his best.

OAKLAND, DECEMBER 24, 1976

They left for San Francisco while it was still dark and caught the dawn just north of Point Arguello. It came up maroon like an Oriental rug, and as the light climbed the sky it faded into a cool, cloudless blue. As usual, Dorothy had wanted to get an early start to avoid the heavy pre-holiday freeway traffic on Interstate 5. Henry, as usual, would have preferred to avoid it by not going at all. He could do without his brother-in-law, Fletcher, and their annual one-week collision that Dorothy called his vacation. You work hard and you need it, she insisted protectively. Henry wasn't so sure. Every time he and the Berkeley sociology professor got together, Fletcher would lecture him—explaining crime and corruption, ridiculing Henry the naif, saluting Fletcher the shrewd, bold, cynical *homme d'expérience*. Henry loathed his sneakers with the three stripes.

Smiling and looking wonderful behind the wheel in her green suede car coat, her green silk scarf knotted cowgirl-style at the side of her neck, Dorothy held the Toyota at a steady sixty. She was eager to get there. She was fond of her sister Betty, her two teenage nephews, their dog Mr. Spock, Fletcher, San Francisco. It was some consolation that she, at least, enjoyed his vacations. Turning to watch the sunrise, Henry sipped his wife's steaming, black-velvet coffee from the Thermos cup. The week off would give him a chance to make up his mind about Harkness.

It was a big well-established investigating agency with seventy years in the business and fifteen offices nationwide. Earlier that month when the art dealer, Hofstedler, was sentenced to a year in jail, there had been an article in the paper that mentioned Henry's part in cracking the case. The Harkness Agency was impressed. They invited Henry to join them and take charge of their Los Angeles bureau. It was a good offer. Henry said he'd think it over and let them know after Christmas, but he hadn't yet told Dorothy anything. He was afraid to hear what she'd say.

Well, come on, expert, she teased him, who do you think did it? Did what? he asked. Dorothy wanted to know who murdered Edwin Drood. Ever since leaving L.A., she had been recounting to him *The Mystery of Edwin Drood,* the unfinished last novel of Charles Dickens that she had just read. Dickens had died in Chapter 23 with the murderer still at large. Why, he wondered, would anyone begin reading a crime story in which they knew from the outset nobody was going to get caught? Henry took a dim view of books with unresolved mysteries. Stories, he felt, should wrap things up, get rid of the mess, tell us who did it. TV could solve a crime in half an hour with three commercials in between. It was a comfort. Life had enough false steps and loose ends. Who needed them in fiction?

Well, she prodded, come on. Henry said, Hard evidence, and pointed out that there is no hard evidence Drood has actually been murdered. In fact, Henry hoped eventually to see the young man happily married to his fiancée, Rosa Bud. Dorothy grinned and made whiskbroom sounds of derision. Dear, dear Henry, she said fondly, you're such a romantic.

The day had turned a brilliant blue-white and dazzling like an arc lamp. Dorothy had put on her sunglasses. Henry watched in silence as the roadside lettuce fields raced back to Los Angeles and wished that he was going with them.

They arrived in San Francisco in the early afternoon and drove through the gray, windy downtown city streets. Betty and her husband lived on a hill that was so steep there were no puddles after it rained. Their house, overlooking the bay, had a spectacular view of the bridge to Oakland. It was a sprawling Victorian structure with stained glass panels, sloping floors, dark woodwork, and more rooms than a provincial hotel. Betty was in the doorway waving as soon as their Toyota pulled up in front.

Go ahead, Henry told his excited wife, and took the keys from her. I'll get the bags. Climbing out, Dorothy called, Don't forget the presents, dear. The two sisters fell all over one another like tears. Opening the trunk, Henry quickly filled his arms with boxes and bags and then slammed the door shut. It was chilly standing there in the street. He spit out his gum to avoid choking on it inside. It's only a week, Henry, he reminded himself, and taking a breath so deep that it rattled his rib cage, he marched to the door.

Fletcher was waiting for him just inside. He was wearing a seaman's black turtleneck sweater, dungarees, and sneakers with three stripes. His graying Afro exploded from his skull in every direction. He was brimming over with health, vitality, confidence, and an utter disdain for failure that Henry found unrealistic. Fletcher jogged. Jabbing two fingers into his brother-in-law's side as if they were loaded, he said, Hello, peeper. Henry cringed. Fletcher howled, and behind him on the hallway table the lacy leaves of an asparagus plant trembled. Hearing the commotion, the family's Irish setter came bounding in. Beat it, Spock, commanded his master. The dog—its tail wagging in ecstasy—circled about Henry as if he were a fire hydrant.

Let me take that stuff from you, Henry. Fletcher was genuinely glad to see him. Go ahead into the living room and put your shoes up on the couch. Dirty the doilies. Was it a good trip? Don't stand there gabbing, Betty, make these people a drink. Dorothy asked her sister, Where are the boys?

The living room was pleasant. They drank, they talked. The sisters—different as stripes and checks—shared with one another a flattering attentiveness as they chatted animatedly, a look that said, How interesting! Tell me more. When have I ever heard anyone speak so well before? Henry listened to their conversation, warmed himself by the fire, sipped a cheerful scotch and soda, watched the tiny Christmas lights flit nimbly about the tree. He should have known that it was too good to last.

Fletcher returned, bouncing athletically into the room on the balls of his feet, and said, Dacks. Norman Dacks. It was the name of a big San Francisco agency. Henry knew something about its reputation in child custody disputes, its work in anti-terrorist planning for corporate executives.

That's right, acknowledged Fletcher, but did you know that all their people have graduate degrees? One of my colleagues at Berkeley just quit to go to work for them. Their approach is completely scientific, the latest methods. Computers, electronic surveillance, infrared photography, voice prints, psychological profiles. For chrissake, Henry—this with a straight face, a contemptuous snort, a hopeless shake of his head—is it really possible that you don't even use a car?

Fletch! It was Betty, calling to her husband. Stop teasing. Henry just got here. Fletcher winked at his brother-in-law, drew closer, cleared his professorial throat *hem-hem-hem,* and, in a low voice, gave him some advice. I think it's a bonehead play, Henry. Operating a one-man cottage industry at a time when the investigation-security field is big business, and trying to do it without a car in a city where a driving license is more important than a birth certificate. It's as if you think you're living in some quaint old-fashioned European walking city instead of those thirty-nine suburbs hanging like garlic bulbs from a string of freeways. The problem, Henry, is that you're a nineteenth-century detective in a twenty-first-century megalopolis. You should get around by jet, by rocket, by lightning.

Henry said, My mind goes fast, and sat down. He began to thumb through the copy of the *San Francisco Chronicle* that was on the coffee table. Fletcher followed him to the couch like an unpaid debt. He said, At least if you lived *here*—a normal-size all-together town with a subway, buses, cable cars—you might stand a chance. *This* is a city. L.A. is a post-urban process inhabited by white leisure suits.

Henry had found that San Franciscans gave a great deal of thought to L.A. Most of it was crap. There was more from Fletcher about smog and blue-haired ladies and the Tate-LaBianca murders and freeway snipers. What can you do with people like that? he wondered. Match them killer for killer and kook for kook. Henry tuned him out.

Looking through the paper, he came upon a small notice that piqued his curiosity. He glanced at his watch, got up, and interrupted Fletcher to inquire about his raincoat. It was in the guest room upstairs. Dorothy asked, Is something wrong, Henry? Nothing was wrong. I'm going for a walk, he told her. I've got to get some gum. Fletcher volunteered to go along with him to the store, show him the way. Thanks, said Henry. I'll find it.

In front of the bus terminal, a buoyant Santa Claus hopped back and forth against the chill wind and shook Christmas out of his bell. Santa knew he had the little guy in the raincoat the minute he saw him. Hurrying after him, he rattled the bell in his ear. The fact that Henry was obviously in a hurry didn't seem to make any difference to him. Henry slowed, stopped, looked him up and down.

Is this where I get the bus to Oakland? he asked. You bet! said the delighted Santa. Slipping a daisy into Tattersall's top buttonhole, he jingled the coins in his small pail and chortled, Ho, ho, ho, how about it? Henry looked at him. The heavily rouged cheeks, the moth-eaten beard, the eyes feverishly bright. You working for Volunteers of America? Santa rattled his pail loudly and pleaded, Hey, come on, it's for poor children. Salvation Army? asked Tattersall. Nope. I'm a Krishna Klaus, he revealed. Henry was impressed. You guys get around, he said, dropping a quarter into the collection. Merry Christmas! called the Krishna Klaus in a tone of such ingratiating servility that Tattersall considered going back for his money.

On the bus, he realized that he had come to a decision about the Harkness offer. Henry wanted no part of it. He had no desire to become a salaried hack working for a large company. He prized his independence too much, his freedom to turn down the cases he loathed and take only those that meant something to him. Freelancing didn't provide much in the way of security, but it provided everything else that was important to Henry. All right, maybe he *was* hopelessly out of date as Fletcher had said, but he preferred to use his own head, his feelings, rather than the expensive technology of Harkness or Dacks. Henry wasn't at all sure that Dorothy would understand all this and thought it best not to say anything. Not being a poet, he might find it hard to explain.

This is it. The bus driver's voice was throaty, nasty, vexed, a surly victim of mass transportation's countless indignities. The swollen face frowned at Henry in the rearview mirror. You asked me to say when we got there, didn't you? Without looking, he skewered the air with his index finger. The Oakland Museum, he called out. Take it or leave it.

Chance. Of course it was only chance that had turned up the *Chronicle* announcement of the Daniel Asher retrospective exhibition in Oakland, but for Henry standing in front of the

316

museum there was an inevitability in his presence here that went beyond coincidence. Once again, their paths had crossed as if fated and irresistible. The museum was buried under vines, shrubs, ferns, dichrondra, and the entrance wasn't easy to find. Henry located a staircase and, like Orpheus, warily descended.

Inside the museum, there was a store that sold prints, postcards, photographs, books. It was selling the retrospective catalogue for a lot of money. Henry observed that there were a lot of catalogues that hadn't yet been sold. The attractive cover was a vivid electric blue and printed in white DANIEL ASHER. Beneath it was a collage. A man in a red beret being pushed off a subway platform by a man in a red beret. Falling into the path of an oncoming train. The engineer not seeing him. Within his narrow, lighted compartment, the engineer in his red beret embracing the naked woman. And the speeding train rushing on.

Tattersall picked up a copy of the catalogue, and it fell open to a picture of the artist. He was leaning against a small streaked column under a weatherbeaten arch with the word FORTUNE painted on it. Behind him were a few palm trees and what looked like the beach at Venice. His feet were bare, and his dungarees were frayed at the bottom, his tee shirt torn at the neck. In his fingers, a cigarette hung loosely. He showed a gap-toothed smile and stared directly at the photographer with a certain intense look that the detective recognized. Knowing Dan Asher the way he had come to know him, Henry guessed there was a woman holding the camera. The mustache, the long hair, the smile and pose gave him the air of a mellow Robinson Crusoe who was going to make out just fine.

The photograph was black and white. It appeared to Henry that it must have been taken before Asher's first heart attack when things began to fall apart for him. First the girlfriend. Then the daughter. Henry felt sorry for the poor sick guy, losing this, losing that, falling into crime, and then, dressed as a flag, getting clobbered by the cops at the Century Plaza riot.

He remembered the shocked expression on the artist's face the last time he had seen him. There was no doctor aboard the plane, but by then it was probably already too late for a doctor. Henry tried mouth-to-mouth resuscitation, tried everything he could think of to save him, or at least to keep him alive just long enough to pry the secret of the Rembrandt out of him, but it was no use. The man who had been sitting beside Asher was nearly hysterical, and Henry volunteered to switch seats with him. Unobserved, he went through Asher's pockets, but there was nothing. He remembered how utterly miserable he felt as the plane closed on New York with the two of them seated side by side in silence as if there was no need of words between such old, dear friends.

Can I help you? The well-dressed woman behind the counter had a pleasant voice, an open face, and didn't look as if she needed the money. She was smiling at his buttonhole. Glancing down, Henry was flustered to discover that the daisy was still there. He stuffed it into his pocket. Just looking, he said with a nervous grin and returned the expensive catalogue.

The exhibition gallery was large, serene, well lighted, but there were only a few people in it. Henry didn't even see a guard. Partitions had been set up for additional hanging space, and the entire gallery was filled with the small collages in their simple wooden frames. On the broad white walls, they appeared to be tiny bloodstains, broken glass, pink flesh, peacock feathers. They seemed to Henry as important as clues. He had no idea that Asher had done so many of these things or how fascinating they were.

The show was arranged chronologically, beginning with 1943, and Henry went squinting along the walls and through the alcoves, from the artist's early dark works to the dazzling pocket-rainbow of color at the end. There were mysteries to be fathomed, remarkable relationships to be explored—a bound young woman and two top hats, a turbaned Sikh armed with a scimitar in a grade school corridor. It was the sort of work calculated to delight a man unafraid of surprises, a man who trusted his intuition. Henry marveled at the delicacy, the care with which each one of these collages had been pieced together from tiny bits of paper or fabric, assembled out of pins, bones, buttons, and shells to form a little world.

In the last alcove among the last works the artist completed he found *La Grande Roue*. Nine years ago on that day when he had dropped in on Asher's studio, it had been an unfinished yellow Ferris wheel. Henry was bowled over by the earthiness of the old guy copping a feel of the bride's young tit, enchanted by the romance of the brave flags in the glittering Paris sky.

It was a shame, he thought, a damn shame that there were so few here to see Asher's extraordinary last show. Perhaps if the collages were larger . . . It often seemed to him that to capture anyone's attention in America it was necessary for things to be large—the Empire State Building, the immensity of the West, the Great Depression, Moby Dick. Perhaps it was just that folks were too busy this afternoon with last-minute Christmas shopping.

It was getting late. Dorothy would be worrying about him. Henry decided to call her before starting back and found a phone downstairs. His sister-in-law answered and said, Sure, Henry, just a minute. She had been giggling about something. When Dorothy got on, he told her that he was in Oakland and he'd explain all about it when he got back. That's fine, dear, she said and hung up. Henry supposed that there was no hurry after all.

Outside the building, he buttoned his coat and turned up his collar against the wind. Then he noticed the pool in the courtyard of the museum and walked toward it. Asher, he thought, how could you? An artist like you! How could you have stolen the painting? It was beyond Henry. There were mysteries in this world even more puzzling than the whereabouts of the missing Rembrandt, problems that perhaps would never be solved. Henry had read in the paper about absolute zero, the impossibility of reaching it, and how each time scientists got closer to their unobtainable goal they discovered something else. Wouldn't it be a pity, said one of them, if nothing new could be discovered because we were already there? Patient though he was and still confident after almost a decade, Henry dreaded the thought that Rembrandt's wrestling Jacob might be his absolute zero.

The pool shivered in the clear wind, and the reeds and tall cattails waved. The green water-lily pads skimmed across the surface like skaters. There were carp in this pool, beautiful fish perhaps as large as fifteen pounds, several of them white and vermilion, one white and gold, some white with black and orange markings. Henry had seen fish like these at the Japanese nursery on Sawtelle where Dorothy had gone to buy a moonflower plant. He had admired them, and the Japanese owner said koi are lucky fish. We call nishiki-koi living jewels. They have been bred for hundreds of years. It is even said that there are rivers in my country in which they have lived forever. Who knows? he said, turning to Henry, and it was hard to tell if his eyes had narrowed against the sun or with laughter.

Leaning over the museum's bronze-colored guard rail, Henry gazed down into the pool. He was thinking about what he had seen inside. He watched his reflection float to the surface. Beneath his eyes and nose the living jewels moved gracefully through the water, untouched by the wind or years or chaos, their apparently random ways an ageless, unforgettable dance that had survived to comfort and exalt the heart. It cheered Henry up. The whole longing for its parts. Life thumbing its nose at the end.